THE DRAGON WAKES:
A NOVEL OF WALES AND OWAIN GLYNDWR

BY

T. I. ADAMS

Copyright © 2012 T. I. Adams
All rights reserved.
ISBN-13: 978-1480119697
ISBN-10: 1480119695

DEDICATION

To my Mother, Father and Stepmother

TABLE OF CONTENTS

THE TESTAMENT AND CHRONICLE OF GWYN AP EYNON 4
RUMORS AND TALES OF MY LORD'S BIRTH 8
CONCERNING MY ORIGINS AND THE FIRST PROPHECY 14
THE GREAT FROST AND THE EVILS OF THE LORDS OF RUTHIN 38
THE STORY OF THE TRAVELS OF MY LORD OWAIN 57
THE TRUTH OUR DEALINGS WITH OWAIN LLAWGOCH 69
OUR ARRIVAL IN THE CITY OF LONDON 89
THE BATTLE OF ST. PAUL'S 102
THE CORONATION OF KING RICHARD 118
OUR ACTIVITIES DURING THE GREAT REVOLT........................... 131
OUR INDENTURE TO ENGLISH GREGORY 173
THE WAR IN SCOTLAND 190
THE BATTLE OF CADZAND 209
THE "WONDROUS PARLIAMENT" 217
OUR TRAVELS WITH KING RICHARD 238
THE "MERCILESS PARLIAMENT" 258
HOW TEN QUIET YEARS ENDED 276
HOW THE HOUSE OF LANCASTER APPEARED LOST 299
THE RETURN OF HENRY BOLINGBROKE 310
HOW HENRY BOLINGBROKE STOLE THE CROWN OF ENGLAND .331
HOW MY LORD DECIDED TO DECLARE HIS KINGSHIP 351
THE EVIL OF THE HENRY BOLINGBROKE 357

ACKNOWLEDGMENTS

I would like to acknowledge the help of Katherine Nielsen for help with editing, Jim Kiessling for advice on medieval weapons, and my daughters Devon and Conner for putting up with me.

A NOTE ON WELSH PRONUNCIATION: THE WELSH ALPHABET

A	B	C	CH
"C<u>a</u>t"	"<u>B</u>alloon"	"<u>C</u>at"	"Ba<u>ch</u>"
D	DD	E	F
"<u>D</u>og"	"Smoo<u>th</u>" (a "d-th" sound)	"T<u>e</u>n"	"Ha<u>v</u>e"
FF	G	NG	H
"<u>F</u>ace"	"<u>G</u>oal"	"Lo<u>ng</u>"	"<u>H</u>ave"
I	L	LL	M
"<u>I</u>nk"	"<u>L</u>ow"	"<u>Ll</u>oyd" ("th-l")	"<u>M</u>an"
N	O	P	PH
"<u>N</u>ame"	"M<u>o</u>re"	"<u>P</u>en"	"<u>F</u>riend"
R	RH	S	T
A rolling "rr" similar to Spanish	"R" + "huh"	"<u>S</u>ea"	"<u>T</u>able"
TH	U	W	Y
"<u>Th</u>in"	"P<u>i</u>n"	"M<u>oo</u>n"	"P<u>u</u>n"

"Give me leave o tell you once again that at my birth
The front of heaven was full of fiery shapes,
The goats ran from the mountains, and the herds
Were strangely clamorous to the freighted fields.
These signs have mark'd me extraordinary;
And all the courses of my life do show
I am not in the roll of common men.
Where is he living, clipp'd in with the sea
That chides the banks of England, Scotland, Wales,
Which calls me pupil, or hath read to me?
And bring him out that is but woman's son
Can trace me in the tedious ways of art
And hold me pace in deep experiments"

Owen Glendower, Act III, Scene I, "Henry IV Part I" William Shakespeare

THE TESTAMENT AND CHRONICLE OF GWYN AP EYNON

I remember the day when My Lord Owain decided that we should begin to kill the English. It is always difficult to decide when the killing day has arrived. At first the day seems like any other. You wake up and say your prayers, eat your breakfast and talk to your family as though nothing is different. But in your mind you wonder if the time has come. You pray or take council but eventually it grows in your mind that today is the day to kill the strangers that live amongst you. Finally, you pick up your weapon, tell your kinsmen what must be done, do what you need to do to bless your endeavor, and begin to kill.

My Lord told me the day had arrived on the evening of the feast of Saint Cynfarch. He was praying in his chapel, and I went to tell him that the visitors had arrived for his ascension. He turned to me.

"Tomorrow we will begin to kill the English" he said. "The Spirits and the Blessed Saints have confirmed by decision." He paused and looked at me.

"We shall take Ruthin and burn it down" said Owain.

"What of the Lord of Ruthin?" I asked.

"Be warned" said Owain. "He must die by my hand. I shall take his head."

I hesitated. "They say old debts are bad debts Owain"

He smiled. "Then they are fools. I shall have my vengeance. I have been promised it."

"Must they all die?"

"Only those who resist," said Owain. "If the men accept me, they may live. If they challenge my rights, I will have them all killed."

"Even the women and children?"

He gestured impatiently. "Am I a barbarian? Am I English? They may go, but I will have the men if they resist. "

We were silent for awhile. The fire crackled and grew higher as the evening chill set in. "What of the Lord of Ruthin's men? What of them?" I asked

"They must all die. I will be avenged. We must provide their heads," he growled. "The Prophet has told me that they will begin to speak to us as they did before the foreigners came."

I hesitated. "The Bishop will not approve."

He shrugged. "The Bishop does not approve of many things, and yet he follows."

"You are not worried for your immortal soul?"

"I will account for my soul before God," he replied. "Anyway, there are more ways to Heaven than the Blessed Fathers know. The Church itself cannot even decide who is Pope. If they do not know who is Pope, how can they claim to know what God thinks?"

He paused, stared at the cross and then began to speak in a whisper.

"I will burn it down, burn it all down. I will destroy it all. I will bring it down upon their heads. They shall see the costs of ignoring my rights. What do they know of my greatness or what is due to me?"

His voice rose as he continued.

"I was born to the beat of dragons' wings. I was prophesized. My coming was foretold a hundred generations ago. I am the redeemer, the Mab Daragon, the Son of Deliverance; I have come to restore the Britons to their rightful place. Doubt me not. The marks have been seen and the signs have been demonstrated."

There was silence for a moment. I heard the door open behind me. I turned and saw the Prophet had entered. He walked to Owain and knelt before him.

"They are all here My Lord," said the Prophet.

Owain nodded to him.

"Is all ready for the ceremony?" asked Owain.

"Yes, My Lord" replied the Prophet, "You shall be the King of the Barons tonight."

Owain nodded. He turned to me, "Come then, let us go and fulfill our destiny."

Thus it began. We killed many Englishmen in the days that followed. The hills were red with the blood of the foreigners, and their towns were burnt and broken. Grass grew in their market places where they had once defiled our land with money.

Thank God the world has forgotten this. Indeed, the world has forgotten my Lord Owain entirely. Once he drove the strangers from Wales and made himself master of the Britons.

He spoke as an equal with the Kings of France and Scotland, treated with the Lords of Ireland, and entertained the Pope's envoys.

He brought low the King of England. Four times the English King brought his power against him, and four times My Lord Owain sent them home sodden and defeated.

He raised the Lords of the North, divided Ynys Prydien among the Northumbrians and the Lords of March and nearly toppled proud Bolingbroke from his throne.

He sent his ships to burn the Southern Shore and joined with the King of France to lead a mighty army into the Lost Lands.

Great was my Lord's power and great was the measure of his triumphs. Yet outside of our valleys, he is forgotten. At best, he is a joke in the taverns of Shropshire or a foil for the mummers on the stages of Ludd's Town. If they remember him at all they will say,

"Why did he do it? He was a rich man. He had everything a man could want. Why did he hate us so much? That's the Welsh for you. They're terrible people."

Is there no one who remembers the truth of Owain Glyndwr, Tywysog Cymru, Princeps Walliae, the heir to Amherawdr Arddwyr and the fulfillment of the prophecies of Myrddin Wyllt? Am I the last to know the truth concerning my Lord's triumphs and struggles?

I, Gwyn ap Eynon, sometimes known as Gwyn Ffyddlon or Faithful Quinn, declare, that though I may be old and infirm, I remember all. I shall tell the world of My Lord. I will write here in these folios the true history of Owain Glyndwr. I call upon the world to take witness to my testament. The words I write are true. There is no one better able to tell my Lord's story, for I knew him from when he was a boy until the end.

RUMORS AND TALES OF MY LORD'S BIRTH

It began with a birth. As is the way with such stories, the Mother and Father were far from home. They were in the South on a pilgrimage to seek the blessings of the Monks of Dewi Sant. They had been childless for a long time. The Mother had prayed to the Blessed Saint that, if he would grant them a child, she would make a pilgrimage to his shrine. And so despite the protests from her husband, she had insisted on going before the birth. She was adamant that the child be born in her lands among her people.

They stopped at a small settlement at the center of her peoples lands. Her family had once been the kings of the South. They had sent their riders throughout the land to carry the law of Hewyl Dda, fought the Saxons, beat the Black Heathens, and conquered Gwent and Morgannwg. Now, her family's glory was all in the past, and they were nothing. The settlement where they ended their journey was nearly all that was left of her inheritance. Still, it belonged to her completely.

I am told that it was the Feast of Saint Mathew. I do not know if this is true. It was two years before I was born. If it was Saint Mathew's Day, the harvest would have been almost complete. The land would have been golden with the cut wheat and simmering under the gentle heat of the last of the summer. The taeogions, peasants as the Saxons call them, would have been taking the wheat to the mills and preparing to scorch the stubble in the fields.

Owain's Mother would have been nearly alone in the manor house, attended only by her ladies. I have been there since, and the house in question is nothing much. No more than a freedman's house really. They were less than ten miles from Dewi Sant's, but she was in no condition to keep traveling. She was not due for two weeks, but she knew her time was coming early. Her labor began in the morning. They called for the local midwife. She would have been terrified by the responsibility of bringing a lord's child into the world, especially when the birth turned out to be so hard. By nightfall, she was still struggling. She screamed and cried. The room was small and hot. As is the practice, the Midwife would have lit a fire in brazier to purify the room and maintain the proper temperature for the birth. With the presence of all of the ladies in the room, and the stifling heat of late summer, the room would have been intolerable.

She squatted and pushed for hours, but the baby did not come. The Midwife had warned her it would be a hard birth; she had given her herbs to calm her and charms to ease the pain, but the child was large and she was small.

Owain's Father awaited the birth outside with his retainers. At home, he would have had things to distract him but here there was nothing to do but wait and pray. The local Priest was called to usher the child into the world. He was a Welshman, for many of the priests in the South were natives taught by the White Brothers from Ystrad Fflur. As with the Midwife, he would have been nervous to attend the birth of a Lord's child and would have struggled to ingratiate himself with the Lord.

I was told that the sky was alive that night. In the North the sky was coloring. Fire rippled across the horizon, turning the night red and gold. I once heard Sionni DauVis claim he was there. He said that shooting stars streaked across the sky, and great rumbling noises flew on the wind from the Northwest. The mountains trembled, and the ground shook. Frightened herds ran through the fields, and beasts moaned and cried in fear.

There was a dragon and a giant somewhere, said Sonni. The giant was throwing rocks and crashing mountains. He heard the dragon beat its wings and roar out its rage. The dragon must have been a powerful one because ash and fire fell for many days from the west and the sun was darkened that autumn.

Of course, Sionni was a drunk and a terrible liar, so it is quite possible there was nothing and, even more likely, he was not even there.

Owain's father asked the Priest if he thought the skies that night were a bad omen.

"No, My Lord, a sign of greatness for your child. Or possibly unrelated?" said the Priest. The Priest was no doubt aware of the importance of Gruffudd Fychan and wanted to keep him happy.

Gruffudd Fychan would have been unconvinced. He had been educated in London and was always skeptical when it came to prophecy. Very un-Welsh was Gruffudd Fychan when it came to truth. He would have pressed the Priest.

"What of a birth on Saint Matthew's Day, the autumn equinox? So close to a day when the gates between this world and the Annwfyn, the Other World, are about to open? Does that have a meaning? Is not Saint Matthew the reaper, the old man that cuts the harvest?"

The Priest tried to evade the Lord's eye.

"Also Saint Mabon, My Lord, the patron saint of wine and the harvest of the grape," he said "Surely a good thing"

Sonni interjected.

"Saint Mabon is beloved on the Tylwyth Teg, the Beautiful People of the Other World. It was he who preached the Word of our Risen Lord to them and converted the Bobl Bach, the Little People, to the true faith with his pipes and his caldron of strong red wine. It is always a good sign to be favored by those from the Annwfyn."

For this bit of pagan wisdom he would have received a scowl from the Priest

Gruffudd Fychan gave up, sat back on his chair and observed the night. Sionni said the sky was lit as never before. Dragons and comets dashed across the night, the hills turned red, and the herds and flocks ran and hid. He said the sky burnt as they played and spat flames at each other. No matter what the Priest said, Gruffudd Fychan would have thought it at best an ambiguous omen.

Some time passed. The men continued to look out at the sky and wonder at the mystery of it all. Then there was a shout and the crying began. The Midwife came out of the house all smiles.

"A son, My Lord" she said. There was the back slapping and congratulations that are always due the Father. Gruffudd Fychan looked to the sky.

"I have heard" said Gruffudd Fychan, "that in Cathay there are wizards that can command such dragons and signs to come to the sky. I have heard that such marvels are called into being whenever an heir is born to their Kahn. Perhaps this is a similar sign." He sighed and turned to the Priest "What is the name of this place Father?"

"Trefgarn Owain, My Lord."

Gruffudd Fychan thought for a moment.

"After Owain Fychan" said Owain, "The last of the Lord Rhys's direct line?" The Priest nodded. Gruffudd Fychan looked around. "So this is all that is left of the great lordship of Deheubenth."

"Yes, My Lord, after the Saxons killed Owain ap Rhys, this was all they left us."

And indeed it was true. Great was the Kingdom of the South, but Henry Plantagenet, then ruler of the Empire of the Aquitaine, conquered those lands from the Welsh and gave them to Flemishmen from across the seas. All he left the descendants of Lord Rhys was this small settlement and the lands around it.

Gruffudd thought for a moment. "Perhaps we should honor Deheubenth. The boy will have firm title to Powys, and it will do no harm to strengthen his connections to the South. What do you think, Father, shall I name the boy Owain?"

The Priest was happy that the Baron had decided to cast the night's phenomena in a good light. "It is a propitious name My Lord. As the prophecy of Myrddin says:

> Owain a fu ag Owain a fydd ag etto
> Owain a rydd gawared I frython
>
> (Owain was and Owain will be again,
> Owain will give deliverance to Britain)

"Let us hope he fulfills his promise then. He shall be called Owain ap Gruffudd Fychan ap Gruffudd Mawr ap Madog."

That is how it is said Owain came into the world. Far from home on a pilgrimage to the holiest place in Wales. What would his Father have done if he had known all that was to follow? What would he have done if he had remembered the rest of the prophecy?

> "Owain shall be a broken shield, a shattered spear,
> Owain shall bring the dragon to the land and the fire to his father's home"

I asked Owain once if this story was true. Had he been born so far away in the South?

He smiled. "That's the story" said Owain.

"But is it true?" I persisted.

"If my birth was in the South and my home is in the North, do I not unite them both? Am I not the true embodiment of all Wales?"

"But is it true?" I asked again.

He thought for a moment. "Shall we say that my family is from the North East? That is many miles from Trefgarn Owain. My Grandfather was a man who liked control. It would have been out of character for him to have allowed his son and daughter-in-law to travel so close to a birth."

"So it is not true," I sighed.

"How should I know?" he said with a sparkle in his eye, "I was but a baby. You should ask old Sonni DauVis what he remembers. After all, he says he was there."

CONCERNING MY ORIGINS AND THE FIRST PROPHECY

There was always Owain. He was always My Lord and I his captain. I cannot remember a time when he was not there. I suppose I must have met Owain when I was about four or five years old. My Father brought me to Gruffudd Fychan's home at Glyndyfrdwy and left me there. It was never explained whether he would return or if I was to stay. He just left me and hoped for the Christian charity of his hosts. He was a hedge-bard; simple and common. He never amounted to anything, though he did probably tell a few good tales. Like many bards, it may have been that he was inexact when it came to times and appointments and simply forgot to return.

He had taken me from my Mother's house. I remember it vaguely. It was a pale, white mud house built part way on a hill. It was probably in the North, for I remember it being cold. If I close my eyes tightly, I can picture a young woman holding open her arms to me. I suppose the woman is my Mother, although for all I know, she may be a sister or some other family member. I do remember a death. It was a cold autumn day. The leaves had fallen and covered the ground. I am standing near an open grave in a church yard. I can see a corpse wrapped in sacking. Two men lift it up and place it into the ground. A Priest stands there, says something and waves a cross. Then he turns to me.

"She is with Jesus now, son. It is a glorious day for her" he says.

I can see my child's hands reaching out in front of me towards the grave wanting her to come out and be with me. I have no idea how she died. Taeogions die easily. The death would have provoked little comment or reaction.

I suppose my family must have passed me from relation to relation until my Father appeared. Bards rarely stay in one place. They make their living from the Barons, traveling from household to household and selling their words. For some reason he decided to take me rather than passing me on to a relation to raise. He got as far as Glyndyfrdwy before he realized how much work a child could be. I imagine him arriving and passing me to a cook or a serving maid, and then going off to spin songs. I am sure that the servants would have understood that I was there to stay. Next morning he was back on the road and off to next hall. I was left behind. Owain's Mother noticed me, took pity and gave me to her son as a companion. She was a good woman and always had a weakness for birds with broken wings.

I never saw my Father again. He was a minor bard. He was never to achieve the fame of Iolo Goch or Sonni Cent. No doubt he was charming and sang a good song. He was probably a good hand with the ladies and left a string of bastards across Wales. I am told he died in a knife fight in Hereford. But he left me my name and nothing else; I was Gwyn ap Eynon when I was young and Gwyn Ffyddlon after I had shown my loyalty to My Lord.

Years later when I was in Hereford, I tried to find my Father's grave. I explored the paupers' cemetery, but I could find him nowhere. Death was common on the roads in those days, and men died easily. He may have been buried in Hereford but just as likely met his end on any one of a thousand roads and tracks that wound around the Marches that divide England from Wales.

I have never resented being left with Owain's family. My Father was without doubt a bastard of the highest order, but if he had left me with my Mother's people, I would have lived a dull life. What would I have been? I would have gone to the fields early, spent my youth watching cows, married a simple girl, raised a brood of scrawny brats, and whiled away my life toiling to keep a Norman lord's cattle fat as I grew thinner and thinner. If I was lucky, I would have died ruined and bent without ever seeing anything beyond the valley in which I was born. If I was unlucky, plague, war, or some petty accident would have taken me to an early grave. Such is the life of taeogion.

Instead, I have seen things beyond anything that a taeogion could see. I have seen the death of kings and the fall of great princes. I have seen great Queen Dick in all his glory. I have seen the mad King of France and the Emperor of the Greeks. I have traveled to Avignon, seen the great palaces of the French Popes, and learned where they hide their stolen wealth. I have seen great battles and watched horses wade through a sea of blood. I have known the bravest of men, watched great champions die, seen a sea full of ships, and a sky full of dragons. I have heard the roar of Hell's and watched the son of the beast batter down the walls of the mighty fortresses. Above all, I have seen that the Devil is real and moves through this world disguised as a friend and a stranger.

I digress. By birth I picked up much of my father's florid language. Like most Welshman, I find it hard to stay to the point when there is a story to be told.

My fostering at Owain's house was a wonderful adventure. Owain adopted me; I was his first solider and he was always my Captain. He appeared strikingly different from other Welshman. As a boy, he was blond and blue eyed. I suspect it was his Northern blood. The Kings of Norway had married into his mother's line and brought their bright hair to the family. He was always bigger than most people around him. As a boy he was tall and rangy. Although we could not be more than a year or two apart, he was a full head taller than me and remained so throughout our lives.

From the start he led me in our games. We ranged across the hills and fields and learned the ways of the land. When he organized the local boys into some imagined assault on a childhood fort, I was his sergeant, his trusted herald, his squire, his page. When lessons were to be learned, I was there with his tutors or the priests. His Mother, Elen Goch, recognized our friendship soon enough and saw that a boy will not concentrate on his lessons if he sees his friends at work or play outside. She realized that by imprisoning us both at learning, she would have a better chance of keeping Owain there. Accordingly, I gained the inestimable virtue of learning my letters and the language of the Priests. I think she also discerned in me some talent for letters and numbers and believed that one day I would make a good steward or bailiff for My Lord. A far-seeing, practical woman was Elen and always anxious that her boy should be protected by good friends. It is a shame she was taken from us so early.

Those were golden times. Every summer day lasted forever and every winter day was deep in snow. The rain never spoiled our games. Life was long and food was plentiful. I remember we would run into the kitchen and steal a handful of dough from the cook. She would shout at us and chase us out with mock anger. The cook was a jovial woman. As I remember she was big and fat with Saxon hair. Her father was a mason from Oxfordshire that had come to do some work hereabouts. She fell in love with some local lad, married him and stayed with us. By the time I knew her, it was impossible to think of her as anything but Welsh. I recall she made fine bake stones and a passable winberry pie.

On summer days we were shooed out of the manor after our lessons and morning service and left to run wild. Owain would lead us up the hills around Glyndyfrdwy. There was a small mound on the ridge overlooking the house that was our special place. This was where the best games were played, the finest rabbits snared, and the most excellent plots hatched.

When is a county boyhood not perfect? Boyhood is that time before labor that will break your back, before passions that do not matter but will ruin you, before the cares of the world will grind you down, before girls will break your heart or wives will nag you to death, before hopes will be dashed and dreams must be abandoned. Boyhood is a wonderful thing. Where are the days of summer past? Where is my youth gone? Why must a man have but one life? Why just one spring and one summer?

As I sit here at my table writing on my tablet and staring at the wall, I wonder where it has all gone and why I was profligate in the spending of my youth. Would I return to those boys on that day and plot out a different destiny for them? Tell them of what was to come and warn them to run away to the Otherworld and Tylwyth Teg, what then English call the fairy people, and stay with them forever? Is it better to remain forever in childlike happiness, or grow and experience the pains and learnings of this mortal world? I do not know. But this I know, and know for sure, I miss that world and would give all the treasure of the Popes to be a boy again, if for only one day.

I wander again. It is a disease to which old men are prone. I shall return to my tale. I remember one day very well. It was a beautiful day. It was the Eve of Saint John, the Midsummer, when the day is at its longest and when the blessed Saint John was born. The Feast of Saint John was much celebrated in those days. It was the time for the hay harvest to begin and for life to shift to harder work. From Saint John's Day until All Saints Day, it is a time for business.

There was to be a great feast and there were guests from all over the Northern March and the Kingdom of Gwynedd. We were given the job of minding the children who were visiting. It was the first time we met the Hamners. Sir David Hanmer was a big noise in the March. He was a judge in Maelor and had just come back from the King's Parliament. His family's lineage was both Saxon and Norman, but they had lived in Wales so long, while taking Welsh husbands and wives that they were counted to be fully human. Sir David had brought his sons Gruffudd and Jenkin with him. They were good boys but very different from the country boys we were. They were not as used to the rough and tumble of country life. Nevertheless, they kept up and joined in as best they could, but it was too much for them. They were just too Saxon.

The game we played that day was simple. The other children ran away to hide while we protected the stump on the mount. They were to run and kick it, and it was our job to stop them. We stood there are looked out over the valley. The sky was impossibly blue and cloudless. The green hills, lush with forests and ferns, stretched out forever. This was Wales at its most beautiful. I stood there with Owain on the top of the mount and looked out across the valley.

"This is the best place in world" said Owain.

I nodded. "Even the King of England has not better place than this" I said.

"But this is the King of England's place. We are merely his tenants. Tadcu says that one day we will gain full rights and the King will go back to London and leave us alone."

"Your Tadcu is wise, but I cannot see the King going without a fight" I said.

"The King's old and losing his wits. Perhaps he will get tired of being lord of our little land and return to us our rights." Owain said.

"He may be old, but his son's a good fighter. Your Tadcu said he saw him kill thousands of Frenchmen when he fought with him in their wars. He'd fight to keep such a fine place as our valley."

Owain thought for a minute. "If you are right, I will have to fight him for it. When I am a man I shall challenge him to combat. Here in this very field. I will raise my banner and we shall fight for my inheritance. "

"And I shall be your trusted squire" I said, "I shall hand you your sword and lance and you shall mount your warhorse."

"Excellent" replied Owain, "But what if he brings his army?"

"Then we shall raise an army from all of Wales and fight them here" I replied.

"And I will make you one of my Captains. You shall lead my archers." He danced around the hill marking out imagined battle lines and directing his army.

"What of Lori?" I laughed, referring to his little sister.

"She shall lead the Welsh women in songs in praise for our triumphs and shall weave garlands of flowers to reward us for out victory. My brother Tudur will lead my navies to great victories upon the high seas."

"When he loses, will you take his kingdom? England is very rich and is yours by right as a descendent of Arthur and Macsen Wledig."

He wrinkled his brow, "I will let them keep the East. As the bards say, "better your own cottage than another's palace". But I will have the West."

It was then that we heard a noise from behind us. At first I thought it was Tudur. He could be light on his feet and was able to often defeat our defenses. Owain leapt up to catch his brother. But instead of Tudur, I saw a grown man.

Even then Crach he was probably the ugliest man I have ever seen. I remember exactly how he looked on that first day. It was impossible to guess his age. His skin appeared to be peeling off like a snake's. Half of his face was burned, his features melted and running into each other. The rest of his face was scared and pot-marked. It looked like leather that has been left out in the rain. His lips were cracked and broken. A massive beard flowed unevenly around his lips.

We Welsh pay particular attention to our teeth, but Crach's teeth were a wonder to behold. The emerged from his gums at all angles. Some overlapped and grew over the others. Not one of them was close to white. Most varied in color from a striking yellow, through brown to an appalling rotten green.

His hair was wild and unwashed. A dome in the front and a mass of knots with twigs and leaves twisted around long strands. As I looked I saw insects and even a small mouse crawling around. His hair was white with random streaks of black.

He wore a dirty grey robe like a Franciscan, although he did not seem to be a monk. More like some skinny old hedge-bard. His robe was stained with urine and old food. He did have good eyes though. They were the deepest blue, almost violet, and darted around intelligently.

He looked down at us.

"I am sorry for my appearance boys, but I have been sleeping for a long time and have only just woken up."

He stretched, scratched his balls, and picked his nose. He noticed the mouse in his hair and shook his head to get rid of it. He focused on Owain and inhaled.

"Am I speaking with Owain ap Gruffudd Fychan ap Gruffudd Mawr ap Madog ap Gruffudd Maelor ap Madog ap

Maredudd ap Bleddyn?" He paused for breath, "Gruffudd Fychan's boy?"

I should explain our names to my foreign readers. We Welsh do not have family names. Instead we identify our lineage through listing our more famous ancestors. Thus, Owain was known as "Owain son of Gruffudd the Younger son of Gruffudd the Older son of Madog" and so on. Normally, we go back two or three generations so as to show where we stand. If you were trying to prove a point or show a connection, it is not unusual to go back five or six generations. Being born of low station, my family's line dies out quickly, but Owain, like most high-men, could recite his own genealogy right back to the Flood.

The problem is that Wales has a great poverty of names. Gruffudds, Rhys, Llewllyns, Tudurs, Maredudds, Madogs, and Owains proliferated in family trees with disturbing frequency. As a result, nicknames were added to distinguish one Dewi or Llewellyn from another. Thus, a Rhys becomes Rhys Ddu, Black Rhys, if he has black hair or gloomy temperament to distinguish him from Rhys Goch with his red Norse hair and loud, angry manners. It serves well to confuse the Saxon but was perfectly intelligible for us.

Owain looked at the stranger.

"I am impressed with your knowledge of my lineage. And you, Sir, who are you?"

He thought for a moment and looked down at his robe. Then he reached up and touched his face as if feeling it for the first time.

"Crach" he said "Crach Ffyinant. Yes, that will do for now." He continued, "I have had many names but considering my current appearance, Crach will do just fine and, as you can see, I have appeared to have sprung from the ground as a fountain springs from the dirt." He was right; it was a good name for him, "Scabby of the Fountain". As I remember him on that first day I met him, it fitted him perfectly.

Crach and Owain stared at each other for a minute. He yawned again.

"I am a guest of your Tadcu's. He has asked me to make prophecy tonight. I was early so I thought I would come to fetch you. Your Mam will be looking for you in a few minutes and I thought I would help her find you before she begins to call."

Owain looked puzzled.

"I have to find the others before we can leave; they're hiding," he explained.

Crach looked around. "The little girl's behind the rock, the two foreign boys are in heather by the twisted tree and your brother is in the ditch by the back of the clearing. Not terribly clever is your brother?"

Owain titled his head to one side questioningly.

"Just being observant" said Crach. "Most things are clear if you look at them correctly. Do you know what this place is, this little hill?"

Owain shook his head. Crach went on.

"The Old Ones, the ones that were here before the Romans, used to have a shrine here to the Goddess Aerfen. She was a war goddess and ruled over our wars with the Romans and the Saxons. Three boys had to be drowned in the Scared River every year to ensure success in battle."

He gestured to the river below our hill. Then he turned his gaze to us and eyed me wistfully as if wanting to begin my drowning immediately.

"I suppose we must have stopped doing it because the Saxons won and pushed us back into our mountains."

He paused and then looked at me and then turned to Owain.

"Tell your friend there to go find the others. Your Mam's just about to call." At that moment we heard his Mother begin to shout for them. Crach smiled and winked. "I told you she needed you home."

He turned and walked away. Owain ran behind him. I collected the others and headed with them toward the manor. At that time, the manor was the biggest building I have ever seen. It was square and compact. The hall ran along the back of the compound facing the river. The walls and adjoining building followed in a straight line from the hall and cut back to form a courtyard. The entire structure was surrounded by a moat. Gruffudd Mawr had given the manor of Glyndyfrdwy to his son Gruffudd Fychan as a down payment on his inheritance. He was giving up his son in order to give him a taste of what it would be like to run all of the family estates. He meant well, but he could not let go. He would ride the circuit around his three manors, keeping them all under his control. Although his base was at Sycharth to the south, he never stayed there for long. He would be there for a few days and then off to the west to Corwen. After inspecting the estate there he would round back to Glyndyfrdwy.

If there were any illusions that his son was Lord of Glyndyfrdwy, they evaporated the moment the Old Man arrived. The Steward would rush out with the accounts, the Sergeant would stand straight and report on the judgments, the Beadle would account for the taeogions, the Cook would uncover delicacies previously unknown in her kitchen, the Forester would materialize out of the woods, and the Huntsman would shake game from the hills where a day earlier he had sworn there was none.

Whatever he said, Glyndyfrdwy was Gruffudd Mawr's center. This was where the family came from. This was where they had endured. Once they had been Kings of Powys but now their kingdom had shrunk until it covered little more than Glyndyfrdwy. Through the wars of Edward Longshanks, through the years of the Great Hunger and the Great Mortality, they had endured. Other families, even those as noble as they were, had waned. Some had had died out or been reduced to freeholders or worse. Not Gruffudd. He had married into the English, learned their ways, and used their law to secure his place. He had acquired Sycharth and Corwen and secured his title to all the lands around Glyndyfrdwy. When the English recorded his name on their titles he contracted Glyndyfrdwy and chose "Glyndwr" or "Glendower" as they said. It suited the English; they liked place names for their nobles. Gruffudd Fychan ruled forever in the Old Man's shadow and would until the day Old Man died.

That night was one for memories.

Saint John's Eve was one of the few feast days when a boy had something to do. We had been building fires for weeks. We would collect every bit of fallen wood we could find and drag it home. Blinking my eyes against the heat, I looked at the bonfire we had built. It reached to the second story of the manor. There were small fires around it in a greater circle. Later, couples would try to jump the fire to prove their love. The boys would roll down burning wheels from the hills. The older boys would ask girls if they would love them and everyone would dance. The fires would reach up to the skies and new hopes would be born.

Crach looked across the glen. He saw the fires and nodded. I heard him talking to Owain, "So its Gŵyl Ifan tonight, is it?" he said. "What do the Christians call it?" he said. He rubbed his temples, "Saint John's eve? Yes, that's it." He paused for a minute.

"Saint John is an interesting character" he said. "Do you know he's called the Oak King? If you look at pictures of him, you'll see he has horns. The Saxons called him Hern the Hunter before they knew him as Saint John. For us he is the sliver hand, Llew Llawgyffes. Of course, then the Christians came and told us who he really was."

"In the old days, a boy would dress as the Oak King and fight another boy dressed as the Holly King. The Oak King would win and we would kill the boy that represented the Holly King." He looked back at me with disappointment, clearly regretting that there would be no boy sacrificed tonight. He continued.

"A girl would ride naked on a mare at the end the fight. She stood for the Goddess Epona. We would sacrifice the mare and the girl would dance in the blood. The Oak King would then copulate with the girl, and the harvest would be blessed. From Midsummer to the Winter Solstice the Oak King would at first grow strong and then begin to fade. On the Winter Solstice, a boy representing the Holly King would fight and defeat the Oak King. Then we would kill the boy who represented the Oak King and a new cycle would begin. It was all very simple until the Christian ruined it." He signed, full of regret.

"I thought that it was impossible to kill Llew Llawgyffes" said Owain. We got this notion from our Cook. She was a good woman but filled with nonsense about the Old People.

"A common mistake" replied Crach, shaking his leathery head. "Llew cannot be killed during day or night, nor indoors or outdoors, or when riding nor walking, or clothed and not naked, nor by any weapon lawfully made."

"So how is he killed?" said Owain.

Crach sighed, "I was told you were a boy with some intelligence" he said. "I would have thought it obvious. Llew can only be killed in the evening, wrapped in a yew with one foot on a cauldron and one foot on a goat by a weapon forged when forging weapons is forbidden."

I interrupted, "Why a cauldron and goat?"

Crach looked at me with annoyance. "You should be very glad boy" said Crach, "That you have such kind and generous lord as Owain or you would be put out on the road as a dullard. The obviousness of a cauldron and goat when dealing with magical entities is so well known and demonstrated that you should be ashamed to ask such a question."

It was clear to me that I was in the presence of a superior intellect and I deemed it best to remain silent. Owain was made of stronger stuff. "How do you know all of this?" he asked.

Crach looked at Owain and smiled, "Why, I was there when they killed the last Oak King."

Seeing the expression on our faces, he laughed and winked.

"Don't look so shocked. I have read books written by the Christian Fathers and other that lived here before they came to these lands. I know about all kinds of things"

Owain looked surprised, "You can read?"

"Oh yes" replied Crach, "I was a monk for awhile and picked up the knack. I even went to Rome and Constantinople to read some of their books. They're not very interesting really. I stopped at a good library in Alexandria once. It was much more interesting, but the Romans burned most of it and then Christians and the Mohammedans finished it off. All the books are lost now." He breathed in and sighed.

He continued, "That's the problem with books you see; too prone to burning, people that don't like an idea in a book can just burn it. It's much better to rely on people's memories, much harder to burn." He tapped his forehead, "Best to keep it all up here. In the past we did without writing. One of the Old Ones could remember and recite all the Lore of Britain. They didn't trust books. It was a shame really. When the Roman's killed them all we lost so much."

Crach fell silent. He was lost in his thoughts. I realized later that Crach had many memories and when he talked about the deep past he could drift off and would disappear into himself for a long time. Owain turned to me, "Come on let's go see if the fires are ready yet."

Saint John Eve is a wonderful night, but also dangerous. It is one of the spirit nights of the year. Along with the Eve of May Day and All Hallows Eve, the spirits of the dead are very close. Ghosts visit unprotected homes. All sensible people collect golden flowers like Saint John's Wort and mistletoe to place over the doors. These keep the spirits out and the Tylwyth Teg from mischief.

Saint John's Eve was one of the few nights when we would be up after the sun went down. Back then our days were ruled by the sun. We rose at sunrise and slept when the sun went down. Only the very rich or people of bad character enjoyed the night.

On the Spirit Nights like Saint John Eve, this changed. Great fires lit the night and people collected around them and danced and celebrated. Gruffudd Mawr's servants had set up tables and piled them high with food. On this night he brought together all of his family, his clan, his tenants and his allies. It demonstrated to all that the Old Man was still in charge and had plenty of life left in him. It was intended to show that only he had reputation enough to command their attendance and the wealth to fill their bellies with fine food and good ale.

As the sun began to fade, the Priests and some monks came out and began to walk around the fires. I can remember them chanting:

"In honor of God and of Saint John,
To the fruitfulness and profit of our planting and our work.
In the name of the Father and of the Son and of the Holy Spirit, Amen."

We followed saying the prayers for the harvest. When the entire party had finished going around once, the older boys began to blow horns and bang on drums. The revelers raised their mugs and sat down to the feast. At the center of it all was Gruffudd Mawr. Even at the end of his years, he was a huge man. Old, but still strong and powerful. He was the picture of the Welsh warlord; his mass of hair and huge beard proudly grown long in contradiction to fashion.

Next to him was his son and Owain's father, Gruffudd Fychan. Owain's father wore his hair cut short in the English fashion. He was quieter and smaller than Gruffudd Mawr; generally a calmer, more orderly man. Gentle and kind, Owain loved him, but I knew he could not help wishing that he was more like his Gruffudd Mawr.

Owain's Mother Elen sat next to him. Elen was a sweet woman. Beautiful golden red hair she had. You could see that she disapproved of Gruffudd Mawr. Like Owain's Father, she was quiet and slight. She always seemed worried and slightly distracted.

To her left was Sir David Hanmer. Thin, tall, and slightly stooped, he was almost a caricature of the Man of Law. Despite years of living in Wales, learning Welsh, marrying a Welsh woman, and having Welsh children, he was still a Saxon. He looked around the festivities as if we were seeing some wild, alien revelry for Tatary. In the manner of the French he was tolerant and understanding, but in his face you could see what he really thought. He was a great friend of Gruffudd Fychan. The two of them had a great belief in the law and would spend hours talking on some arcane argument that Sir David had encountered at court.

For all his foreign ways, his wife was definitely Welsh. She was tall, with a hook-like beak in the way of some of the people along the coast. She gossiped along in Welsh with the other women. The rest of the table was filled out with merchants from Oswestry and local landholders. There were even some relatives from as far away as Anglesey led by Tudur Vychan. There was the normal mixture of Pulestons, and Pickhills; all powerful Welsh families along the Northern March. Owain knew them all and could explain the complex web of kinship and obligation that tied them all together. If one was harmed or threatened, every man, woman and child in the March could tell exactly how the insult would affect their families and what would be owed of them for redress.

Crach began talking again. He looked at them dismissively.

"Look at them, boys, they think they have power. Since our last king was killed, they are no better than taeogions. They are all Arundel's dogs." He was right. The Earl of Arundel dominated the Northern March and decided who rose and fell. He touched everyone in the March. Believe me; you didn't fart in those parts without his Lordship's say-so.

"The Earl has been good to our family" Owain interrupted. "He helped Tadcu get his rights back to our land. My Father says he is a powerful man with the King, and we are wise to retain his friendship."

Crach snorted, "Mark my words boy, Arundel will lead you nowhere. His fate is sealed. He is a great criminal and will end his days on the block." He touched his nose indicating that prophecy had been made, "Trust me, I have seen this."

Owain nudged me, "Who's the Saxon?" he said pointing at a short, portly man sitting to the left of Gruffudd who was definitely confused by the proceedings. I shrugged. He tugged on Cook's apron.

"Who's the Saxon next to Tadcu?" he asked. There could be no doubt he was an Englishman. He had the superior bemused attitude typical of Saxons.

"He's a Scudamore" replied Cook, "Related to you through your Manggu L'Estrange family down South in Hereford." Owain turned to me. I looked blankly at him. I knew most of Owain's family connections, but the relationship with the Scudmores and the L'Estrange was a little confusing. He saw my confusion and explained.

"Grandmother died when I was young," he said, "I barely remember her but I know her death hurt Tadcu Gruffudd badly. She was an L'Estrange. They're an important family in the South. They were close to us but moved away after his Manggu's death. Perhaps having this Scudamore here today was Tadcu Gruffudd's way of starting to build new alliances and patch things up?"

"Perhaps" I said, "They say Gruffudd Mawr always thinks before he does anything big."

The star of the gathering was Iolo Goch. He was the family bard. Iolo was a young man then, but, unlike my Father, had already established himself as a major bard. He spent the year traveling around the courts of Welsh nobility writing odes to them and their magnificence and drinking their wine. In between these stints at court, he actually wrote some poetry of unsurpassed beauty and wonder. It was easy to see where he got his name. His hair was bright red and flowed down over his shoulders. He amused the crowd by relating a comic poem about a fat monk, a bandit and a shire reeve. He waved his arms and mimed the actions, nodded and winked to the ladies as he showed the actions of the bandit, and shrank and hid as he portrayed to cowardly reeve.

The servants brought out jars of ale, beer, and mead for the tenants and the farm workers while others brought out spiced wine for the nobles. The tables were weighted down with meats and pastries. Huge roasts of venison, mutton, and pork were displayed. The taeogions rarely ate meat, and this meal was a treat for them. It was a gesture of respect that Gruffudd was prepared to share his bounty with them. The nobles ate more rarified food. Starling, herons and swans covered their table.

As the sundown approached, the smaller fires were set. Couple would jump over them to prove their love. If a couple jumped the fire on Saint John's Eve, they would marry before the end of the year. Maidens were ready with flowers in their hair waiting for the beloved to call them. The girls giggled and laughed while the boys urged on each other and drank ale to bolster their courage. Our job was to roll the fire wheels. We would climb to the top of the valley and roll down burning wheels into the bonfire, causing it to spark and burn. Then the party would dance around the fire and sing.

Crach moved toward Gruffudd Mawr, taking a place behind him and whispering into his ear. Gruffudd Mawr nodded and occasionally spoke softly. Eventually the sun sank down and the adults shooed us up the hill. We lit torches from the small fires and climbed the hill. There Owain and I looked down at the Vale and at the Sacred River, winding its way through the Valley snaking through their land. I could believe what Crach had said. The land was magical on a night like this. Spirits were alive in the land, and the Tylwyth Teg were abroad. The big bonfire was still unlit but the smaller fires glowed. The household servants played the harps and banged drums and Iolo sang and recited. We waited as the last rays of the sun fell behind the hills.

The Forrester and his men watched the boys to make sure that they didn't start a fire. Finally the sun fell behind the hills of Blewch Goch. The Forrester nodded to us to light the wheels. We touched the straw around the wheels and they blazed into light. I saw Owain kick his wheel and take off after it whooping and shouting. I followed beating my wheel to catch up with him. At the bottom of the hill around the bonfire, the music picked up volume and speed and the crowd began to clap and shout. We raced down after our wheels hitting them with the torches to keep them running. The Forrester and his men followed behind making sure that anyone who fell was separated from the fire.

The wheels picked up speed as they plummeted towards the bonfire. The revelers parted and let them in. Owain's wheel passed through the crowd and crashed into the bonfire. It burst into flame. The fire reached up to the sky, the Priests recited a prayer to Saint John and blessed the flames, and the people cheered and shouted. They began to dance and throw themselves around the fire. The Priests chanted hymns and prayers in Latin, Iolo sang a poem to light and nobles raised their goblets for a good harvest and kind autumn and winter. At the height of the festival, Gruffudd Mawr jumped onto the table and smashed his great stick down with a thunderous crash. The noise stunned everyone into silence. He waited until everyone looked to him, and then he began to speak.

"Friends and Kinsman, we are here tonight to pray that Saint John bring us a good harvest and light the way for our bounty as he lit the way for our Lord to bring us his spiritual bounty."

He nodded to the Priests. They acknowledge his piety and crossed themselves.

"We also pray that Saint John keep up safe from the spirits and demons abroad this night." There were more nods of approval from the Priests and a murmur from the crowd. "Further, we pray that Tywelth Teg will see our fires and know that we still honor them by keeping the truce our forefathers made with them and seeing that we live in peace with our Scared River." I knew that would not go down well with the Priests, but the taeogions required that the Tywelth Teg must be acknowledged.

"I pay tribute to our noble guests tonight." He raised his goblet. "Especially our good Friends from the South" he lifted the goblet to the Scudamore, "the East," to Hanmer, "and the West" to Tudur Vychan. "It is good that we come together and remember that we are all kin and connected. I have not many summers left." There were shouts of "no" and "you'll never die you old rogue." He waved them down. "It is good that I see that we will continue on into the future. I commend my son Gruffudd Fychan to you and ask that you show him the same honor that you have given me."

They raised their goblets, "Further, I called upon you, to remember that my Grandson" he gestured to Owain, "is rightfully Brenin ar y Barwniadd, King of Barons. In his veins runs the blood of Powys, Deheubenth, and Gwynedd." The crowd looked at him solemnly and nodded. He continued.

"Much has happened in my life. My Father saw the fall of Gwynedd and the last Prince. When I was a boy, I saw the Great Hunger carry off most of my family, and I saw the Great Mortality take most of what was left. I have seen the world grow cold and the great storms come to our land. I have seen families rise and fall, but we have endured and will continue to endure." There were nods and murmurs of approval. "We must look to what is to come and prepare ourselves for things yet unknown."

Gruffudd Mawr turned to Crach, "Seer, make prophecy for us this night when the spirit world is so close. Call on Tywelth Teg to tell our future."

I could see Gruffudd Fychan look disapprovingly. He would be upset that his Gruffudd Mawr was encouraging such superstition; especially in front of the Saxons. Gruffudd ignored him and motioned for Crach to come forward. Crach scuttled like a crab in front of the table over the fire. The crowd parted. He bent over and pulled some bones from under his cloak. He threw them onto the fire and began to mutter. Then his took some powder from a pouch, poured it into his hand and blew it into the fire. The fire shot up in a bright white, light and smoke poured everywhere. The crowd applauded. He parted his arms, looked to the sky, and breathed in deeply. Then he let out his breadth and bent forward. With his staff he traced some glyphs in the dirt. He closed his eyes and made motions in the air.

A wind whipped the flames higher, as the full moon rose and lit the Valley. The crowd began to make the mark against the evil eye. The priests crossed themselves and the Saxons shook their heads in disapproval. The wind blew harder and harder. Tables and benches tumbled over. Then, Crach raised his hand and the wind stopped.

There was absolute silence broken only by the crackling of the fire. Crach began to speak. His voice reached beyond the fires and out into the night, filling the glen.

> "Ben gunlehont meirview datlev bichein.
> Anudon a brad gulad veibonin."

I could hear Hanmer whisper a translation for Scudamore in English, "When the jailers hold their court. Perjury and treachery of the sons of the land." Crach went on:

> "The foreigners begin the slaughter
> And yoke a Prince's wife and daughter
> And we will plough never reap
> And kin for kindred shall not weep
> Bishops then are strange speech,
> And lack the faith the truth to preach
> Poets without rightful their space
> Stand at doors now in disgrace
> Better now a grave than a life
> When all our days are filled with strife"

He stopped and breathed, the risen moon playing across his face. Then he looked directly at Owain:

> "Etto benn llew goronir
> Ywein Beli ywein holing I gyd
> Ywien gwedi biau kymry Cymro hyfryd"

Hanmer whispered: "Again the lion's head will be crowned, Owain of war....no Beli. A Welsh pagan god I think" said Hanmer. He continued to translate "Owain of all of the clans Owain will possess Wales...a fine Welshman." He paused. "It makes no sense. It's just a drunken man's meandering" said Hanmer.

Gruffudd Mawr shushed them. I saw him turn and focus on Owain. He looked back at Crach.

> "To Saxons pain he now will bring
> And steel and strength will be as nothing,
> On water strong wood hides them not
> And all their happiness will be forgotten.
> Noble poets sing his fame,
> And all shall know Lion's name.
>
> A shining lion in red and gold,
> Like Arthur whose return is told.
> The dragon white shall be put to flight
> The dragon red with flame so bright
> The curled comet will not fall
> And he will come concealed from all."

Again he halted. His brows wrinkled as though he was listening to voices from far away. Then he said

> "He will not seek peace from beginning to end.
> On the blue hill,
> High the bows of Briton over the Saxon"

He opened his eyes as if he had suddenly understood what he had been told. He began to walk around the crowd, gesturing and pointing at the land to the southeast. The taeogions' moved back. I felt their fear as well. In fact, at that moment, I could have sworn that the crowds were filled out with many of the Tywelth Teg.

> "Now a leader of men he is,
> But cursed by the crazed women,
> Hair wild and screaming at the sky,
> Mourning their dead,
> Demanding revenge
> Picking the corpses as the ravens
> As Morgan, Morganna, and Machu,
> Soothing the Strangers
> He stands there lost and alone
> And begs forgiveness to a foreign bishop"

He halted for a moment and pointed due South. "There", he said, pointing at the hill we had played on.

"The Kings of Gaul and Little Britain come to Badon.
On an ancient's hill, they stand
But no blood shall flow."

He shook his head in disapproval.

"That year
The Lion cub, the Lion's brother
Battle with the false lion of the great hill
The great walls of the sea will descend
And Owain, a shattered shield for Britain,
Shall be a as a thief
The stranger will never find his final stand"

He pointed at Scudamore. "You, Saxon, listen well" he said.

"His daughters home
In golden hills
Prepare his way
The mason's guide, the temples lost
Priests' robes shall hide the warrior's fate
His face in the wall
The Devil's friend buried half in a holy place"

He smiled and continued.

"The False Lion shall fight in mud.
His ape shall die under the burning flame.
He shall cut the cord and Gaul shall fall.
But he shall not wear the crown.
Poison shall eat him.
Idiot children will follow."

Then he stopped and looked confused. He muttered a question, "Two Owains?"

The Tywelth Teg were listening too. They nodded and smiled. Then his eyes clouded over again.

"The wars will follow and widow becomes a wife.

> His Grandfather's call
> From the region of his great-great grandfather,
> Unconcealed he will be.
> The darkest, dark,
> Betrayer, blood mixed and war uncivil
> Under the red dragon
> A crown in a hedge
> Lost and found
> A son's son wears the golden crown of Rome
> But no peace does it give him in his marriage bed
> For seven times he will not find his joy
> Even his daughter shall be forever barren
> Only Alban shall be her heir"

He stopped again. He looked around and stared at Gruffudd Mawr and Tudur Vychan as if uncertain. Then he looked once more at Owain with renewed certainty.

> "Owain's children, kings of Britain
> Owain was and Owain will be again
> Owain will give deliverance to Britain."

He stopped and stared at the ground. I looked around and saw that the Tywelth Teg had gone. Crach took a deep breath and looked up, saying "I am done." There was silence for a minute and then slow clapping. I looked over to the Iolo.

"It seems that you have milked many cows to make that prophecy; I hear bits of the Prophecies of Merlin and a little bit of Taliesin too? You are an old fraud why can't you at least come up with something new?" Iolo mocked him.

Clearly there was a rivalry between them. Iolo was the better poet of the two, but Crach seemed to be much closer to Gruffudd Mawr. Crach looked at him.

"I may milk many cows, but I churn my own butter. I make no claim to be original. When I commune with our guests from the Otherworld, they take me to the verse I need. I take from the past and the future. I might even take some from you, Iolo, if you are not too involved in praising your masters for you dinner."

"What does it all mean?" I heard Scudamore ask.

"Nothing but entertainment" replied Hanmer, "Simple games for simple country people. More verse than prophecy. It rhymes much better in Welsh than English and my translation did not do proper justice to beauty of the language." He bowed slightly to Gruffudd Mawr.

Gruffudd Mawr looked annoyed but saw there was advantage in Hamner's words. It was better to keep the foreigner confused than understanding our ways.

"Yes" he said, "Simple country games." He raised his glass and shouted, "More ale, more wine."

The crowd applauded and the festival atmosphere returned. I jumped up to watch the fire, but looking back, I saw Owain staring at the bones Crach had thrown.

THE GREAT FROST AND THE EVILS OF THE LORDS OF RUTHIN

It would have been better if we had killed a boy that summer. Our prayers to St. John brought no relief. The harvest was poor and the winter was worse. The Great Frost came in December and lasted through April. Rivers froze solid. The Seine was as hard as iron, the Rhine was a still as a rock, and frost fairs were held on the Thames. Boats were trapped in harbors, and those that set to sea were menaced by mountains of ice.

The ground was too hard to dig and game was scarce. Animals wasted away as they ate the meager fodder from harvest. Food and warmth became an obsession. Even the rich and powerful went hungry. The roads were impassable. Many a foolish man ventured out on the roads that winter only to become victim to the cold or the frost spirits. Eira Mawr, the great snow giant of the mountains, pushed huge drifts of ice and snow down from the high places, destroying many buildings that had been built on their lands. Those with sense stayed close to their homes and moved little. They drank their ale, warmed themselves by their fires and prayed for spring.

It was during that winter that Owain first encountered the De Greys of Ruthin. The Lords of Ruthin had come with the Conqueror to the lands of the Saxons four hundred years past. They were granted lands in Wales for their service to Longshanks when he defeated the Kings of Gwynedd. He gave them the Cantref of Deffrencloyt which they now called Ruthin.

In that terrible winter, De Grey decided that that whatever pain God sent he would not feel it. It would be felt by his tenants and bondsmen alone. He insisted that rents be paid to the full, all tributes and boons delivered, and all services rendered. When taeogions hid their food, the De Greys sent the bailiffs and beadles into their homes to find it. When the taeogions resisted, they nailed them up on trees as a warning to others. When they ran into the woods to hide, they were hunted down and killed like wild beasts. There were those who said that the De Greys carried the bodies back to their halls and ate them.

Despite it all, Gruffudd Fychan tried hard to keep the peace. He knew they were well connected and had no desire to pick a fight with stronger neighbors. However, the De Greys saw the world differently. They had tried to take my Lord's land in the time of the Great Mortality when the infant Gruffudd Mawr had been the sole survivor of his line. They had failed due to the intercession of the Lords of Arundel, but they coveted my Lord's land and waited for the day when they would steal it from us.

In that winter, it came to Gruffudd Fychan's notice that de Grey's men were hunting in our forests. At first, he did nothing and told our foresters to mark our boundaries more clearly and stand watch along the tracks to turn back trespassers. They came back with stories that the boundary markers had been destroyed and de Grey's retainers trespassed freely into our lands.

Gruffudd Fychan came to Owain after morning service.

"We are going to see the Lord of Ruthin" he said. "We will settle this with him once and for all. Food is too precious this winter, and we cannot spare the loss of game. There is a danger that if we do nothing, a precedent will be set and, once established, a precedent has a habit of becoming law. If we do not register our compliant now, the Lord of Ruthin may claim that our land is his by use and abandonment. I have sent messengers and he has agreed to see me. We will travel there and discuss this as civilized men should."

"I don't want to go to Ruthin. It's full of Saxons" said Owain.

"The Lord of Ruthin's son may be there" said Gruffudd Fychan "He's a little younger than you, but it's important that you develop a good relationship with him. One day he will rule in his Father's place, and it is vital that you and he are on good terms."

"I don't want anything to do with the Saxons, I have my own friends" said Owain nodding to me.

"It doesn't matter whether you like him or not. You need to know him" said Gruffudd Fychan. "The De Grey's are a reality that we cannot afford to ignore. They may be small in the great scheme of things but they are a power in our little world. If we continue to be on bad terms with them, they will continue to oppose and undermine our advancement. We are too dependent on the goodwill of the Arundels and need to find other allies if our family is to consolidate and grow our power in Powys."

Owain was unconvinced.

"We should take your telu and punish them" said Owain, "If we burnt their stores De Grey would learn his lesson."

Gruffudd Fychan wrinkled his brows in frustration and sighed.

"Those days are gone, boy. Your Grandfather might still cling to the old ways, but the law is the thing today. Welshmen and Saxons will no longer settle their arguments with swords. In the future the law will decide disputes. We will go to the Lord of Ruthin and I will inform him that if he does not respect our boundary, I will be forced to go to court. Remember, we are well connected. Sir David is an influential man in the law, and our family has been loyal to the Lords of Arundel. If Ruthin refused to deal with us, the courts will not go well for him."

Poor Gruffudd Fychan; he was a lovely man but too trusting. He had a very un-Welsh belief in the law and common sense. He could never stop believing that if you sat down with a man, showed him the proper legal documents, and reasoned with him, he would agree with you. In short, he never could understand bastards like the Lords of Ruthin.

Gruffudd Fychan was very aware that Owain was always temperamentally closer to Gruffudd Mawr than to him. Gruffudd Mawr was a great rogue. Despite his fancy French and passable Latin, the old boy still lived the good life of a mountain chieftain. He drank his ale from a mug made from a bull's scrotum, kept his horses indoors, loved his bards and his women, and relished a good fight or, even better, a cattle raid across the border into the Mortimer lands. In war time, he would pack up his spear, raise his men and head off to join the Lord of Arundel in France or Scotland. It was always the Lord of Arundel, for he always remembered that the Arundels had protected his lands when his was young, and he was their man forever after that.

Gruffudd Mawr would say, "The Arundels are a bunch of bastards but I know them and they've been good to us. As a boy, I gave them my oath. I promised that if they returned my lands to me, I would swear my loyalty. I have kept my oath and the world will know that I went to my grave and always did my duty."

Despite Owain's complaints, we left the next morning along the old Roman road to Corwen. Gruffudd brought a small escort with us; just a few men from the estate that could pass for a telu. We planned to ride fast to Ruthin along the old road, and then over the pass towards the town. Once there, Gruffudd would conduct his business quickly and return home the next day. Such are the ways of honest men. They believe life is made of straight lines and simple plans. Experience never teaches them that the road is crooked and that life is rarely what we expect it to be.

We started just after the sun had risen. It was one of those crisp, clear days. The air is so dry and clear that you can see forever. The road was frozen and hard, so travel was easy and we made Ruthin by late afternoon. Ruthin is a small town in comparison to those I was to see later, but back then it was huge in my eyes. I remember riding over the hills and seeing it for the first time. I could see the castle at the center on a mount. It was built on a red sandstone ridge high above the Clwyd Valley guarding a river crossing. The Englishry was snuggled around it for protection. The walls were high and thick to protect them from the heathen Welsh who lived outside on the other side of the ditch.

As we rode down towards the town we caught our first sight of the gibbets. A long line of them guarded the road leading into Ruthin. The Lords of Ruthin had decided to decorate the entrance to their stronghold with bodies of the Welsh.

Gruffudd nodded at the gibbets

"See what we are up against?" he said. "The Normans will do anything. The only power we can raise against them is the law. They and their Saxon dogs have brought their power against us for more than four hundred years and in the end they win. We have lost on the battlefield but they respect their laws and that is our opening. We can use their laws to defend our rights and our people."

Owain nodded, but we were unconvinced. It seemed to me that any man who was prepared to string up his tenants along the road would not be persuaded by argument. The law is a weak thing for men with a taste for brutality. If the law was our only protection, I could foresee that there would be more Welshmen in gibbets.

When we arrived, we saw that Ruthin was different on the inside from what we expected. It was a real little piece of England; a bustling market town with prosperous merchants, fine wood and dab houses, and neat cobblestone roads. Despite the harshness of the winter, the people there did not look too thin. They had been sucking the countryside dry through the winter. The castle dominated the town. The closer you got to the castle, the more important were the people who lived there.

Gruffudd Fychan's party wound our way around the town to the castle gate. It was an impressive looking place. A giant twin tower gatehouse dominated the entrance to the castle. Gruffudd Fychan turned to us.

"Prince Dafydd ap Gruffudd built the first castle here," he told us. "Back then it was Castell Coch yn yr Gwernfo. Longshanks took it from him and gave it to the De Greys."

We tramped across the drawbridge to the gate. Gruffudd Fychan looked down at the guards from his horse.

"Gruffudd of Glyndyfrdwy" he said, "I have an audience with Lord de Grey."

The guards were wrapped in heavy fur cloaks and stood around a brazier. One looked up at us with contempt. He sneered and returned to his brazier. Gruffudd Fychan became annoyed.

"Do you know who I am? We are expected" said Gruffudd Fychan, "I am a guest of the Lord of Ruthin."

One of the guards looked back at us. He was a big brute with a scar cutting into half of his face. He wiped his nose on his sleeve and spoke to us in English.

"I don't bloody care who you are. You're a fucking Welshmen and rules are that no Welshmen can enter the castle with weapons."

He looked at Gruffudd's telu. "Tell them ugly buggers to stay outside with the dogs. The boys can come with you. But the rest stay outside."

He led us into the inner court. Gruffudd Fychan nodded at the walls.

"Nine foot thick, boys" he said to us in Welsh "The Normans build to last. Once they locked themselves behind these walls, we were never able to get at them. As long as their castles last, any man that rises against them is a fool. The bards can whip the taeogions up into a fury, but what would bows and spears be against these walls? Trust me, time has moved on. The law is the future. War in Wales belongs to the past."

As I say, Gruffudd was a lovely man.

We crossed the second moat up into the upper bailey. It was even more strongly defended. I remember thinking that Gruffudd probably did have a point. This would be a hard fortress to take by force. Even as a young boy I could see that a lot of good men would be lost taking this bugger. We crossed through another set of gates into the second court and walked towards the hall. Once there, we were conducted into the solar and told to wait.

If Lord of Ruthin had wanted to see us, we would have been escorted into his presence quickly. However, we waited and waited. The longer we waited, the more agitated Gruffudd Fychan became. It was clear that we were being humiliated. Time passed, we fidgeted, Gruffudd sighed and paced. Servants came and went, guards and officials wandered by on some mission. Each time they would give us a curious glance. You could tell they were wondering what the Welsh were doing this far inside the castle.

You see, that was the problem that Gruffudd never grasped. He believed that we could deal on equal terms with the Saxons, that they would be reasonable and talk things out fairly. He never understood that despite his fancy education, he was still only a Welshman to them. Like the old joke says, "What do you call a Welshman with a hundred head of cattle to his name? A thief." Whatever we had and however we were, the Normans and Saxons would only ever see us as barbarians and thieves.

Eventually a servant came out. "Come to see His Lordship have you?" he asked.

"I am Gruffudd of Glyndyfrdwy" said Owain's father.

"That's what I said" said the servant, "You're the Welshy that wants to speak to his Lordship." He nodded towards us, "Are they for His Lordship?" he asked.

"That is my son and his servant" said Gruffudd.

The servant looked at us, "So they are not a present for His Lordship?" he asked. Seeing no confirmation he continued, "Pity, for they're His Lordship's type. You should bring them in with you. It might make him look more favorably on you petition."

The Hall itself was a good place to spend a cold winter. Two huge fires roared at either side of the hall, heavy tapestries hung from the wall, and it was packed with De Grey's retainers. Altogether, they kept the hall quite warm.

I will say they the company was not to my liking. De Grey's retainers were a vicious bunch, bruisers every one. Since the beginning of the French Wars, old King Edward had allowed the magnates to provide soldiers rather than money when it came to a fight. The result was that every lord worth his salt had a gang of heavies with him all of the time, capable of jumping to the King's defense at a moment's notice. The reality was that lords ended up with private armies to pursue local arguments.

Gruffudd turned to us, "Stay close boys."

De Grey was seated on a raised dais at the end of the hall with his cronies. Gruffudd spotted him and pushed through the crowd toward where he sat. De Grey was a god-awful ugly man. A great whale of man, he was. His fat and blubber boiled out of every orifice. It was rumored he had once been a very active man, but he broke his leg at a joust. It had healed badly with the poison underneath. Ever after it was not right. He moved less and less until he virtually had to be carried everywhere. However, as he moved less, he ate more. In time he became a great mountain of a man.

Gruffudd came before him and bowed. De Grey looked at him with red rimmed eyes.

"Are you the horse thief's son? Gruffudd's boy?" he said in French. He was one of the older generation that regarded it as a sign of low breeding to speak English, let alone Welsh.

Gruffudd replied in French. As a people are good with languages.

"I am the son of Gruffudd Mawr of Glyndyfrdwy. I am known as Gruffudd Fychan of Glyndyfrdwy."

De Grey snorted. He turned to his cronies.

"The Welsh have only three names among them." His retainers laughed. "See how they preen and cling to their barbarian customers. They are so proud."

"My Lord" said Gruffudd, "I am here to raise the issue of the boundary markers. They have been accidentally disturbed, and your men have come onto my lands."

Before he could continue, De Grey interrupted.

"That land is mine. We would have taken it all when your father was a boy but for Arundel."

He turned to his retainers as if rehearsing an old argument.

"Arundel thinks he's better than our family. He likes to keep his Welsh pets to torment me. He allows that cattle thief Gruffudd Mawr to set up as a gentleman at Sycharth."

Gruffudd Fychan bristled. "We hold our land directly from the King. We are tenants-in-chief. No man save the King can dispute our rights" said Gruffudd. "Before the Conquest we held our lands directly as the Princes of Powys and we're recognized as such by the Longshanks. We have fought with the Lords Arundel, but we owe them nothing."

De Grey sniffed. He turned to his cronies again.

"See how Arundel sends them to torment me so? This one even speaks French. I bet it can even read and write. They are like trained dogs. They pretend to show intelligence but they are nothing but brutes. Old King Edward made a great mistake when he let them live. He should have declared them a species of game and allowed us to hunt them."

Gruffudd ignored his insults and pursued his case. "The boundary markers have been moved. Your men drove our cattle off. I could take this to court but I would prefer to settle this between us and avoid the expense."

De Grey interrupted again, ignoring Gruffudd Fychan and lecturing to his retainers.

"See the Welshman my friends. He is more of a beast than a man. All he ever wants is more. Set a boundary and he will move it. Give him a lamb and he will take a sheep. He is an inveterate thief and liar. He excels in all things venal and deceitful."

He leant over to his Chamberlain.

"They have no notion of property. They do not think the same way we do. Only the lash and the noose keep them under control. It has been my experience that there is no problem concerning the Welsh that cannot be made better by hanging a few of them."

His Chamberlain nodded, obviously impressed by the depth and wisdom of his lord's insights.

De Grey's eyes' focused on Owain and me.

"They are well formed boys" he said licking his lips.

"Yes, My Lord may I present by son Owain and his page. I had thought to present them to your son my Lord."

De Grey laughed.

"My son has no time for such trifles. He is visiting my friend the Duke of Lancaster." He was putting on great airs now and full of himself. "He and the Duke's son are fast friends. I have great hopes for the future. An association with the Duke's house will bring advantage to our family."

He smiled.

"I, however, have considerable use for young pages. You should leave them here as token of your agreement to respect my boundaries much better."

Gruffudd looked at us.

"I am grateful for the offer My Lord, but my son will be sent as a page to the Lord Arundel in the spring. After that, I have great hopes for my son gaining his training as a man-of-law. Such things are of much importance to the future of our family."

De Grey snorted.

"The law is for fools and thieves, typical that a Welshman should be attracted to it. We are the law in this land and always will be." He gripped his goblet. "Your son would do much better with us here. Education never did the Welsh any good. Regardless, you should stay awhile with us. The roads are dangerous. We can find room for you. We will continue with our discussions concerning your grazing rights on our land tomorrow. I have much business to deal with now." He smiled. It was clear that Gruffudd was not happy, but he was in a difficult position. He was in De Grey's power and it was not easy to stare down a man of De Grey's authority.

"I welcome you invitation, My Lord, and thank you for your hospitality," Gruffudd said. De Grey waved us away. We backed out of the hall, bowing, and followed the retainer to the door.

Gruffudd whispered to us in Welsh, "Stay close to me boys. I have no intention of staying in this tomb tonight."

Owain looked at his father, "But isn't it too late to travel?"

"Nothing will compel me to stay in this place tonight. His interest in you tells me that De Grey is a man of unnatural appetites. He intends mischief to us. We will wait and watch for our chance to leave."

We followed on into the courtyard and waited. The retainer pointed us to a tower. He paused. "Please wait here. I will see to the bailiff concerning your accommodation."

Gruffudd gathered us near to him and spoke softly. "Owain, go to the stables. Find someone who speaks Welsh. Tell him who you are and that Gruffudd Fychan of Glyndyfrdwy requires mounts." He turned to me. "Gwyn, go to the kitchens. Find the lowest of the servants there; those that only speak Welsh. Tell him who you travel with, and that we require a diversion. A small fire will do nicely. Go quickly boys."

We ran to our assigned tasks. It was easy to find Welsh people willing to help us. The Normans' greatest weakness was that we were invisible once we were in service to them. Once in a castle doing their bidding, we disappeared as far as they were concerned. They assumed we were no better than mindless beasts that could be ordered to do their bidding.

We came back to find Gruffudd still waiting for the retainer's return. They took great pleasure in making us wait in the cold.

Gruffudd looked down at us. "Ready boys?" he asked.

"Yes My Lord," Owain replied. "There will be two mounts saddled and ready. They will be left for us with no guard." Gruffudd nodded. "And you Gwyn?"

"A kitchen boy taken from our land promises a fire." Gruffudd smiled.

"Then let us wait boys and hope for the best."

We did not have to wait long. Soon we heard shouting from the pantry. Shortly afterward, men ran past us toward the kitchens. Then a bell sounded. More men and women ran. Fire always posed a particular fear for those in a castle. Its stone walls could keep invaders out, but the interior was made of wood. An uncontrolled fire would catch and before you knew it, the entire structure would be engulfed in flame.

"Now boys" Gruffudd said. "Let us go to our mounts."

Let me tell you how to escape from a castle during a fire, for I have had occasion to escape many a time in my life and have gained considerable expertise in the matter. The essence is to move with deliberation and speed but never to run or hide. If you do things out in the open and with confidence, people will naturally assume that you are meant to be there and will let you do what you will. At the time, I was ignorant of this, but, being a man-of-law, Gruffudd Fychan was well schooled in the art of fooling the Saxon and educated us in the ways of flight.

We moved quickly but openly towards the stable. The horses were ready, and we led then out into the inner court. There were other grooms leading horses out to avoid their panic from the fire. We simply walked with them into the outer court. Once there it was a simple matter to continue walking and lead the horses straight past the guards. As I was later to see, guards can only face in one direction. They are either good at keeping people out or keeping people in, but they cannot do both. The men at the gatehouse were of the outward facing sort. It never occurred to them that anyone walking their horses out of the castle would be engaged in no good. As a result, we walked straight past them and out into Ruthin. Once in town, we headed straight for the main gate. If we were to escape, we had to go fast and small. The town was focused on the alarm bells at the castle and we provoked little attention, so we mounted and rode calmly out into the country. Gruffudd turned to us.

"Boys, we will have to take the bandits' tracks through the forests. The journey will be hard, but the Saxons won't follow us. They will stick to the roads and the lowland trackways. We will be safe from them, but we must be quick. The night is coming on and the cold will be out biggest enemy."

With that he wheeled his horse off the road towards to hills and set off at a canter. Owain and I followed quickly. We wound around frozen brambles and bushes and headed into the forests that covered the hills and mountains around Ruthin. Within a few minutes we had disappeared and merged with the forest. All Welshmen knew the forests well in those days. Since then there has been much destruction of our ancient woodlands. In many places the trees have completely disappeared but in the old days the trees where everywhere. Once the Saxons cut them down, their cursed sheep were let loose on our lands. Their incessant eating kept the trees from growing back, and every day they threaten to turn more of our beautiful tree-covered hills into bare, thin, grassy peaks.

Back then, the forests were still thick in most of Wales. A woodsman or forester would know many paths through them and would always leave signs for the knowing to find and follow. Gruffudd Fychan was able to quickly see such signs and learn the ways of this greenwood. He led us down one ravine and over another. We would turn at one great oak and pause at a beech tree to consult the way. Slowly he threaded his way through the forests to peak of the mountain.

"Keep up boys," I remember Gruffudd saying, "If my memory serves me well there is an old forester's hut somewhere on the other side of this mountain. It's normally well stocked with wood and will make a safe place to wait the night away. In the morning we can continue on to Glyndyfrdwy."

The night became colder, and the chill settled into our bones. The sun, which at best was a rare phantom in that terrible winter, began to fail and dip. The trees slowly closed in around us. As the darkness came, Gruffudd judged that it was too dangerous to ride. We dismounted and led our horses, walking closely together in the lengthening darkness. Without a torch and with no moon, the forest is a dangerous place to go abroad at night. On a dark night, a man can walk ten paces in the forest from the house he has lived in all his life and be as lost as if he were in the wilds of Ethiopia or Cathy.

Gruffudd continued on, but I noticed that the farther we went; he had to stop more often and look more closely for signs.

Shivering, I turned to Owain. "Are we lost?" I asked.

"Hush" said Owain, "My Father knows his way. We must be patient."

The sun sinking behind the trees was eating away at the time we had. The cold clawed its way through our clothes until our hands and feet became numb. I started to shiver and my mind and body ached to stop and sleep for a while.

Gruffudd looked back at us. "This is the right way. We will be at our rest soon." On we walked, tripping and stumbling over tree roots and rocks as we went. Now it was completely dark. As I peered through the darkness, I saw a dim light leading our way. I realized that the Ellylldan, the spirit lights of the mountains, were leading us, and Gruffudd was following their path.

Finally Gruffudd cried out.

"Here it is" he shouted, and he rushed towards a small hut that was all but buried by snow. Owain and I stumbled after him to the hut. It was partially collapsed by the snow and frost. It had never been a sturdy building, and the weight of the snow had proved too much for it. One side had completely fallen in, and the door had collapsed in on itself.

"Quick" said Gruffudd, "Tie up your horses and help me clear the snow from the inside." We did as told and threw ourselves into the hut, digging with our hands at the snow. Gruffudd dug out the roof and tried to balance it on the broken beams. We piled the snow outside to strengthen and insulate the walls. Gruffudd looked around and found a small pile of kindling and firewood near the door way. He cleared a space in the snow and brought the wood inside. With his pocket flints he started and small fire.

"Go bring the beasts inside" he said to Owain. "They will die out there in the night, and we need their heat in here."

It is the practice of the poorer Welsh families to sleep inside with their beasts. This warms their house and ensures that their animals are safe from robbers and thieves. While this is a sound practice, the hut was barely big enough for us all. I remember forcing our horse against the far end of the hut, and the two horses pushed and whinnied being so close to the fire. The three of us crouched around the fire and snuggled closely for warmth.

"What shall we do, Father?" asked Owain, rubbing his hands together.

"We will wait the night," he said. We will sleep in turns and keep the fire going. If it goes out tonight, we will die from the cold. In the morning we can make the old Roman road and reach Glyndyfrdwy by noon. I will take the first watch and then Gwyn. Owain will take the third watch. When it is your watch, mark that the others are breathing well. If it seems to slow, wake them immediately. In this cold a man may drift into a sleep so deep that his soul will leave his body and be lost in the Otherworld forever. If you find yourself falling asleep, poke yourself with your blade. Pain is a great way to stay alert on watch."

Owain and I huddled together and drifted off within a few minutes. I fell into a deep, empty black sleep. It seemed as if I had slept for less than a moment when Owain shook me.

"Gwyn" he said, "Wake up. My Father has fallen asleep and will not wake up." I shook myself and looked around the hut. The horses were still tied at one end of the hut, their heads sagging against each other, and seemed barely alive. Gruffudd Fychan was slumped against the door. His eyes were closed and his face had taken on a terrible bluish tone. Owain was shaking him. Dawn was beginning to break.

"Did he wake you for your watch?" I asked.

"No, he must have fallen asleep in the night." Owain pulled his Father's tunic back and pressed his ear to his chest.

"His heart is still beating. Let us pull him close to the fire." We took hold of him and dragged his body over to the fire and sat closely by him.

"What shall we do?" I asked.

"We must try to make him warm. If he does not wake, one of us will go out at dawn to find help."

And so we sat and waited for the morning. Gruffudd did not wake up, and it became clear that one of us would have to go for help. We argued over who should go.

"I will go," I said. "You must stay with your Father. I will take a horse and ride down hill as fast as I can towards the old road. If I am lucky I will meet a traveler and bring help."

Owain nodded. "I will guard Father. You go, but take my jerkin to help you stay warm." I took his fur and leather jerkin and selected the strongest looking horse.

My breath came out in frosty white clouds. "I will be back soon, My Lord" I said.

I opened the door and was met with an icy blast of cold air. The horse shrunk back towards the inside of the hut and planted its hooves against the snow. I pulled her outside, and led her downhill through drifts of snow. In the dim morning light, the path out of the wood was easier than the way in. All I had to do was follow the incline, and it would eventually lead me into the Valley of the Dee. Once there I could follow the Dee until I came to the Roman Road. The Dee had been frozen solid all winter so it would be easy to cross. I set off with every hope of success, and indeed my plan worked. Before long the trees began to thin and I was able to mount my horse and ride. Eventually I came upon clear ground and saw the Dee ahead. I spurred my horse on and reached the banks of the river, following it for a mile or so before I found a place to cross on the ice. Once on the other side, I remounted and we headed up the bank and onto the road, heading east towards Glyndyfrdwy.

Around mid-morning I came upon the. The watchman saw me and raised the signal, and I saw servants and My Lord's household running towards me. As I got closer I could see that they were led by Elen Goch. She came straight to me.

"Where are my Husband and my Son? Where is my Husband's Telu?" she cried, her face ashen.

My breadth came thick and fast. "The Telu has been detained by the Lord of Ruthin. The Lord Gruffudd, Owain and me escaped and slept last night in a woodsman's hut upon Bwlch Coch. The Lord Gruffudd is ill and needs attention, and Owain sent me to get help."

With my words, Elen turned to her Steward and the others accompanying her.

"Prepare a search party immediately" she said

The servants pulled me from my horse and half carried me into the manor. They prepared a hot bath for me a in a barrel, stripped my clothes and thrust me into the warm water. My body burned and tingled and I cried out in shock. I looked up to see Crach peering down at me.

"Steady boy," he said. "You're half dead from the cold, and it will take some time for you to return to life."

"I will go with the party to find Owain and Gruffudd," he said. "I am skilled in the ways of the forest and will find them. You rest. You have done great service to your Lord and the whole of Wales today."

I can remember no more. I suppose I must have fainted from the shock of the warmth. I awoke hours later to find the house in an uproar. I roused myself from my bed and walked to the window.

In the distance I could see the party returning. A group of men rode fast towards the manor. I strained my eyes to see and caught the shape of a man slung over a horse.

As they came closer I picked out Crach. His long white hair flapped in the wind and he carried a bundle in front of him on his saddle. As he came closer I saw it was Owain. That he was not hung over a saddle like his Father boded well. I pulled on my clothes and stumbled and limped downstairs. By the time I had reached the inner court, the riders had dismounted.

I looked at Owain's still, pale face. "Will he live?" I asked Crach.

"Aye, he will" said Crach, "Though he may lose some toes."

"Gruffudd Fychan?" I asked.

"We were too late" said Crach, "He was gone to the Otherworld by the time we arrived. Owain had tried to keep him warm but he was past saving." He looked at me grimly, "It seems that Glyndyfrdwy has a new master today."

Crach hurried into the kitchen carrying Owain, and laid him down upon the cutting table. One of the riders turned to Owain's Mother. "I think he's gone, Mistress" he said, "I couldn't feel his heart beat".

Crach ignored him. "Bring blankets, boil some water and keep that bloody fire going," he shouted to the servants. "We must warm him up gradually." He tucked blankets around Owain's arms and stomach, and then leaned over and listened to Owain's chest. He rose and breathed into Owain's mouth, listened again at his chest, and then repeated the process, stopping every few breaths to massage his chest.

The household gathered around. Suddenly, Owain shuddered and began to breathe, haltingly at first, and then normally. I heard Cook talking, "Crach has brought the breath back to the boy. He has raised him from the dead."

THE STORY OF THE TRAVELS OF MY LORD OWAIN

Long were the days after that death. A great quiet fell upon the manor. Nothing moved but the mice in the rafters. All through the rest of that Great Frost, the household went in upon itself and, as frozen as the Dee, waited for spring to come. The death of the Lord Gruffudd tore open the hearts of all at the major, but the Lady Elen was inconsolable. The day her husband's lifeless body was brought home was the day she began to die. Although she was to be with us for many years afterwards, she was never truly alive again. Each day she slipped a little more from us until she became no more than a ghost moving silently around the manor.

In the absence of his Mother's care, I feared that Owain would slip into a fatal melancholy too. He was silent for many months and rarely went outside. He attended his lessons as charged, did his duty, and attended chapel but the joyful spirit in him was gone. The only one he warmed to in those terrible times was Crach.

They would spend long hours together talking of the old prophecies and the tales of the ancient kings of Britain. I believe it was during that time that Owain first began to believe his destiny and understand the role that he was to play in the future of Wales. From that time onward, he was always much interested in prophecy and never traveled far without taking Crach with him to interpret the signs that he saw.

Eventually, he winter ended as all winters must. By March the grass began to grow again, and by May the trees budded and bloomed. But still My Lord continued in his melancholy. Then one morning, I heard the sound of horsemen arriving at the manor. I went outside and saw Gruffudd Mawr and his telu dismounting from their horses. He looked down at me.

"Gwyn ap Eynon," he said solemnly. I remember that he always called me by my full name, for Gruffudd Mawr was very proper.

"Go find your Master and the Prophet. Tell them to come to me. We are to make a great journey, and I wish that he attend to me."

I dashed away to find Owain with Crach in the chapel. Crach had nothing against chapels of any kind and often spent time in them conversing with God and his angels. He was definitely a wizard and heretic, but not the sort the Church cared about. He kept his thoughts from the Saxons and spoke his heresies only in Welsh. Crach looked up at me.

"Has he come?" he said. I looked at him questioningly. "Gruffudd Mawr? Has he come yet?"

"How did you know?" I asked.

Crach laughed, "Boy, don't you know yet that I am aware of almost everything that happens or will happen? Besides, I sent a message to him that he should stop here on his journeys."

I turned to Owain, "He calls on you both to attend to him."

Owain shrugged and walked slowly toward Gruffudd Mawr, who was waiting in the courtyard.

"I have heard that you have been much in mourning for your Father" Gruffudd Mawr said. "That is right and proper, especially in the winter when Saturn is abroad and men turn their thoughts dark things. But the spring has come, and it is time to awake from your gloom. I have planned a great journey to the Abbey at Bangor. There I intend to endow the Brothers to say masses for your Father and give praise that you were returned to me. Because of your return from the dead, our tribe still possesses the heir to Powys and Deheubenth in your person. You shall come with me."

At first I thought that Owain would resist, but Crach placed his hand on the boy's shoulder and patted him gently.

"You must go with him, Owain" said Crach, "It is foretold that this year shall be a great awakening for you, and you will gather many allies for the later work of which we have spoken."

Gruffudd Mawr looked at him. "You will come too, Prophet. I desire some entertainment, and I cannot rely on Iolo" he jerked his thumb over towards Iolo Goch, "to entertain me. Your prophecies will keep me amused when I become bored with the Bard."

And so it was that we joined Gruffudd Mawr on his great journey through Wales.

The next day we set off westward along the Dee towards the Cantref of Arllenchwedd and the great mountains of Eryri. From there we rode through the passes and trackways north to Conwy and for the first time gazed out upon the sea and saw the Mor Iwerddan. We then followed the road south and came to the great Episcopal seat of Bangor. Once our business there was completed, we traveled southwest to Caernarfon along Sarnau Eln to meet with some of Gruffudd Mawr's friends at Dollellau. We then turned inland to head towards Bala and home.

I should take a moment here to educate any foreign readers who are not familiar with the wonders of our land.

Wales has two geographies. One is imposed upon us by the Normans and the Saxons. It consists of royal counties and the lands of the Marcher Lords. The royal counties comprise the old territory of the Gywnedd, what the Normans called Walli Pura, that were conjured by Longshanks when he treacherously defeated our blessed Lord Llewellyn the Last.

The Marcher territories were established when the Normans first came to Wales more than three hundred years ago. At that time William the Bastard and his brigands were too busy fighting the Saxons and the Danes to consider advancing into Wales. Instead, he empowered some of his most vicious and murderous bandits to create a string of territories along English border. This boundary region, known as the March, was outside England proper and was not be bound by English or Norman law. The Barons held it entirely free of Royal control. The only thing that bound them to the crown was their fealty and homage to the King himself. Thus, in each Marcher lordship, the Baron was sovereign while still a loyal subject to the King. The ruling Baron took as much land as he could hold and was free to extract whatever revenues he could take. The only rule was that he must defend his own lands and could not rely on the crown or the feudal host for support. This created a shield between England and Wales that acted as a cushion against Welsh forays into England.

In time the Marcher states grew until they encompassed all of the north east, the center, and the fertile valleys of the south. The Norman Lords who ruled the March governed as Welsh princes of old, maintaining traditional law and extracting revenue and military service from their bondsmen and free taeogions. So rich and powerful were these lands that many of the great families of England, the Mortimers, the Fitzalans, the De Clares, and the Carletons, based there powers in the March and recruited permanent standing armies that challenged the crown's power unless the king was clever enough to find profit for them in foreign wars.

Yet beneath this Saxon map there was a second Wales that had hardly changed since the days of Arthur. This Wales was a land of cantrefs, commotes and kingdoms.

From ancient times Wales had been divided into twenty-seven cantrefs. Each cantref contained one hundred trefs. A commote contained fifty trefs. In turn the cantrefs and commotes were assembled to make up the kingdoms of Wales.

This was the world in which we moved. We ignored the Saxons and their boundaries and moved silently between cantref and commote, ignoring the foreigners' claims. This was easy to do for the Saxons and their Norman masters had kept to the lowlands. They never ventured into the bleaneau, the highlands, and its wild forests. They build their towns and castles all along the lowlands and avoided our places in the hills. Thus, most of Wales remained effectively ours. As long as we stayed quiet and avoided the Saxons, we could live free in the bleaneau and mountains and never see the strangers.

Unfortunately, it is a poor life on the high ground. When the world was warmer in my grandfather's day, it was possible to scratch a living from the peaks. But by time of King Edward the Frank-Killer, the world had grown cold, and even the hardiest taeogion knew he must leave the highlands in the winter. As such, while we could travel and hide in our mountains and hills, we could not live there forever and were forced into service for our masters.

In those first days of our great journey though Wales it did not seem as though we would ever see the Saxon again. We crossed from Gruffudd Mawr's lands into the cantref of Penllyn and into the flinty vastness of Eryri and the cantrefs of Arllechwedd and Arfon. Along the way we avoided the roads that would have led us through the Englishries and traveled the mountain trackways known only to our people.

Every night we would sleep at the manor of some uchelwyr who was related to Gruffudd Mawr and Owain. We passed our evenings consuming strong ale, listening to tales from Iolo and Crach and sharing news from the outside world. Gradually I began to understand just how big our little country is. For while Wales is a small place in the great scheme of things, but, to those who love it, a vast empire of the mind. Every rock carries a story, every hill and mountain a legend or tale to inspire the worthy, and every tref its great hero and tales of conquest and victory. In our people's minds, Wales has grown from a small patch at the edge of the world to a vast empire of the imagination.

And great and glorious is its beauty. Once on our travels I remember Gruffudd Mawr turning to us as we looked out over some particularly beautiful valley and saying, "Look boys. Iolo and Crach say we await a sleeping king to save our people, but is not the land so beautiful and fine that it yet may be that king? Is not the beauty of Wales sufficient to cause any true Welshman to rise up of his own accord and defend this great land?"

I have traveled to the eternal city of Rome itself and seen the mighty Alps, and I can attest that there is no pass more beautiful and greater than those saw in the valleys of the North. Green are our hills, dark and thick are our forests, old and hard are our rocks and deep and dark are our lakes. This is what the world looked like before the first men came. When we were given this place by the Lord God, he trusted that we would not harm it or destroy it as the foreigners have done. We have kept our bond, and when we must account for ourselves at

Judgment, we will be able to say that we have protected and cherished our legacy and can return it to him as he gave it to us to use.

This is an important point. Other countries were made or founded by some ambitious tribe or prince. But Wales was not made. It was given to us, and we do not rule but hold it in trust until our Lord calls. Of course, in truth, it is not ours alone. We have always shared it with many other creatures like the Tylwyth Teg, Bendith Y Mamau, Coblynau, the Gwrach Y Rhybin, and, of course, the trees. Many of them have proved to be worse tenants than we are. The trees are far too boisterous for a small country like this and constantly war against each other. Oak and elm are particular vicious and fight each other constantly.

The journey did open our eyes, for not only did we see the beauty of our land, we also saw the pain. We saw the terrible Iron Ring of castles that the Kings of England built to keep us down. It is said that there are more castles in Wales than any other place in the world. After that journey, I believed it, for we did not travel more than half a day before encountering a castle built by our oppressors. So much do the Saxons hate and fear us that never do they live outside their walls. Thus, what is a manor in England must be a castle in Wales if a Saxon is to feel safe in his bed. Every town is in truth a garrison of soldiers defending the Saxons from the heathen Welsh. More than that, the Saxons have built some of the mightiest fortresses in the world to keep us down. They hide behind their walls and sally out to lord it over us. Lord, how I do hate them.

But strangely I do not hate the Normans as much as the Saxons. The Normans are decent enough people, and have a proper contempt for the Saxons. A good Norman knight can be a fine drinking companion and good hunting company. They are not averse to learning our language. I have noted that wherever the Normans go, they have a tendency to blend in. In England they became English, in Ireland they are more Irish than the Irish, and in Naples and Sicily they are pure Italians. I suppose it comes from being Northman themselves. After all, they settled in France when they came down from the North and became Frenchmen within a few generations.

I promised that as my story continued I would be more focused, but I have wandered again. It is my age. My mind wanders, and more than ever I find it difficult to stay on one topic. So where was I? Our great trip around Wales; yes, that was it. Well at first I assumed that the reason for our journey was to visit a great many of Gruffudd Mawr's old friends. Slowly, however, we began to discern a deeper purpose. Gruffudd was seeking out alliances. We saw Gruffudd Mawr sounding out his acquaintances on this or that issue. Gradually he would turn the conversation to the situation in country. I would hear him say:

"What did they think of the Mortimer's efforts to get their lands back? Had they heard the tales of that greedy bastard Earl Humphrey of Hereford? What about King Edward's sale of Welsh offices to his cronies? What about the French? Would the truce last? And what about the Bretons, the Duke of Brittany had freed them from the French, a free British land? What did they think of that? You'd wonder why it didn't happen here."

He would listen carefully to their responses and mark them down as loyal or rebel. If they fell in the rebel column, he would pull them aside and they would disappear for some nefarious purpose. The next day we would part, and Gruffudd Mawr would exchange a hearty handshake and a promise that he would send messengers soon.

"What do you think it is?" asked Owain.

"I have no idea" I said, "Although clearly there is some plan afoot."

"I shall talk with Crach about it," Owain offered. "He has a loose tongue and is always ready to talk."

We discussed this with Crach as we neared the coast by Bangor. We found him as he was standing at the shore to the Western sea looking out toward Inys Mon.

Owain walked up to him, "What are you thinking of, Crach?"

"Just remembering" said Crach. "Do you know this is where the Romans faced the final battle with the Druids? They came into our land in the time of Claudius the Lame. Do you know they brought elephants with them? They didn't reach here until old Claudius had become a god and Nero the Mad was their prince. It took the Romans nine years to hack their way through Britain to get to this place. They came here because they knew that this was the place where the Druids hatched their young. If they could break us here, they would break the hold of the Wise Ones over our people."

I looked up at him. He was staring off into the past. The Island of Mon was barely a mile away from here, and the coast was clearly visible in that flat, dreary, lifeless light, so common to the Menai Straight. From where we stood, I could see the silent beaches and the clumps of oak and yew.

"The Legions reached this point and looked out. The far shore was thick with thousands of Wise Ones. They filled the horizon. Their hair was bleached with lime and mare's urine and pulled up into spikes, and their bodies were tattooed and painted with the secret signs of the old gods. They were screaming and bellowing to the sky, shouting out their curses on the people of Rome, calling the secret words, and begging the gods to come and destroy the foreigners. Their women were there as well, all dressed in black, shouting invocations and calling down the gods on the invaders. The sky was filled with ravens and eagles sent by Morganna and Macha, enough to blot out the sun. The Wise Ones had captured some Romans and the positioned them at the front. When they were sure they had the Romans' attention, they removed their heads and drank the blood. Others they skinned alive, and the Old Ones went about with the skins pulled over their bodies. It was an incredible sight. Even the Legions, the masters of all of Europe, Africa, and Asia hesitated. They had never seen a sight so terrifying."

"What happened?" asked Owain, his eyes wide.

"What do you think? They were Romans, they followed orders. That's what made them great. Their captains gave the order to advance and off they went. They brought forward their artillery and fired across the strait. It is said that the eagles and ravens flew down and snatched the missiles from the air, but there were too many and our boys began to fall. When there was space enough for them on the beach, the Romans brought forward their boats and floating bridges.

"Great engineers were the Romans," he added. "They swam their horses across and ran them onto the beaches like the warriors they were. We pushed them back into the sea, but they came again. Each time they came they took more of us than we took of them. So many men died that day that the Strait turned red. The fight was long and painful, but the outcome was clear. Even Macha manifested to fight them back and Morganna's ravens came down and mobbed them as they crossed. The Legions kept coming. They pushed us back into the forests and onto our scared groves. Our boys fought them hard and begged Lludd and Beli Mawr to manifest but they were in the east with Boudicca as she burned Lludd's Town and it is well known that gods cannot be in two places at once. They must have thought that she stood a better chance of defeating the Romans there and that Beli Mawr's daughters could defeat the Romans on their own. They were wrong, of course. All of our people were killed. The Romans cut down our holy groves, smashed our caldrons, stole our talking skulls, and broke the altar stones. At the end of it all, the old ways were finished. Ten thousand years of history lost in a day; all our knowledge and wisdom gone. It was a terrible thing."

"Did anyone escape?" I asked.

"The Romans took some prisoners, men that had been wounded in the fight. They tortured them to make them reveal the magic of the Wise Ones, but they died before they would talk. The few who survived were sent to Rome in cages to show the Romans had defeated the Britons forever and then executed them in the arena. They say Myrddin was there but escaped. He went under the hill and slept until Arthur came to free his people. I cannot vouch for the veracity of that story. Myrddin is said to have been in many places, and he comes and goes when he is needed. There is a rumor that he was not even here and instead fought with Boudicca's armies and helped her daughters escape the final battle with the Romans."

"You describe it well" said Owain gazing out over the beach.

Crach smiled. "The stories are well known. There's a Roman called Tacitus who wrote a good tale about it. I read it when I was in Rome. It was a good read, although far too sad and he got certain things wrong."

"So did it really happen like that?" asked Owain.

"Close enough" said Crach. He tossed a stone into the strait. He looked at us and smiled,

"We should go and ask the Great Toad of Cors Fochno in the bog land north of Aberystwyth. He is the oldest thing on Earth and will answer one question for each person once in their life. I've already asked him mine, so perhaps you can use yours by asking him about the Wise Ones and the day the Romans came to the Holy Island."

We nodded and walked on discussing what we would want to ask the Toad.

After Bangor, we turned south and headed back into Eryri. To you foreigners who are reading this account, Eryri is a wild place full of brigands and outlaws. It would take a brave man to cross it without a strong escort. Gruffudd Mawr plunged in as if he was going to church on a Sunday morning. He led us into all manner of wild and lost places. We pushed deeper and deeper into the mountains, staying on the high tracks and the places where no foreigner ever goes. We passed around the south short of Bala and headed north up towards Dinas Mawddwy. We stayed a night at the LlewGoch Tavern and then plunged up the mountain on the track to Llanwchllyn which climbs up through the mountains to cross Bwich y Groes.

We headed up the pass until we were almost at its highest point. It was a flinty, dark place. I remember Owain turning to me and saying, "This is just the place where I would expect outlaws to lurk."

As is the way when such things are said, hardly were the words out of his mouth when an arrow flew towards us from the rocks and thudded on the ground in front of our party.

Gruffudd Mawr raised his hand to halt our little column. We scanned the pass and saw no one. Then, out from behind a rock, a small, wiry man appeared. He was not much to look at. Short, thin and with short red hair and skin as pale as a ghost,

"I am here to request toll for your passage. The paths here are treacherous, and we are willing to provide you with guides and protection for your journey." He smiled.

Gruffudd Mawr looked at him. "You honestly expect me to pay for transit? I, the true Prince of Powys Fadog, the great and renowned Gruffudd Mawr of proud and distinguished decent? Why should I pay for anything?"

The brigand smiled. "You have an excellent point My Lord, and were I alone I would agree that my request is foolhardy. But I am not on my own." He waved his hands and the upper levels of the pass were full of men, all of them armed with the long spears that were the chosen weapon of the men of the North. The outlaw continued, "So you see, My Lord, I have made sure to add a little weight to my argument."

The air was very still. I began to feel that something terrible was about to happen. I looked at Gruffudd Mawr. He eyes were alive, and his eyebrows twitched and flicked. I expected a sudden explosion of violence. Just at the moment when the storm was about to break, he burst into laughter. He leapt from his horse and threw his arms wide.

"Sionni Mawddwy, you are a brigand, a wolf's head, and an outlaw, but you have a fine sense of humor. Come and embrace me and meet my Grandson" he said.

The bandit walked forward and embraced Gruffudd Mawr as an old friend. Gruffudd Mawr turned to Owain. "Boy, come and meet the finest spearman and cattle raider in all of Gwynedd."

Owain climbed down from his pony and walked toward the bandit. Sion Mawddwy looked down at him.

"He's a fine boy, Gruffudd. Sorry am I to hear that your son was lost to you. It is good that you have such a fine grandson to continue your legacy."

Gruffudd Mawr smiled. "He is a fine boy and will be a good solider for Wales one day."

He turned to Owain. "Sionni was with me in Flanders and Aquitaine when I was young. He was just a boy then and anxious to gain some experience in the ways of the world and find his fortune in the French Wars. He was an honest thief and a good fighter but was not comfortable taking orders from the Saxons. He got bored and went home to perfect his thieving skills on the Saxons and Normans hereabouts. He has proved to be very successful."

Sion bowed. "Gruffudd Mawr, you praise me too much. I am a simple bandit. I trade in stolen cattle, robbery, and small time hostage taking, the gentle country pursuits of our people." He turned to Owain, "I come from a long line of bandits. My family has the distinction of being known as the Red Bandits of Mawddwy. We have been noted robbers here for many generations. We have served the Kings of Gwynedd in wartime. Since the Saxons came to our mountains, we have devoted ourselves to fighting their wars against the French and stealing their cattle. Our goal is to make a profit for ourselves and make life as uncomfortable as we can for the Saxons. If we are lucky, they will be tired of losing their cattle and portables and go home back across the Dyke. Then the Prince of Gwynedd can return, and we go back to our old ways of sealing cattle from our neighbors."

Gruffudd Mawr roared with laughter and slapped him on the back. "Enough of that for now" he said. "We will speak more of the Prince after we have rested."

And so we met the famous Red Bandits of Mawddwy.

THE TRUTH OUR DEALINGS WITH OWAIN LLAWGOCH

The Red Bandits were a pleasant bunch of lads. They treated us well and gave us a good time while we stayed with them. They had established their base in the Dugoed Forest in the Mawddwy Valley. According to Crach they were descended from the Bright Northerners or Norse as the English call them. This band was so violent and unpleasant that their comrades asked them to leave. They finally washed up on our shores and soon found their way here. Rather than settling down to a life of farming as many of their fellows did, they decided to continue their old ways and taught the crafts of robbery, cattle stealing and general brigandage to the people hereabouts.

We followed them deep into the forest through a winding path, where we were welcomed to their village. It was nicely laid out. I looked around the camp and the reason for their name became apparent immediately. Every bandit had bright red hair; it was clear they were sprung from a common stock.
At that time I was very afraid of them, but since then I have gained a great respect for bandits. They are hard men. They live in the worst of circumstances. The cold and rain are their friends. They live in the wild for most of their lives with rocks and dirt for their beds. Most will have lost a finger or toe to the cold at some time. But they are good boys and useful to know.

There were other men there too who were not bandits. Listening to them talk, I could hear the soft accents of the men of Gwent and Morgannwg, the flattened, clipped voices of the men from Inys Mon, and the almost Irish sound of the speech of the Southwest. There were also foreigners, men from far across the seas. I could pick out at least two who spoke French and one who spoke a language that sounded like Latin but wasn't.

Owain and I discussed what might be happening and why these men had traveled so far to meet with men that were little better than common thieves. Eventually, Owain decided to ask his Tadcu.

"Why are we here Tadcu?" he asked Gruffudd Mawr.

"I have much business with these men" he replied. "You will attend with me in my discussions. It is important that my heir be present at so important a meeting. You will learn that bandits are good friends for a man to have. I have maintained strong ties with our local bandits for many years and, if a man looks to expand his influence further, he must strengthen his ties with bandits elsewhere. Remember as is well said "A fo ben, bid bont" (if you want to be a leader be a bridge).

"But why are all these other men here too?" Owain asked.

"A bandit camp is a good place to have a discussion when you want no one to hear. Bandits are not known for their love the law, and it is one place where you can be sure that no Saxons or their agents will be found. Like me these men have business that concerns Wales and I thought it best for us to attend to it here where no one will spy upon us."

He dismissed us. We left to explore the camp and busied ourselves by getting into small troubles.

Suddenly, there was a great commotion. We rushed to the camp's entrance, where Crach and Iolo stood. Owain looked up at them.

"Who is come?" he asked.

Iolo's face was full of smiles. "Tudur Vychan is here and some men from the Inys Mon. Praise the Lord, the time has come."

"What time has come?" asked Owain.

"The time of our deliverance, Little Lord," he replied, "The tribes are gathering to prepare for his arrival. Your Tadcu has been preparing the way. He has traveled far and made many alliances. Our deliverance is at hand, Glory to God."

I was confused by all of this. It was clear that something momentous was to happen, but all of this made no sense. We stood with Iolo and watched as Tudur Fychan and his band arrived. As with Gruffudd Mawr, he had brought his oldest sons. I say sons because Tudur Fychan's oldest sons were twins; Rhys and Gwilym. That was the first time I saw them. Both were pitched on one horse. The two red-haired beasts grasped each other tightly, simultaneously fighting, arguing and laughing as they entered the bandits' camp.

I knew the Tudur Brothers for many years, and I never once saw them at rest. They had a boundless energy and were constantly fighting with anyone who would have a go. When there was no one else to fight, they would spar with each other.

Their horse drew near to us. The moment they spied Owain, they pulled their horse to a stop and jumped down. One ran to Owain.

"You are Cousin Owain" they said. "Da told us we would meet you. We are the Sons of Tudur Fychan. Your people were once Kings of Powys. Will you be a King again when Owain LlawGoch returns?"

We looked at them, quite lost.

One of them continued. "When Prince Owain returns from France, will you be a King again, or will you swear loyalty to the Kings of the North?"

Confused, Owain looked around until Crach intervened.

"Quiet cubs" Crach said to the Tudur boys. "Did not your Father tell you to keep your council? These things will be decided tonight." He swatted at the brothers and they scampered away.

"What is going on?" asked Owain.

"Do you know of Owain LlawGoch?" asked Crach.

"All the world knows of the exiled Prince" said Owain.

And indeed he was right. The entire world knew of Owain LlawGoch. He was the last of the Kings of Gwynedd. Rather than accept the lordship of the Kings of England, he had fled Wales and gone to France. Of course, many men had taken the road to France. But unlike them, he had gone to work for the

King of France. He had gained a great reputation as a fighter and was known for his bloody ways. He was much distinguished for his campaigns in France, Castile, and the Empire, and particularly for his wars in the lands of the Swiss while in the French King's service. Many men said that he was the Mab Daragon and that he would return to free Wales.

Owain looked up at Crach. "Is he returned? Will we fight with him against the Saxons?"

Crach looked grim. "He says he will come, but he has said that before. I have seen what is to come, and this is not his path." He turned around and walked to the camp.

"Come" Owain said to me, "There will be a gathering. We must see what will be decided."

He was right. That night, in front of the great fire, all the Lords of the North sat together and discussed the future. Gruffudd Mawr was there to represent Powys and the men from the South arrived to hear proposals. Tudur Vychan was the speaker for the Northerners. I remember him standing there in the firelight, his arms raised to draw everyone to listen.

"Brothers and comrades," he said. "We are here because our Lord has called us from across the seas. We have emissaries from the King of France and the King of Castile. They both have sworn help. They promise men and money. Aye, there will be gold, for we will need to sweeten the way. Is it not said that money is the key that opens all locks?" There were nods and murmurs of agreement. "I will let them speak and you will hear their promise."

One of the foreigners stood up.

"I am Jean de Loubert" he spoke in French with Tudur Vychan translating, "I am a true subject of his Royal Majesty Charles of France. I bring great tidings for you. His Majesty has known long your oppression at the hands of the barbarous Saxons and has shed many tears for your pain. He is a good friend of you true Prince Yeuain de Galles."

"He means Prince Owain" interjected Tudur Vychan.

"He grieves at your sad condition and the indignities that your brave Prince must suffer. Your Prince has attended the King in Paris and has gathered around him many brave Welshman who have aided the King in his struggles with the English. He has proclaimed his intention to reclaim his kingdom, which is his by right of succession, kindred and inheritance."

The men around him stamped their clubs on the ground and waved their torches in the air. He continued.

"The King of France has given Prince Yeuain ships and arms. He has provided him with gold and silver to reward his friends for their loyalty. He has assured him that he may leave France and return to Wales to seek his rights. He has given him soldiers from his own household and horses from his own stables. He is returning, my friends. He has come for your deliverance."

There was a great roar. The men raised their torches and began to chant. "Deliverer, Deliverer."

Then Gruffudd Mawr stepped forward and held his hands up. There was silence.

"You all know who I am" he said. There were murmurs of assent.

"We are Kings of Powys" he said.

There was a shout from the back, "Powys Fadog only. The heirs of Gwenwynwyn are the Kings of Wenwywyn."

Gruffudd Mawr glowed. "The heirs of Gwenwynwyn lost their rights because of their treason against the Kings of Gwynedd" he shouted.

Whenever was it different in Wales? When one man stood up, another tried to cut him down. We are a family of quarreling siblings. Each time a man succeeds there will always be someone to say he does not deserve it or that "his brother was better but he never got the chance." We are always undermined by our arguing and our inability to accept a single leader.

Tudur Vychan stood. "I stand by Gruffudd Mawr. He is the rightful King of all Powys." There were grunts of approval. "Heirs of Gwenwynwyn betrayed Llewellyn. The Heirs of Gwenwynwyn were approached to come to this gathering but showed no interest. They have sworn their allegiance to the Lords De Charlton. Whatever were their rights, they will forfeit them when the Prince returns."

Gruffudd Mawr continued.

"As I said, I am rightful King of Powys. My Grandson is rightful King of Deheubenth. I swear that if Owain ap Thomas ap Rhodri ap Llewellyn ap Llewellyn, known to the world as Owain LlawGoch, returns to Wales and reclaims his lands, I will swear allegiance to him. Furthermore, I will place my estates, my fortune, my kin, and my tribe at his service. He comes to fight for Wales and free us from the tyranny of the Saxon. I will fight with him."

There were more shouts, and then he said, "But, I will not fight against the Lords Arundel. I have sworn peace with them, and as long as they stay on the English side of the border, I will not fight with them." There were nods and murmurs. After all, each man there had allegiances and it was always our weakness that we do not break our promises. So unlike the English we are.

Tudur Vychan stood up and shook his hand. "Can we hear from our other visitors?"

The men from Gwent, Brecon and Morgannwg stood in turn and made their oath. It was clear that this would be a rising of national proportions when the Prince came.

Then a man stood up who wore the tonsure of a priest or a monk. He was clearly a man of importance and wore the pale robe of the White Brothers.

"My Children" he said, "Be it known that our order favors your endeavor. Furthermore, the Bishop of Bangor and of St. Aslph's has also received word and blesses your cause."

This was the final word we needed. The crowd went wild. Men applauded and danced. The Holy Church blessed our efforts. What more could a man want? The bandits produced and a band of harpers and pipers stuck up a tune. With all of Wales at our back, the blessing of the Church, the support of the Kings of France and Castile, and a rightful heir to Gwynedd, how could we lose? We feasted long and hard into that night, and made a many promise for our great campaign to come.

The next day is was over. The men had sore heads to nurse and messages to carry. They departed one by one and set off for home. We also returned to our lands and waited. We waited all through that summer. We waited all through that autumn and into the next year. The men trained in secret. The women made arrows and collected food in secret places. After our lessons, we no longer played but practiced with the bow or holding the rock to strengthen our arms. Gruffudd Mawr brought a master of weapons to Glyndyfrdwy, and Owain trained with him day and night. Winter came and still we waited. By now, everyone knew that the Red Hand was returning. You could see his symbol everywhere if you knew where to look. The hand of a man smeared in blood or red berry dye on a tree or a wall somewhere. Banditry increased. Wild men came down from the mountains and struck across the border to bring out cattle and sheep. The Saxons could not travel from one colony to the next without being accosted or shot at by some lonely archer. We would hear that the Reaves of this or that shire had spotted a Castilian agent spying out castles or a Frenchman had been arrested counting pikestaffs in an armory. Everywhere the country was coming to life. But still he did not come.

Then one day a rider came to the manor. He rode up the old road from the east. As they say, nothing good ever comes from the east. He wore the livery of the Lord Arundel. I remember he came into the courtyard and asked to see the man of the house. Owain and his Mother came out.

"I am he, sir" said Owain.

The messenger looked at him suspiciously. His Mother spoke

"I am a poor widow. I hold these lands in trust under the protection of the Lord Arundel for my son until his majority. My husband died but two winters ago."

The messenger nodded.

"Then I give you my message, My Lady. The Lord Arundel, Barron of Cirk wishes it be known that the outlaw, pirate, and traitor known as Owain of the Bloody Hand, made an attack on the King's processions on the island of Guernsey. Be it known that the pirate left France from Harfleur with several ships provided him by the so-called King of France. Further, be it known that he revealed his traitorous intend by ravaging the said islands and breaking the King's peace. He remained there many days before the winds and the commands of his master called him back. Be it known that he retreated utterly defeated by the good people of Guernsey and, such were his injuries, that he will make no other attack upon our lands. God save King Edward."

He looked up from his scroll. "My Lady you are instructed that this message must be spread among all your tenants and kinsmen, and be read out from the pulpit in both English and the natives' language for one month. Furthermore, be it known that any man caught promoting or passing tales concerning the imminent invasion or return of Owain of the Bloody Hand, will be judged a traitor and acting contrary to the King's and the Lord Arundel's peace. Any such offenders must be immediately turned over the Lord Arundel's authority for judgment and punishment."

He bowed and asked for directions to the next tref.

So that was it. Owain LlawGoch was not coming. Later we were to learn that the winds had pushed his ships back and he had been forced into Guernsey. He had waited there for the winds to turn, but then a message from the King of France had arrived calling him back to face some new menace to France.

France was saved and we were left to hang. Suddenly, men who had been Owain LlawGoch's staunchest partisans disappeared. Red hands were no longer seen, bandits went back into the hills, and Castilian spies and French agents set to sea. There was also a great burning of documents and letters. Agreements that had been made were destroyed and friends were cursorily absent at feasts and fairs. In the March, the high men ran to their Lords to show their loyalty and to testify that they had always been their strongest supporters, while others were rumored to have spoken treasons. Tudur Vychan was particularly adept at changing sides and quickly became one of the leading men in searching out traitorous bandits.

However, some were too badly incriminated. Such a man was Gruffudd Mawr. His sympathies were an open secret. He was known to have dealt with bandits and traveled far across the North the preceding year. He was a marked man from the day the news came that Owain was not coming. But he was a brave and a clever man. He knew the Lord Arundel favored him and would not move against him without evidence. Further, he knew that that evidence would appear in time. So, one day, he determined to go hunting in an area known for his dangerous cliffs and crevasse and its ferocious wolves and wild boar. He went alone with only a single spear, leaving early in the morning. It was said that it must have been a wolf or boar of great power the killed him, for when his body was found at the bottom of a ravine the next day, it had been clawed and bitten as if he had attacked the beast with his bare hands.

It was a hard time for Owain and his family. Without a male heir who had reached his majority, the possession of land is always unsure and unsafe. But it turned out that shortly before his death, Gruffudd Mawr had visited the Lord Arundel and secured his agreement to respect and defend our rights. In return, he had transferred lands in the south into the Lord's procession. Further, Gruffudd Mawr had met with Sir David Hanmer and secured protection from the law over our lands. Sir David was then a jusdiciar and a respected man. He had secured contracts with Sir David to take our land in trustee until my Lord's majority. Thus, Gruffudd Mawr had defended My Lord's lands from the vicious encroachment of other Marcher Lords through Arundel's good graces and predations of lawyers and the Crown through Sir David's protection.

But there was a price to pay. I recall another visit, just after the funeral of Gruffudd Mawr, when Sir David came to the manor. I watched from behind a door open ajar.

"Your Grandfather made provision for you," he said to Owain. You will come with me and live with my family and learn the ways of the English. Then you will attend the Inns of Court in London to study the law. Your Grandfather was a great man, but he belonged to a time past. He wanted me to tell you one thing and bade you to follow his council. He said, 'Tell Owain that I was wrong. His Father's ways were the best. Learn the law and study hard. Books and words will be our new defense'."

Sir David left the room to make arrangements for our journey. I crept out from behind the door.

"What shall we do?" I asked Owain.

"Just as my Tadcu said. We shall go with Sir David, and I shall learn the law," he said.

"But what of the great campaign to free our lands?" I asked

"I have not forgotten" Owain replied, "Tadcu said that books and words were our defense. What Sir David never heard was that he also said that swords, bows, and bandits will be our best offense."

CONCERNING OUR SOJOURN AT HANMER MEER

Hanmer Village; how English it was. It was just a few miles from Wales, but totally different. Yeomen in orderly homes arranged around a green with a fine great oak growing in the middle, boys playing stick ball on quiet evenings, and men drinking ale in the tavern when work was down. Money, yes coin money, was changing hands. All Welsh men know that money is evil and best left to rich men, such as Flemings and Jews. The idea that a common man would have and hold money and use it in exchange was strange to me then. I was shocked and surprised that common men would use coins. It was then I decided that the English were an alien race and that they must be removed from our Holy Land before they polluted and contaminated our people further.

The Hamners lived in a fine hall that fronted the green. Behind it were a good orchard and a very pleasant kitchen garden. The church snuggled close by. It was a good church built in stone by the Normans. The great lake, Hanmer Mere, dominated the hamlet, a "mere" being the word that the English of these parts used when referring to a lake. A very odd language is English; so many words for the same thing. In Welsh we have the opposite problem. We use the same word for many things. Thus, "pwll" means a pit, a hole, a lake, and a pool. It depends on where you mean and who you are talking to. I mean, Wales is a small country and everyone knows what you mean.

The Hamners were a mixed family. The old man was English, but the rest of them were properly Welsh. Sir David Hamner's mother had been a Welsh woman, so she had beaten some civilization into him. His wife, Angharad verch Llewellyn Ddu, was a good woman from Cirk. She was the daughter of Llewellyn Ddu ap Gruffudd ab Iorwerth Foel. Black Llewellyn was much respected, although a bit of a bastard. He was one of those men from a past age, of the world before the Great Mortality. His great advantage was that he lived longer than any of his contemporaries. In the end he became quite interesting simply because he was so old. His children remembered him in all of his glory, though they had little good to say about him. I saw them cross the road rather than speak to him. Angharad bore three sons: Sir David Marged, Gruffudd, and Jenkin. They grew up in Wrexham and were very much town lads. I shall talk more of Marged later.

What can one say of old Judge Hanmer? When I knew him back then he was not yet at Sergeant-of-Law. He did not reach that position until we were in London. He was every inch the man-of-law though. He was prudent, wise, and greedy as the day is long. If there was money to be made from a client, he was up early and after him all day. Whenever I saw him at town he would be at the porch of some church touting for clients. He was very good at his job, very discrete and dignified. He had a fine way of talking. He stitched his words together so that they had the sound of being much cleverer taken together than individually. I will say that he had a good knowledge of the law. He seemed familiar with all of the cases dating back to the time of the William the Bastard. He could write a pleading on any subject, and no man could stand against his argument. He was always in the company of landowners. He had no feel for the common people outside the assizes and preferred to stay out of their company.

What else? Well, he was frugal in his appearance. I believe he only had one good robe. I remember him best astride an old piebald horse, wearing a motley coat with a narrow, white silk belt. On his head sat a plain white skull cap and he wore a grey hood around his shoulders to keep the wind out. In truth, he saved his money to buy land, of which he was known to be a great purchaser. Yet whatever his wealth came to, it did not seem to make him happier. The richer he got, the busier he became.

The Hanmers had a complicated ancestry. They were originally Flemish, but somehow had found their way to Scotland, sided with Longshanks and then came south and settled in Hanmer. Until the Great Mortality they were petty tenants without much to their name. They had held the office of beadle for the Arundels and had presided over the hallmote. After the Great Mortality there were few left who could read and write and even fewer that knew the law. The King reached out to anyone who could keep order with a measure of justice and common sense. Sir David was one of those men. From being the son of an impoverished country knight, he was able to rise in the service of the law. He became a juror and, in time, a justice. He used his fees to purchase land from the Arundels, who were only too happy to unload it as they had had not the men to work it, and established himself as a presence in land. I suppose he was a good man, but he and I never got on too well. He was too cold for me, and I was too common for him. If it was left to him, I would have been sleeping with the servants in the kitchen, but Owain and Elen were insistent. I remember Elen saying the day we left with him, "David, take care that Owain has Gwyn with him. He has been through many deaths in his life and needs some constancy. Gwyn is a good boy and will be a great aid to Owain in the years to come. Keep him as if he is my son and see he has his lessons. Owain will need educated men around him." Sir David looked confused, but didn't have it in his heart to hurt a widow. He agreed and was as good as his word. He took me and treated me well, though he did keep me at arm's length.

Although Elen was willing enough to send us out into the world, she was not willing to let Tudur or Lori go. Lori was always the apple of her mother's eye and was never far from her sight. Even when she was a grown woman she did not stray too far from home. Elen would have smothered Tudur too if she had had a chance. She wanted him to go into the Church and pushed him mightily in that direction. However, Tudur was not for the bookish life. While Owain was as quick as a whip when it came to book learning, Tudur ran from books as though they carried plague. In the absence of a strong father, Tudur ran wild, and by the time we returned to Wales, he was sorely in need of discipline.

Crach, of course, came with us. He never had a proper place in the Hanmer and spent most of his time going back and forth between the Tavern and the Hall. He became quite a local character, and during our time at Hanmer was well known as a horse doctor and cunning man. Sir David clearly disapproved of him and initially tried to cut off his allowance. For a time he was successful, but when he saw Crach was establishing himself within the villages and was striking up a business as a money diviner and finder of lost things, he decided it would be better to keep him on a shorter leash. Sir David reinstituted his allowance and allowed him to sleep in the shack in the Hall's kitchen garden.

After a year or so we were fluent enough in the foreigners' tongue that we could fit into their world. We learnt our lessons, said our prayers, and got into all the trouble that boys get into. It was around this time that I recall that love and longing first entered our world.

Owain was the first. The object of his affection was young Marged Hanmer. Now Marged and Owain had been promised to each other for many years. Gruffudd Fychan and Judge Hanmer had sat down one day soon after Marged's birth and worked out an arrangement. Both men saw advantages for an alliance. As all the world knows, the richer a man is, the less likely he marries for love. Only the poor can marry for love alone. Everyone else must consider his family's interest very carefully and calculate how the match will advance his house.

Marged was a few years younger than us and was not there for the first few months of our time at Hanmer. As with most girls of her state, she had been sent off to a nunnery for her education. She returned towards the end of the second year of our time at Hanmer. Her father determined that she had learned all a woman needed to know; that is, reading, writing, some knowledge of sums, embroidery, music, French, and the preparation of perfumes, balsams, simples and confectionaries. Accordingly, he brought her home.

The moment Owain saw her, he fell in love. Marged as I remember her then was a beautiful girl. Golden hair tumbling over a compact, curvy little body, with the palest blue eyes and pure, white skin. Owain suddenly found himself in awe of her. In a minute he turned from being the most desired young man in the village to the most hapless dog in the county. He took every excuse to be with her and was, for once, completely tongue tied when it came to speaking with her. She was well aware of the effect she had on him. It has been my experience that girls who have been boarded up in nunneries emerge much more knowing of the ways of the world than girls who remain on the outside. I have little idea of what happens behind those walls, but I have come to the conclusion that some strange magic is practiced when women are gathered together in large numbers.

Slowly over the months, Owain and Marged grew. Marged became Owain's obsession. He followed her everywhere. When she spoke, he was struck silent. Everything she did was wonderful, and every action was perfection. Of course, she was changing too. She repaid his attention in full and soon they were sweethearts. It was fairly disgusting for an outsider: long painful looks at mass, sweet smiles at meals and stolen conversations when her Mother was distracted. Of course we all thought that no one noticed. If we had had any sense we would have seen that Marged and Owain's families had fixed them together years ago. They pushed them together and waited for it to occur to them. If nothing had happened, it would have made no difference to the outcome. It's simply easier in these matters if you can persuade the two young people involved that it was their idea.

Of course, all of this didn't mean that their parents were anxious for carnal expression of their love. Marged's mother kept a stern eye on her. But young love will always find a way. Slowly they began to meet and exchange kisses and touches. As they matured their passion flared, and I could see what was going to happen. This was not a common love of the kind that Owain had had with a dozen maids around the village. This was a serious thing.

Finally he came to me. "I will see her tomorrow by the old barn," he said. "You must keep watch and make sure we are not seen. I must protect her honor. Her maid will hide her absence. You must watch to ensure her honor is kept."

The next day we waited by the barn. At the appointed time Marged came. She saw me and stopped dead.

"Why is he here?" she asked Owain.

"He's my friend," said Owain.

"He's your servant," she countered, not looking at me.

"No," he insisted, "he is my friend. I've known Gwyn since we were children."

"Well, I don't like him," she said "He makes me nervous." I could see that she really did dislike me. I couldn't understand why back then, but she had hated me from the moment she first saw me.

"Come on, beloved," said Owain, "Gwyn will just keep a watch for your father."

She looked a little mollified but was unconvinced. "Well, I don't want him listening," she said. "He must stay down here."

"I don't want to go up there" I said awkwardly, "You can do what you want. I'll wait here."

"See," said Owain, "Gwyn's a good lad. He's just doing a favor."

Although she wasn't happy, she saw the sense of a lookout. So off they went, and down I stayed. I sat back and passed the time by throwing stones at a tree and eating an apple I had brought with me. After awhile they came back. Her golden hair, which had been pinned into a braid, now flew loose about her head and Owain looked like he'd had the cream.

"All right then?" I asked.

Marged blushed. "Keep your thoughts to yourself," she said. She turned to Owain and kissed him. "I must go," she murmured and off she went. Owain watched her go and then turned to me. "I will marry that girl," he said.

I nodded. He probably would, I thought, and when he does it will make my life hell.

It continued on like that all summer. They would meet by the barn. I would keep watch while they disappeared into the loft. I became very good at sitting against the wall of the barn and throwing stones at that tree. I could hit just about every branch.

Toward the end of the summer they were discovered. I was on watch, but it was hot and difficult to stay awake. Of course, I dropped off and gave up the watch. I was woken by Sir David shaking me.

"Where is my daughter?" he said.

"Fuck," I thought. "I don't know," I said.

"Don't lie to me boy," he railed at me, "Where is your Master? I know he never goes anywhere without you." And then he said, "He's with my daughter, isn't he?"

I was lost. We hadn't worked out a story in case we were discovered. Of course I knew that Owain and Marged would have heard my conversation with her father and would be working things out. I suppose my eyes must have looked up, and Sir David saw my eyes flicker upwards.

"Up there are they?" he said, he face red with anger.

Before I could reply Owain emerged from around the side of the barn. "You are looking for me, Sir David?" he said.

"Where is my daughter?" Sir David shouted at him.

"Not here, Sir," said Owain, quite calmly. "I was looking for Gwyn, but the lazy bugger had run off rather than do his chores."

"Don't lie to me. I have seen you look at my daughter. I know what you think. I returned from the assize today, and I find my daughter gone. I am not a fool, young man. I have searched the village. I remember this stop from when I was a boy. Disreputable young men would attempt to dishonor maids in this barn. I came straight here and found your servant asleep and no doubt keeping watch."

Owain played ignorant, "I have no knowledge of such things" he said. "I believe Marged is at her prayers. Have you checked the church? You may search the barn, but you shall not find her."

Sir David appraised Owain. He was a good enough lawyer to know when the accused had escaped through a false alibi.

"I suppose if I go now I shall find her with the maid and she will vouch that she had been there all afternoon?" he said.

"I cannot say, Sir," said Owain, "I have been searching for Gwyn."

Sir David looked at him, "You have me now, boy, but I shall have you. I am a man of law and believe that punishment must follow evidence of guilt. I will have you if I smell one drop of corruption. My daughter is my property and no man, no matter who his father was, shall have her before marriage."

He glared at Owain and stamped off.

"Sorry, Owain," I said.

Owain grinned at me. "Don't worry about it," he said "The old man was bound to find out. This just means we'll have to find a better place."

And so they did. They fucked all over the village that fall. It was a miracle she didn't end up with child. I propped up more walls and sat under more trees than any boy in creation. Owain and Marged were good at their deceptions, but my role meant that I was inevitably on show to the world. In time Sir David stopped following them and started to have me followed. I could not venture anywhere without Sir David or one of his men watching me and waiting for me to attend to my sentry duties. In the end, it became too much. Owain and Marged were mad for each other, and Owain decided he must speak to Sir David on the matter. He must have been about fifteen years old then and was of an age when many young men with property could consider discussing their future prospects.

He went to Sir David to discuss the future. He found him in his counting room at the Hall. Before he could speak, Sir David held up his hand.

"Owain," he said, "I know of your interest in my daughter and I have no objections. However, I am concerned that you may have inherited your Grandfather's wild ways rather than the ways of moderation practiced by your father."

"I would do anything to prove myself worthy of your daughter, Sir," replied Owain.

"Well," continued Sir David, "It was your Father's dearest wish that you should study and enter the law. All young gentlemen now-a-days need knowledge of the law. It is our only defense against the power of the great. If you are to protect your lands and support my daughter in any future agreement between our houses, then you need to understand the law. I strongly urge you to consider attending and reading the law at Inns of Court in London."

Owain thought about it. "If I did this, would you look well upon my suit, Sir David?"

"If you studied the law and returned with the basics of a legal education, I would see no problem to your suit. You could even become betrothed now."

Owain immediately brightened. "We could be married when I complete my education?"

"Indeed," said Sir David, "I would have no objection at all. You will have reached your full majority and you will have full title to your lands."

"How long would I have to study?" asked Owain.

"Seven years is satisfactory to gain the basics of a legal education."

Owain's face fell. "Seven years without Marged?" he asked.

"No, of course not," said Sir David, "You would return here for major feast days and we would visit you in London. I frequently plead cases at Court in Westminster and I could bring Marged with me when I attend. You would see her often and, because you are betrothed and contracts have been exchanged, you could even spend time alone with her, or at least with minimal supervision."

That was all he needed to say. He had Owain. Owain would have done anything to be alone with Marged and the promise of betrothal and marriage was all his young heart needed to hear. I recall meeting him after he had spoken with Sir David, and he told me the news.

"So we are going to Lludd's Town?" I asked him later.

"Yes, we will all go. Sir David said he will send Gruffudd and Jenkin with us."

"What will I do?" I asked.

"You will come and learn a measure of clerking. There is much to be known in the court of Chancery, and Sir David assures me that your prospects are secure."

Just at that moment Crach entered into our room. "Have you spoken with Old Man Hanmer yet?" he asked. As with many things, Crach often knew things before they happened.

Owain nodded and was about to speak. Crach held up his hand. "I know he has traded you his girl for the law. A good trade and one that you were bound to make. I will finish my work here and we can leave for Lludd's Town any time after that."

"Is it a good move?" asked Owain, for he was by then addicted to Crach's prophecy.

"My boy," said Crach, "every young man should live in Lludd's Town for a time, but no man should stay there too long less he become too addicted to excess."

"So we should go? It will be good for us?" asked Owain.

"Oh yes, we should go. But I tell you, there will be great adventures and important meetings there, and we will all need to stay close together if we are to weather the storms that are coming."

And thus it was that we went to Lludd's Town and began upon the road that led us into the service of the great Queen Dick.

OUR ARRIVAL IN THE CITY OF LONDON

Let me tell you how you know you have come to London; you smell it. Before the sight, before the noise, you have the smell. All of the commerce and bustle of London make a fine bouquet. Slaughter houses, glue makers, tanners, candle makers, fat renders, vinegar makers, and fishmongers all combined with animal dung and the waste of thousands of people to make a smell so ripe it is a wonder that any man can stand to live within ten miles of the place. So awful was the smell that we, poor country lads, were forced to stop at the village Hamestede, a full four miles from the city, and buy posie sacks to protect us from the vapors.

As we came down Watling Street towards the city, we began to hear the noise of the place. Blacksmith's hammers, hawkers' cries, haulers' shouts, beggars' calls, church bells ringing, arguments brewing and the thousands noises of a city at work.

After the smell and the noise, you finally see the Beast. When ever has a man not be shocked by London on his first viewing of it? The size alone would be enough to stun all but the most jaded traveler. I have heard that more than twenty thousand people lived crammed into that space and I can believe it. It is beyond me why men ever decide to live in such close quarters. It is truly a sign of the madness of the English.

The first thing a traveler sees is the great wooden spire of St. Paul's. Then, as he grows closer, numerous other spires and towers come into view. London, despite its reputation for evil, must contain more churches, monasteries, convents, and holy places than anywhere else in Christendom, or so I believed then. If one looks down the Strand towards Westminster, one can even make the Abbey there and the Royal palaces about it. After the churches, you become aware of the walls. London has a fine wall and, although not much used in these latter days and in need of work, it could still provide a good defense to any would be attacker.

Coming from the northwest, we traveled down Holborn, crossed the River Fleet by Chicken Lane and made straight for

Newgate. No sooner had we passed through the walls into London proper when we discovered we had walked into a charnel house such as the Devil must keep in the lowest depths of hell. Newgate runs passed the home of the Grey Friars and opens directly onto the Shambles, as the butchery is known. The great cattle pens at West Smithfield channel an unending supply of beasts into these small streets. There they are killed, cut, and sliced by the butchers of London. The beasts' blood runs directly into an open drain in the middle of the street and on to the River. Along the street we could see all manner of beasts hung up in the shops, whole pigs and lambs, great flanks of beef, huge sturgeon and pikes, whole cod and all other beasts that walked on four legs or swam in the sea. Dogs, cats, and all manner of vermin chewed the rotting vittles that merchants threw into the street, and with the smell of death is everywhere. Poor Jenkin was quite overcome and vomited in the gutter. We pressed our posies to our noses and pressed on into the heart of the Beast.

We were much surprised by the height of the buildings. We had seen impressive homes before at Wrexham and Oswestry, but nothing like these. Three- or four-story buildings were the norm. They jutted so far out into the street on the second story that it seemed that they would meet in the middle. Unbelievably, almost all had glass in the windows. In Wales only the richest of the rich could boast glass in their windows. Most people would make do with nothing at all or, at best, an oiled and scraped skin.

I will also say that I was struck that London must be a very fine place for cats. Of dogs we saw many, but they were mere tenants and wayfarers in the kingdom of the cats. Now it is well known that cats, despite their usefulness as huntsmen and trappers of mice and vermin, are distrustful, dishonest, and deceitful beasts. Therefore, they are to be viewed with suspicion, even if they become friendly, and should always live outside the homes of men. However, the denizens of London have thrown all caution to the wind. Cats wander everywhere are a free to come and go from any house. On our first day there, we saw so many cats that I thought that for certain we had come to "cat land" rather than greatest city in England. They eyed us from barrel tops and from behind windows; they wound around our feet begging, and skulked in dark corners, no doubt conducting their hidden business and lecherous practices.

We saw toms pull their wives into the secret places, for it was their time of love, and we heard the screams that followed. Everywhere we saw cats; pusses and toms, cats and kits. It was thus that I first realized that London would be a place where much mischief could be found.

On we went, fearless travelers, determined to uncover the mysteries of London. Through the pigs and pig shit, past the horses and horse shit, and through the people and people shit we pressed on. With each step our feet sank deep into the dung of a thousand beasts, as well as their blood and entrails. As thousands of visitors have done before, and doubtless thousands will after us, we were accosted by barkers, street merchants, tricksters, hucksters, beggars and whores. We had the wide-eyed look of lads newly arrived from the country who could be easily fleeced and taken. No doubt we would have been had not Crach stepped up and with his great stick beat them back and uttered vile curses in both English and French to fend them off.

"Come lads" he said, "If you wish to get a belly full of London on your first day, follow me and I shall show you the sights."

And so we set off behind him and saw the greatness of the City; for there was indeed greatness to be seen. It was amazing to consider that the year before, the city had been ravaged by plague, and we were seeing the rump of London's multitude. We were told repeatedly during our stay that London was much diminished in the years since the Great Mortality, and many properties were still empty. We could not have imagined it that day. In London all manner of people live cheek by jowl with each other. Thus, the whore walks next to the monk, the beggar with the rich merchant, the juggler and the clown with the penitent, and the knight with the bondsmen.

Everywhere one could see the colored robes of different orders that dot London. If one were to look down any street, one would see the black cowl of the Benedictines, the white of the Cistercians, the grey of Franciscans, and the brown of the Dominicans. They go about the city as if they owned it and, in many ways, they do, for most of the City is indeed owned by the various orders. It seems strange that such goodness should march alongside such evil, for it is well known that the Devil is commonly a resident in the City. Crach told me once that he had seen the Devil many times walking around London. I saw him once myself. He was walking up towards Smithfield on Aldgergate Road. He was tall, well dressed and had a very nice hat. He definitely had the look of the Devil about him. I have also heard that he regularly attends many mummers' plays around London and often plays the part of the great Tempter in person.

As we moved into the City away from the smell of the Shambles, we saw the maze of wealth and business that is Cheapside. First we saw goldsmiths, saddlers and harness makers. Next came the makers of milk and cheese, then bread, then soap then cobblers and cordwainers, then drapers, mercers and tailors. Each new cross street produced new smells and mysteries with merchants stalls all arrayed with their ware. Each laid out their wares in open stalls and in banks in front of their shops. Some pretended indifference; others called out their wares and tried to drag customers into their shops. Apprentices wandered the streets with signs advertising their masters' stalls and indicating the way to marvelous prices and goods of unparalleled wonder and quality. At the end of the Poultry, where, unsurprisingly, bird meat was sold, we came to the Stocks Market. Crach pointed to the stalls selling herbs, fruit, flowers and roots.

"There is much of great medicinal value to be found on this stall, boys" he said, "When last I was here, I was able to find everything from black opium to unicorn's horn. It is not something to be missed."

We turned south and headed down Lombard Street towards East Cheap. Longshanks had thrown the Hebrews from the City as a gesture to his piety. Having deprived himself of their services as moneylenders, he was required to invite the Italians in to play the Jews' role. They were much hated by Londoners, who held them to be worse than the Jews. From there we turned on East Cheep, passing more poultry stalls, then down Pudding Lane and onto the fish wharfs that backed off of Petty Welsh.

"Why is this known as Petty Welsh?" I asked.

I was treated to one of Crach's withering looks. "This is where they kept us once, the Little, Unimportant Welsh. We were either here or up by the skinners' yards at Walbrooke. When the Saxons took the City from us, they confined us in certain streets and districts, much like the Christians do with the Jews. This was our place. We were not permitted to live as the Saxon did. We had to skulk amid the fish and the docks. When they first came here, they could not read or count and needed us to run their trade. They kept us here until they had learned enough, and then kicked us out."

Finally we came to the great tower itself and the bridge over the Thames. The bridge itself was a marvelous sight. It was composed of a dozen smaller bridges, each arched to meet the next, with a drawbridge in the middle. Great houses and home had been built upon it, as well as taverns and other places of entertainment. Rising up in the distance we could see London's Great Tower. It was impressive enough, but for anyone who has traveled around Wales, it takes a lot to be impressed by castles. Compared to Caernarfon, almost any castle looks a little small and uninspiring.

Crach raised his stick to point at the Tower.

"See that Boys, the Romans built it when they first came. Of course, there was something there before that, but it has been forgotten. Some say that Merlin the Wild brought the ravens there and told them stay, since should they leave, the kingdom will fall."

He laughed.

"They are in error" he continued, obviously much pleased at his wisdom and knowledge. "I know for a fact that the ravens came with Bran the Blessed. He was so strong that even after he died, his head was cut off and carried away by his army to continue to help them in battle. It was finally brought London and buried where the Tower now stands to defend the city from invaders. The ravens were the Druids' special creatures. They arrived shortly afterwards to give sign of their master's commitment to the City. It is not they that keep the City whole, its Bran's head under White Hill."

We nodded, although it is fair to say that neither of us understand anything that Crach had said.

"Come, lads" he continued. "We must find our lodgings. If my memory serves me well, we must head towards St. Paul's and out of Lludd's Gate to find the Inns of Court. They will be by the old Templar Priory."

With that he took off to the west and we, foot sore, and exhausted, followed to begin our new lives as students of the law.

When has ever a student's life been different from what it was when I was young? Does it not consist in equal measure of drunkenness, poverty, and excessive and overly passionate argument? I say poverty for every student knows that their allowance is never enough and somehow it all seems to disappear shortly after it arrives. Sir David was generous enough, but he was concerned that Owain should not fritter away his inheritance, so he kept us on a tight leash. He insisted that I come with him as a student and I tagged along, part student and part servant.

Every student arrives at college scared and uncertain of their position. Before long they are at home and as drunk as ever a group of young men will be. For the young are blessed with an energy that the old can only stare at and wonder. A young man who enjoys the easy energy of a body still untested can study from dawn to dusk, drink all evening, argue and fuck all night and wake the next day ready for more.

When I think back to our time at the Inns, I realize now that it was among the best in our lives. I remember one day in particular. I was crossing through the gardens of the Middle Temple on a mellow summer's evening. It was that time of the day when the world takes a breath and rests a little before plunging into the evening's entertainment. As I walked, I could smell the new cut grass and the roses that grew heavy in the garden. I heard music of a pipe being played nearby looked up through an open window to see a student practicing his scales. It was a perfect moment. I thought to myself then that if I lived to be a hundred, I would remember this moment and all promise of youth.

But it is not just such sweet moments I recall. I remember great drunken nights where we seemed to drink buckets of beer and still stand and sing. I remember evenings and nights spent in taverns with men and women of all kinds. We would debate the law, argue for or against the case of Lollardry, dispute the rights of Parliament, and re-fight the wars in France. We would gossip about our fellows, our masters at court, and which girls could be taken most easily. Youth is indeed wasted upon the young.

It was an interesting time to be in London. The year before the plague had come again to the City, the death carts had trundled the streets, and the lime pits were piled high with the unlucky. If you looked to the east, you could see the smoke rising from Gravesend where the French would raid to show the King of England his time as lord of the Narrow Seas was over. In the City the Victualars and the Drapers Guilds' warred for control of London, and both fought with the Johnny Gaunt for the right to maintain order within the walls. Aye, these were great times for a young man to be in London.

For all our time there we lived at one of the Inns near the Temple where apprentices at law stay and learn the rudiments of their trade. Nowadays, the presses are making books plentiful and boys can learn with their own books. Not in my day. At class, one boy would be chosen as a reader, and he would read the law from our text. The apprentices would listen and try to memorize the arguments. Later the master would examine the apprentices, and they would argue points in counterfeit court. This would go on day in and day out. The apprentices would sit for hours with sore heads from our night of drinking and desperately try to focus on the lesson at hand. Sometimes a Master would lecture us as to the law. Many of the Masters were poor teachers, but some stick in my mind.

I recall a great fat man from the North. He wore his beard short and his hair long at the back. Robert Watchman was his name. He was an awful Lollard. At the time Lollardry was quite the rage. These believers held that the Bible should be written in the tongue of English, doubted the magic of the mass, refused homage to the Pope, and counted all priests as charlatans. They would wander the country in red robes preaching heresy and attempting to convert the English. Master Watchman would attend the Inns on weekdays. On Sunday he would travel back to his home in a village outside London where he would play the Paterfamilias for the day. Then he would return to a week of teaching, drinking, whoring, and arguing. He was a great one for holding court in his rooms at Grey's Inn. He would collect his disciples together, share his ale and preach the gospel according to Wycliffe.

As Welshmen we were always a little confused by the Lollards. Their insistence on an English Bible and their hostility towards priests had little appeal to us. After all, why should we care if the Bible was translated into another foreign tongue, and what did we care whether a Priest was a fraud? To us, it was enough that a Priest be Welsh. Our hatred of most Priests in our homeland came not from doctrine or the role of the Host, but the fact they were English and had been forced upon us. However, we enjoyed a good argument and spent long hours disputing the finer points of doctrine with our fellows.

I should stress that the Inns did not teach only the law. They made sure that we apprentices received a full education. In addition to the law we studied dancing, rhetoric, history, music, and divinity. I recall that the Hanmers were particularly light on their feet in those days and fine dancers. Owain and I, being Welshmen, were particularly fine singers and had a strong appreciation of music.

"But what of you?" you may say, "Surely a simple bondman's son was not treated to a gentlemen's education?"

And indeed you are right. During my time in London I was part student and part servant. Officially I was part of Owain's retinue and performed the thousand tasks a gentlemen needs when he is present in London. Although no more than a boy myself, I hired servants, selected laundresses, procured ale and food, managed our finances, and generally ensured that Owain and the Hanmers' lives ran smoothly. When not working I perfected my grasp of many games of skill and chance, including all the various games of dice, French squares, Twelve Men's Morris, Merrilles, and shove penny. When not gaming I explored London, and occasionally attended Owain at his studies. Owain nourished the idea that one day I would become his chief steward and secretary. He had taken his Mother's words to heart that a man must have men around him who are bound to him for life.

"You are the first of my Telu," Owain would say to me.

"Never doubt Gwyn," he said, "You and I will see great things. This work may be dull, but it is preparation. I promised my Father I would learn the ways of the law, and learn I will, but I also promised by Grandfather that I would restore our inheritance as Kings of Powys. You will learn as I do here, for the law shall be one of our weapons in the struggle for my rights, and I will need men around me that are educated in the ways of the Saxons. Be patient. This will not last forever and we gain important intelligence here."

So I was patient, learned and waited. I will be honest though, it was a terrible effort for me. It was especially awful when we would have to attend the courts in Westminster. We would walk down the Strand, turn at one Longshanks Cross or Charring Cross as it is sometimes known, and headed towards the Palace at Westminster. As Owain was still an apprentices-at-law, we had to pay to pass the bar into Westminster. Once an apprentice had served out his time with his master and became a Men-of-Law or Sergeant-at-Law, he could pass the bar without payment. We would then go past the Royal Abbey towards the King's Bridge and enter into the King's City. By that time the Court of the Common Bench had settled in London and taken up permanent chamber quarters in Westminster Hall. Nearby were the Courts of Chancery, the King's Bench, and the Exchequer. All provided excellent experience for a practicing student. We would attend the courts and listen closely to the pleadings and arguments. I did not learn much from these pleadings, but Gruffudd, Jenkin and Owain were much impressed and listened intently to the cases.

I shall pause and describe the King's City. Westminster was not only a palace; it was a city, the King's city. It was a beautiful miniature city surrounded by walls, rivers, and moats devoted to the whims and ways of one man - the King of England. There are no shops or taverns; everything is for the King. Thus one would see all manner of servants, craftsmen and artificers at work for the King. On a single day you could stroll through the big gate on the strand and see carpenters, coopers, blacksmiths, whitesmiths, goldsmiths, spicers, bakers, butchers, cooks, gardeners, barbers, blood-letters, bonesetters, trumpeters, messengers, heralds, minstrels, illuminators, readers, scribes, bedesmen, grooms, stable-boys, jewelers, engineers, pavilioners, armorers, artillers, gunners, masons, tillers, bowyers and fletchers, furriers, heaumers spurriers, lorimers, brewers and not one of them plying his trade for anyone but the King. They were all his servants and lived there behind the walls. With them came their wives and children, all living behind Westminster's walls and all devoted to the King. For all of the women worked for the King too. They cleaned and washed, darned and mended, cut and embroidered, and weaved and spun; everything for the almighty big arse himself, the King of England. Of course that big an operation didn't run itself. All of them are managed by the King's men, and they are everywhere too, all of the ushers, sergeants, scriveners, notaries and clerks, running around and overseeing every aspect of his household.

It was a miracle that anything worked. If it had been Wales, nothing would have worked. We don't believe in too much organization and know that things are best left to the goodness of the spirits and the blessings of the lords. Years later when Owain held court in Harlech and Aberystwyth, Gruffudd Yonge ran everything without the help of a single servant. Of course, he did have Marged, and no one messed with her.

I am getting ahead of myself. The other thing you noticed when you stepped past the bar was how crowded Westminster was. Everyone knows the famous buildings, the Great Hall, the Painted Chamber, the White Hall, the Queen Chamber, the Abbey, but few know of the hundreds of smaller houses and buildings that fill the city. All of the great men wish to be close to the King, and there is only so much space. Westminster was full of secret tunnels and passages. The King and his most important servants could pass through the entire palace without ever being seen. This was a subterranean and private world where the King dwelt and from which he could appear at a moment's notices.

It was all too much for me. I never liked the place. The law made it worse. I have never understood why right and wrong are not enough for the courts and why lawyers are needed. I took every opportunity to escape Owain's contemplation of the cases and wander to the comparative peace of the Abbey to clear my head.

It was during just such a break that I discovered my life's great project. One day I was lost in the complexity of a case and headed out to take a breath of fresh air. It was late autumn, and the air was cold and fresh. I stretched my back and looked up at the cold, clear sun.

"Escaping from the pain of the law?" I heard a man say. I looked down and saw a monk.

"Indeed Brother" I said. "I am not made for the law. My Master wishes that I attend him at his studies for he believes that a basic understanding of its rule will help me in my duties as his steward one day. I confess I do wish to be of aid to him, but it is hard for me."

The Monk nodded. "It is hard to pursue a trade for which one has no vocation," he said. "When I was a boy, my father was much interested that I join the family in the wool business. I come from the Cotswolds, and we produce the finest wool in all of England. He worked with Italian merchants in Bristol to sell the wool to lands to the South. I struggled with it, but never could I understand the ways of the trade." He sighed. "No matter how much he beat me, I never could get the trick of it. Finally he despaired and packed me off to the good monks of St. Benedict."

"My Master does not beat me." I said. It was true, for Owain was unusually kind and reasonable. "But he does not see that what is easy for him is hard for others. I would prefer he go to war and take me as a squire than go to law and take me as a clerk."

"Well" said the Monk "These are dangerous times. You may well get your wish. If things continue to go badly in France, the French may be here in Westminster soon."

"I hope they do. At least it would free me from the law," I said.

"Careful what you wish for young man," said the Monk "I have made a study of the actions of our armies in France. We have been hard upon them, and they will undoubtedly avenge themselves. Look how close they come to us." He pointed down the Thames. "They have raided along the southern shores for years now."

"You are well informed," I said.

"Indeed I am. I have made it my place to record the events of the day. I have made a general chronicle of these years. See, I am a history maker and am much annoyed by the lack of true detail concerning the real events of past times. I once began a history of Britannia during the Romans, but I was forced to abandon it for lack of reliable sources. I decided to ensure that this did not happen for later historians and began a chronicle of my time in Westminster. My hope is that I will make a full history of all of the days of my life, such that future historians will have the record I have been denied."

This struck me as a sensible idea and I said so. He thanked me. "A people must also have a clear record of their past that cannot be disputed" he said.

"I am a Welshman," I said. "We have great memory but no real record. Our bards record our greatness in song but no record is produced. It is often difficult to determine the reality of an event and men spend a great deal of time arguing over what occurred or embellishing tales until the truth is forgotten."

"Perhaps that should be your vocation," said the Monk.

"You are literate and aware of the need for such a record. All a man needs to make a chronicle is a pen, something to write on, and time. It costs little and provides much to your posterity."

"Maybe I will one day," I said, "But it seems a job for older men. I am young and must live life before I write it."

"Well taken," said the Monk. "But remember my words. Each people need a chronicle, and there is always much to write."

He smiled and wandered off towards the Abbey. Thus, the idea took root in my mind to create this chronicle and, though it has been many years, I have never forgotten his admonition. When the time came and I had finished living my life, I sat down to write the events of my days. So I thank that unknown monk of Westminster for it was he who provided me with the final weapon to avenge My Lord, the truth and real happenings of his life.

THE BATTLE OF ST. PAUL'S

Enough of our time at school; I shall tell you of the more interesting parts of a student's life, which is, our adventures in the taverns of London and the great politics that occupied the English during our stay there. Our first great adventure was in the summer after the death of Prince Edward.

Now our guide to the world of the tavern was our fellow student known as William Brown. He was a Londoner himself. Though a commoner, his father was a clerk and sergeant in the King's Great Wardrobe. This provided him with monies, for bribes are always plentiful for a man in the King's service.

William took us through the city into the bowels of Eastcheap to a tavern on Crooked Lane. William always had something of the sodomite or bæddel about him. It was the fashion of the day for men to affect Frenchified manners. William was tall and thin with very rose cheeks. He was dark in his looks and had grown a beard to make his face look manlier, but the gentleness of his manners and the softness of his skin and hair ruined the effect.

"Come, gentlemen," he said. "We will visit a tavern where you will see the most notorious thieves and the cheapest whores in all of London."

We left our Inn and walked to the river. It was the practice of watermen in those days to gather at various places along the River to solicit business. One of these, The Temple, was a place where many lawyers gathered who needed to make regular trips to Westminster. Tupence would buy a trip from the Temple to Westminster and trepence for a ride to the Bridge. We procured a boat and headed down river to the docks around the Bridge. We hove in at Oystergate and headed up past the meat and fish stalls of Bridge Street to Crooked Street. It gained its name either from the way it wound and curved or from its fame as a safe place for thieves, robbers, night-walkers, footpads, reafers and tricksters who dared cross the river from Southbank. The smell of the fish and the meat from Eastcheap, the brewing and dyeing of St. Michael's, the shellfish of Oystergate, and the fish at Botolph's Warf made it an undesirable residence and thus appealing to low types. It was a dark and dirty place. The buildings rose four stories high and fell forward into the street. Soon we arrived at The Hog's Head, a terrible tumbledown place, with the windows at all angles, the door blown in, and the smell of old ale and rotten food wafting into the street.

Our spirits lifted at the scene inside. Drunks slumped on the tables, minstrels banged out tunes on pipes and lutes, and whores and tavern women milled round in a great crowd. A fat woman of middle years recognized William and called out to us.

"Master William" she said. "Come over here and give us a kiss." She floated across the room, grabbed William, and planted a great, wet kiss on his lips.

"We are ready for a fine time here today," she said, "We have new wine in from France, fine Kentish ale, and whores a plenty from the Bishops Palace across the river."

She referred to the whore houses that the Bishop of Canterbury owned across the river on Southbank. Quite illegally the girls would take a time off from the Bishop's service to earn some money for themselves across the river in the afternoon before the evening's peak hours.

"I see you have brought your friends," she said looking at us.

"Will you introduce us?"

William bowed deeply as if she were Joan of Kent herself. "Mistress Wriggly, this is Owen Glendowery, a Welshman and fellow apprentice-at-law." Owain bowed deeply and ignored the mispronunciation of his name. William continued. "Next are the Hanmer brothers, Griffith and John, English gentlemen all from Shropshire, but much contaminated by their closeness to Wales. Rumor has it, they have a mother who is Welsh and can even speak the Devil tongue." He winked and laughed.

"And last, this is Quinn, a sometime retainer of Master Glendowery."

Mistress Wriggly curtseyed low. "Charmed, I'm sure," she said. "Well lads," she continued, "I shall bring ale and a jug of wine. Would you like some girls?" she asked.

Young Jenkin blushed. Mistress Wriggly saw that and poked William in the ribs. "Is he a virgin? The little one. I have just the girl to make a man of him. But not all of you, I'll be bound. This gentlemen," she nodded at Owain, "is a fine figure and I'll wager has broken many hearts." She cackled. Looking around she nodded to a group of strangers.

"You are in luck today," beamed Mistress Wriggly. "We have a great hero with us, a veteran of the Battle of Poitiers, Sir John Droppole himself; just returned from France."

We followed her gaze over to the fireplace where a handsome, vigorous man held court in front of a gang of followers.

"Sir John," she called, "Say hello to our visitors from the Inns of Court." The gentlemen looked up and there, for the first time, I saw the famous Sir John Droppole.

And what shall I say of Droppole in those early days before he was old, sick, fat and disillusioned? He had once been a gentleman who held high the virtues of knighthood. He loved chivalry, truth, honor, freedom and above all courtesy. He had set out from our lands to fight in his Sovereign's wars. He had wanted to fight in Aegypt against the Mohammedans and in Poland and Latvia against the Pagans. He would have even settled for Granada and the great siege of Algeciras and Belmarie. In the end he had landed in France where he fought fifteen battles and three duels. Rumor had it that he had traveled as far as Palestine and the land of the Great Turk, although there was never any evidence of it. He was even then well known, with a reputation for being strong, brave and wise. He was of a good temper, as meek as a maid amongst his friends, and had no vileness in him. I would have said when we first met him that he was a perfect knight. In appearance he was not gaily dressed. He wore a tunic of simple cloth that was discolored and stained by the mail he had worn over it for many years. His hair curled down from under his cap in great ringlets. He face was covered with a rough beard and framed a face of great humor and kindness.

However, the roots of his later decline were already evident, for he was even then a great lover of food. I have never seen a man eat as much as Droppole could. He could sit down at dawn and eat till dusk. There was no stopping his appetite. If there was food on the table, then it would be put into his mouth. He also had an enormous taste for the drink, and a great capacity for wine and ale. I have seen him with my own eyes guzzle more than ten buckets of beer over a single day. He also had a prodigious thirst for wine and strong liquor. He was particularly fond of the strong red wines that were much about the City at that time due to the English successes in France.

His downfall was that no matter how much he drank, he kept his head. When other men would fall asleep from drink, he was still up and about and holding court. Accordingly, he would continue to sup until all were gone in drink and he would then away to bed. Despite this ability, all men know that drink wastes the man in time, slowing his reactions, wasting his muscles, increasing his gut, and rotting his brain. Thus, did drink make what in later years we all came to know as Sir John. That is, a fat clown who was the butt of jokes, and whose name is synonymous with debauchery and decay. But that was many years in the future.

On that day he was still a great paladin and a man much to be admired for his worldliness and his chivalry. I will choose to remember him as he was in those days and forget what he was to become, the lickspittle and toady of Bloody Henry himself.

"Come here, my good fellows," he called to us. "I am always much enamored of young men wishing to learn the ways of the law. Come Peestel," he said, pushing a skinny young man away, "make way for our young friends. Where then do you hail from?"

Owain straightened and looked him in the eye. "We are Welshmen," he replied, "from the Northern Marshes near the towns of Wrexham and Oswestry."

"Welshmen indeed," replied Droppole. "You are a bold but barbarous race. I served much time with them in the service of the Prince Edward, though those fellows were from the Black

Mountains of the south of your country." He glanced toward the rest of us and Owain gave introductions.

"Wondrous it is indeed to see so many young men from the Marchers come to London to learn the law," said Droppole, smiling amicably. "Why if this trend continues, there may even one day be a race of gentlemen in Wales." He and his cronies erupted into laughter.

"There are many gentlemen already in Wales, Sir John," said Owain. "And all those men would be none the better for a London education."

"Come now," replied Droppole. "I mean no harm. There are many fine men in Wales. Why in my late employment in France, I shared many an evening with your countrymen and saw ample evidence of their refinement and education."

Again his cronies erupted in erupted in laughter.

"Let me introduce you to my friends," said Sir John. He turned to the men who sat around him, "The is my loyal Corporal Nam, next to him young Whistler, a fine servant at war, and these young lads," he pointed to some young men guzzling a jug of ale, "are Master Pons and his friend Master Gladhills. The gentleman over by the window is Long Will," he said, gesturing toward a tall man by the door, "a scribbler of verses and clerk at the Wardrobe. Our other new arrival is Davy Dodd, a Cheshire man by birth and much traveled on the King's campaigns in Flanders. He is a good man with a bow is Davy, currently enrolled in his Majesty's service at the Tower. All fine men and boys."

Owain spoke up, "You were recently in France?"

"Aye" said Whistler "Sir John, myself, and Corporal Nam went to France in the service of Prince Edward, May God Rest his sole. We did our duty and then went a routin' when his highness went home. We were with a gentleman of your country, Sir, a Sir Gregory Sais. He joined up with Sir Hugh Caleley and went south. Very profitable is routin' in France. I quick ride through the country, a little arson, the occasional fight, and plenty of booty and hostages to ransom. However, the Frenchies have shaken themselves recently and we judged it time to come home."

"You were with Prince Edward in his last campaign?" asked Gruffudd.

"Yes Sir" said Droppole with a long face. His mood was immediately changed. "He was a fine and terrible man. We were with him at his last campaign in Aquitaine, and a brutal and terrible thing it was. The worst was at Limoges. The Prince was much upset that the Bishop of that town had turned traitor and sided with the French. He swore revenge again the people of the Limoges. We mined the town's walls all autumn. Then one morning in November, the wall came down and, wouldn't you know it, the moat was filled up with the rubble. We poured through and had the whole town in our procession before the Frenchies knew what had happened. Then the Prince was carried into the city on his litter, for even then the rot had set into his legs, and ordered us all to give no quarter. Women ran from their homes with their babes at their breast and begged the Prince for mercy. He would have none of it. He had every one of them killed. More than three thousand they do say. The streets ran red with blood. But here's the joke lads, he never got the Bishop. Old Johnny Gaunt ran into the Bishop and took him in gave him protection." He laughed and poured more ale down his throat.

"Gaunt's a troublemaker," continued Sir John. "A narrow man, I think, hot tempered and with small ability. He has defeated Prince Edward's old friends. He locked up the Commons Forespeaker De La Mare in irons and packed up the Earl of the March the continent. Oh, we all know what he is doing. De La Mare is Mortimer's man in the Commons, and the Lord of the March is next in line to the throne after Prince Richard. He wishes to do away with everyone who stands between him and the throne. He will be the death of this country. Thank the Lord that the old King still lives and may live long enough to pass his empire intact to Prince Edward's son."

"Evil days upon us," said Whistler. "We are defeated in France, and the realm is much impoverished."

"Aye," nodded Droppole. "It is true. The City itself is full of factions. Master Northampton's mercers and drapers fight daily with Master Brembre's fishmongers. Even the whores take sides. I should stress, young sirs, that considering our location," he nodded towards the river, "and the customers of the house," he nodded towards some fishporters drinking in the corner, "we favor Master Brembre. We are all strongly aligned with the Fishmongers." He downed some more ale and continued. "To top it all, Black Johnny Gaunt threatens to take London's liberties away and place his bum-boy Percy in authority over the City. Furthermore, it is well observed that Lollardry is everywhere." He took a sip of his ale, put his tankard down and issued a statement loud enough for everyone to hear.

"We are all orthodox here, sirs, and will have no heresy spoken." The Fishmongers raised their jugs and cheered. He nodded and acknowledged their support. Then Sir John continued.

"In fact, you may say that we are for Brembre and Bishops." He laughed to himself at his joke. "Further, we are opposed to the King's whore, for we believe she exercises a malign influence on of all his affairs."

"Is it true" asked Gruffudd "that Mistress Alice runs all his affairs since the death of the Queen?"

"Indeed, young sir," said Droppole. "And a greedier bitch there never was. She has robbed the King blind and has become Queen of Bribes, the Lady Meed herself." He nodded to Long Will for, as we were later to learn, he had written a poem about the Mistress Alice and had coined for her these names.

"It is true," interrupted Long Will. "Every day her demands come down from Westminster or the Palace at Sheen. She has an insatiable appetite for money. The Wardrobe is meant to pay for the clothing and stores for the army. Instead we are sending money to Alice and buying rubbish from her favorites. I tell you all, Good Sirs, if the French were to come tomorrow, we could barely clothe or provide for a soldier, much less arm him. It is a sorry state of affairs."

"She works hand-in-hand with Johnny Gaunt, she does," nodded Droppole. "These are dark days. They have removed all the good men from the Council. They have taken away our ancient liberties. Why did not Parliament see their sins and banish Awful Alice when last it met? It would have stood too, had not Johnny Gaunt turned it on its head and demanded the Parliament be sent home."

"I'll have no such talk in here," interrupted Mistress Wrigley. "Alice and I came up to London at the same time, and she was a good girl."

"Surely you do not claim to know Awful Alice herself?" asked Sir John.

"Indeed I do," said Mistress Wrigley. "And a fine lady she is. She came up from Essex with me to serve in the Queen's household. She was an honest girl pursuing a decent trade."

"Before she snagged and king and stole the kingdom," said Long Will.

"Nonsense!" cried Mistress Wrigley. "The old Queen wanted her for her husband. Let me tell you boys, there never were a man and woman who loved each other as much as Queen Philippa and King Edward. They were together since they were boy and girl, and she gave him a good twelve children. Now, when she realized she was sick and dying of the rot, she realized her man would be alone and bereft of female company. So what did she do? She had all the girls shown to her each year as they entered her service, and she picked the ones that looked most like her in her youth. Then she kept them about her until she could spot one that was most like her in manners and had the wit to amuse the king. After a year or two, she settled on Alice. She was a simple country girl, unlettered but a beauty and well-educated between the sheets.

Sir John interrupted. "Madame, what nonsense is this? You claim Queen Philippa invited this viper into the King's bed? Tripe, Madame, bollocks, shit. I will not accept this. What woman would do this?"

"Sir John," said Mistress Wrigley, "You may know the ways of men, but you know nothing of the soul of a woman. A man could no more give a woman a lover than he could give her his own balls, but a woman can do such a thing. All women know that men are fickle. In time you all tire of us and go off following some young heifer simply because she is young. But a clever woman will see that when this is inevitable. She knows she can retain her position if she controls the choosing of her man's affection. A clever woman will pick a girl so like herself that in that girl's every action, every pose, she will remind her husband of her in their early years. He will be trapped in memories of their love. Guilt will consume him, and though he will be addicted to the touch of the young one, he will return again and again to the old one. And if she dies? Well, she will have him trapped by her image and enthralled by her love. A clever woman was old Queen Philippa. She knew what she was doing. Kept Edward happy, kept him close, and made sure he could never stray from her."

"An interesting theory, Madame," said Sir John. "I must defer to your expertise on the womanly arts. The soul of a woman is inevitably a foreign land for men. We may explore, we may travel but we are always foreigners and always uncertain of their ways."

"That's as may be," said Long Will "But she is ruining the country."

"Master Will," said Mistress Wrigley. "She's a country girl and without a shilling to her name. What's wrong if she wants to make herself a little scratch? There's not much a woman can do in this city without a husband and capital."

"You have a point Madame," agreed Sir John. "Those of us not born to money must do as needs demand."

Owain turned to Mistress Wrigley. "You said you came up with her. What did you mean?" he asked.

"We were both Essex's girls. Alice was a tiller's daughter and I was thatcher's. We came up from Essex together and entered the Queen's service. We were there a few years, but she was meant for better things. I didn't have her looks and knew not a word of French. The King doesn't know much English so all his ladies have to speak French if they are to hold his interests for long. Alice was raised a by nurse to some highborn family and learned French. The nurse thought that if Alice could speak French it would help her get along in the world, and I suppose it did."

She paused for a moment and drank her ale. "While she pursued Kings I became friendly with a brewer, and in time we married. My husband bought an inn when a spot of the pestilence cleaned out these parts and the taverns were going for a song. Poor love. Didn't last the year and he left me with this place and a nice brewery in the back. I had no choice but to make a go of it."

"And a fine go you've made of it," said Sir John "This is the finest ale in London and you serve the best fish and pig in all of London."

He raised his mug and we all saluted Mistress Wriggly.

"More ale," called Sir John, and a young girl came in with a new jug.

"Eleanor," said Droppole, "Perfect timing. Just when a man needs a fill up I can always count on my Dear." She was a beauty was Eleanor. Jet black hair, pale white skin, a slender frame, nice tight arse and plump red lips.

"Gentlemen," said Droppole as he pulled her on to his lap "Meet Mistress Eleanor Rykner, a wonderful girl with a great career ahead of her as a whore. She has the specialty of servicing the many men of the cloth in our fair City. " She slapped Droppole and he guffawed. "Would you gentlemen do the honors?" he asked.

William pulled out his purse, "Why of course, Sir. Mistress Wriggly, bring ale and wine for all our friends." With that a cheer went up and a great day of drinking began.

So we continued all through the rest of the morning and into the afternoon. We consumed many a jug of ale and wine, scoffed down several good chicken pastries, and continued our talk on the ills of the Kingdom, how best to resolve them, the virtues and strengths of various wrestlers, and the likely winners of various dog races to be held in Southwalk.

Towards three of the clock we heard a great commotion outside the tavern. We were of course all in a great state of disarray by then and anxious to become involved in any trouble and misrule. Like a good Captain, Droppole dispatched Nam to determine the origin of the commotion. After a few minutes he returned.

"The fish porters from Oystergate are heading to St. Paul's. Nick Brembre called his boys out. They are saying that Bishop Courtney has brought that heretic Wycliffe to St. Paul's to answer charges. Johnny Gaunt is right pissed off. He says that Wycliffe is his pet and the Bishop has no authority. As the Fishmongers say Johnny Gaunt and his lads are off to St. Paul's to arrest the Bishop and to free the heretic Wycliffe."

There were general exclamations, for the Bishop was of an old London family and despite his affectations he was much admired by Londoners. Gaunt was known to favor Wycliffe and had a continuing hostility to the liberties of London. There were clearly complicated politics at work here, but the mob did not bother with the details. They were simply responding to the impingement of their ancient liberties by the hated Gaunt.

"To arms men" shouted Droppole. "We cannot let the Dark Prince protect his pet heretic and disrespect our Bishop." He jumped up and raised his hand pointing out of the tavern. Sir John led forward, kissed Mistress Eleanor, took a swig of ale, grabbed a flagon of wine, and charged out. We followed after him and into the mob outside.

A London mob is a great thing. I have seen many in my times and they always follow the same pattern. One minute the streets will be clear and all is normal. Then in the distance you hear the first faint murmur. Suddenly the street fills up. No one gives the signal, no one knows from whence it comes. It is a great medley of people. Old men in their dotage, drunks, such as ourselves that day, insolent youths, apprentices, men from their trades, painted whores, scolds, and goodwives. All come into the street and surge along seeking the object of their anger and a resolution to their grievances. Spectators that one moment ago were there only from interest are dragged along and become loyal followers. The apprentice boys shout out their call to arms, "Cudgels, Boys, Cudgels," for whenever have there not been boys ready to run from their work and rush to a fight?

The most surprising thing is that the mob always seems to know exactly where it is going. In this case it was to St. Paul's. On we went up St. Michael's and then west on Candlewich Street to Bludge Row and on to Watling Street. We arrived at St. Paul's as a full mob and smashed into the Church to watch the confrontation between the Bishop and the Prince.

In we barged shouting and screaming.

"Down with heresy!"

"Hang the Heretic!"

"Boil him alive!"

All the noble sentiments of a mob, but we were happy. There is nothing like the prospect of a hanging and the violation of sacred space to brighten one's day.

We would have pushed on there and then and hanged the bastard Wycliffe if it were not for the presence of Black Johnny Gaunt. There he was in all his glory and he stopped the mob with one glare and a few dozen men-at-arms. No doubt he was an impressive looking man. He was tall, more than six and a half feet, with jet black hair and a neatly trimmed beard. He had riveting eyes, very dark and knowing. They seemed full of suspicion and guile.

What we saw was that day was one of the first great displays of Johnny Gaunt's arrogance. He stood there with his lapdog Earl Percy and told us to shut up. The miracle was that we did it. We would have all melted away if it hadn't been for that prick Earl Percy. He was emboldened by his master and shouted out at us in his thick Northern brogue.

"Get out of here you fucking scum. Your betters are determining matters of great estate and you are not needed. I am taking Master Wycliffe to safety at the Duke's Palace."

Northerners were as good as foreigners to a London mob. He was barely understandable to them. While they might take shit from a Prince of the blood like Johnny Gaunt, they would not take that from a foreigner. The mob roared and screamed abuse. Percy's men moved to the front and pushed us back with their pikes.

Bishop Courtney stepped forward. "Marshal Percy, I'm in authority here." He spoke in a broad London accent and was clearly a local boy so he got a cheer from the mob. He continued.

"If I had known what you were up to, I would have let you in."

There were cheers and applause from the mob. He turned and bowed slightly. Successful churchmen are also good performers.

"I have business with Master Wycliffe," said the Bishop. "He needs to attend his spiritual masters and defend his words."

Gaunt interrupted. "Bishop or no Bishop, I will have the Earl Marshall maintain order. You have limited rights in this matter Sir." Now he was speaking fancy and the mob did not like that, but they were beginning to enjoy the show and thus held back and booed and hissed at this display of arrogance.

"Pay heed Sir," said Percy addressing the Bishop. "Your authority is limited as long as the King is present. I am the Marshall and have authority to arrest anyone causing a disturbance within twelve miles of the King's person. I believe he is present in Westminster as we speak and thus I have authority here." He nodded to his pikemen. "Provide a chair for Master Wycliffe as he is to attend to us."

"He is under examination, Sir," said the Bishop, "He shall stand and answer like anyone else. It is contrary to law and reason that the accused should sit in the presence of a Prince of the Church."

The mob applauded. Gaunt flushed red with rage. He turned to the Bishop.

"Sir," said Gaunt, "Have a care or I will have you dragged out of your Church by your hair."

That was all it took. The mob roared and pushed through Percy's men and crowded around the Bishop.

"To arms, to arms," shouted Droppole. "Good Welshman" he turned to Owain, "Gather with me and guard this Prince of the Church."

Owain always tended to orthodoxy and was much affected by men speaking against the Church. We gathered around the Bishop. Percy's men fell back around Gaunt. Percy stepped forward to command and hustled his master out of the Church via some side door. In the confusion Wycliffe, who had caused this commotion in the first place, disappeared.

Now the crowd's blood was up. It poured out of the Cathedral and into Ludgate intending to sack Johnny Gaunt's Savoy palace down the Strand. Their efforts were wasted as the Dark Prince had taken himself off to a friend's house in the City to dine after his exertions, but at the time we knew none of this.

We were obliged to remain with the Bishop and were not able to get out and enjoy the sacking. The Bishop looked to us, saw we were of the better kind, and wrongly assumed we favored public order.

"Lads, we must go and stop the mob. They cannot be allowed to do damage to any person of Royal blood. No matter if he is a black hearted pig like Gaunt."

Owain looked at him. "Your Grace, I have no love for the English, but I will not stand by and watch any man stand against his better." As I say, Owain was a traditionalist in many things, especially as a young man.

"Excellent, good Welshman," said Droppole. "Bring the Bishop and we must end this madness."

So off we went, carrying off the Bishop, and cutting our way through the crowd to Carters Row.

There we commandeered a wagon, threw the Bishop on board and set off. With his regalia he cut quite a figure. The mob allowed us to pass thinking that he was blessing their endeavor. We finally arrived at the Savoy, but not before the Mob had killed a Priest they found at the gate of the Palace. Later it was put about that they believed he was Earl Percy, although how they could have mistaken a priest for the Lord of the North is a bit of a stretch.

They did not know it then but the Marshal's men-at-arms had already found Gaunt at his Steward's house and rushed him and Percy off in hiding to Kensington.

When we reached the Savoy, the Bishop reached out to calm the mob.

"Lads!" shouted the Bishop, "Leave Gaunt alone. He's not worth it. We'll get that bastard Wycliffe later."

The mob cheered. He continued.

"He might have pulled the wool over Gaunt's eyes, but he can't fool honest men like yourselves".

There were more cheers. He had measure of the mob.

"I thank you for your protection. Percy is no better than a foreigner and it is a shame and a sign that the Kingdom has fallen on bad times when such a man can be Lord High Marshall. Now in recognition of your bravery, I will open my cellars to you. Escort me to my palace and I will see that you shall all have wine and ale."

There were great cheers now. The Bishop knew that nothing quiets a mob like the promise of drink and the killing had satiated their anger and they were ready for enjoyment. Off we went with him to his Palace up by St. Paul's. It was a good day and we all drank our fill and celebrated our victory at the Battle of St. Paul's.

THE CORONATION OF KING RICHARD

I shall now tell you of the coronation of Good Queen Dick or, as he is better known, Richard by Grace of God King of England and France and Lord of Ireland. We had been in London two years when Richard the Magnificent ascended to the throne. He must have been about ten or eleven years old at the time so he was well qualified to rule a kingdom or two. His Grandfather Edward the Frank-killer had died a few weeks before. I never had much love for the old boy but, as with any well known figure that has been there all your life, I felt bad when he went. After all, he did his job well. He killed a lot of French, kept troublemakers out of his realms, and made sure taxes stayed low. What more could you want from a King?

In his last years he was in a pretty bad way. He never got over the death of his son. I speak from harsh experience that the worst thing in the world for a man is to see a child go to the grave. A man prepares himself for misery in his life but when a child dies, a portion of him will dies with them.

So after Edward's death, the King withdrew and took no part in government. In his dotage, Alice took him off to Sheen and did her best to keep the poor bugger happy. In the end he died on the warmest day of the summer of seventy-seven, alone and afraid. It is said that when Awful Alice was told he was dying, she rushed to his room and began her mourning by stripping off the King's rings and jewels and heading off to London to protect her wealth. Others say that she was with him through the old man's final crisis and kept his spirits high with stories of their good times together and promises that he would soon regain his health and go hunting and hawking. Believe what you will. No man knows the truth. As for Alice, little is known of her after those great days. Parliament was quick to strip most of her wealth away, but Queen Dick restored some of it. She ended her days where she began them, in Essex. Like many commoners who have tried to rise too high, she took to the courts to obtain her rights and went Law-Mad. I have seen this madness in many people. They go to court determined to correct all the injustices heaped on them and end by emptying their purses and losing their wits. Alice was no different. She ended as a mad old woman engaged in endless lawsuits against powerful men who didn't care tupence for the law. Never trust the law, I say. Put your trust in the sword and the torch. A common man is more likely to find justice with these than with an ink pot and a piece of parchment.

Old Edward's funeral was good enough. We Welsh like a good funeral. We are a morbid people much given to thoughts of death and take great pleasure in a good funeral. The death of a king is particularly good. We cannot stop ourselves from swarming down and gawking at the hearse. Then the wailing breaks out. It has been my experience that grief is like laughter; one person will cry and we all cry. As a result, we Welsh lose all control and end up screaming like mad things.

Edward's journey from Sheen was nicely done. They made a wooden effigy of him and glued a good wig on his head. They stuck the effigy on top of the hearse, put a gold pillow under his head, and hung a canopy of fine silk. The hearse came up from Sheen and was brought over from Southwalk. They added some more gold cloth and good smelling herbs when he got to London, as he was getting a bit ripe by then. Owain and I went down to see him at St. Paul's. He was all draped in black. It was very tasteful.

We went out the next day and followed him down the Strand to Westminster. The hearse left St. Paul's at dawn. The City was so quiet. All of the Londoners stood outside, very still. More than four hundred esquires, all in black, marched in step by the hearse. Each carried a torch to light the early morning gloom. When they got to the Abbey at Westminster the Cathedral was hung with heavy black cloth and the throng was draped in black silk. It was a good service. I will say something for the English, they do ceremony well. All the Lords secular and ecclesiastical turned up, most likely to suck up to the young king. They wrapped Edward in red samite, laid a white silk cross on him and stuck him in his coffin. Everyone said a mass and crossed themselves and went back to work. As I say, a nice funeral.

About ten days later they held the coronation. Between the funeral and the coronation, the City got properly tarted up. People came from all over Richard's realms. Judge Hanmer turned up with Marged. That put Owain on his best behavior, but he and Marged managed to run off for a bit of slap and tickle.

The festivities began the day before the coronation. A great procession took Queen Dick from the Tower down to Westminster. Following the Norman practice, the men from Bayeux followed behind him. After them came the Aldermen from each of London's wards. They were dressed very nicely but they still looked like a gang of thieves. They were all far too fat and far too pleased with themselves to really be honest.

For some reason, a corps of German mercenaries came next and then a delegation from Gascony. It was all very confusing. After them came all the brutes and bullies of the realm. Thus, we saw, in order, the Earls, barons, and knights.

In that crowd came the King's his famous uncles. I shall pause for a moment for to describe them, for they will shape My Lord's story more than any other men in this tale.

At the time of the Coronation four of Edward's sons were still alive. Queen Dick's father was dead, of course, and the second oldest of Edward's sons, Lionel, had followed him to the grave a few years before the coronation.

It is worth noting why there were so many royal peoples there on that day. It had been the great fortune, or misfortune as it turned out, for Edward the Frank-Killer and Queen Philippa to be blessed with many children. Now like most families, three or four of their children died early, but most grew to adulthood. So Edward and Philippa ended up with five adult sons and four grown daughters. All but one of the daughters died in early womanhood and left no heirs. However, the sons proved quite healthy and left many heirs; Johnny Gaunt himself had more than fourteen children from his various marriages. Therefore, from this one family were to burst a great abundance of royal persons, all with some claim to the crown. As the years went on, these many uncles and their progeny would all come to argue over the throne and claim some right to the crown. It was, I believe, the main reason that England has been racked with civil war

At the head of that group on that day was the oldest: John of Gaunt, Duke of Lancaster, Black Johnny, the Prince of Darkness himself. He was in his prime then. A tall, imposing man well made in body and with those dark looks that were so unlike the rest of the Plantagenets. His hair, beard and eyes were as black as Newcastle coal. When you stared into those eyes, you saw there was always something going. He could no more stop scheming and planning than he could stop breathing. That was his downfall. He thought too much. Whereas most men will act without thought or only think a pace two ahead, Johnny Gaunt was thinking a mile or two down the road. An admirable talent, you may think. Indeed, it would have been if he were he a lucky man or one blessed with good judgment. Unfortunately, while he took the long view, he was frequently wrong as to what would be the best course. His schemes became too involved and too complicated. He tied himself up in knots and ended up being stuck and unable to move without hurting one or other of his interests. He saw so well the likely outcome of all actions, both good and bad, that he was unable to decide which way to turn. When on the odd occasion he was able to make a decision, it was almost always the wrong one. If he decided on a campaign in France or Spain, it was sure to end in a defeat, an indecisive stalemate, or a victory that would benefit some other person. I have been in his presence when he would explain to the King all the consequences of a proposed action. He would neatly sum up the situation, identify the forces acting upon the decision at hand, and lay out all the courses of action and their dangers and advantages. Then, just when you expected some great breadth of wisdom to clear away all darkness, he would either collapse into uncertainty and doubt claiming that all courses were too risky, or propose some complex, torturous plan that any fool could see would fail.

It was this tendency that made him so unpopular. From the richest merchant and greatest lord to the poorest rustic, it was well known that Johnny Gaunt was a plotter and a schemer. His every action was questioned and seen as evidence of his duplicity. When his plots failed, it was either seen as evidence that God had intervened against him, or that his failure was only seemed so and some deeper plot was at work.

He was, however, very good at making money. Throughout his life he was the richest man in England, richer than the King himself. He started off rich and ended up richer. His Father set him up well and made him Duke of Lancaster. I should add that in those days the King could move around titles and lands like the pieces on a board of French Squares. However, Johnny Gaunt was not just willing to sit on his inheritance. Following the Great Mortality, the land was much changed, and if a man was willing to take advantage of the new world he could make a fortune. Land that had been worth a king's ransom became worthless. The men and women who had worked it were gone and fields languished overgrown and empty.

Johnny Gaunt was a young lad when the plague first came. By the time it was safe to venture out again, he was of age and in charge of his lands. He picked up empty lands for a song. Men were only too happy to convert their vacant lands into coin. With his wealth he was able to hire laborers to work them and turn them to profit. When he could not cultivate his land, he turned farm land into grazing pastures for sheep. As a result he became a great power in the wool trade. When he could find no men to work the land, he was among the first to rent it on long-term leases. As a result in a few years he created a whole class of men who were loyal to him and dependent on his good graces to maintain their wealth.

Each time the plague returned, he followed the same pattern, so that it seemed to the common people that Johnny Gaunt made an unnatural amount of money out of others' suffering. His mere presence could be counted on as a sign that death was coming and the common people would soon lose their land. So while his oldest brother, Edward, and his Father fought the French, he stayed home and made himself a new world of wealth and bound a class of prosperous men to his ambition.

But it did not stop there, for he was also a great one for the courts. Many families had completely died out after the Great Mortality, and there were endless disputes as to the ownership of the land. A man with the resources and connections to pursue his rights in the courts could normally outlast the opposition and end up the owner of these lands. That was exactly what Johnny Gaunt did. He would litigate over any holding to which he had even the slightest right. Nine times out of ten he would win and bring the land into his holdings.

On top of all this, he was very shrewd at sniffing out an advantageous marriage. He married well himself and fixed up his sons nicely too. He managed to bring a good deal of land and money into his family that way. As is ever the way, money breeds money. The rich become richer simply by virtue of having money in the first place. Thus, his fortune grew, and he gained the impression of being unstoppable. He simply had to begin some new endeavor and men would flock to his banner, sure that somehow they would make money out of it.

But despite his great wealth, he lacked something that could never be bought. In our world a man may be richer than God and can only rise as far as his birth will allow. It was Johnny Gaunt's fate to be the third son. Despite his ambition and wealth, he would never be anything more than a third son. Barring another plague that would take off Edward's entire family, he would forever be third in line the throne. For a time it seemed possible that God might favor him with the succession. His brother's oldest son died leaving only the young Richard. Then Edward himself died, and the boy became King. When Edward the Frank-killer finally died, he was among the young king's protectors. In time he was lucky enough for his other older brother, Lionel, to die leaving only a girl child. So if Richard were to die, he would be King. But that was the problem. A more evil man would have contrived an accident and taken the throne himself. But Johnny Gaunt was stuck between his ambition and his love of his brother. He idealized dead Prince Edward; all his life he felt bound to him and was determined to honor his brother's memory. He'd not move against Richard and was determined to secure his brother's son upon the throne. If only the people had believed this.

It is well known that rich men are always hated and are sinks of evil. Johnny Gaunt was no different. His naked ambition, his pursuit of wealth, and his endless plotting for advancement in foreign lands, convinced common Englishmen that he wanted nothing more than to be King. As a result, they hated and feared him. He wanted to be loved, but never could manage it. Over time his bitterness hardened into a fear and hatred of the people. He came to live surrounded by his guards and feared someone would try to murder him whenever he traveled. This only led people to fear and hate him more. "Look at him," they would say, "going about as if he is the king with his toughs and bully boys. Does he wish to scare us? What is he planning?" Poor Johnny, a rich man trapped in a world that saw wealth as a sure sign of corruption and evil.

Who came next? Edmund of Langley, Duke of York. Never had a man given so many high titles and so much power done so little with it. While his other brothers and sisters sparkled and burned, Edmund seemed to fade into the background. He had the potential to be as rich as his older brothers, or to be as well loved as his younger brothers, but somehow, he was forgotten. He was a boring, capable man who seemed content to live in others shadow. There was always something insubstantial about him. Even as I think back now, I cannot really remember his looks. I know he was there, but I remember nothing about him.

Edmund will play an important part in this story but for now he will be remembered for not acting rather than acting. So unambitious was Edmund that both his nephews would place the Kingdom in his hands when they went to war. Whatever happened, they could always count on plain old Edmund to do as he was told and be certain that their kingdom would be waiting for them when they returned. The one time he did what was unexpected, he plunged England and France into a war that even to this day continues.

Next came the beloved Thomas Woodstock, Duke of Gloucester, Plain Tom, Honest Tom, the last honest man in the Kingdom, people said. He was about twenty at that time and a fine- looking man. Unlike the other great lords, he avoided fancy clothes and jewels; most of the time he wore a plain rustic tunic, the clothes of a simple man. He took great pleasure in the pastimes of the country lords and had little patience for court or the ways of magnates. He preferred ale to wine, pork to fowl and bread to cake. Unusual for the time, he spoke mainly English and had much trouble with his French. He always spoke it with a heavy accent and the bum-boys around Richard's court would make fun of him. However, behind these simple ways was a man as ambitious as any. He dreamed great things and had no doubt that it would all he dreamed of would come to him in the end.

Despite being the youngest, he had the easy confidence of a first born. He expected everything and received it as his right. He felt none of the competition that his older brothers thrived on. Most of them had grown and gone out into the world by the time he arrived. Queen Philippa was left to dote upon her little boy and filled him with confidence and entitlement. As he was far from the throne, he had few expectation placed upon him and lived most of his life away from London and the court down in Oxfordshire. All his life he rolled his "Rs" like Oxfordshire men do. After his mother died, he was left alone to make his own way. While the other sons were away building fortunes or fighting the French, he ran wild with the sons of Woodstock manor tenants. He lived the life of a country boy and acquired the manners of a lowborn rustic. While this made the gentlemen and ladies of court laugh at him, it greatly endeared him to the common people. They loved their Honest Tom and took pleasure in his awkward ways.

Now, while his distance from the throne reduced the pressure on Plain Tom, it also opened the door to his ambitions. His older brothers might feel some loyalty to their brother's son or some obligation to the will of Edward the Frank-Killer, but Plain Tom felt none of that. Edward was away in France while he grew up and dead in a box by the time he was a man. The old King had little time for him after Philippa died and so he spent most of the time under the thumb of Awful Alice. As a result Plain Tom felt no great love for Richard. He believed his uncles were cautious old men who were enslaved to the memory of dead men. In contract, he was only too willing to propose that Richard step aside for a better man. So while Johnny Gaunt struggled to support his nephew, Plain Tom struggled to see him fall. As is always the way, the people saw this situation only on the surface without knowing the underlying causes, and so they got it wrong. To them, Johnny Gaunt conspired for the throne and plain, Honest Tom upheld the ancient rights of the Kingdom and acted as his nephew's protector against the evil councilors.

There were many others who followed, but I will not waste time describing them all. I will only draw a picture of those who are to be important for this story. The uncles of course came with their departed brother's wife, Princess Joan. Fair Joan was a little past her best when I first saw her, but she was still an attractive woman. When she was young it was said that her beauty surpassed that of all women in the Kingdom. But people believed that Prince Edward had married her for love only with no thought of the value of the marriage. At the time of the Coronation I remember her as a tall, thin woman, a little too thin for my taste. Her light red hair flowed and curled around her face. She carried herself with immense grace and had the look of someone born to the purple and quite sure of her position in the world.

She was well liked by the people. They always like some royal bitch that will treat them like shit. I will say that I was not well enamored of her. Her manners were too Frenchified and foreign for me. She may have been elegant and fashionable, but hers was an outward beauty only. She was an evil bitch underneath it all. Joan was the one member of that strange family who truly hated the people. In fact, she could barely stand to be near them. If she had had her way, she would have lived Aquitaine and left the cold shores of our island forever. I believe that she was to blame for those times in her son's reign when most blood was spilt. She held human life for little and would do anything to advance the interests of her son. I should add that I blame her for the fact that her son was a sodomite. She paid far too much attention to that boy and brought him up with too much regard for the ways of women. Some say that men are born that way and others that they can be made. For myself, I believe there is a little truth in both of those views. Richard may have had inclinations that way, as did many of the Plantagenets, but his mother did little to dissuade him and much to encourage his unnatural womanliness.

Who else do I remember? I recall the Arundel brothers were there, Richard and Thomas. Richard had come into his inheritance. He was a rather uninteresting man, typical of the magnates of his day. Rich and anxious to show you he was in charge. His brother was more interesting. He was Bishop of Ely back then. Never did I know a man more venal, grasping and evil than that bastard. All of the problems of my dear Wales may be placed at that cunt's feet. Although he wore the Bishop's miter, he was far from a true bishop. His Father bought him a Bishop's hat when he was nineteen. He was then retroactively ordained and declared a priest. He lived as a rich noble and had a string of whores and women throughout his life. I suppose he must have known the words of the Mass, but I never saw him speak them. He had one religion and that was power. Everything he did was meant to advance his power and position in the world. If any man got in his way, he would do him in with a rare joy and force.

He had at that time not begun his career as a great burner of heretics, but it was he who introduced this continental idea to our Island. By the time he died, his control of the church and our world was such that burnings had become a common sight in England and Wales. Even now as I remember him, my quill shakes. The very memory of the man fills me with anger. I hope that there is a special place in hell reserved for him where demons create new torturers for him daily.

The Earl Marshall of England must have been there, Henry Percy himself, but I do not remember him. No doubt he was riding around and swearing at everyone to keep them in line. He was a great, rough man, a Northerner through and through. Blunt, direct and forceful. He was quite difficult to understand. He spoke English in the way Northerners do, and there was much of the Scot and the Dane in him. He was a wild man with hair sprouting everywhere. He did much to affect the appearance of a barbaric Marcher lord that was used to the way of battle and could be counted on to be firm, trustworthy and loyal. Despite his bluster, he was something of a ditherer and coward. He was always willing to change sides when he saw the advantage and suffered from a permanent case of the "slows." That is, when danger beckoned, he could always be counted on to find some pretext to wait and prepare a little more. When the danger was past, he would turn up with his retinue all arrayed for battle and ready to fight. It was not a bad strategy. He made a good living out of just missing battles until he jumped to My Lord's side and brought the whole House of Percy down with him.

If you had looked closely at that procession, you would have been able to pick out a few more faces that were to be important for our story. You would have seen the young Henry Bolingbroke, the son of the John Gaunt, all fresh-faced and full of promise; not the evil old leprous slug he was to become. You might have seen the Earl of Mowbray walking with him; a fine boy and friend to Bolingbroke. Little did they know how their fates would be intertwined, and how they would bring each other down into death and exile. If you looked even closer you might have seen the Mortimer heir, still too young to play a proper part in drama, but tied to My Lord as few other men have been.

If you looked even more closely you might have spotted My Lord. He would have been with the Welsh baron and untitled tenants-in-chief who came towards the end of the procession. If you had a keen eye, you might have noticed that those untitled Welsh barons held back and let one of their number come to the front: a young, handsome and extremely tall man with red hair. That was My Lord, of course. The English did not see it, but the Welsh barons acknowledged him. To them he was the King of Powys and Deheubenth and, if the King of Gwynedd and Prince of Wales had no issue, he would be heir to all the Welsh Kingdoms. But the English had no eye for the Welsh, and there were few Welshmen in London in those days. If the crowd noticed them at all, it was only to comment that at least they looked a little more civilized than the Irish who followed, and perhaps they weren't as bad.

However, one day they would all pay attention to My Lord and know his anger. When they did, few would remember that he was there that day or even that the Welsh barons had paraded. They would only remember the boy King and the last time all the family of Edward the Frank-Killer were seen together in such harmony.

In front of them all came Queen Dick. He was a good looking boy; he had a nice royal flare to him. Tall and thin with very pale skin and flowing blond hair like his mother. So much of this story will be about him that I will say no more of his character and appearance. In fact, there is little more I can say, for he was always a mystery to me.

The procession wound up Eastcheap and turned on Westcheap to leave the City. It cut south onto Fleet Street and took the Strand to Westminster. Of course everything got out of control, and Londoners crowded into the streets. Johnny

Gaunt was on hand to spoil the day and had his men cut through the crowd. Luckily he was still sparring with the Alderman and, anticipating that he would do something vile, they had set up an effigy of one of Gaunt's bum-boys, Master Robert Belknap, vomiting and shitting. It must have annoyed Johnny Gaunt, as there is no way that he could have missed it.

They had really done Westcheap up well. The drains flowed with wine, mixed with the normal shit and offal that went down them, while the procession went by. It was pretty disgusting, but the crowd loved it. I saw Sir John in the parade busying himself by scooping up cupfuls as they he went past. Around the turn to Paternoster Row they had built a model castle. Little girls of the King's age, all dressed in virginal white, saluted him from the towers and rained down gold and silver leaves as he stopped. Then they came down and offered the new King a golden cup full of the finest wine. In retrospect I suppose it was a mistake to have girls. A few tasty boys would have been much more to her Majesty's tastes. The bæddels and sodomites of Cock Lane picked up on it right away. They all came out from the bog-hole taverns around Grey's Inn and were all rouged up and waving at him.

With Owain in the parade, I was free to wander round on my own. I took up with the boys from the Hog's Head and watched the show with them. We were all in a good mood, apart from Long Will. I nudged him in the ribs.

"Come on, Will," I said, "Have a drink and enjoy the day."
We looked at me mournfully. "This is not a happy day for the Kingdom," he said.

"A boy king is not what we need right now -- Vae terre ubi puer rex est – 'Woe to the land to which a boy is king'."

"Come on," said Whistler "He might be young, but that means that he hasn't been spoiled yet and his Dad was a good sort. A bit of a bastard, but you need a king that's not frightened of using the rod."

"I don't know," saw Will, "You've got the French barking at our heals in the South and Flanders, they raid along our coasts, we're got evil Uncle Johnny Gaunt looking after the shop till the boy is grown. It will be a rough time. I wouldn't be surprised if the king had an accident before his majority. Mark my words; Johnny Gaunt will move heaven and earth to make himself King of something."

Fearing things were becoming too serious; we took advantage of the free wine to get completely pissed. At some point we decided to have some fun and headed off to St. Pancreas and Cock Lane to find some girls for the evening. Along the way by St. Paul's we ran into Eleanor; she always made a good living from the priests and monks around there. I had always had a warm spot for Eleanor and her being in a good mood and willing to give it away for free, I took her along to Cock Street. I recall Whistler shouting something at me as we headed into the back room of a tavern. I should have listened. She informed me it was her time so she could not take me. However, she serviced me with her mouth. I reached down under her skirts and she much resisted. Of course, my passion was up and I ignored her. I pushed my hand in and to my shock I encountered a little extra. Now my knowledge of the perversities and strangeness of the English was at that time much underdeveloped. We Welsh are tolerant enough but are lost to this kind of thing. I was shocked and withdrew my hand.

"You didn't know?" she said.

"I knew nothing," I said, a little embarrassed.

"Don't hurt me," she said, "I'm just trying to make a living."

I thought for a minute. What did I care? After all she was serving me and life was hard in London.

"Alright," I said, "Let's finish up, but no kissing."

So she finished me and we wandered back. No one ever mentioned it again. Later she married a tailor in Bishop's gate and lived a good life. So I ended the Coronation day a little wiser and much more educated in the ways of the English.

OUR ACTIVITIES DURING THE GREAT REVOLT

Now I must turn to our adventures during the Great Revolt or what the English calling the Hurling Times, due to the great violence of the actions that occurred then. My Lord's loyalty to the otherwise foolish King Richard was rooted in the events of these times, and in some measure explains why, after Richard was overthrown, he took it upon himself to free Wales and avenge that King.

We had been in London almost seven years when we first heard rumor of the Great Revolt. As with all strange things, the first indication we had that something was coming was through Crach. In the months running up to the Revolt, he was much back in our presence. During our stay in London, he had spent most of his time at the homes of various sorcerers and cunning-women's homes around London. Crach had little time for men educated in the ways of magic, sorcery and alchemical knowledge.

"They are liars and frauds," he would say. "They claim knowledge from ancient sources, but they know nothing. The best they can do is conjure up the odd demon or angel and perform a trick or two."

While he himself was not above casting a circle or conjuring an angel to perform his bidding in the way of court sorcerers, he favored simple country magic and would always turn to a local village cunning woman rather than a man educated in the ways of classical sorcery.

"Country people are the only people left that remember the ways of the old ones," he told us. "You want to cure a case of dropsy, make sure your prick stays hard or clear a croup from your chest, find the ugliest woman in the village and ask her for a remedy. Ask a sorcerer and all he can do is help you understand the mysteries of the planets. They're a useless bunch of farts."

Thus Crach took great risks with the witch-finders, even going so far as to seek out Old Mother Red Cap at Camden Village. He also spent a good deal of time in the river in Mortlake, which was a pond off the Thames. In ancient times, swords had been offered to the river and, he told us with a glint in his eye, human sacrifices. Crach was approving of human sacrifice and insisted it was an important part of religious practice that had been sadly forgotten.

Now around the time of the Great Revolt, Crach returned often to the Temple. He was much in need of money to finance his travels across much of the South and the East of the Kingdom.

"The Great Society is meeting," he would say, "and I must be present."

"What is this Great Society?" I asked.

"A fraternity of masons that boasts decent from the builders of Great Temple of Solomon," Crach said. "They know the secrets from the desert spirits and demons that Solomon enslaved to build the Temple and later chained within its walls. Their treasures were returned to this land by the Templers, and they now circulate among guildsmen throughout the south."

It sounded like a pile of crap to me. Every guild I have ever heard of claims access to ancient mysteries or decent from some famous magician, but they are all liars. Men have an irresistible love of ritual and always find it necessary to explain their action by reference to some ancient precedent. The masons and guildsmen of the Great Society might have got a little gold from the Templers to build a church or two, but that that was all. In my opinion they had no more knowledge of the Holy Land than did any rustic. I blame it all on Wycliffe and his English Bible. As soon as the Lollards started telling people what the Bible stories actually said, every fool in the Kingdom began claiming unique knowledge of the mysteries of the Scriptures. Leave thinking to the Priest and learned doctors, I say; philosophy is not for the common sort.

I should also say that it was during that time I noticed a strange thing about Crach. While we seemed to grow older, he did not seem to age at all. If anything, his skin was slightly smoother and his hair was slightly more abundant as the years passed by. He was still ancient and twisted, but I would swear he looked better. I supposed at the time that the climate of London agreed with him. In the years ahead, he came to look almost human, and when I reached my middle years, I swear he and I looked about the same age. I suppose it was a mixture of his potions and my own aging, but I must say that it only added to the mystery of the man.

The event that triggered the Great Revolt was, of course, the third effort to levy the Poll Tax. At the end of the Edward the Frank-killer's reign, the exchequer was empty. Greedy Alice and her friends had managed to seize it all. Of course, the great and good explained it was all because of our reverses in the wars in France. In King Edward's time we had made so much money from the rape of France and the ransoming of rich prisoners that almost all taxes had been rescinded. However, corruption and the incompetence of the young King's guardians meant that new taxes had to be imposed. Being idiots, fools, and evil men, they decided that the best way would be to tax each man and woman regardless of their wealth. I do not know much about governing but this I do know: no man likes taxes, but men will only pay them if they feel they will get something for them. A man will hate taxes the most if he has to pay them all at one time and sees no benefit. That is exactly what the Poll Tax did. The Commissioners would come to a village and demand payment. No benefit was offered in return.

Of course in Wales we felt little pain. Most of the Welsh lands were in the marsh, and the Barons who controlled those lands did as they wished. They already had so much in tax revenue that they did not need a new tax. In the Welsh Royal counties the taxes were already stacked up high, and the people were so poor they barely had two pennies among them. Even Johnny Gaunt couldn't get blood out of a stone.

In the late spring, Crach came back from his wandering.

"Been out in Essex," he said as we gathered in our rooms.

"They're not happy out there. I will be surprised if we don't see some trouble before the summer's out. They'll be here. The Great Society met to consider calling a rising."

"There's no such thing," said Owain as he nursed a jug of ale and stared out of his window across the street towards London and the lure of its taverns.

Crach was annoyed. "No such thing, you say. Well, you are much mistaken. The Great Society has been in operation in this Kingdom for more many years. Its Grand Master lives and works in the City of London itself, its Captain is a man from Maidstone and its history in these lands goes back to the time of the first crusade."

Long Will was with us that day spinning gossip from the Wardrobe. "I know nothing of any Great Society and I too doubt its existence but I will tell you that times are hard enough for the common man. They are much put upon by the taxes, they starve and the great lords keep them at their as slaves. They are filled with anger and all it will take is one spark and the land will be in flames."

Crach nodded. "He is right. The land has never been so angry. I will say no more other than that when the time comes and the streets are full of rebels, they will first and above all seek the destruction of the Hospitallers of St. John for the Society was a great opponent of the Templers."

"The Templers have been gone these fifty years. There is no vestige of them left," said Owain.

Crach shook his head. "The Templers are everywhere." He looked around as if they were watching. "They were suppressed, but their memory and their power lives on. Never dispute their power, for they lurk in every secret place. Again I say, mark my words, this City will be in flames and chaos by harvest time."

Of course he was right. The spark was applied to the tinder by the appropriately named Judge Bumpton. He turned up at the village of Brentwood to collect taxes. He took along a few sergeants-in-arms from the Tower to make sure he was obeyed. When the locals refused to pay up, sent in his boys to collect by force and arrest the most vocal of those in opposition. The result was predictable. All men know that June is a good time to put ideas into the head of rustics, for June is a quiet time; the straw harvest has yet to begin and the planting is over. Men have time on their hands and leisure for idle thoughts. If you present them with a cause to riot and rebel at this time, they may consider it for they know they will have time to act before the must collect the harvest. Thus good Judge Bumpton planted the idea of rebellion in these villains' heads at just the right time. The villages of Fobbing, Corringham and Standford-le-Hope rose and chased him out of town. The good Judge scurried back to London to cry to his masters and scream revolt everywhere.

Johnny Gaunt was up in Scotland causing trouble at that time, so it was left to his lapdog Bobby Bealknap to keep order. He set out for Essex to show that he was in charge and end the rising there and then. The result was predictable. He hadn't been there more than a few days before he had set the whole county on fire and brought the revolt down on everyone's heads.

Before June was out, more than fifty thousand men had risen in Kent and Essex. The Kentish men rose when royal agents attempted to take a man they claimed belonged to them. I should explain that in those days, many Englishmen still were bonded to the land and could not move to seek work without leave from their master. There were always bond chasers abroad who were trying to track down runaways and hundreds of men on the tramp looking for new work.

It was at that time that I began to credit some of Crach's tales of a Great Society, for it was plain that there was some sort of organization. The men who rose in Essex and Kent made their way towards Dartford. Villages that were within twelve leagues of the coast did not rise. They were somehow instructed to remain quiet so as to guard against French invasion. It became clear that this was an organized revolt.
At Maidstone their leader revealed himself, a certain Wat the Tyler. He took charge and headed off to London with his chief captain. Each day we heard they were closer and each day we saw more evidence of their organization. The Essex men went straight for any property owned by Johnny Gaunt and burned it to the ground. The Kentish men captured Rochester Castle and headed north to London. They reached Blackheath over the river by the middle of June and readied themselves to take the City.

"What are they waiting for?" Owain asked as we viewed the scene across the River from the Temple.

"They are waiting for the men from Essex to arrive," said Crach.

"It won't matter," I said, "They'll never get into the City."

"They have agents within the Walls," said Crach, "and they will be here within the week."

The next day they marched up to Southwark, opened up Mashalsea Prison, and sacked the Archbishop of Canterbury's Palace at Lambeth. Then, in what was to my mind a completely unnecessary action, they fell on the Flemish whores' houses around the bridge. I saw no reason to attack the girls. They were hard working young women and as much as the "King's True Commons" as ever the rebels were. At about the same time, the Essex men arrived from the east Aldgate. They moved around the City wall and set up camp in the northwest at the Smithfield cattle market.

We discussed whether we should stay at the Inns and defend ourselves or go into the City. Master Watchman was clear.

"Glory to God, Brothers," he shouted to us when we encountered him in the garden pulling on his hat and tunic, "The day of judgment comes. Let us sally forth and join our true Brothers have come to save London from itself."

"Silly bastard" said Crach. "Nothing will so quickly disillusion a gentleman who favors the mob as will close association with them. I predict he will either be back here before night or dead. A mob does not take kindly to a man of learning who offers his services."

"Should we stay at the Inns of go into the City?" I asked. Owain, ever active and anxious to head into the fight, answered.

"We shall go in and observe these English rustics. Let us see if they are enemies or friends."

That night Owain and I disguised ourselves as rustics and paid a frightened wherry man three pennies to take us across the river to see the rebels. It was an outrageous price, but he would not move without seeing silver. We arrived in the evening when the day was cooling and the rebels had lit their fires for the night. As we walked through their camps, we saw that the fires were made from the wood of the Bishop's Palace they had destroyed that afternoon. The priceless carvings and solid timbers of the Palace cracked and ticked as good as any simple kindling. We heard snatches of conversation as we moved about.

"I tell you, the Great Society means to make a new commonwealth and turn the old world upside-down," said one man as he sat by a fire.

Another poked the fire. "We need it. I tell you England's never been a good land since the Norman came." They spoke in the soft rolling burr of Kent.

The first man nodded, "Fuckers think that handicraftsmen is nothing."

"It'd all be different is the King's Council were workmen," opined a third. There was general agreement, and it seemed that they were of the same mind.

The first rustic replied, nodding his head.

"True, it would be better if the Council was made of laboring men and we were all magistrates."

They all nodded and the second and oldest man replied
"You've hit the nail on the head there, Brother. There's no better sign of a brave mind than a hard hand."

We walked on. We saw a Preacher speaking to the Mob from a cart. Torches burned around him, and a pale cross was planted in the ground behind him. A crowd thronged around him for entertainment.

"Be brave Brothers, for your good Captain Watt vows a great reformation of this realm. When we rule, we shall make bread available for every common man; we shall ensure that all beer is brewed to strength, sold in true measure, and never watered; we shall take the Great Whore of a City that sits on the opposite bank and end all tyranny. Cheapside shall be raised and left to go to grass. There shall be no money, all men shall eat and drink as they need, all may wear whatever apparel they choose and they shall worship the Lord as Brothers. There shall be no more lawyers and nothing written by unjust men. For is it not a bad thing to take the skin of an innocent lamb to make parchment? And that parchment, being scribbled on, should be used to bind a man?"

There were murmurs of approval.

"Some say a bee stings, but I say it is the bee's wax; for I once I have sealed a thing, I am never mine own man since."

There were more grunts and murmurs of approval. He was just getting warmed up, but we had heard enough. We moved on and found a quiet place. Our intention was to stay there that night and then in the morning make out way up river and cross at Westminster if we could find a wherry.

Around dawn we were woken by a great commotion in the camp. We joined the others and ran to where we saw Knights and Bannerettes who had converged there.
A Knight shouted, "Where is your Captain?"

A Priest pushed his way to the front.

"He is not here, but I am John Ball his Vicar-in-Chief and may speak in his absence."

The Knight eyed him dismissively. "You all should leave here. Sir John Knolls and a great power are near at hand. They are all loyal to the King and will set you to flight."

There were shouts of confusion. Ball laughed loudly.

"If there were such an army, then we would not be given warning. This is an effort to scare us into retreat." He turned to the crowd and raised his voice.

"If knights are coming to send us off, then I shall make all of you knights so that you can stand against them. For what is a knight but a man like you with but with the money to buy a horse and a sword? Do you not have swords and knives? Have you not fought for your King with your bows? Aye, all of you have. You are all knights and should have no fear of these lies."

With this the mob gained strength and moved menacingly towards the Bannerette. The Knight responded.

"You rebellious dogs and sons of whores," shouted the Knight. "You are the filth and scum of Kent. You are all marketed for the gallows if you do not lay down your weapons. Go home to your cottages and forsake this mad priest. You should know that the King is merciful and will forgive your revolt."

There were boos and hisses but the Knight was not easily put off and he continued, "If you ignore my warning and persist in angry, wrathful ways and remain inclined to blood, you will all die, we will burn your bodies, and you shall not hear the last trumpet."

Ball ignored him and turned his back on the Knights. "I shall not speak to these silk-coated slaves. I speak to you, good people."

The Knight interrupted. "How dare you? You wear a priest's cassock but you are nothing. What was your father? A plasterer? A shearman?"

Ball looked back, "So what? Was not Adam was a gardener?"

The Knight looked confused, "And what of that?"

"Adam was a working man as we. There is no shame in work. For is it not well said that "When Adam delved and Eve Span, Who then was the Gentleman?"

The mob roared in laughter. The Knight reddened. "What gross and miserable ignorance."

"A clever argument," Ball taunted him. "I am impressed with the depth of your thought. Perhaps I should let my Brothers have your head to see where such arguments come from."

The Knight has reached the end of his patience. "Well, seeing that gentle words will not prevail, I warn you that if you do not move, you will be assailed by the full power of the King."

He pauses and pulled out a parchment. The very sight of it caused boos and hisses. The Knight read from the proclamation.

"This shall be read in every village and town," began the Knight. "You shall be proclaimed traitors with the criminals Watt the Tyler, Jack Straw, and John Ball. Those who continue to support these men shall be hanged up at their doors within sight of their wives and children. If you turn back now, you shall be taken to be friends of the King and no harm shall attend you."

The crowd booed and shouted. Ball yelled above the noise of the crowd.

"Do you men believe him? The King is our friend. We will never go home until we have recovered our ancient freedoms." Gesturing towards the Knight, he went on. "They enjoy our slavery. They break our backs with burdens, take our houses over our heads, and ravish our wives and daughters before our faces. All of you who love the commons follow me and show yourselves to be true men. We will not leave one lord or one gentleman. Spare no one dressed in silks and finery. Those who wear simple clothes are judged honest men and are our friends. Come, my Brothers, let us take this Knight and his friends for punishment"

And with that the crowd closed in on the Knight's party, dragged them from their horses and beat them to death. Ball called out.

"Look, they fall like sheep and oxen. I grant you all a great boon and reward you all. You shall all have a license to kill for ninety-nine days. Do your worst Brothers."

We saw the killers carrying off body parts. One said, "This shall be our monument to this victory. We shall drag these bodies into London itself and post them hard on the Mayor's Sword itself."

The rebels' captains and sergeants then called for their men to form themselves up and head toward the Bridge in organized companies. We held back and joined the local rabble and the disorganized mob that followed the rebels. As we crossed the Bridge, I saw one of the rebel's Sergeants guiding us across, for some agent in the City had let the draw-bridge down for them to enter.

"Where do they go, Brothers?" Owain called out to the Sergeant in his best impression of Kentish rustic.

"We are off to the see the King," he replied. "Our Captain has promised us that the King has agreed to hear our grievance and free all men. In return, he only asks that we free him from his wicked councilors. By week's end all men will be free and there shall be no lords between the King and Commons, Glory to God, Brother."

"Glory to God, Brother," said Owain.

"What do they expect to happen?" I said.

"They act in the interests of the King," said Owain, "I have observed that the English will never do anything unless they are directed to do so by a king. If some rabble-rouser wants to work up the English to do something violent, he must tell that he is acting for the king. Once so informed they will do almost anything. It is quite disgusting. Note, they are not interested in Parliament, they know nothing of the disputes between the City and the King Council, and yet they act as if they are fully informed in these disputes."

"But they know nothing;" I said "They are prepared to turn their lives upside down and risk everything on a mere whisper of a rumor.

Look at them," I said, indicating the orderly columns. "They probably started out egged on by a few low, dishonest men but now they are ready to risk their lives in the pursuit of some insane dream."

"Watch and learn," said Owain "Think what might be possible if people so inspired could led by a disciplined group with a single vision. For are not most men sheep and easily seduced by promises of advantage? What could we do if we could take advantage of these simple peoples' ways and turn the English upon one another? I make no suggestion. I simply recommend that you think on what we are seeing and consider how it may be of use to us."

He stopped for a minute. "Come Gwyn," said Owain, "Let us go to the Hog's Head and see what the boys are up to."

We turned west and headed to Crooked Lane and the Hog's Head. There, as with all places of business in the City, the windows were closed and the door boarded up. Owain banged upon the door.

"Mistress Wriggly," he called "Mistress Wriggly, open the door. It is Owain and Gwyn."

A window opened from the upper levels of the Inn and Mistress Wriggly poked her head out.

"Master Owain, is that you?" she asked.

"Indeed it is My Lady. We were concerned for your safety and the disposition of the patrons in these troubles."

"Oh, Master Owain," she said. "You are a good man to be concerned for our safety. We are secure and I stay to protect my property. As to your party, Sir John, Whistler, and Nam have gone with the Mayor and the loyal Aldermen to the Tower. As for Poins and that rogue Gadshill they have betrayed us. They are gone to the rebels. They hope for mischief."

"What is going on at the Tower?" Owain asked.

"The King has rallied his knights and men-at-arms there. Sir Robert Knolles called upon Sir John and the other Routiers in the City to rally with him and the King. The Mayor is trying to call the City militia to him but the chaos is such he has not the power."

"You are well informed Mistress," said Owain.

"Indeed I am," said Mistress Wriggly. "I was laying out Sir John's lunch and a messenger came to the Inn. "Is Sir John here?" he says. "Yes," I says. "Well he must come," he says, "Why," I says. "The rebels are to surround the City and Sir
Robert Knolles wishes all men formerly under his command in France to come to the Tower. The King has but few good knights and men-at-arms and needs all loyal men to come to defend his person."

"So I tells Sir John and, quick as a rat on the cheese, he jumps up, snatches up his arms, and is kicking Whistler and Nam awake and ordering them to action. I begged him, begged him I did, to stay and protect us here, but he would have none of it."

"Mistress" he said, "I go to defend my King," and he kissed me, grabbed a leg of mutton and headed to the Tower. Eleanor and I cleared out the customers and barred the doors. We will wait until good order returns, and then we will reopen. I would go to the Tower or leave the City, Master Owain. These rustics will kill us all."

"We must return to our friends and kinsman at the Temple.
They are preparing our defense. We swore we would return with intelligences of the rebels' movement."

"Godspeed Sirs," she said. "Remember we shall be open for business when order is resolved. If trouble happens, I shall send Eleanor as a messenger."

We saluted her and headed back towards the Temple. When we reached there, we found our fellow students had barricaded the streets around the Temple.

We found Gruffudd working with his students to block Chancellor's Lane between two buildings. Owain quickly informed him of our intelligences.

"It confirms what we have heard. They say the rebels are intent on hunting down all those that support Johnny Gaunt and are hell bent on liberating all the criminals and violent men in London," said Gruffudd. "We are arming ourselves and preparing to defend the Temple. The rebels will make their attack on the Temple and the Courts tomorrow."

We joined with our fellows in building the Temple's defenses. All day we worked piling up barrels and stacks of furniture as barricades. We armed ourselves with whatever weapons we had at hand. Almost all students had swords or daggers of some kind. Many had bows or crossbow and had practiced regularly with them at the butts on Sundays. We were far from a professional force, but we believed ourselves able to mount a good defense and slow down the assault. After a day's labor we collapsed into sleep. The Wardens of the Temple established a watch to protect us through the night, and we rested for the battle tomorrow.

Owain woke me at dawn. "Gwyn, I want to see more of these rebels. Let us see if the men from Essex are any different from the Kentish men we saw yesterday," he said.
We pulled on our tunics and stockings and headed north on Church Street towards Smithfield. As we neared the rebels, we were met by watchmen guarding the entrance to their camp. They questioned us as to our purpose and asked whether we were agents of the Knights of St. John or Johnny Gaunt.

"Hold it there lads," said one in a broad tidewater accent.
"Are you with Captain Watt and the King's True Commons or St. John and Johnny Gaunt?"

Owain stepped up, "We are with neither, Sir," he said "We are drovers from the Marches." This was a mistake I thought, for it was never good to mention you were Welsh to

Englishmen. "We have come to market in London with our master's cows and wish to see they are unmolested by your men."

"Then you're out of luck," said one of the Watchmen. "We were hungry and have had to dine upon the stocks held here. If your master is still in London, tell him that the chances are that his cattle are gone."

"He urged us to inspect the stock and bring evidence, for he doubts our words and believes that we might sell the cattle ourselves and say they were eaten by the rebels," said Owain.

"We are not rebels Welshey," said the Watchmen. "We are all members of the King's true commons. Many of us are freedmen or guildsmen. We have apprentices and masters here. Nor are we rebels, for we are loyal subjects of King Richard. Neither are we heretics. We are all true communicants and support the one true Church."

"I beg your pardon, my friend," said Owain. "I was ignorant as to your purposes and the composition of your host. We are simple men from the country and have but the words of the gossips of London to inform us of you."

The watchman was somewhat mollified.

"Well, that's as may be, but we can offer no admission to our camp unless you have the approval and marks from our Captains, or if you know our pass and watch words."

Owain looked at him, "Well I know neither your Captains nor your secret words, thus we must return to our master and hope he believes us."

"I mean no offense lads," said the watchman. "Go back and stay low. There will be many happenings this day and foreigners such as yourselves should consider making scarce."

We assured him we would and headed back down the road toward the Grey's Inn.

"What now?" I asked Owain in Welsh.

"If there is to be great deeds done this day, I say that we wait in a concealed place and observe these members of the 'Kings True Commons.' When they leave their camp, we will join with the straggles and hangers on and observe their actions."

I nodded knowing that My Lord had chosen the right plan, for it was worthy of us to see what these rebels intended. We headed to a cop of trees that hid the road around Holborn. Once there he climbed the highest tree and looked out across the camp.

"What do you see?" I called up to him.

"More men that I have ever seen in one place," said Owain. I climbed up next to him. He was right. They stretched more than an English mile from St. Bartholomew's right down to the River Fleet. They were like a great crawling mass of brown and green all moving with one purpose. They drifted across the hills of Smithfield and Clerkenwell rising out of the morning mists and moving through the pens and barns of Smithfield. They were organized in tightly ordered camps. Watchmen were stationed at each of the roads leading to their camps, and we could see lookouts on the higher buildings.

"This shows organization," said Owain. "This is not a disorganized mob of rebels as those we saw south of the river. This is an army that bares command. There is a head somewhere that is directing the body in this mischief."

"Crach's Great Society?" I said.

"It could be," said Owain, "but even a Great Society must have a leader, and no leader of statue and power would let such an army assemble without being close at hand."

Owain was right. This was clearly a great force disciplined and regimented by a single marshal or constable. Then we saw the army begin to stir. In the north the various camps began to line up in rows and draw together. Their captains could be seem raising and rallying their men as a drover would whip his stock and move them towards the pen. Across the shimmering heat of that early summer morning we could hear horns and whistles calling commands. Once the battalions had been rallied, they moved off towards Clerkenwell.

"I think they must be sighting towards the St. John's Knights Hospital," Owain said.

"What would they want there?"

"What did the watchman say, "Are you for St. John and Johnny Gaunt"? Perhaps they believe that there is an alliance between the Dark Prince and the Order of St. John. If so, I believe they are greatly mistaken. Johnny Gaunt is up in the North causing trouble with the Percys and the Scots."

As we spoke we saw the Essex men begin to enter the grounds of the Hospital of St. John. Even from this distance it was clear that no quarter would be given. We watched them batter down the Abbey doors and pour into the courtyard. Across this distance we began to hear the screams and shouts of the good brothers who had made resistance against the Essex men. With the screams came the noise of glass breaking and the rising rumble of men's voices when there is violence to be done. Within a few moments we saw the snapping flames of the first fires. They began to lick up from the outlying buildings and gradually consumed the fronts. Where the priory would not burn, they took their hands to destroying the buildings with implements, swinging axes and hammers to bring down the doors and arches. When that was done, they dragged out the monks and began to beat and whip them. It was clear whatever grudge they had against the Order of St. Johns, they felt it very deeply.

As the Priory fell, the rebels began to move south. Slowly they gathered their forces as more detachments of the rebels began to rise themselves and form into groups.

"They are coming for us now," said Owain. "We must prepare the defenders of the Temple."

We climbed down the trees and ran back towards the barricade the students had built. When we arrived it was clear the students had already heard of the rebel attack. They had finished the work on the barricade and now defended it with a mixture of bows and spears.

A Master-of-Law at the Temple called out to us. "Stay close boys," he said. "We will defend here as long as we can. When we cannot hold the barricade any longer we will fall back to the Temple itself. We'll hold the gate house for as long as we can. We must protect the records and charters held in the Temple. The Court at Westminster is sending boats down and we are trying to remove these to the Palace."

Then the rebels came. As a throng, they poured down the streets and lanes around the Fleet. Down Fleet Street they rolled, hitting the Fleet Prison like a strong wind. It held for a minute before the gates broke down and in they went. As with the St. John's Priory, they fired it down within minutes. It is truly amazing what a mass of men can do when their blood it up. The criminal and footpads were freed and more evil flooded out to join the mob. On they came, they had tasted flesh and they were ready for murder now. The Inns of Court went next. I saw one home of five years crumble as the rebels hit it. The firebrands threw up their torches into the thatch and cheered when it caught. We could hear them shout:

"Now is the time, now is the time."

"Kill the Lawyers and Avenge the Templers."

"Down with St. John and Johnny Gaunt".

"The Templers?" said Owain in confusion, "Why are they so concerned about the Templers?"

On they came. Our boys began to pull their bows and fire into the mob. We were of poor discipline and there was no effort taken to coordinate the arrow swarm. Rather than a sky full of arrows, we sent the occasional flip and flop. This will not stop a mass. If you are to halt a gathering of men, you must fire all your arrows at once and fire in unison for several minutes. Doing this can put thousands of arrows into the air and take down whole battalions. They will fall and cause their comrades to fall, slow the advance and allow you to hit them again. Seeing their comrades' fall, the remainder will be frightened and, as the deaths mount; they may doubt the right of their cause and retreat.

Our put-put of arrows was not enough to keep them back. Before we knew it, they were on out barricade and swinging their axes and hammers. We climbed up and hit back, but it was clear we were losing. I saw Owain strike down at least half a dozen of rebels, and I dispatched as many myself but it did no good. There were simply too many of them.
I heard one of their leaders shout:

"The only laws of England shall come from an honest man's mouth. Burn all the records of the realm. All things shall be in common."

The students began to crumble. "Back, back!" I heard someone shout. "We must all go to the Temple. Defend the gate."

So back we went, abandoning our barricades and running to the gate. We were among the last inside. We slammed and barred the door. Once inside we hove to the gates and began to pile up boxes and crates to further protect the Temple. It was to no good. Outside we could hear the mob banging with their axes and hammers on the gate. We heard them, "Now is the Time, Kill all the Lawyers, Avenge the Templers."

Gradually the door gave way as the rebels swung their axes. Then it cracked and opened a little. Owain pushed the tip of his sword through the crack and stabbed at the rebels. I could see blood spurt and men scream, but nothing stopped them there were simply too many of them. The gate twisted and yielded to the rebels and as before they flooded in. Owain and I ran back.

"To the river," he said, "All is lost." We ran back to the river. I could see that the normal clutter of lawyers' boats and wherries had gone.

"Where shell we go now?" I asked.

"There," said Owain pointing to a long boat in the river. From it Hamners gesticulated to us. We threw off out bucklers and dove into the river.

Now the Thames is a funny river and has many strange moods. Though a man can swim in it, the River has obscure currants that can take a man down quickly. Thus, all men avoided swimming in the Thames if they could. Once in, we discovered that indeed it was a good idea to avoid the river for no sooner was I in the river than off it took me.

"Owain," I cried. He saw me struggling and despite the many arrows and rocks thrown from the bank he swam towards me. Taking my hand he pulled me from the currant that had caught me. We swam together until we neared the long wherry. The Hanmers reached down and pulled us aboard. We climbed onto the deck and looked back at the Temple.

"Are they destroying the Temple?" I asked.

"No," said Gruffudd, "They seem to be respected it. Look." He was right. From the Ferry we could see no fires coming from the Temple and no damage being done to the structure. However, they had brought out the chests of legal documents and were building a bonfire on the river bank.

"They are burning the legal titles and records, but they show no interest in the Temple."

"Perhaps it was because it was the Templers' building once?" I suggested.

We watched as they continued. The mob killed all of the students and lawyers they found and destroyed all legal documents, but the Temple remained undamaged. As we drifted down river we could see in the distance that the rebels were moving onto the Savoy.

No man knows the Savoy today as it was when the rebels destroyed it that day. It was Johnny Gaunt's greatest palace in London. Greater than any palace the King of England ever had and seen by one and all as evidence of the corruption of Johnny Gaunt. Back then it was known throughout England for its beauty. Its luxurious furnishings and Italian gardens were known everywhere. I have often imagined that Heaven must resemble the Savoy. On that day it went down. If the rebels had been angry before, they were furious now. They took to the destruction of the Savoy as if it was their masterpiece. They smashed every window, broke every statue, and burnt every drape. Gangs of rebels marched in disciplined fashion and pulled out all of Gaunt's wealth. Everything was thrown onto one of pyres and burnt. Systematically they destroyed each layer and level of the Palace. When they reached the roof, the tillers and masons among the mob climbed up and smashed the roof tiles and guttering.

"Amazing," said Owain "They are not looting the Palace, they are destroying it." He was right. From the river we did not see one item stolen. Everything was destroyed in a disciplined, organized fashion. I have heard that when two men did try to steal, they were arrested by the rebels and hanged. More and more it became clear to us that there was method to this mob's madness. They were not the simple rustics bent on destruction, but a disciplined army intent on a single purpose and determined to complete destruction.

We talked of this as the wherry floated down the River toward the Tower. We hove in at the Watergate and were dragged off the boat and told to wait in the Tower courtyard. There a man from the military wardrobe passed out surcoats with the badges of loyalists. We were to wear these to distinguish us from the rebels if they broke into the Tower. I pulled mine on and looked down to see the twisted double "S" and the red rose of the House of Lancaster. I looked over and saw Owain had the same. We had been unlucky enough to end up as Johnny Gaunt's men.

Having been hurried to the Tower, we found, like most military operations, that expediency and fast work leads to long periods where nothing will happen. Thus we cooled our heels and milled around with no great purpose waiting for orders and direction.

Every person of substance or power was in the Tower that day. I saw more Lords, Ladies, Earls, Dukes, Duchesses, knights, Archbishops, priests, aldermen, and guild masters than I have ever seen in once place. If a rebel had managed to burn the Tower down almost every powerful man in England would have disappeared.

While we were waiting there was a great commotion. A tall striking woman came striding from the Watergate with her baggage in train. She was quite a looker; red hair and pale white skin. She was obviously some rich man's wife, for she behaved as if she was the Queen of England herself. She looked around for someone to help her. Her eyes settled on us.

"You two, you're wearing the Duke of Lancaster livery aren't you? Come here I have baggage for you to carry." We stared at her like lost lambs. She pointed at us, "I mean you two. Holy Mary, don't just stand there gawking. Don't you know who I am?"

Strictly speaking the answer to that was no, we had no idea who she was.

"Well, come on," she said. "If we don't get a move on, there'll be nowhere left for us. I've already been thrown out of one palace and I have no intention of being thrown out of another.

There are some people that it is best to just go along with, so we picked up the bags she indicated and walked off behind her. At the time I assumed she must be some great lady, perhaps the wife of a prince of the blood or some earl's wife? She carried her head high like she was the most important woman in the Tower that day, and the men-at-arms behaved as if she was.

We followed her as she went off into the Tower. She waved the guards away, climbed up the second floor and began to walk through the corridors looking for a good room. Nothing held her back. She poked her head in everywhere and acted like she owned the place. She paused at one room, sniffed the air and walked in. "This is good enough," she said. She looked back at us, "Well come on, get in here."

In we went. "Put my baggage there," she said gesticulating at a nook by the window. We turned and were going to leave when another woman walked in. She looked a little familiar. I knew I had seen her somewhere before.

"Lady Katherine," said the older woman. "I thought the mob had caught you at the Savoy."

The other woman crinkled her face in an almost smile.

"Your Highness," she curtseyed. "They were kind enough to eject me before they took to destruction. They seem uninterested in me and only wanted to destroy the Duke's property."

"Are you not the Duke's property?" said the older woman with a smile. "Perhaps they recognized a fellow country girl?" said the older woman.

"Whatever it was, I survived with my skin. Let me tell you, when the Duke gets back, I will have him hang every one of those rustics" she said.

The other woman nodded. "I hear the Duke is hiding in Scotland. I would not count on him returning too soon. The Scot's may decide to keep him." She laughed slightly.

"I will rely on the goodness of your son to protect him. As we speak I am sure he is preparing an army to return to London," said the younger of the two.

"Indeed," said the older woman. "We shall see. By the way, is your brother-in-law with us? The wine dealer? I always think it is good to know that we shall well prepared in a siege and wine is so important."

That was a nice dig, I thought, the nobility depended on trade but hated tradesmen. She went on, "For one such as yourself with connections in trade, I am sure it must be reassuring to know you are needed." They smiled icily at each other. Ye Gods I felt uncomfortable. Give me a sea fight or a bad day under the arrow than being between two grand ladies fighting with words.

The older woman turned to us, "My I borrow your men?" she asked. "It appears we are forced to share. The Archbishop is lecturing my son, and I believe they are in need of a muscle."

The other woman wrinkled her eyes, "Your Highness, I realize that a great lady of your age requires extra assistance, please take them with you." She smiled.

The other woman nodded, "Lady Katherine."

"Your Grace," said the younger woman.

The older woman turned to us, "Come, then, I need you to attend on me in my son's chamber."

And so we met, and followed, Princess Joan, the Fair Maid of Kent, the once-upon-a-time most beautiful woman in England, the King's mother and the wife of the late Edmund Prince of Wales. I didn't recognize her from the coronation. Important people always seem different when seen close up.

We followed her into a huge chamber. Men were hunched over the table arguing. At the head of the table was a young boy slumped back listening to old men shout. Princess Joan walked in. She pointed to a map of London and the surrounding counties.

"You two, fetch that down and bring it to the table. I wish to review the situation with my son," she ordered us.

The men stopped their arguing and bowed to her. We hefted the map down from the wall and brought it over to the table. Joan walked to the table and looked fondly at the young boy sitting at its head. There he was, Richard, King of England and France, Prince of Wales and Lord of Ireland. He didn't seem that impressive at that moment. More like a resentful, confused boy being bullied by adults.

"What are your plans, dear?" She asked him.

"The Archbishop feels that it would be best if I talked to the rebels, Mother," said Richard.

"You must do what you think is best," said the Princess, "but I think it is a bad idea."

"Your Highness," said the Archbishop. "We are surrounded and need to buy time until we can rally our forces. If the King gives the rabble an impression that he will consider negotiating, perhaps he can persuade them to leave."

"Nonsense!" said Joan, freezing the Archbishop with a steely glance. She turned to Richard, "Your Father would not have talked to them. He would have mounted up and fought them on his own before even considering talking to them. They are a disgusting mob of unwashed bondsman and slaves. You should have no time for them. I tell you, placing yourself before them only demeans your office and shows that you are not worthy of their respect."

Richard sighed, "What would you have us do Mother? You might have noticed that we are surrounded and cut off from the rest of the kingdom. Do you wish me to conjure an army from nowhere? Should I tell them to go home and stop bothering me?"

She waved her hand in irritation. "Your Father and Grandfather would have done so," she said, "and what's more, they would have ridden out with the knights to put this rabble down. Furthermore, need I remind you that I, a woman and your mother, was able to walk straight through that mob unharmed?"

Richard was no match for her. "Very well, Mother, we know that I am not a patch on my Father and Grandfather and, if I was half the man they were, I would never have let this happen. However, I am here and while you are lecturing me, I see that the mob is busily finding any person of quality in this city beheading them and burning their entrails."

Joan look annoyed, placed her hands in her lap and sat back in her chair.

"Well, My Lords, we have heard from my Mother. What do you recommend?" said Richard to the group assembled at the table.

"As I said, Your Grace, we need to buy some time," replied the Archbishop, glancing at Joan. "Meet with the rebels. Agree to everything they want. I will absolve you from any oath you make have to break."

Joan broke in again. "I see that whore Katherine Swynford is present in the Tower. Can you not eject some of the vermin? She and her ilk would blend perfectly with the mob."

"Mother, please do not provoke people," said Richard, clearly annoyed. "We need to stand together."

Joan turned to the Archbishop, "Where would you have my son meet with this scum? Have you any plans to protect my son, or would you prefer to have the King cut up into pieces by these maniacs to buy some more time?"

"Your Highness," he said, pointing to the map, "I plan to have them meet at Milesend. The King will travel by boat to Westminster accompanied by a guard from the Tower. There, he will gather a considerable force of loyal soldiers and travel to Milesend."

Joan was clearly alarmed. "And leave us all to be killed by the rustics?" she squeaked, her eyes wide.

"Your Highness," the Archbishop said, frustrated but trying to calm her, "the mob can no more enter the Tower than I can jump to the moon. We hold the Tower and the river. We are safe. Time is on our side. The longer we wait, the more the situation swings in our favor."

She interrupted, "Does it? I hear rumors that all of Norfolk is on fire and towns between here and York have been captured by the rebels."

"There have been outbreaks elsewhere, but you exaggerate, My Lady" said the Archbishop, only slightly patronizing. "The Bishop of Norwich is a martial man and is very capable of dealing with rebels. Our intelligencers tell us that even now he is rallying his forces to strike back at the rebels. Whatever the case, we must protect the City. If the mob set fire to it, the loss would be irreparable. Look what they have done to the Temple and the Savoy."

Princess Joan made a dismissive noise, "That is the one good thing they have done. The Savoy was a monstrosity. Gaunt has no taste. I tell you, Richard, everything he has done is an effort to show up your Father and raise himself above you."

Now the Archbishop was clearly frustrated. "Be that as it may, Your Highness, we must keep the mob calm and lead them to believe that the King will assent to their demands. When he has led them out of the City, Mayor Walforth has plans to close the gates and assert control over the City. You will safe here."

"Well, I doubt the truth of that, but you seem intent on this course of action, so I shall remain here," said Joan.

The Archbishop said, "Your Highness is under the protection of Lancaster's men, and I can lend you a few more. You will be safe here." He turned to us, "You men will stay with the Princess until I command you otherwise. Your Master will hold it well if you obey me."

I would have spoken up and told him that we were not Lancaster's men, but Owain waved me down, "We will stay with the Princess, Your Grace" he said.

Joan rose from her chair and stamped her foot impatiently. "I don't need these fools. I faced this mob down before, and I will do it again. Send them to the walls where they can do some good."

The Archbishop indicated for us to leave and off we went. Outside the chamber, I turned to Owain, "Who have we just seen?"

A fat middling man was leaning against a wall regarding us coolly. "I believe, gentlemen, you have just seen the King of England, the Archbishop of Canterbury, and the Princess Joan. As for the woman I saw you with earlier, I believe she is the mistress of Johnny Gaunt himself, Mistress Katherine Swynford."

"And who would you be, Sir?" Asked Owain.

"I, Sir, am Geoffrey Chaucer," he said, "A sometime poet, royal intelligencer, wine seller, soldier, diplomat and servant of the King." He bowed. "I take you lads to be Welshmen and not normally in the service of Lancaster?" he said.

"Not normally," said Owain, "We were students are the Temple but retreated here when the Temple was destroyed."

"An understandable but futile action on their part," said Chaucer. "These rustics have such a belief in the power of letters, but parchment is not the power. They can burn all they want, but as long as the lords exist, they will be back."

What shall I say of the great and immortal Master Chaucer? Not much. He was nothing much to look at and he had a big mouth; just couldn't shut up. He was middling fat, middling height and middling in years. He showed no evidence of his genius as a writer, a spy and a diplomat.

"You know her?" Owain asked.
"Oh yes," he said, "My sister-in-law, no less." He smiled.

"You are a well connected man then," observed Owain.

"I was, but perhaps will not be if the rebellion continues," he said. "Then, we may see a very different world, or we may all be dead by the end of the week." He paused for a moment. "Come," he said, "and I will show you the way to the walls. We shall observe the world the rebels would make for us."

He indicated the way and we followed while he gave us his interpretation of the political landscape.

"Katherine is the widow of Sir Hugh Swynford," said Master Chaucer. "Sir Hugh was an undistinguished knight but the marriage got Katherine out of the nunnery and into Queen Blanche's household. From there it was an easy step into Johnny Gaunt's bed," he said.

I think we must have looked surprised at his bluntness, for he laughed, "Don't worry boys, I tell 'em as I sees 'em. Everyone knows Katherine's story, and there's no shame to it."

"She doesn't get on too well with the Princess," Owain observed.

"Those two are like peas in a pod," said Chaucer, shaking his head. "So alike that each reminds the other of her failings. They can't stand to be near each other because it makes them remember where they came from. Joan married up a couple of times before she found her way into Edward's bed, and Katherine did the same thing. Both are country girls under their fine manners and have worked bloody hard to get where they are today. They know full well what each other is and what they both had to do to get where they are now. Given their similarities, they know exactly what each is prepared to do, and it scares them."

"But Joan is the King's mother," I said. "That gives her a position and power that Katherine can never have."

"Don't be too sure of that," said Chaucer. "Katherine has the ambition of Satan himself. If she can't put Johnny Gaunt on the throne, she will manage to make one of her children a king. Mark my words, lads," he continued. "Katherine is a woman to watch. She will remake this entire Kingdom by the time she is done."

"Nonsense," I said. "No man would let himself be so led by a woman." I was young and naïve at the time and unskilled in the ways of women.

He looked at me with a smile. "Perhaps I am wrong," said Chaucer. "Perhaps none of this matters and we will all be dead by the end of the week."

We reached the battlements and looked out over London. Chaucer gripped the stone, turned to us and waved his hand to indicate the city.

"Behold the best of England," said Chaucer. "The plain, simple Englishman is the finest fellow in the world and will endure almost anything without complaint. He has labored under the Norman yoke for four hundred years without compliant. He has endured slavery, famine, plague, war, and seen his language defiled, but did nothing. As long as he has a lord in his manor and a king on his throne, he is content. But he is an earthly being and has his limits. After sixty years of war, famine and plague, even he will become a little frustrated. God's balls, they were uncomplaining still and made no move to protest. So what did the great lords do? They decided to tax and squeeze these Englishmen until they could contain themselves no more."

"You sound if you are with them, sir," said Owain.

"I am with no one but the King," said Chaucer, "but the King has not been well served by his councilors. These great lords do not act in the King's best interest. These people," he gestured to the City, "love King Richard but they hate the great lords. They wish only to be dealt with fairly. If the King will show himself to them, this could be over very quickly. Instead, the King's Councilors will plot and conspire and we will be lucky to escape with our lives."

He looked back out at the City. "I have taken up too much of your time. I must go to find my wife. I need to tell her that Katherine escaped the Savoy and is here. That will please her."

He nodded to us, "Good day gentlemen" he said.

We nodded back and took up our posts as guardians of the Tower. While it was entertaining, there was nothing for us to do. The sun had set when I heard someone coming. I turned and saw the Lady Swynford. We bowed. God's balls, she was a beauty. Her red hair flowed in soft curls past her shoulders and she wore a silken gown of blue and gold woven in an intricate diamond pattern. No doubt about it, the nobility breed a fine looking bit of trim.

"I wish to observe the rebels," she said, "Escort me to a safe place." She treated us like shit and we loved it. What do you say to a woman like that?

Owain came forward and led her to a parapet with a good view. She climbed up and looked out across the City. It was a riot, a celebration. The poor and rotten, the forgotten thousands took the night. Throughout the city we could see taverns that had been ransacked, fires burning, and mobs swirling through the streets. The flames lit her face with a warm pink glow. God she was a beautiful woman.

"Look at them," she said. "If they had the chance they would kill us all."

She turned to us and said, "I grew up with them you know, in a little village in Essex. Just after the Great Mortality. The village was almost empty. Life was so uncertain that it didn't matter who you were. We had to stick together if we were going to survive. I got to know the common people back then. I saw how they hated the rich fat men who rode past our village, and I heard what they wanted to do to them. I would've done it too. I was hungry enough to kill all of Essex if it would have brought me a mouthful of bread."

She turned to Owain, "Where are you from?"

"The Northern March, My Lady," he said.

"You're a Welshman then?" she said.

He nodded.

"Well, you understand then. All the Welsh hate us. Oh, I know you bow and scrape, but you hate us. If you could only learn out how to get into bed with them," she indicated the mob below, "you could be done with us in a day."

She looked back to the scene beyond our walls. "I warned my Johnny this was coming," she said, "I could see it. After the Great Mortality, those who were left did whatever was needed to place themselves at an advantage. Johnny and his brothers just didn't understand. They thought they could go on living in the world that existed before the Pestilence. Rich men are always stupid. They don't understand that people will break if you keep pushing. Now look at us, hiding in the Tower with that bitch Joan and my Johnny run to the Scots. Worst of all is that bitch Joan. Why do I have to die with that woman? She's just like me you know, came from a small village in Kent and married good. The only difference was she caught her prince when he wasn't married. And I've got to wait for that silly bitch Constance to die."

She sighed. "Why do I care?" she said. "We could all be dead by the morning." That seemed to be a reoccurring theme.

"No, My Lady," said Owain "We're safe here. The Tower has never been taken."

She held up her hand. "Don't be silly. The enemy is not out there. There are plenty of servants and apprentices within these walls who would be more than willing to open the gates if they get the chance." She smiled. "No, if we are murdered it will be treason. Fear the ones inside, for they'll kill you dead just as they smile and scrape."

She nodded and looked out. "Yes," she said, "we'll be lucky if we make it out alive."

She turned to Owain. "Take me to my apartments, Welshman," she said. "If they are to cut my head off tomorrow, I wish to look my best."

Owain reached up to her and escorted her away while I remained on the battlements. I do not know what happened that night. All I can say I did not see him until the morning. I suppose he was detained guarding her chamber while I froze my balls off.

It was that day that the rebels came at us. Under cover of night, the King had left with his guard and had traveled by boat to Westminster. We were left secure behind the Tower's walls. Then, at mid morning, I began to espy a great gathering of the rebels on Cheapside by the Stocks Market. Once again, I saw the strange discipline which with the rebels moved. One by one their sergeants raised their companies and rallied them into a disciplined force. Some of them lifted banners showing the various lodges of the Great Society, and horns blew the signal for the attack to begin.

Owain arrived on the walls smelling very fine.

"A tough night protecting the Lady?" I asked.

He nodded. "Hard work but a task honorably done," he replied.

He looked out. "What are they doing?" he said.

"They've been at it for awhile," I told him. "They look to be preparing for some new mischief."

And so they were, for they now moved in the direction of the Tower.

"They cannot mean to attack the Tower?" said Owain.

"If they do, this will be over quickly," I said grimly.

A force without siege weapons cannot take a castle such as the Tower. They must starve it out. In the case of a well provisioned fortress like the Tower, located on a river, this is impossible. Disease and pestilence will take the attackers before such a castle falls. If an army without siege weapons attacks a strong point, they will hurl themselves uselessly at the walls and present an easy target for the defenders.

However, these rebels were reading from a different book. They formed up and poured down the streets straight at us. The crossbowmen and archers quickly positioned themselves and began raining arrows and bolts down on them. The rebels hit the main gate and paused for a moment. Then, we saw that they continued on. Someone had opened the gates and let them in. While the Tower was full of the King's loyal men, we had all forgotten the many servants and apprentices who worked there. They were with the rebels, not with us, and were happy to ensure their passage.

"That," said Owain "is how you take a castle without a siege." I nodded and thought back to Gruffudd Fychan's warnings about the impregnability of the English castles in

Wales. We should learn this lesson, I remember thinking; this is the way Edward Longshanks' Iron Ring will fall.

The rebels poured in quickly. Most of the Tower's defenders were not trained to fight but were aldermen and townsmen. Men who could do well enough under command to defend a wall, but who had no stomach or training for a straight out fight. The real bruisers had left with the King for Westminster.

I looked to Owain for command. "We must go to the Lady Swynford and the Queen Mother," said Owain. "Our duty lies in defending the women."

We dashed off through the maze of the Tower to the Great Ladies' chambers. They had taken refuge in the great hall and were attempting to barricade the door. The Lady Katherine saw us.

"You two, Welshmen, find something to bar the door."

We busied ourselves by pulling furniture across the room to form a barricade. The King's ancient and heavy Great Table went against the door.

The Lady Katherine reached up and looked through a window.

"Look," she said, "They have the Archbishop and the Prior." Owain and I ran to the window and saw she was right. The rebels had taken prisoner the Lord Chancellor of England, Simon Sudbury, the Archbishop of Canterbury himself, and the Treasurer, the Grand Prior of the Order of St. John's Hospitallers. They had bound them and were manhandling them out of the Tower, stripping them of their vestments and ornaments as they drove them away. I could see this would not end well for them.

"They are taking them to Cheapside," said one of Katherine's ladies. "They will be on us next and will kill us all." She began to cry, and soon the other women took up the wailing. Katherine looked at her. She reached back her hand and struck the woman with such a force it sent her flying.

"For Christ's sake, shut up you silly woman," she shouted. The crying stopped.

"Well done," said Princess Joan. "At least you can keep order in your own house." Katherine curtseyed and Joan nodded. I took this as a bad sign. Things must be bad if these two gorgons had decided to call a truce.

I did not have much time to consider this before there was a great thudding and banging at the entrance to hall.

"The rebels are upon us," shouted Owain. It was the scene at the Temple all over again. A door cannot hold all of Essex and Kent. We held them back, stabbing and pushing, but in they came. This is it, I thought, we're on our way to Jesus. We fell back to the woman. I saw Katherine had pulled a dagger from somewhere and was brandishing it with holy fury. She caught my eye and nodded. As she said, she was a country girl at heart and willing to kill and gut when it came down to it.

We were ready to throw ourselves in when Princess Joan shouted above us all in clear rustic English, "What exactly do you think you are doing?"

The shock of it stopped them dead. She rose from her chair and walked to the rebels. She looked down at the first one, "Take your cap off when I am present and get down on your knees." He hesitated for a moment and then she stared down at him.

"I am the King's Mother, Princess Joan, wife to the great Prince Edward. I expect your deference. My royal dignity demands acknowledgment."

That was enough for him. Down he went and the room followed. Hats came off and eyes were downcast on the floor. We were left like two ships marooned at low tide. She saw us and motioned us to the wall.

The leader of the rustics spoke, "Begging your pardon my lady," he said.

"Did I give you permission to speak?" she roared.

"No, my lady," he said and looked down.

"Good. Well, you make speak and please explain why you are here and disturbing my ladies at our weaving." That was a nice touch. Nothing impressed a rustic like women hard at work for their men.

"We only seek Johnny Gaunt's whore. She is rumored to be hiding in the Tower," he said.

Katherine looked at her. She knew this was a moment when Joan could be done with her. Joan smiled. I swear she was tempted for a moment.

"All the women here are in my service. They are honest virgins. We are all loyal to my son and deplore the machination and conspiracies of the Duke of Lancaster."

"Amen," said the rustic.

"Leave us," said Princess Joan. "We must return to our labors. I have promised my son a new shirt, and I will make it with my own hand." Another nice touch; the rustics looked favorably upon a great lady working for her son.

They bowed and began to leave. Then one spoke up, "My Lady, may I touch you?" he said.

She looked at him, her eyes glinting steel. "Pardon?" she said.

"May I touch you?" he said again, "No disrespect, Ma'am. I just would like to say that I once touched the Fair Maid of Kent." He smiled.

She looked at him amazed and then held out her hand. He came forward and touched it. Then one after another they came. Each one knelt before her and reached to touch her hand. Some reached up and touched her hair. After each was done they bowed, said "God Bless you" and left the chamber.

Joan looked around the room. "Well" she said turning to her ladies, "Clean up this mess." She turned to Katherine. "Luckily the rustics are now as good a judge of quality as are their betters," she said.

The Lady Katherine nodded. "Well played, My Lady," she said Gesturing to her serving women, she raised her voice and said, "You heard the Princess. Clean up this mess."

Thus it was that Princess Joan quieted the mob and pushed them back when the walls of the Tower had been powerless to do so.

While we were defending the Tower, the King treated with the rebels at Milesend. Following the Archbishop's council, the King decided that it would be wise to give them what they wanted and hope the rebels would go home. Thus, he met with Watt the Tyler, Jack Straw, and John Ball and promised that all men would be free and had charters drawn up to that effect.

Rumor reached the City quickly about what had occurred, and everywhere we would hear the chants of,

"All men are free!"

"No man between King and Commons!"

"Now is the time, now is the time!"

But others forces were also at work. It was rumored that the Great Society was meeting at Clerkenwell to decide the new order of the Kingdom. Among the expected results were that there would be no Bishops and all Bibles would to be written English. The great lords' lands would be shared out among the common people and, in fact, the title of 'Lord" would be abolished altogether. There would be no man between the King and the Commons. Parliament and all courts of law would be abolished. Lawyers would be outlawed, and any man found to be practicing law would be hanged. All taxes save those for the war in France would be stricken. All properties of the Templers would be restored, for it was rumored that secret Templers had been the force behind the Great Society and that they had organized the rebellion to restore their position and avenge themselves against the Knights of St. John, who had led the assault on them.

How much of this is true? I do not know. I simply report what I heard. It was a time of madness and rumor. I also heard that they wanted no more than the end of feudal obligation and the freedom to work. All things could have been true and all things could have been lies. I know one thing for certain: they believed in the King and loved him with a fierce devotion. They saw him as their shining light and constant brother. They simply could not believe that he could do other than support their needs.

So we come to the final days of the revolt in London. We heard that the King would meet with the rebels at Smithfield and Clerkenwell on Saturday after the Tower had fallen. He would attend the rebels there and issue a formal and public announcement of his proclamation of freedom for all men. He and his party would then surrender themselves to the rebels who would become his bodyguard and ensure his protection from his wicked uncles who they believed had distorted the Royal will. In preparation for this great event, it was put about that all men loyal to the King should rally to his party to protect his purpose and ensure that the rebels could not take him by force. Thus it was that on that morning we marched out from the Tower through the empty streets of the City and met with the King's Party at St. Paul's. How great were the mighty now fallen. The King had with him but a few knights and men-at-arms. Sir Robert Knolls was at that time building a great army outside the City, but it had yet to arrive. The loyal aldermen and the City militia numbered only a few hundred. The King himself looked young and vulnerable. He did not inspire confidence that he was indeed a strong leader.

We formed up with the Militia and headed out of the City towards Smithfield. When we reached Smithfield, we saw all of the rebels in and around London had arrayed themselves there. I would guess there were well over twenty thousand men in all, but I do not know for sure. All were armed to the teeth and seemed well schooled in the arts of murder and destruction. We men of King Richard formed ourselves up in opposition. The King sent one of his men to the rebels to tell them that he was ready to meet with them. A gentleman, who may have been the Lord Mayor himself, rode out and called out, "Watt Tyler of Maidstone, attend your King at his pleasure."

A sturdy man astride a small pony separated from the crowd and rode toward the King. He wore a large dagger in full view. This was not normally a thing you did in the Royal presence. Once he was close by, he dismounted and came to the King, extending his open hand.

"Brother," he said with a great smile "be of good comfort and joyful this day. In the next fortnight you will have forty thousand more of the commons than you have at this moment, and we shall be good companions together. We will put an end to these Lords who imprison you and come with you to France to secure all the rights your Grandfather was promised."

Clearly there had been secret conferences and conventions concerning the future of the Royal estate. Then Watt turned to his companions who had ridden up behind him. They were a ragged bunch, all violent, hard-looking men. One carried a great banner of St. George.

"God's teeth," he roared, "it's fucking hot. My mouth feels like straw. Bring me a jug of water." One of his placemen brought a jug to him. He took a great gulp, swilled it around his mouth, and spat it out on the ground in front of the King's horse. "Ah" he said "Now my throat is clear, but I need some ale."

One of his confederates brought him a flagon of ale and he downed a great mouthful. He turned and remounted his horse. Then, he pulled close to the King, and unsheathed his dagger and began to play with it, telling the King an elaborate story of the executions of those he said were the King's enemies the previous night.

Sir John Newton came close by him.

"Put your dagger away," he said. "Have you no regard for the Royal person? No one but the King's Champion can show an open blade in the Royal Presence."

Watt looked at him. "Fuck you," he said "By day's end no gentleman shall order any man how he shall behave before the King. My Brother the King has no fear of his True Commons," he said, and he raised his dagger.

The King held out his hands to both of them. "Countrymen, do not argue. We are here this day to make peace and prevent further bloodshed. Master Tyler is playing and Sir John is over excited by the events of the last days."

Watt sheathed his dagger, "You are right, My Brother" said Watt. "Today is a day for celebration, not rancor. I will inform my people that you are come to join us."

Then he pulled his horse about and headed back to the rebels.

"Look," said Owain loudly, "there is that great thief Gadshill with Tyler," and he pointed at one of the men with Watt.

"This shows the measure of the rebels if this is one of their chief ensigns."

Before I could stop him, Owain called out, "Look, the greatest thief and robber in Kent," pointing at Gadshill. Tyler pulled up his horse and looked to where Owain stood.
Tyler then turned to his attendant carrying the banner of St. George. "Take that man and strike him down now," he ordered, pointing at Owain. "Cut his fucking head off."

The man with the banner looked to Tyler, "He weren't talking about you, Watt; he was talking about Gadshill." Owain shouted back, "I have said nothing of you, Master Tyler. I meant only your accomplice."

Tyler started towards Owain. He was stopped by our commander, Mayor Walworth, who cautioned him. "These young apprentices and valets are not worth your attention Master Tyler. They are ill-disciplined and prone to excitement."

"Fuck that," said Tyler "They have insulted the Captain of the Commons. All traitors must be punished."

He moved towards Owain and into the King's party. Seeing that Watt was surrounded by the King's supporters, Richard called out.

"Arrest him. He seeks to do harm to our person."

Tyler was close enough for us to see him clearly. He face flushed in anger. He pulled back his horse and struck at Mayor Walworth with his dagger. Walworth was wearing armor under his tunic, and the blow skidded off his chest with a clang.

Owain rushed forward and grabbed Tyler's horse. Other men, seeing his action, crowded in on Tyler. He turned to beat us back. Then Mayor Walworth recovered his balance, pulled out a dagger and struck him with great force in the head and the neck. Blood gushed everywhere. Owain pulled his sword but slipped in the blood and fell near Tyler horse. As he fell, a young esquire who had been standing next to us, a certain Ralph Standish, pushed forward and slashed at Tyler with his sword.

Tyler was knocked from the saddle and fell back. Even with his wounds, he was able to ride. He reached up and pulled himself back onto his horse. Tyler's companions cut through the crowd surrounding him and pulled his horse away from his attackers. Then, gathering his strength, Tyler rode across the gap between the King's party and the rebels.

I heard him call out to his men. "I am murdered. Cut them down, avenge me."

The rebels began to murmur and moved forward.

"We're for it now," I said as I helped Owain to his feet. "They will come at us for sure."

Then, just as Tyler disappeared into the rebel host, the King roused his horse to life and rode out towards the rebels. Before his bodyguard could move, he rode straight at them. When the King was in front of the rebels he called out in English, which was a great surprise, as at that time all noble persons spoke French,

"Gentlemen, what are you doing? Your Captain may have fallen, but now you shall have me as your Captain. I am your true King, and I ask you to remain at peace."

This calmed them greatly, and the more timid of the rebels began to fall back. Then, riding closely to the most heavily armed and aggressive of the rebels, he called,

"Gentlemen, I am concerned that my Brother Watt has been harmed. Return with him to the Hospital at St. John's. I will attend to you there and come to you are Clerkenwell."

With that he rode north towards St. John's. Seeing the King was so clearly on their side, they broke and began to return to the North. Then the King turned back and rode towards our party.

"To arms, My Friends," said the King. "Sir Robert Knolls comes with three hundred men." He pointed to a group of knights arriving from the west. "We will make short work of these rebels if they dare challenge us."

We cheered as Sir Robert and his knights arrived and formed a phalanx around the King. I heard Sir Robert say, "Is Tyler fled?" He turned to his knights. "Some of you go and follow him. Whoever brings back his head to the King shall have a thousand crowns for his reward."

"No," said the King "Back to the City. We are weak here. More loyal men are arriving at the City, and we shall shut the gates to protect us from these rebels." With that the King's party turned back to the City and galloped away. And so the tide turned. The King's bravery had turned a potential disaster into a great victory.

"There," said Owain his eyes shining in admiration, "is a true King. As long as he lives, I shall not turn against him and shall follow him whether he commands." Thus, did My Lord form his attachment to King Richard, and so were the English spared from the wrath of the Welsh for another twenty years.

OUR INDENTURE TO ENGLISH GREGORY

All revolts end badly. Whether they triumph or fail, there is always blood. The Great Rising was no exception. In the aftermath of the events at Smithfield, the King regained control of the City. Those who had been prominent in the rebellion were rounded up, tried, and executed. In the Kent and Essex countryside, the King's Sheriffs regained their courage, rallied loyal men everywhere and led out their forces against the rebels.

Unfortunately for the rebels, news of the early successes of the Rising only came to them after the events of Smithfield had occurred. Unknowing of the failure of their Captains at Smithfield, they rose in great numbers. Throughout East Anglia, Leicestershire, and Hertfordshire the agents of the Great Society finally reached their appointed places, spread the word the time had come, and the commons rose. As far as Chester and York there were risings. They were all in vain though. Now that the London rising was smashed, the Magnates and the King were strong enough to strike back. Throughout East Anglia, Bishop Despenser was particularly active and gained a great reputation as a killer. The King's Council revoked all the charters the King had issued and new proclamations were made that bondsmen remained un-free and Statues that bound laborers were still in effect.

We stayed in London for a few more months. There was, in truth, little for us to do. The Temple was unharmed but many of our teachers were fled or had died in the Rising. All of our titles and books had been burnt. We remained with the militia and worked with the King's men to enforce order in London, but our work was easy and required little effort.

Owain attempted to enroll in the King's forces, but his lack of connections held him back. In particular, the absence of the Lord Arundel at Court meant that was no room for a man of Owain's loyalties. Owain's part in the fall of Tyler and the final confrontation with the rebels went unnoticed. Whereas many of the main players of that day were knighted, Owain remained unrecognized.

Still, he was unperturbed. "Do not worry," said Owain. "I am convinced of this King's greatness. There will be many opportunities for me before his reign is over."

Finally, when the roads were safe and we could travel north, we quit London and headed back to Hanmer.

Now there are those who will tell you that not many died after the Hurling Times were over. They point to the records and the rolls and show how few men were tried and punished. That, they say, is the true measure of those times. They are wrong. They did not travel the roads of England, where you could not go a mile without finding some poor soul swinging from a gibbet or rotting in a ditch.

Every town and shire had its killing ground where the rebels had been taken for slaughter, and it was common to see poor men walking the highways with some terrible injury that came from the revenge of the lords. This was a time when the law was forgotten. Rebels were not tried and judged, they were cut down where they stood. The mere suspicion of rebellion was enough to receive a visit from the reeve's men late at night. Any Lord or knight with suspicions could take a man and deal with him as he saw fit.

In the aftermath of these killings, things quickly returned to normal. It was as if the entire realm decided to forget what has happened. No man spoke of where he was or what he did during the rebellion. No man told tales of how his village had followed the Great Society or how his shire had risen at Captain Watt's command or Constable Straw's direction. In the quiet that followed, men went back to their fields and kept their own council. Equally, the Lords and the Reeves kept silent. They were anxious to maintain the fiction of the law, for all men know that the law's power must seem infinite or it may be easily overturned. They were not anxious for rustics and apprentices to be reminded of how close they came to pulling the lords down.

Thus, it was to be many years before I heard men speak of those times. When I did it was in the taverns where men began to sing songs of Captain Watt's adventures and heroism. In time he became as great a hero as Robin Hood and was forever remembered as the man who twisted the lords' noses every chance he got.

On our arrival at Hanmer we saw that the district had remained quiet during the recent rebellion. Owain found his beloved and embraced her with true love. Sir David entered in upon him.

"I see you have returned, Master Owain," he said.

"Yes, we are back from London and back for good," replied Owain, his eyes on Marged.

"But you have not finished your education at law. You are barely an apprentice, much less a man of law," said Sir David.

"There is no law to return to," explained Owain. "The Temple stands, but all the records of the realm are burnt. There are no teachers and no books to learn from."

"I have heard there is much destruction, but that can be remedied soon," argued Sir David.

"I think you misunderstand the extent of the destruction," replied Owain. "The rebels burnt the holdings of Chancery, the Exchequer, the Temple, Lambeth Palace, and the Duchy of Lancaster at the Savoy. In the counties they burnt the records of the Countess of Hereford and Essex, the Bishop of Norwich, and the University of Cambridge. But it is not just the books and parchments of the law that are gone, but the spirit of the law has been killed in your England."

Owain continued, "The King's Council ignores the King's pleas for moderation and murders men daily on the streets. Men swing from every gibbet in London and along all the great roads of the realm. I have seen more than five hundred men in a single grave outside London. Everywhere there is death and disregard for the law. I did not support the rebels and was with the King himself at Smithfield, but I do not believe this to be right. The King might be a friend of the law but, his magnates are not; they seek only to expand their power. This is not a time for law; it is a time for power. I must return to my estates and defend the ambitions of the great magnates who surround us."

"I am of age and have reached my majority. I ask for your daughter's hand in marriage. If you agree, I will marry her in the Church here and take her back as soon as possible to Sycharth."

Sir David sighed. "If you must, you must," said Sir David. "I knew that it was inevitable. You were always more your Grandfather's son than your Father's. You have my permission, but remember Owain: in such time as these, it ill behooves a man to run from the law. In disorder powerful men will always seek advantage, and they will take that advantage from weaker men -- people such as you and me."

"The only protection we have is to work towards the restoration of the law, for that is the only thing that will restrain these great beasts that roam our land. You are young and feel that you have great power and strength, but you do not. In this land only the patron of great men or the protection of the law can bring strength to little man such as ourselves," Sir David said.

Owain started to protest, but Sir David raised his hand to stop him. "I know you are a great Prince of Wales, but all of that is in the past. You must either secure the patronage of great men or return to the law. You may take my daughter as I promised, but I urge you to take care in choosing your alliances."

With that the marriage was approved. Owain and Marged were married in the parish church at Hanmer, and afterwards they set off for Sycharth. When our party arrived at the great castle of the Princes of Powys, it was much reduced in its status.

Sycharth had been built in the shadow of a small mountain on the Welsh side of Offa's Dyke not far from Oswestry. Later in Owain and Marged's tenure it was to become a fine palace, but in the beginning it showed evidence of many years of neglect.

As with many of the castles along the border, it was made of timber but plastered to look like stone. When you approached it from the South you would first see a high timber wall that had been plastered, daubed and painted to do a good impersonation of stone. It was surrounded by a moat caused by the damming and diverting a small river that ran close by. The gatehouse was strongly build and defended by two guard towers. Our party, Owain, Marged, Crach, myself, and the Lady Marged's servants, came to the gate.

Owain called out in Welsh. "I am returned. It is the Master of Sycharth come to claim what is his."

There was silence for a moment and then an aged watchman limped to the walkway over the gate. "Who is there?" he called out to us.

"It is Owain ap Gruffudd Fychan ap Gruffudd Mawr ap Madog, Master of Sycharth, Prince of Powys and Lord of these Land."

The old man squinted at Owain.

"Is that really you, Owain Bach?" he said. "It is I Ehangwen ap Medyr. I was your Tadcu's Steward and Castalan. I have been waiting for your coming. I shall go down and open the gate."

He hurried down as best he could, for the Castalan had seen better years. Finally the gates swung open. "Welcome Lord of Powys" said Ehangwen with a flourish. "I have kept this fortress safe for your return."

So we entered into the castle of Sycharth. It was a simple mote and bailey castle: a walled enclosure with a blacksmith's shop, a church, stables, and the cottages of the household, as well as a mount with another wall and a strong wooden building at the top.

"There it is, my Lord," said the Castalan pointing to the bailey, "your hall in the sky."

It was a grand word for a not particularly impressive hall. We climbed the mount through a covered passage as the household emerged from their homes and workshops to see us. They were a skinny, dirty bunch that lacked the discipline of a good lord. As we moved into the castle, the Castalan called out,

"The Prince has returned. Gruffudd Mawr's Grandson has come back to us. The Mab Daragon dwells amongst his people once more."

We mounted the steps and climbed towards the Hall. We came to the door and it opened slowly.

"No one has lived here since your Prince Gruffudd left. We have kept everything as it was from that day, My Lord," said the Castellan.

What a broken down place it was. The Castellan spoke up.

"I have kept it safe for you, My Lord. It is untouched."
Indeed it was. Nothing cleaned, nothing changed. It looked terrible. I saw Marged's eyes roll across the room. Owain caught her glance.

"I know it is terrible. You will have the income to repair it as you would like."

Thus it was that Marged went to work. She whipped her servants into work and cleaned every surface that could be cleaned. Within a few weeks, the Castle began to look much more habitable. She sent her ladies to Oswestry and Shrewsbury to buy tapestries and carpets and brought in glazers to measure the windows so she might replace the oiled skins with glass. Carpenters and shinglers came in to fix the roof and plankers began work to strengthen the floors. Craftsmen in local workshops and artisans from Shrewsbury set to work making exquisite new furniture.

Outside the hall she claimed the garden for her own. New plantings of sweet smelling herbs and cuttings of leeks, cabbages and beans were set into the rich brown soil. Elsewhere, the beehives tended and the dovecote restocked.
Owain and I busied ourselves with reviving the estates and the structures below. He brought Tudur down from Glyndyfrdwy, and the two worked tirelessly to put the Castle in order. We patched the walls, hauled in timber for re-framing the walls had tumbled down, and called in his tenants and kinsmen to clear out the moat. He threw himself into the affairs of his estates. His grandfather's aging stewards, beadles and the

bailiffs came to him and reported that the mill needed improvements, the fish traps had fallen into disrepair, and the lord's lands lay in waste.

Owain took command quickly. He inquired as to the hardest working tenants and granted them free-tenantry for money rent, gave them the land he lacked the labor to cultivate, and broke up his herds among them. He sent agents to Oswestry to buy sheep and studied his lands to see which could be turned to grazing for these unholy beasts. He called in the tribesmen and customary tenants and told them he would increase their share of the harvest if they would grant him an extra labor boon to put the affairs of the estate in order. When he heard they could not use the forest because of outlaws who ruled the high place, he pulled his telu together and struck out to find them and bring them under control.

We spent a good six months chasing down outlaws and running them off. Most were easily put down or brought into My Lord's service. When he could not achieve their compliance, he beat them badly enough to show that his land would be unprofitable for them. He then promised them free passage and sanctuary as long they laid off his lands and the lands of Arundel.

Quickly his reputation spread. The rules were clear. The Charleton's lands in Powys were fair game for outlaws operating from My Lord's lands. Stealing and raiding the Grey's lands was encouraged, and anything belonging to Lancaster and Johnny Gaunt could only be taken if it could not be traced back to Owain. My Lord took a cut of the outlaws' profits, helped run the cattle stealing rings, paid off the Arundels and kept things safe. The merchants in Oswestry quickly came to realize that Gruffudd Mawr's grandson had returned to his grandfather's old ways and enthusiastically joined with him to revive the cattle stealing trade.

Soon Owain began to follow his grandfather's habits, riding to Glyndyfrdwy, Cowen and back to Sycharth. He was an impressive figure in those years, tall, strong and well-built. He ignored the fashion of the day and grew his red hair until it reached past his shoulders. His red beard grew into a strange double fork shape that became his mark. He affected the dress of a tribal lord: plaid kilt, leggings and leather jerkin, rather than the brightly colored robes of the English gentry. To the tribesmen and tenants he seemed like the very image of the Old Man reborn, and they accepted him quickly. When he rode into a tref, they would call out "Owain Bach, you've brought your Tadcu back to us." It was a good time.

All might have gone along a different road had not the Scots and French determined to assert their power. In the summer of our third year at Sycharth, a messenger arrived from the Court at Westminster. I was busy working on restoring the walls when I heard he had come. I rushed up the motte and into the hall, where My Lord sat in conference with Tudur and Crach.

They looked up at me.

"The King wants money," said Tudur.

"It is more complicated than that," said Owain "Parliament voted the King a subsidy for the war in France, but the French have undermined our plans. They have assembled an invasion fleet at both Sluys and sent an army to Scotland. The King does not believe that there is enough money to fight the French in Scotland and defend the South Coast. Parliament won't vote more money, so he's imposed a scutage of us."

"Scutage is obsolete," I said drawing on my memories from the Inns of Court. "One hasn't been levied since Longshanks"

"Yes," said Owain, "but the King is in a hard place, and he'll do anything rather than try to levy another poll tax and risk revolt."

"Can we pay?" I asked "All the improvements of the estates will make it difficult."

"I can't slow the improvements," said Owain, shaking his head. "Marged will have my balls." He waved his hand around. "This is not a hall for a woman that has seen an English town. Do you see she has ordered windows? Glass for every space, she says, and she's redesigning the top floors for wardrobes. She wants chimneys, too. The expense is ruinous."

"So what shall we do?" Tudur asked.

"I advise soldiering," said Crach. "Your grandfather regularly supplemented his income by joining the wars in France. The outlaws always provide a good supply of men. Besides, it has been foretold that you will fight with the Saxons before you proclaim your regality. I have prophesied this myself and therefore I know it to be true." He returned to a cup of ale he had been working on and continued.

"I have seen that there will be a few good fights in the near future, so I believe you should seek employment," said Crach. "Go ask English Gregory. He's back from France and looking to find men and a new war somewhere."

"Who's English Gregory?" asked Tudur.

"He's a Saxon from Cheshire and a captain of a free company," I said.

"He only recruits Welshmen," said Crach "His grandfather settled in the March and married into the Hanmers, so we are connected. He did well under Edward the Frank-killer and ended up with a few castles in France. The French have kicked him out and he's trying to restore his fortunes."

Owain thought for a moment. "It's worth a shot," he said and with that we prepared ourselves to enter the service of English Gregory.

English Gregory's manor was on the boarder of Shropshire and Cheshire where the land flattens out and the forests fall back to the rich farmland of the Northern Plain. Once upon a time his manor had been a distinguished building, but by the time we arrived it was ramshackle and overgrown. Grass grew long and wild all around the house. The orchards grew without harvest. The stable, which was built along one side of the house, slumped sadly, as its roof had collapsed and no one had come to repair it.

Owain dismounted and went to the door. He banged on it with his fist and waited for an answer. After a few minutes a great hulking brute of man came to the door. Although we were all relatively tall, this lad stumped us. He was more than six heads tall and about the same across.

"I am Owain of Glyndyfrdwy come to speak with Sir Gregory," said Owain.

"Dad's not seeing anyone today," said the man. "If you're here about recruiting, come back tomorrow. We're holding a muster then."

"I would prefer to meet with your father beforehand," said Owain. "We have traveled far, and I have some dignity with my people. It would not be right for me to muster as a common solider."

The man looked at us.

"Welsh are you?" he asked.

"Yes, good Welshmen all."

"I fucking hate the Welsh," the man said, "but my Dad fucking loves you. Says you're tough bastards, but I think you are sneaky cunts. I lived with on the Lynn Peninsular in the west when my Dad was in France. They used to make fun of me because I didn't speak Welsh good; fucking stupid language if you ask me. You need a bucket full of spit to be able to speak it properly."

Owain eyed him calmly. "I am sorry my countrymen did not treat you well. We have a custom of treating the simple and slow with generosity and kindness. Clearly you merit such treatment."

The man looked at Owain. "Think you're fucking clever do you?" he asked, a sneer on his face.

"No cleverer than any Welshman," replied Owain. "This makes me several times wiser than any Saxon."

With a roar, the man launched himself at Owain. Owain jumped back as the man hit. He raised his hands up and swung them down on his neck. The man grunted and fell to the ground. Owain circled back. The man raised himself and ran at

Owain like a bull. He grabbed Owain around the middle and pushed him down into the grass and began to pound him. I dismounted and ran to My Lord. I was about to dive in and try to pull the brute off when a great shout came from the door.

"Peter!" it said. "Leave those men alone. They may be of use to me."

From the door came a thing of myth, a thing of tales gone by. It was a man, after a fashion, but so bent that it seemed to have long passed the point where it could stand. Wispy light blond hair issued from every part of its uncovered body. The beard alone seemed to be more than a head long and wrapped around its body as a scarf. What struck me most about him were his vast hands; great monstrous things, beaten and scarred by a thousand fights. The Beast looked at out from behind snowy blue eyes and spoke in Welsh.

"I am English Gregory. You boys looking for work in the King's wars?" he asked.

"Indeed," said Owain picking himself up. "As I told your son here," he motioned to the man we now knew as Peter,
"I am Owain of Glyndyfrdwy. I bring my telu and seek contract with you for the King's Wars. I am sworn to the Lords Arundel and hear you muster livery for them."

The Beast looked back at us. "Ever fought before?" he said.

"Just against bandits and thieves," said Owain.

The Beast sighed. "The trouble with this fucking country nowadays," he said, "is we have no decent fucking wars for a young man to learn his business. When I was your age, I had been at war in Flanders and France for half a dozen years. I had at least one castle and my own company. Now look at me. Look at me now." He shook his head. "I was kicked out of France and sent back to this shit pit with my wife. It's not even mine. It was hers in dowry. She holds clear of me until her death. Her father was a fucking lawyer. Smart man he was. He tied me up in knots. If she dies before the boy here reaches his majority, it goes to the church. If I pack her off to a nunnery, it goes with her. If I get the marriage annulled, it goes to the church. So here am I, stuck with some ugly old bitch and this shit house."

I interrupted, pointing at Peter, "You say he has not reached his majority yet?"

The Beast looked at his son. "Big bastard isn't he? He's only sixteen summers. When I went away he was a mewly babe. Came back and he'd become that great monster of a thing. Don't know where he gets it from."

He looked us over. "You lads come in and let me negotiate with your master," he said.

Then he turned to his son and said, "Peter, attend their horses."

"You have no grooms present?" asked Owain.

"Don't allow servants here," said the Beast. "My wife does not deserve such luxuries. If she is willing to render me the property without conditions and accept a place in a convent, I will grant her an income. But until that day, she may starve for all I care."

We exchanged looks. Clearly this was a man of considerable determination and our negotiations would be difficult.

The inside of the house was as bad as the outside. Wood panels came away from the walls and tapestries hung thread bare. From what we could see, the solar and the hall had no furniture. The Beast saw our looks.

"I have sold everything that can be sold to the Jews of Flanders. I am short on funds, and I have a desire to make my wife's stay upon this earth as painful as possible."

He waved for us to follow him into the kitchen, where he indicated a barrel of ale.

"Help yourself," he said and settled down at the table supping from his own ale pot.

"We have a mind to go to war in Scotland," said Owain.

"What men will you bring?" asked the Beast.

"My telu and those bound to me in service on the land who can be spared, and any hillsmen that are sworn to me, some thirty to fifty men in all, depending on the disposition of the hillsmen. I can also raise others from beyond my lands who accept my authority as chief of my tribe, perhaps a hundred at most."

The Beast nodded. "How many of these men have fought in a war?"

"Of the younger ones, none," said Owain. "Most of the older, perhaps half, have seen some war in France."

"And they are Welshmen all? I will only take Welshmen. They are the only men I will trust in a fight. One Welshman with no experience of war is worth ten Englishmen who have warred all their life."

"Every one of them will be from my estates in Glyndyfrdwy, Sycharth, and Corwin and my patrimony in Powys and Deheubenth. My kinsmen at Hanmer Mere may also bring their sworn men."

He looked at the Hanmer boys for the first time. "Are you David Hanmer's boys?" he asked.

"Aye," said Gruffudd, "English born, but Welsh raised"

"I believe I am some form of cousin to you," said the Beast.

"If memory serves me, your mother was the granddaughter of my grandfather's brother? Close, but not close enough to matter. I met your father once in France when he was carrying documents from the Old King. I remember little of him apart from he had no taste for the war and wished to be home as soon as he could."

He turned back to Owain. "What are you terms?" said the Beast.

"First, we will only fight under the banner of Arundel," said Owain. "I am his sworn man and cannot fight with any man that seeks to harm him or to diminish his house."

The Beast nodded impatiently. "This is obvious," said the Beast. "We are all Cheshire men here and know no lord but Arundel. Arundel gets his cut from anything I make. Even the King's Sheriff has little power in these lands."

"We will take French rates for the work," said Owain, referring to the rates for soldiering that all Welshmen knew. "All moneys will be paid to me as their captain. I am baron and Uchelwyr. I shall take the rate of a bannerette -- four shillings a day. Sir David's sons will serve as knights bachelor and will take two shilling a day; as for the rest, a shilling a day for the men-at-arms with weapons and armor and sixpence for archers. A hundred marks for each thirty men for expenses, food and fodder. Any loss of horse shall be compensated."

The Beast snorted. "You hold yourself in high regard for a man that has never been blooded," said the Beast.

"We are all Welshmen," said Owain, "As you say, we are worth many Saxons."

"That is true, but I will only be able to charge to the Lord Arundel and he in turn to the King for your men as titled. Thus, while I respect the validity of your title, the Lord Arundel may not, and even if he did, the King's Jews may not. I cannot promise you the pay of the bannerette or the Master Hanmers the pay of a bachelor knight. The best I can get for you is a shilling for a man-at-arms. Your retainers will be under a reduced rate, nine pence for a man-at-arms and thruppence for an archer. If a man-at-arms comes without armor or with only a spear, I will judge him a Welsh Lancer and he will get tupence. This is not France, and Parliament has not granted a new subsidy for Scotland. As for the quarter marks, I will hold them from the King and provide for all food and fodder. All horses maintained and, if harmed, replaced at value. Furthermore, I have title as Captain. You will have to earn the title. However, I promise that your men will only serve under you and will take no order directly from any other man except those officered by the King and the Lord Arundel."

Owain grunted. "If this is all you offer, I would be better staying at home or paying the scutage."

"Then go and pay the scutage," said the Beast. "There are plenty of bloodied men back from France with much time on their hands and desperate for work. I have two sons myself with nothing to do. I can use them for free."

We all knew that this was nonsense. The rates were set by the old King and fixed by statute. He would charge us at three-quarter rates to Arundel and pocket the rest. In turn, Arundel would charge us full to the King and pocket the remainder. When it came to the quarter marks, the King's Chancellery would hold them back and cheat Arundel. When they came to Arundel, he would hold back and cheat the Beast. The Beast would then hold back what he could and cheat us. This we all knew. It was simply the way of the world.

Owain thought for a minute. "If you keep the quarters marks, what assurance do I have that you will provide for my men as required?"

"You may set a man with the Master of my Wardrobe. He may view accounts and join him on supply days."

"That's reasonable," said Owain "And I will be present when horses are judged due for replacement."

"But I will have the last word," said the Beast.

"Naturally," Owain agreed. "However, the rates are low. I demand my dignity. I will be paid as a baron and my telu as full men-at-arms. As for my people, I acknowledge your difficulties. Perhaps we can make up the difference on ransoms and booty."

The Beast waved his hand noncommittally. "You know the rules," he said. "All prisoners above the rank of Duke or Earl go to the King; any titled prisoner goes to the Lord Arundel. We take a third share of the ransom. If your company is responsible, I will take a third and you two-thirds. Any one below the rank obliged to Arundel, I must surrender a third to the crown and Arundel to divide between them. Of the remainder, we will split one third to me and two thirds to you. All booty, monies, gold, silver, jewels above ten marks, one third to the crown and Arundel, one third to me, and a third to you. Anything below ten marks we split one third for me and two thirds for you. You may divide the remainder among your men as you see fit."

"How long to you offer the indenture?" asked Owain.

"One year from the date of your mark," said the Beast, "with condition to be extended on agreement of all parties for one quarter year thereafter."

"I can live with this, but I am concerned that there will be few opportunities for ransom and booty. After all, Scotland is a poor place," said Owain.

The Beast smiled. "I have a plan," he said. "I will enroll my command as the outriders. We shall be ahead of the main Army. I am known for this, and Arundel will grant me this status for a small fee. We shall ignore the body of the Scots and pursue the French. This will grant us the best opportunity for ransom. We are going after the big prey; I will not waste my time ransoming plough boys. I will hold and sell to Arundel. He will manage all negotiations.

"Furthermore, my sons and my retainers will sweep out around us. My older boy, Paul, and my servant Daniel are much experienced in the extraction of booty from lands. Paul can get money from a stone. They will strip whatever they find. My daughter's husband is a salt merchant from Nantwich. He deals with the outlaw trade and the salt thieves. He has good connections and is used to dealing in routed moveables. He will be with the army to ensure they are received, valued under ten marks, and directed straight to the appropriate market.

"Wherever possible I will move any gold, silver, or jewels through London before the Arundels see it. I am already in negotiations with a number of border traders, and we will move any beasts through the border markets, especially after the Army has moved north and the King's agents are no longer present.

"Above all, we must avoid the Percys," he warned. "Whatever their current titles, the Percy family runs the border and the Northern Marches. If Old Man Percy sees we are bypassing his agents, we will be in the shits. I have entered into agreements with Lord Neville's agents. Gaunt's made him Warden of the Middle March and Neville's new up there and knows that he cannot hold it for long before Percy takes it back, so he's anxious to take what he can before he loses it. Consequently, his agents have made it known that we shall have his protection in the markets of Middle March."

"So," said Owain, "you are saying that as an accomplished thief you can ensure we will have blood and booty and take the lion's share before the Army can arrive."

The Beast stared at him. "I will ignore the insult," he said. "I am proud of my trade. It is dirty work but the best you can get. We are not chasing outlaws, and you need me. We will go directly after the French. They are not the womanish sops that they are made out to be. They are hard men. They have been fighting all their lives, and they have kicked us out of half of France in the last ten years. If you stick with me boy, you will learn more in a year than you would with any other routier in five years. I will bloody you and let you know the way of the sword and the axe."

Owain considered. He looked down, thought for a minute and then looked out. "I will take these terms. But be advised, I am not a man to be cheated or crossed. I keep my word and I will pursue any oathbreaker to the ends of this earth."

The Beast raised his hand and spat in it. "Lad, you have nothing to fear from me. Once I make a deal, I keep it." They shook and we were sold to the Beast for a year.

Thus is the way of war. Before blade will strike plate, before man will fight man, before blood will be spilt, there will be deals struck, bargains made, and men's lives and goods traded away. In these sordid deals, where men are bought and sold for a penny, glory is built and reputations are made. Such is the way of the world and such are the evil times in which we live.

THE WAR IN SCOTLAND

It is often said that England is two kingdoms: the soft luxurious, rolling land of the South, where even a fool can grow a bounty; and the hard, cold land of the North. I will say that my first journey to the Scottish Marches confirmed this view. The North is a hard land. The mountains match our own, the grass is thin and the land rocky and unforgiving. The men are tougher and more taciturn than the ignorant Southerners and show more closely the imprint of the Norse.

I was much struck by their language. It was a much harder, more guttural sounding thing. Many was the time when I would have to pause and listen carefully to grasp their meaning, and often we found ourselves lapsing into French when their English became incomprehensible.

However, I found that I liked Northern men. They have a streak of practicality and directness that is often missing from the Southern English, and I found them honest and true in their dealings. I took great pleasure in learning that they despised the English of the South as much as we. I believe that it was this realization that first suggested to My Lord Owain that this distinction might be important for our people, and that one day we might exploit it.

"You know," he said one day, "I think that if these English were ever given half a chance, they would rebel against their Southern masters. They have almost as much hatred for them as we do, and, if they were ever to be deprived of their oath to the King, they would as soon raise their own standard as serve under a new Southern King."

"Right enough, said Crach. "They have risen so many times against the Kings of Westminster and Winchester. Watch closely the ways of the Earl of Northumberland when we are with the Army. If any family will claim the crown of the North, it will be them. They are Lords of the North as it is and hardly resist plucking the crown."

Crach was right. As we moved North we began to encounter a great stream of armed men coming from every hamlet and village that owed allegiance to the Earls of Northumberland. All of them were hard men, armed with an impressive array of weaponry. If the Lords of the North were ever to call upon these men, they would pose a great challenge to the Kings of the South.

By the time we arrived at the Scottish March, we saw the full host that the King of England had assembled for the great invasion of Scotland. The host itself was impressive, but the actual army of the King of England was a weak thing, barely more than two hundred men. This was nothing compared to the Johnny Gaunt retainers that numbered more than five thousand men. The Lords of Northumberland themselves brought more than three thousand men. Thus, between them, the two great Lords brought with them almost half the muscle of the host.

We settled ourselves down under the banner of Arundel and awaited the order to move. We had been there no more than a day when we encountered many of our old friends from London. Here was Sir John with his gang of cut-throats, and Dodd the Archer in the King's retinue. We caught up on goings on since the Hurling and how they had found their way north. Sir John was convinced this war would be short and sweet. Interestingly, he had forgotten his previous hostility to Johnny Gaunt and was now in the pay of Lancaster.

"Lancaster provides steady work, boys," said Sir John. "With the absence of a reliable war in France, a gentleman must seek out stable sources of income. The House of Lancaster is rich and always in need of a strong arm. As such, I thought it best to swallow my pride and care for my flock by taking the red rose and the twisted 'S'. However, I fear I will get little for my troubles on this jaunt."

He paused and rubbed his belly.

"I tell you, boys," said St. John, "there's nothing worth taking in Scotland. We'll have nothing to steal, and we'll no doubt starve to death in that freezing cold shit hole."

What he said made good sense. I had never heard Scotland called a wealthy country and could see little sense in invading it.

I believe it is a sign of the Saxons' madness that they have attempted to conquer and subdue that wild barbarous place. Even the Romans had the good sense to leave it alone, and they would try to conquer any place that wasn't underwater.

The host began to move and we rode out over the open moors that divide the land between England and Scotland in search of the French and Scots. As promised, Sir Gregory had established us in the vanguard. We were well placed to steal but, as warned, there was little to take.

"Bloody Scots," said Owain, "the bastards have driven off all their herds."

When we looked ahead there was nothing beyond the empty moors. Not a house or village of any size.

"They're poorer than us," said Tudur. It was true. The Welsh might be poor, but these lads made us look like kings.

When we did encounter some wretched settlement, what wealth might have been there was long gone. The folk on either side of the Scots March were used to war. They knew that the arrival of either the King or England or the King of Scotland meant that their livelihoods were at stake, and that it was time to retire to the mountains. Furthermore, the Kings of England had been invading Scotland for more than three hundred years. The routes of invasion were well known, and the locals avoided them. In fact, so well known was the path of the English advance that I half expected to see sign posts and mile marks directing us along the invasion route.

"This is what our fathers did when the English came," said Owain as we rode over the moors. "They picked the land clean and left the foreigners to starve and battle against empty air."

I could tell he was thinking that one day this would be our way again. It was true that being on the receiving side of this stratagem showed its value. Day after day the army advanced, and day after day our supply lines became longer. In France the army would have been able to live off the riches of the land. In Scotland, the land was so barren that the Army had to bring all of its wealth with it. As soon as our lines were more than a few days long, the Scots sent down their raiders and moss troopers to pillage our baggage. Slowly the Army saw its power drained away through the necessity of protecting our line or searching for food.

Our role as routiers was similarly limited. The highlight was when we came upon an Abbey. We were lucky enough to find it undefended and were able to take most of its movables. After that there was nothing more until we reached Edinburgh. Anticipating our arrival and seeing the size of the King's host, the Scots determined that Edinburgh was best left open to us. The King of Scotland's power was gone and all the portable wealth had been taken off into the highlands. What of the French? What of the great threat that we had come to Scotland to dispose? They had gone with the Scots. Not one Frenchman was to be found.

Then, one day along the approaches north of Edinburgh, we finally came upon some action. We were a small party: the Hamners, Tudur, myself and a few of Owain's telu. We came down into a glen following the trail of some cattle that had been driven to the north. At the far end we espied a party of armed men. In the distance we could see they were arrayed in much finery. I rode close to Owain.

"What do you think?" I said.

He strained his eyes. "A party of French engaged in an action similar to ours," he said. It was good to know the French were criminals and equally devoted to robbing the Scots.

"Will they stay and fight or run?" I asked.

"Either way we shall have them," he said. "Order the men to form up and follow me."

We drew up into a line and prepared to charge the French. It seemed the French decided at the same time to charge us. As we formed a line, so they matched us. Now they were clearly in view. It was plain that in terms of numbers we were slightly superior to them. However, from the reflection of the sun off their armor, I could see they were better protected.

"We shall have them," said Owain. "They will be charging into the sun, and we have the advantage of the ground. They must ride up hill, and we will come down on them."

Then he raised his hand and called out, "For Powys, Saint David and King Richard." His telu shouted in agreement. "Come on lads," he said, "let's show these foreigners what Welshmen can do." With that he brought down his hand and began to move forward. We joined him at a trot. The French began to move towards us as well. We rode closer, our horses beginning to catch the scent of the hunt, knowing that battle was upon us. Owain raised his spear leaned forward. As one we joined him and kicked our horses to a canter.

The French followed but were slowed by the gradient of the land. I could see them raise their shields and bend forward into the classic seat of a man preparing to take the lance of another. This was the kind of war at which the French excelled: head on charges with no care or preparation. We preferred the bow and the spear on foot but if this was My Lord's chosen strategy, then so be it.

We came closer and the line began to bend away from the center. This is always the way. The captain tends to spread out in front of his men. They will fall and try to catch up, with the slowest and least attentive falling behind. Faster and faster we urged our mounts on to the French. They came up the hill with screams and shouts and then suddenly we were upon them.

Now, it is a well known and little commented upon fact, that horses will not charge each other. When faced with a direct charge, horse and rider will move away at the last minute and prevent a direct collision. If they did not, all charges would end with massive piles of men and horses. Thus, as we closed on the French, small gaps began to appear in our lines as each man fixed upon his opponent. The French had longer and stronger spears than we, for ours were better suited to throwing and fighting off mounted riders. However, our horses were smaller than the great French beasts being the small, study ponies that our men use on these long rides. The French found themselves having to tip their lances down and at the same time avoid plunging them into the ground. It turned out that we had something of an advantage over the better French weapons.

Suddenly we were on them. As always in a battle, each man's field shrinks to what he can see from his helmet. His world is the thin slit through which he can see. The field of battle is that which his body can feel. All concentration and thought goes into his own desperate fight to kill the enemy and survive. Blows glance off, sharp edges stab and noise is everywhere. A battle of ten men seems like the fight of a thousand, and the fight of a thousand narrows to a war of one. In that moment there is no fear. There is only the exhalation of battle and desperation to survive. I have no clear picture of what happened. I know we came together, I know men fell and I know I survived. I was one of our band who rode through the French and cleared the line. I wheeled my horse and looked back. I could see that we had come off equally. Some of our men had fallen but so too had some of the French. Owain was in the heat of the battle. His spear was shattered, but he was using it as a sword and was parrying off a French knight's attacks. He seized his moment and thrust the broken lance into a Frenchman. The man fell back and Owain withdrew his lance and swung it around to bash another Frenchman's head in. I kicked my horse to life and rode toward Owain. I could see he had discarded his lance and unsheathed his sword. He swung wildly, cutting his way through the French. I pulled out my axe and began to cut a way to My Lord.

It is a beautiful thing to see a man possessed by a battle as Owain was that day. He was not a trained man like the great knights, but he was a natural fighter. No man could touch him. He acted under the blessing of some Holy Angel. I remember him that day, yelling and screaming in joy as he swung his sword and unhorsed one man after another. I too joined him in the fight swinging my axe to cut my way through to him. Of the others, I could see nothing. I saw the French were now encumbered by their longer lances and were casting them aside for this closer fight. Finally I came close to Owain. The Hanmers and his brother were near him. We joined and formed a wall against the French. One by one they gave ground or fell from their horses. Then I heard a command called out in French. The Frenchmen began to disengage and pull back. However, this was not a rout. They were falling back in good order and were preparing for another charge.

"On them" I cried.

"No" Shouted Owen. "They wish us to follow them. They will have others waiting for us."

He called us to order, and we watched the French ride down the valley. Seeing them run, we cheered and looked to our wounded and the fallen upon the field. The men wished to kill any prisoners in Welsh fashion, but Owen ordered them to halt so that we might ransom them.

We gathered ourselves and prepared for another charge. However, none game. As the afternoon wore on, it seemed the French had left us. We dismounted and began to take stock. Then, at the far end of the glen near some pine trees, we espied two Frenchman coming towards us with a flag of truce. Owain saw them and, tying a similar banner around his shattered lance, proceeded forward and urged me to follow.

He turned back to his brother, "Tudur, if I do not return, you are my man. Take the men back to English Gregory and form a party to have our vengeance."

We rode to the French. The two knights who met us were fine examples of the French knighthood, well arrayed and riding fine mounts.
The older of the two addressed us in broken English. "I am Allain du Loudeac. My companion is Jean de Auray. We wish to discuss the terms of your surrender."

Owain smiled and answered, "I am Owain of Glyndyfrdwy. This is my sworn man Gwyn ap Eynon. We have no need of surrender. I thought that you had come to discuss the ransom of our prisoners."

The knight who had spoken first smiled, "Glen-diff-dewy?" he said, "Gwyn ap Enyon? These are not English names. You are Welsh," he said. He turned to his partner and said, "Ils sont Gallois." The other Frenchman looked at us and said in French, "Gallois? Impossible. Where are their tails?"

It is a well known fact in France that all Welshmen have thin leathery tails that fall down our arses. These are of course the scabbards of the daggers we carry to kill French knights that have been tumbled from their horses, and it is a great joke for the French to ask to see them.

The first Frenchman laughed. "Perhaps they are hiding them in their breaches," he said. Then he continued in a language that sounded very close to Welsh, "We are brothers, you and I. I am Breton. I speak the tongue of the Gaels. My people are not Frankish. We are at the command of our Duke to oppose the King of England. Why do you fight for this man? He keeps your people under his boot. Why do you not join us and take back your lands?"

Owain looked at him, surprised. "I am sworn to King Richard and must hold my oath to him and his successors. Were it not for my oath, I would fight the Saxon, but in the absence of a true Prince of Wales, I am bound to the King."

The Breton signed. "This I understand. I was sworn for many years to the King of the Franks. Until my Duke returned to our lands, I was forced to obtain his orders. However, my Duke has returned and we are a free people again."

Owain smiled. "I have never met Bretons," he said, "Your language is like ours, but closer to the tongue of the Kernow," he said referring to those people the Saxons know as Cornish.

"I have heard this before," said the Breton. "We both spring from the same root, but our language has diverged with the span of years. However, interesting though this conversation is, I must urge you to surrender. While we talk my Scots allies are moving among the hills around us." He indicated the high places along the glen and we could pick out bands of lightly armored men moving among the hills.

"In a short time they will surround you and escape will be impossible. Then they will demand attack. They are barbarians. Not like you and I. They will want blood and they will not respect the rules of warfare. I urge you to surrender to me and I will see to ransom."

"But we have your prisoners," said Owain, "If there is an attack by the Scots, I cannot count for their safety. In the heat of battle accidents may occur."

"This is true," said the Breton. "I know I can count on you to behave as a civilized man, but events can complicate the situation."

He thought for a minute, "What do you propose?"

Owain replied, "A bargain. The prisoners for safe passage from the glen and your agreement to hold the Scots back until we are clear and on the high-ground. They may pursue us when we are clear. We shall leave a prisoner every hundred paces until we are clear of the glen. Then you may enter and retrieve them. We shall take only the bootie we can carry and will leave the prisoners with their horses and weapons."

The Breton thought for a moment. "This is a good bargain. I have no love for the Scots, and I feel you are my comrade. There land is cold and wet and their women are ugly. They have little wine and we have had no booty from the campaign. I have no desire to see my comrades killed in some meaningless, crude fight, especially one with a brother Gael and a gentleman. The way you were willing to meet our charge on equal terms shows you are a man of honor and not one of these barbarians. I will agree to your terms. Let us shake upon it."

He withdrew his glove and reached his hand out to Owain. Owain rode forward and grasped his hand. "We shall begin to retreat the moment we are back at our lines," he said.

"I will send a messenger to order the Scots back and will ride alone to recover my comrades."

"You are an honorable man," said Owain, "I hope we may meet again under better circumstances."

"I return the compliment," said the Breton. "Perhaps one day a true Prince will return le Pays de Gales and I shall sail to these islands again to fight with you?"

"Perhaps," said Owain, "but for the time being we must say our goodbyes and hope we do not meet again on the field of battle in this war."

The Breton laughed, "There will be no battles here," he said. "The King of Scotland is too frightened and the King of England is too slow. They will chase each other around until they are bored and then go home," he said.

"Goodbye Sir," said Owain. "Goodbye My Lord of Glen-Diff-Dewy," said the Breton.

With that we saluted each other and rode back to our line. Following our word we retired leaving a prisoner every hundred paces. The Bretons followed and recovered those men, checking their wounds and helping them mount. At the head to the valley we released our last prisoner and Owain turned to wave to the Breton, "I shall see you again My Lord du Loudeac," he shouted.

The Breton waved back, "Call upon me when you are tired of serving the King of England."

With that we were gone and over the crest of the glen into the high country. Owain called to us, "Come on, and let us make haste. I trust the Breton, but not his French and Scots allies. Let us away to our camp and out of this place. We have earned much glory this day and need to inform our captains of the position of the French in this area." With that we were gone and returned to the host.

The rest of the campaign was slow and boring. We rode farther north, and every day the Scots fell back. The land was empty and picked clean. The enemy was absent and only appeared at our rear to raid the baggage. Every day things grew worse. The rain began and kept up for days. Rumors began that that the Earl of Douglas had formed an army separate from the King of Scotland and was moving South to cut our supplies and ravage the border towns. Then we came to the great city of Edinburgh, only to find that it had been abandoned. All that remained was the great castle where the Scots looked down on us, hurled insults and threw down buckets of shit and piss.

The Castle was impossible to take without a long siege. Although it was held by only a few Scotsmen, their small force was enough to keep us out for months. If we were to attempt to take the Castle, we would be trapped in the City and dependent upon a long supply train. At any moment the Scots might return and trap us in the City, the French fleet might cut off our escape to the seas, and the besiegers would become the besieged. The King faced the decision as to what to do; should he stay in Edinburgh or move further north and attempt to bring the Scots to battle?

In response, the King called an assembly of the Great Lords to review the situation and hear their mind. Owain, as a tenant-in-chief, was called, and I attended as part of his retinue. We met in a hall in Edinburgh that the King had chosen for his councils. We were led in by various sergeants and were stood in order of our regality. As always, Owain, though deserving a position near the front, was pushed back with the minor lords. Once we settled, the King entered in procession and sat down on a throne that had been brought for such occasions.

He still did not look the great martial lord that was required upon such occasions. He was weak and delicate in appearance, and was clearly better suited to the rituals of court than the field of war. He was clothed in gold and wore a small signet to signify his position. One by one the great Magnates trailed after him and took up their positions near the throne.

It was clear from the public nature of this council that the King, or his favorites, wished everyone to hear these discussions. They wanted all in attendance to know that any decision the King took, he took with good council. Further, they wished all to know which council arose from which lord. If there were to be factions, they wanted all the powers in the land to know the origins of the debate and share in the outcome of the decision.

From where we stood, we could see all the Great Lords. At the front, closest to the King, were his uncles and their children. Closest of all was Lancaster, Johnny Gaunt himself, and his son the Earl of Hereford. Next to him the King's other uncle, the Duke of Gloucester, and the Duke of York. Another of the King's uncle, the Duke of Clarence, had been left behind in Westminster against the threat of French invasion. Next to them we could see the Greatest Lords and the King's favorites. Foremost was the Great Marshal of England, the Lord Percy and that mad bastard of a son, Henry the Hotspur. Next was our lord, the Lord Arundel with all his finery. Behind him were the Earl of Mowbray and the Archbishops of York and Durham. Behind the throne were the King's favorites, De Vere and De Pole.

All the conspirators and plotters were gathered in one place. At times they would give good council; at other times they would offer only as much as would hurt their enemies. Whatever they said you could always be sure that it would favor them and their interests. If the King had been wise, he would have sent the whole crowd packing and made his decision alone through prayer and exploration of his heart.

After the preliminaries had been observed, the King turned to the royal uncles.

"Gloucester," he said gesturing to his Uncle Tom, "what is your council? What do you think concerning our position here?"

Gloucester drew himself up, flushed with importance.

"Your Grace," he began, "I believe that we have no choice but to withdraw. All we have won here is an empty city. If we remain here, the Scots will raid our supply lines and frustrate our movements. In time, all we will possess will be this City. Then the Scots will simply wait and starve us out. The French will take advantage of the situation and invade from the South. The King and the host of England will be trapped here in this freezing, worthless city.

"Eventually we will be forced to surrender. Your Grace will be taken, and all the Great Lords and their retainers will be captured. The French will march to London and take the City. Once there, the King of France will sleep in the Tower and dine in the Great Hall at Westminster. The North will be open to the Scots and they will pour down and take Northumberland and York. All will be lost."

The King considered this and then he asked, "What if we leave and pursue the Scots?"

Percy interrupted. "This is the strategy Your Grace," he said impatiently. "We must follow the Scots into the north and force them to battle. We can shatter their army and remove the threat to the North for a generation. We can then turn south to deal with the French. Speed is of the essence. A quick pursuit will capture them before they have the chance to move deep into the Highlands. We can catch them with britches down and destroy them before they can prepare their defense."

Arundel shook his head. "My intelligencers suggest they have moved across the lowland to the west. Already my vanguard has tangled with French raiding parties," he nodded toward Owain. "I believe that they intend to fall back behind us and move down into Northumberland and to York. If I am correct then they will have cut us off completely. As My Lord Gloucester says, then the French will invade and the two may link up and challenge us in the Midlands. We must move their host to the west and confront the Scots before they are behind us."

Then the venerable Lancaster, old the Great Johnny Gaunt himself interrupted.

"We must finish what we came here to do," he said. "We must push across the Forth," referring to the great river than cuts through Scotland into the western lowlands. "We must cut off the Scots before they can threaten any invasion of the Northumberland. If we delay they will move south. There are rumors that already they move against Carlisle and Penrith. If we move west, we can cut their supply lines and force them to move north. Then we will meet them in battle upon ground of our choosing in the lowlands. The King of Scotland will see that we have destroyed half of his army, and he will have to come to their aid. We will face them while our strength is intact and defeat them one at a time."

"Madness," said Gloucester. "My Lords mistake the Scots' strategy. My brother Lancaster is too optimistic. If we pursue them, all they have to do is withdraw into their mountains. The King of Scotland will disappear into the Highlands, and the Army of Douglas into the mountains of the March. We must pursue one or the other. We go west, we move away from our supplies and the eastern road. We will follow them into a land that is empty of provisions and expose ourselves to the King of Scotland's army in the north.

"He will come down when we are weakest and rally the Earl of Douglas's host with his own power, trapping us in a place of their choosing. If we move North, Douglas will come east to harry our supplies while we move further into the Highlands. We will not catch the King of the Scotland. He and his forces are light and we are heavy. We move slowly, the Scots move quickly. We will not catch them. Your Grace, they will be moving into friendly territory. The Highland chieftains and wild mountain men will support them. We will follow them across a wasted land. Not one cow or grain of wheat will remain. They will pick the land clean and we will be dependent on an ever lengthening supply line. As we move, they will send their Highland savages south to destroy our baggage.

"When we are exhausted and starving and winter is coming on, they will fight. But they will not fight upon good land. They know the land and believe me that land is made for defense. In some lonely place far from our homes, we shall be cut off from retreat and surrounded by the wild Scots. They will choose a place where we cannot bring our host to its full power. There they will bring down all the Highlands upon us and we shall be destroyed."

The room was silent. "My King," said Gloucester, "I fear that if we follow unwise council and pursue the Scots it may well cost Your Grace your crown and all your lands."

The speech clearly made an impression. The whole assembly was silent. The King turned to his favorites, "What think you De Vere? De Pole?"

The King's bum boys groveled for a moment. Then De Vere said, "Whatever you decide, Your Grace, your safety must be of the first regard. You are England, and if England is harmed or falls, then all your realms will be vulnerable. I would council that Your Grace move toward the greater threat. These Scots are wild men; they run around half naked or barbarously clothed, speaking an uncivilized language. They are not worthy of Your Grace's martial attentions. Such is Your Grace's reputation and glory that they have run away at the very mention of your name. You have chased them from their greatest city and forced the King of Scotland to shelter like a rustic in some stinking hut upon the empty Highlands.

"You have shattered their power. Even now their French allies skulk and hide in the ferns of the Highlands and wait for their ships to take then back to France. You have accomplished all a King could accomplish; even more than your great-grant Grandfather, the Great Edward. I would imagine that even now in heaven he looks down upon you and says, "Truly do I give up my well earned title,' "Hammer of the Scots,' and give this unto my great-great grandson the Great Richard."

He paused for all this shit to sink into the royal head.

"You have defeated the Scots," said De Pole. "Now it is time to turn south. Even now the Scots beg you to end this punishment and leave. Show mercy and leave them to their wretched land. Travel to Westminster in your glory and make your victories known. Why, I would say, that after this triumph the very news of Your Grace's presence in the South will be sufficient to affright the French and quash all talk of invasion.

"If the French are still stupid enough to brave the Channel, then you will challenge their power and bring down this mighty host upon them. Thus, I urge Your Grace to quit this ugly and ill-stationed dung-heap forthwith and return to the adoring arms of your people. The host should follow as soon as possible and reassemble, if necessary, to challenge the French in the Scott."

It was obvious that De Pole had had enough of the cold of Scotland and wished to return to the comforts and tender arses of Westminster. Perhaps it was more difficult for him to attach his mouth around the royal prick when they traveled in their gilded coach and he wished more a more familiar place to service the King's member.

De Vere now stepped in. "Your Grace, your good friend speaks the truth. Your body is too precious to risk in combat against these rank barbarians. You should only wage civilized war against great lords, not against such as these savages. I urge you to retire, sure in your victory in this land, and prepare for the challenge in the South."

The King thought for a minute. "What think you of this council?" he asked Lancaster.

It was plain that Lancaster despised De Vere and De Pole. It pained him to agree with them in front of the assembled lords. "My Lords De Vere and De Pole speak well, My King. I am convinced by the arguments that have been made. Your place is in the South ready to confront the French. Withdraw with the host and bring your power to the south coast to ready the land for the French."

Northumberland could see his position was failing, he was anxious to secure himself a place in the winning side, reaping any glory or profit that was to be had from defeating the French invasion. However, his interests were all in the North, and the North would be vulnerable unless the Scots and French threats were quelled.

"Your Grace," said Northumberland. "The Scots remain a threat. I urge you that if you decide on such an action, you should leave such forces in the North to dissuade the Scots from raiding into your lands. Garrison Berwick well. Place patrols along the March lands and ensure that the treacherous Scots do not take advantage of Your Grace's mercy by coming from their hiding places to ravage the North. I must move South with Your Grace as Marshall of England, but I will volunteer my own dear son, the martial Hotspur, to act as warden and commander in my place and guard the March in your absence."

The King's eyes fell on Hotspur. He was not quite the King's type. He was too hard and manly. From observation I had deduced the King preferred a softer and womanly man for his companion. However, Hotspur's body was fine enough to warrant the King's attention.

"Come forward Hotspur," said the King. Hotspur moved forward and knelt in front of the throne; always a dangerous thing for a man to do around Queen Dick. He was likely to get a cock in his face and invitation to the Royal bedchamber.

"May I trust you to defend the Northern Marches and all my conquests while I go to defeat the French in the South?" said the King.

"My place should always be with you, My Lord," said Hotspur, "guarding your Royal presence and extending the breadth of Your Grace's domain. However, if your Majesty commands, I will abjure my desires to be with you and guard your lands. I will be as good a watchman as ever was. No Scot or French-paid man will dare set foot in your lands while I am here. If they come, I will simply mention your name and they will run away in fright. I will give chase, calling all the while your great name until they skulk once more amongst the heather."

It was clear that if the House of Percy could not have the war they wanted, then the next best thing was to get the King and his playthings out of their lands. If there was no booty or lands to be gained in among the Scots, then they wished to make peace quickly and return to their old arrangements with the King of Scotland. A strong force in the March, funded at Royal expense, would bolster their position among their rivals, prevent a Scottish incursion, and possibly allow a more advantageous arrangement to be made with the King of Scotland or the Earl of Douglas on the Scots side of the March.

The King laughed in an almost girlish manner. Her Majesty was obviously quite titillated by all this praise from these manly men. "Sir Henry, My dearest Hotspur, faced with such assurances of protection, what can I do but rely upon you."

He turned to Northumberland. "My Lord Northumberland, your boy is almost as well equipped with a golden tongue as he is with armor and weapons." He paused, no doubt contemplating that golden tongue up his own arse hole.

"It is decided," he said. He turned to his uncles. "You great Lords sit with full bellies and do not see not the danger that we face. If we go north or west, the common solider may perish along the way. I will not destroy my power by driving it into the wilds. I must keep the army intact and ready to fight the French. Therefore, I shall leave immediately to rally powers in the south. The host will retire from this City in good order when all is ready. As a punishment to the French and Scots, I order this City should be put to the torch before you leave. I will station a force at Berwick to protect against further insults from my vassal the King of Scotland. My Lord Arundel will detach his power to support Hotspur and his power." I could see Arundel wrinkle his forehead; no doubt he was wondering who would pay and how he could cheat the Royal purse to maintain any men he left.

The King turned to De Vere and De Pole. "Come, my friends, let us prepare for our departure and decide upon the vestments we shall wear to celebrate our triumph as we travel south."

Thus the great assembly at Edinburgh ended. The King was back in Berwick in ten days, and the host followed soon after. Edinburgh was pillaged but not fired. In the King's absence, Lancaster and Northumberland made a pact with the King of Scotland in return for a substantial payment and an agreement not to venture south of the March for the rest of the campaigning season. They left the City intact and moved south in good order. What of the French? They tired of the cold, the rain, and the lack of action and turned their ships back to their homes.

"See," said Owain when we received news the French had left. "The French are not well adapted to this form of war. They are an aggressive and impulsive race. If they come as allies, they must be used straight away or they become bored. If I had been the King of Scotland, I would have sent them South into the March and beyond to raid our baggage and drive deep into England. They are not used to our little wars of the hill country and need constant fighting if they are to remain steady allies."

I saw in later years that Owain had taken many lessons from this experience, for when the French came to Wales, he followed this strategy exactly to burn and loot the English.
Unfortunately, the end of the expedition did not signal glory for us. Due to English Gregory's conspiracies he ensured that we were left behind in the garrison at Berwick. There, safe and warm, he could continue to collect our pay and send our raiders to steal and loot the land of the Earl of Douglas under the protection of the Lords of Northumberland who had returned to their old ways. All that summer and the next winter we waited in fruitless duty. Crach cast the bones and examined

sheep turds to see what next the fates would bring us, but it seemed we would stay there forever.

Owain received regular reports from his lands and tracked the progress of the rebuilding at Sycharth. It seemed that Marged was now much in power and was enforcing her will upon the servants and retainers who remained. Owain made some trips back to see Marged and ensure the estate continued to flourish. Shortly after he returned, a message came that Marged was pregnant. I never knew a woman more fertile that Marged. All Owain had to do was go home and remove his britches and she was with child. There were so many children over the years that it sometimes seemed that he intended to raise his own army from his loins and populate all of Wales with his children.

Then, in the first stirrings of spring, we had word to quit our position and travel south to Southampton. There we were to join the Earl of Arundel and the navy he was building to secure the Channel. We packed our things, left English Gregory to continue his arrangement with Northumberland, and headed south to join the great fleet that the Lord Arundel, Admiral of the Seas and Commander of all the King's ships, now prepared along the Southern Coasts.

THE BATTLE OF CADZAND

We arrived at the base of the Lord Arundel's fleet just as the winter was ending. At that time the King kept most of his ships at London to guard against any French attack. The Lord Arundel had assembled his own fleet at the Port of Sandwich and prepared to use it to strike out at the French and attack their ports before they could set sail. By the time we arrived, the fleet numbered some sixty ships and he determined that it was sufficient to challenge the French.

We Welsh lads were unfamiliar with the ways of the sea and the use of ships in war. The port was a great wonder to us. The harbor was a forest of masks and cranes as supplies and weapons were loaded onto the ships. Most were cogs of the kind used my merchants; wide bottomed low-slung ships but with the bows and sterns build up with castles from which men could shoot. Archers were placed upon these towers while armed men would be held for attack on the lower deck. We were told by our captains that the goal of the enterprise would be to catch a French ship and weaken her by arrow fire. Then, when we close enough, grappling irons would be thrown and the two ships would close together. Our men would then bring down a bridge between the ships. We would run over and fight the French in battle upon their ships. We were told not to damage the ship or use fire. When all was secure, the ship would be captured and returned by our crew to England. It all seemed quite simple, but then so does playing the flute when first you see it; you simply blow down and move your fingers.

Our Captains' dealt with our ignorance by playing war in port. Each day we would be gathered on a ship tethered to dock and another ship would be brought alongside. We would be split into two sides; half on one ship and half on the other. Once assembled we would take turns attacking and defending. It was great fun. We would fight with wooden swords and mallets. Our Sergeants would shout an order and selected men would swing a grapple and catch the ship. The defenders would try to push them off but eventually one would get over and secure a place. Then we would push the board over and run over it like mad things. Once we were over our job was fairly simple; fight our way up to the castles on the ship and take the high ground. We would trap the crew and our archers could take them out at their pleasure. We were told that we must take the castles. Convention stated that the moment a ships castles were taken the crew would surrender as there was no point in fighting any longer.

"What if they don't?" asked one lad. "I mean there are some mad bastards out there. I've seen men so riled up they just don't know it's time to stop."

He got a hard look from the Sergeant. "We will be fighting trained men that are used to sea-fighting. They will know how to behave and respect the rules of war."

"Trained men like us" said one man. That got a laugh. We had all seen some action but we were far from hardened sea-fighters.

However, despite our inexperience, it was all the Arundel had. The French had dominated the Channel for a generation and there were few men left that knew how to fight. There were pirates of course; men that made a good living raiding anything that moved in the narrow seas. However, the few pirates that we still operating on the English side ran their own ships in the Earl's fleet and were not willing to split their men up among the other crews to buttress our inexperience. It quickly became apparent that not only had we not fought at sea but few of us had ever been in a boat before. I was fairly typically. I had crossed the odd river and paddled through a lake once or twice but I never been to sea or faced the rolling waves. Before we left for the big fight they sent us out, one ship at a time, to get our sea legs.

Never was a boat so full of vomit. Our boys puked their way out in the sea and back again. Men begged for the French to come and slit their throats or for them to be thrown overboard to drown. I put my head over the side and puked until I thought I must vomit everything I had ever eaten. Owain was a little better than most but even he lost his normal dignity and stayed unnaturally still staring at the floor and away from the horizon.

After a few such trips the vomiting had fallen to a manageable level and we were judged ready for war. Rumor had it that there was a big fleet coming up the Narrow Seas and the Earl had a plan to catch them just off Margate. Men said that it was a Castilian fleet sent up from the South to pick up the French in Flanders. If they made it to Flanders there would be nothing to stop them pouring over the narrows and landing on the south coast. We were told that we were the only thing that stood between the King and the hordes of French cut-throats ready to rape and pillage their way throughout England.

Of course, the entire world knows that the truth was different. Arundel had gained intelligence that the French invasion army had dispersed months ago. With little to do the fleet had been sent south to La Rochelle to pick up the wine harvest. It the plan was for the fleet to transport the wine to Sluys in the spring. There was some idea that the fleet could then be reassembled for a new invasion if the French King had a mind to do later that year. The problem was that most of the fleet was made up of Flemish, Genoan, Castilian, and Burundians captains. They had been hired by the King of France for a season's raiding and to transit his troops to England. Beyond that they had little allegiance to the King of France. Arundel seized upon this and realized that such men could be easily swayed. He formed a plan to seize the fleet when it was in transit. His agents went about the captains at La Rochelle. One by one the captains came to an agreement whereby they would minimal resistance to the Earl's attack. They would allow him to catch up to the lead ships that contained the French King's men. The Earl's men would then overwhelm these ships. Once resistance ended, the remainder of the fleet would surrender. The Earl would take the wine harvest, sell it cheap in London and split the profits with the Captains of the Wine Fleet. The ships would be held for a few months while the captains spent their money. Then they would be released and left to go on their way. Noble prisoners would be held and ransomed and the ransoms would split between the Captains and the Earl. When the French saw the fleet had be taken they their invasion plans would be over. When the Earl was sure that the French were gone, the wine fleet would be released and he would begin raiding along the French coast. If the recently captured ships wished to take part, Arundel would license them as privateers and they could join in the raids as long as they kicked back the booty to Arundel.

It was a nice plan and typical of the state of war in those days. While war has ever been done for profit, it has reached its high point in the English wars with the French. No one Englishman will leave his island lest he sees profit. That was why the King Richard became unpopular. He saw the French Wars as a costly and dangerous waste of time. If he were too loose a campaign, he would come home poor and broken. On top of that he would be forced to go to Parliament and request a further subsidy. As he knew, subsidies came with conditions that little by little chipped away at his power. Thus, he was ever opposed to new wars.

His subjects saw the world in a different way. All Englishmen, from the poorest ploughman to the richest magnate, saw the wars as a way to line their pockets and live free off the French. Regardless of whatever battles were won or lost, the average solider had a good chance of making a little scratch. Most captains could count on a few decent prisoners to ransom and most magnates could count on a few bribes to leave a town or two alone or the profits from sacking a less well defended castle. The merchants of London could count on all the plunder taken being funneled back through them and sold at a decent markup. Indeed so profitable were the wars that towards the end of Edward the Frank-Killers reign, England had become one of the richest nations in the world. Travelers from all over would marvel at the wealth of the English and not realize that most of it had been stolen from the French. So rich did the English become that all but the poorest stopped drinking beer and developed a taste for cheap French wine.

Aye, but there was a cost and the King saw it. Great profits came with great risk. At the height of the old Kings power after the battle of Poitiers when they took the French king prisoner, England was rich. The French King was held and ransomed for twice the total yearly income of the Kingdom of France. In those times, the Parliament was never called for subsidies and no Englishman paid duty or tax to the King. However, when the war went bad, then the king was burdened with debt. It was as if the entire Kingdom of England took all its wealth and placed it upon a single throw of the dice. The young King saw the folly and wanted peace but everyone else disagreed.

Well enough of that. I meander.

Let me return to the story of the Great Wine Raid or as it is known, the Battle of Cadzand. It was in early March when we got the word the French fleet was coming. All of our ships bustled out of the harbor and we made for the sea off Margate. As predicted the French fleet appeared on the horizon around mid morning. I believe that never had there been so many ships on the sea at one time. Later I was told that were over three hundred. We were less than eighty. However, Arundel's spies had told him that there were less than twelve hostile ships.

According to plan, the Arundel's allies in the French fleet saw us and began to break toward the English coast as if they had panicked at the site of the attacking ships. This pushed the French ships to the fore. Realizing they had lost the ships they were escorting they bore down on the English hoping that by defeating them they would remove the threat to the wine fleet and be able to pull it back toward Cadzand on the Flemish coast.

Arundel's fleet took up the challenge. Our ship picked out one ship and went after it. The captain jostled and moved about until we were in bow range. From the deck we could see that the French had crossbowmen in ship's castles. Our boys had a distance advantage over them and also the longbow is better suited to indirect fire. They notched their arrows, fired, and began to shower the French ship with arrows. We could see the sailors falling from the rigging. The crossbowmen began to fall and drop from the towers. Gradually we came closer. The captain turned the ship and we moved in alongside our opponent. We crouched down behind the wall of the ship and waited. As the ships came together, the archers turned to direct fire letting their arrows fly directly into the French resisters. Then our fellows ran up the masts, swung their grapples on to the French ship, and jumped over. Once there, a couple of our lads grabbed the boarding ramp and pushed it over. The men with the grapples jumped down around it and began to try to fight off the French as they attempted to push it back. The moment it landing boards were secured, our Sergeant shouted, "Alright lads, let's get at them".

Up we went and charged across the board like a pack of dogs at the hunt. We screamed and yelled and uttered curses that to this day make be blush. More than a few of use fell straight off the board or were picked off by crossbow blots. Then we were over and cramped into a tiny place to fight our little war. As ever in battle a man's world shrinks to that which he can see. All is chaos and screaming. Somehow we began to push towards the towers. Owain dashed up one ladder, smashing his way through the French. I followed the leaders and beat back anyone attempting to slow me down. Then suddenly we were up on top of the castle and fighting the crossbowmen. Our archers had done a good job most of them were already dead. Those that were left were in no mood to fight. They threw down their weapons and gave us to understand they wished to be taken as prisoner for ransom. I looked up and I saw that the ship had taken fire. Our Sergeants were showing that the fight was won and were heading the prisoners onto to the main deck. Our scavengers began to disappear below deck to drag any loot over. We marked our prisoners so it would be clear we were due ransom from them and began to look around for any loot. The prisoners were looped together and taken back across the board to our ship. At the same time I could see our sailors reaching down into the sea to pull out men that had fallen overboard. We picked what we could and they cross back to our ship. . The French ship was too far gone to save. Our sailors lashed the wheel to send it out toward the French coast. The fire caught the wind and began to consume the ship we backed off and looked around for new fight.

But there was no need for that. Arundel's eighty against the French's mere twelve was an easy fight. The big ships in Arundel's fleet were now turning to remainder of the fleet now hovering near the coast. They signaled them and harried them into a pack. Slowly they moved close in and began to follow Arundel's ships back toward Sandwich. Cheers began to go up as one ship after another realized that the fight was won.

Owen embraced me, "This is a great day Gwyn" he said, "We will live rich off this raid for many years."

And so we did. When Arundel got the wine fleet back to port it was discovered that we had taken more than nine thousand tuns of wine; almost all the wine produced that year for the north. Arundel had wine merchants waiting and had it packed to send straight up to London. They sold it in London for a bargain price and made a fortune and brought the loyalty of the citizens of London for years to come. Owain got a share and did very well for himself; at least enough to keep Marged quiet.

As for us, with the French cleared from the Narrow Seas, we went on the attack. Arundel took us across to Sluys. They were unprepared for series fighting but we took a few castles and towns. We spent the rest of the summer raiding along the coast and into Ghent. I must say we made a tidy profit from captives and looting but there was no serious fights. It was said that more than two hundred thousand francs worth of booty was taken in that summer. The Earl had hoped to trigger a rising by the Ghentois but they were sick of the English coming from across the seas and stayed at home. In less than a month we ship back to England and docked at a port on the Orwell near Ipswich.

As we landed we could see many of the German and Flemish ships that we had seized sitting a port. Their sailors cheered us as we arrived; thanking us for removing them from the danger of participating in the invasion and allowing them to spend a month at rest in port. We had failed to achieve the Earl's big goals of reigniting the war in France but we had made a tidy profit and ended the threat of any French invasion for that year.

Owain had demonstrated his value as a man of war and had made a good enough return to establish himself in Sycharth as a successful man.

"You'll see" he said to me "This is the beginning of everything. The Earl and the King cannot ignore my achievements. Arundel will rise and the King will acknowledge me as a man of value in my own right."

I wish that it were so. Instead of triumph, the next months would see the end of Owain's political ambitions as a loyal subject of Queen Dick.

THE "WONDROUS PARLIAMENT"

Knowing nothing of what the future would bring, we were in a happy mood that summer. My Lord's fortunes seemed assured, his patron was rising, and we had blooded ourselves and could return home as respected men. However, we did not know that we were prisoners in a larger scheme of treason and oath breaking.

When we first set food upon England again, we were all happy to be Arundel's men. Our mission was not as successful as we had hoped, but we had saved the King's realms from invasion and made a pretty penny in profit. Our sergeants came to us and told us to form up and join the march to London, where we would be celebrated for our victory.

After a week's march we reached London full of good spirits. London had changed much since our last visit. In fear of invasion, the good citizens had roused themselves to action and had repaired the city's walls. They had also demolished many of the buildings outside London, lest the French should use them as bases to gain access to the City. London was now standing alone as a guarded city ready to defend herself.

We expected glory, but there were no cheers or award for us. The city was glum and silent. We found our way to the Hog's Head Tavern to inquire as to our old friends.

"All gone, Master Owain," said Mistress Wriggly when Owain asked her where the regulars were.

"Sir John and all his lads have gone with Johnny Gaunt on his Castilian adventure," she said. "All the Lancastrians are gone. I recall it clear," she said. "Sir John was holding court in his usual place when in walks one of Lancaster's place men. "All right you lot," he says, "The Duke of Lancaster invites all his sworn men to join him in a little trip to Portugal to stop the Castilians. There'll be plenty of booty, fair rates for fighting, and all the wine you can steal. If we're lucky the Duke may manage to make himself King of Castile. If he does, we will all be lords and will soon be living in the sun in our own castles."

"And what of the French?" asked Sir John.

"The French?" says the Placeman. "Once the Duke's King of Castile, the French will have to fear an enemy in the South and one in North. They will crumble like a block of dry cheese. King Richard will hold court in Paris and his uncle will be King of Castile by Christmas. We will then join the armies of all Christendom together and drive the Moors from the rest of Spain. We shall be heroes and the entire world shall remember our triumphs."

She stopped and looked around at us. "I tell you the truth Sirs," said Mistress Wriggly. "I do not think that Sir John's boys were very interested in the opportunity. They had been up to Scotland with Johnny Gaunt and had got no farther than Berwick when they were told to fall back. They didn't get paid neither, and they were suspicious of Lancastrian promises. But Sir John rallied them. "Come on lads," he says, "Portugal's the place for us; cheap wine, loose women, and gold aplenty. I say we collect our belongings, kiss our women, and march down to the docks." Then he turned to the Placeman, "We are sworn men of Lancaster," he said. "I assume we will take rates for normal overseas service?" he asked, and the Placeman says yes.

"Well," says Sir John, "I shall work out our terms of service and you may be assured that you shall all share in the booty fairly". The men cheered and he led them all out.

"It was a sad day for me," she said. "My business has not recovered, and with so much fear of the French afoot, the King has taken all the young men down to the coast. I am so glad you're back. Now I can count on all you good Welsh lads to drink my ale and sup on my wine."

"What of the City?" asked Owain "Is all calm now we have put the French to flight?"

"No Sir," she said, "The city is full of fraction and conflict, even worse than normal. The drapers and the victualars are at each others' throats. Master Brembre still leads the fishmongers, but he is no longer Mayor. Master Exton of the drapers' guild now controls the city, and it is said he is an enemy of the King. Master Brembre favors the King and rallies his men to dispute every action by the Drapers.

"It has reached the point where every ward has declared for one faction or another," she continued. "A man cannot travel to one faction's ward if he is too closely associated with the other. The apprentices battle for Cheapside almost every day in order to take territory for their masters. I tell you, Master Owain, I wish the French would come. Perhaps they would calm these disputes and unite us against a common enemy."

"What of the King?" asked Owain.

"It is said that he has been about the Midlands and the March all summer. Rumor has it that he tests his strength and recruits more Cheshire men to protect his person lest there be rebellion. I hear now he is at his place at Eltham and waits to hear the result of the Parliaments inquiries."

"I did not know the Parliament was called," said Owain. "That may mean that my father-in-law is at Westminster. I will call on him and ask him for his council on these matters."

Owain would have sought him out the next day, but he received an invitation to attend the Bishop of Ely at his Inn up on the north of Holborn Street. The Bishop was Thomas Fitzalan, the Earl of Arundel's brother, and even then a growing power in the land. He had collected all the great magnates at his London residence, and he called them and their captains together at his Inn to inform them of the plans he and his brother had made for the following months. Owain had been raised to the top of Arundel's rolls due his courage at Cadzand and Arundel and sought to secure his loyalty in the forthcoming actions.

I accompanied Owain to a dinner hosted by the bishop, acting as his servant and retainer. While there I watched the great magnates wine and dine and attempt to embroil My Lord in their conspiracies. I recall the scene clearly. We entered the great hall of the Bishop's Inn and saw several rows of benches draped in red cloth, and silver plate and cutlery set at each place. Elaborate salt sellers and sauce dishes were spread across the tables.

There were more than twenty captains and their retainers milling around drinking goblets of wine. At the front was a raised dais with a fine oak table set upon it. A red velvet cloth covered it with even more elaborate tableware. A large tapestry showing the defeat of the dragon by St. George hung behind the table. The walls of the hall were painted white and blue and edged with gold. Lances, shields, and swords decorated the walls in a display that proved the Bishop saw the Church as a martial institution and wished to make clear he was a man of war.

Owain sighted a few of his comrades and went to talk. I fell back to the walls with the Captain's retainers and listened.

"What is the news?" asked Owain of another Captain.

"The Bishop and his brother have a plan concerning the King, and they wish to test our loyalty," said the other Captain in a low voice.

Owain scowled. "I do not hold well with Royal politics," he said. "I have given my oath to the King, and I will follow him and his loyal successors."

"Times change, Master Glendowery," said the Captain, "The King is surrounded by wicked advisors. In the past such situations have led kings to ruin. Did not the King's great-grandfather fall after he was led astray by the sodomite Gaveston?"

"This is not the same situation," said Owain. "Edward was an oath breaker and purposefully humiliated many of the great men of the realm. King Richard is still but a boy. He has not even reached his majority. Further, Gaveston and King Edward engaged in many unnatural and sinful acts. To my knowledge, King Richard is innocent of all such accusations."

The captains around Owain broke into laughter. Owain always was very trusting and gullible when it came to rumors of sodomy. Not me. I can smell a sodomite a mile off. It's a peculiar talent I have. The captain turned to his fellows with a grand gesture towards Owain.

"My friends, observe the simple honest Welshman. He hears nothing but good and is happy in his simple rustic ways. He misses the obvious and ignores the gossip of court. Would that we were all as simple and honest as this man."

There was much laughter. Owain's face reddened, "What is your meaning?" he asked.

The Captain turned to him, "Master Glendowery, I mean no offense. In fact I complement you for avoiding the gossip of the court. But I should tell you that it is widely said that the King favors his friend De Vere because the two of them share physical affection."

Owain looked surprise. The Captain continued.

"Oh come now Master Glendowery, you cannot be so innocent that you have not seen the signs? Look how the King dresses. He covers himself in the finest cloth and gold jewels; his hair is colored, curled, and cared for by Italians studied in the arts of beauty; he paints his face and powers his cheeks. He avoids war, the natural sport of kings, and instead busies himself with the decoration and building of his palaces. Why, he would rather see a new roof on his Palace at Westminster than a new invasion of the Low Countries. In all things he has an unnatural love of beauty. Such things are not right in a man. They speak of a dangerous attachment to womanly ways. It is a clear sign that he is a sodomite."

"But he is married," said Owain. This raised another laugh.

"Master Glendowery, how charming. Of course he is married. He must produce an heir even if he finds the act disguising. Anyway, that German cunt he married looks more like a boy than a woman. It is said that the Lady Katherine fucks her more than the King."

Owain looked truly shocked. "I will hear none of this," he said. "The King is the King. The manners of the divinely-chosen are different from our own and cannot be judged by our standards. I saw him at Spitfield when he faced down Watt the Tyler. He was as brave and as strong as any man ever was.

Had he not ridden out in front of the mob after Watt's Tyler's death, they would have been upon us and all those who were there with the King would be dead. I tell you, Sir, when I saw that I swore that there was a man to lead us. Even though I be a Welshman, and know well the pains and indignities your nation has visited upon my own, I knew that day that King Richard was a good, brave man and could be counted on to see us fair."

The argument would have continued, but at that point the Chamberlain entered to announce the entrance of the Bishop and his guests. In they came, walking toward the dais at the head of the hall. The Captain bowed, scraped and kissed the Bishop's ring as it was offered. When they reached their tables, they sat and signaled for the captains to be seated.

The Bishop was surrounded by all the hard men at court. Next to him was his brother, Richard the Earl of Arundel. On his other side was Thomas Woodstock, the Duke of Gloucester. The dais was filled out with Thomas Beauchamp, the Earl of Warwick, and Arundel's son-in-law, Thomas Mowbray, the Earl of Nottingham. Gaunt was of course absent in Spain, but his son Henry Bolingbroke was there and, if you looked closely, you could see that weasel Reggie Grey, sometime known as Reynald de Grey, third Baron of Ruthin, hiding near the back. This was not the old man who had killed Owain's father, but the fucker's son.

Jesus and all the saints, I wanted to jump up and kill him there to settle the blood debt. I restrained myself for the sake of decorum, but promised myself that I would have his liver one day. De Grey was enjoying himself in conversation with Bolingbroke. It seemed that his dad's strategy had worked well, and he had managed to ingratiate his brat into the good affection of the House of Lancaster. If I had any doubts as to whether the Lancastrians were our enemies, it disappeared that day. Anyone who was close to the Lords of Ruthin was clearly our enemy.

Bolingbroke himself was looking very flush with cash, and was dressed even more gaudily than normal. Before Gaunt had left he had married Henry off to some rich bitch, and his potential wealth already marked him out as one of the richest men in England. I believe at that time he had not been elevated to the Earldom of Hereford and was styled the Earl of Derby.

The English are much confusing in this fashion. The great lords take their names from their place of birth until they are awarded a title. Then they insist on being called by their title. Thus one man makes take many names in his lifetime. Henry Bolingbrook was variously known as the Earl of Derby, the Earl of Hereford, the Duke of Lancaster, Henry of Lancaster, and the King of England. In each case he insisted that everyone call him by his current title. The main reason for this custom seems to be to confuse chroniclers and make sure that school boys and students will never properly know the history of the English lands.

The Bishop rose and spoke the Pater Nosta to bless our conspiracies. We bowed our heads and waited for the cross and the signal to eat. When he finished, he looked up at us.

"Good Captains," he said, his face flushed with pleasure. "I bring you here to celebrate and reward your actions in my brother's campaigns in France. I pray that we will soon be allowed to return and continue to take back what is rightfully ours for the mutual profit and glory of the King and all his loyal subjects."

Cheers echoed in the hall.

"Later we will speak more of our intentions, but for now please enjoy my hospitality and take pleasure in the entertainments."

So the celebration began. Dish after dish was placed before each guest, the wine and ale flowed, and musicians and fools entertained us. Then as the dinner was finished and a general feeling of charity and well-being had spread over the crowd, the Bishop's chamberlain came forward and called for our silence. The Earl of Arundel then stood and began to address us.

"Captains," he said, "you have shown yourselves to be good, loyal men. You fought with bravery and skill. Never has anyone crowded a harbor with as many ships as you brought to England. We returned with threescore of tall ships and six great carracks full of oil and wines. Such is the abundance of wine that a tun of highly-prized French wine is worth hardly a mark of English money. I count myself to be lucky to have been your Admiral and to have led men such as yourselves."

Of course Arundel did no such thing. He stayed safely in port and waited for us to arrive with the booty, typical of the bloody nobility.

He continued.

"However, now I must call upon you for even more dangerous work. As many of you know, the King is surrounded by a bunch of evil fuckers, many of them in the pay of the French, determined to distort his will and persuade him into ill-advised acts. Let me tell you, if these men had not persuaded the King otherwise, we would still be in France and preparing our march on Paris. Instead we were called back for want of funds. This isn't the King's fault. He's still a young lad and not used to the ways of the world. His good nature makes him open to the trickery and the lies of these traitors. I will name those men. I speak of the King's Treasurer and general-in-thief, John Fordham and his Chancellor, the Earl of Suffolk till recently Michael de la Pole. Further, I call upon the King to exile his false friend the sodomite Robert De Vere."

There was shock and murmuring in the hall. We were all Arundel or Gloucester's' men, but this was dangerous talk. At the same time we felt honored to be included in the conspiracies of great men.

Henry Bolingbroke spoke up, "I'm with you, My Lord. I'd give my blood to take down these treacherous bastards. I don't care how many of them there are or how tough they think are, we can take them. If we die in the doing, so much the better. Their captains and their men will die with us. Indeed, ten thousand souls shall keep us company in heaven sure that we have died in a Holy cause."

I thought it was very nice of him to offer our lives in his fight. In his mind we were no more than props to the bloody scene he had in mind. He would do all the dramatic killing, and we would die defending him. Like I say, it was nice to know that we were valued members of his fantasy.

The Bishop interrupting him, sensing that the room was not ready for such warlike talk.

"Patience, Henry," He cautioned. "I understand your feelings, but we must approach the matter calmly. How does my friend the Duke of Gloucester, the Lord Protector of the King during his minority view the situation?"

He turned to the Captains. It was time for him to play to audience.

"Everyone knows the Duke for his plain dealings and simple ways. Others will wear silk and gold, but not him. He wears a coat of simple English frieze, and he is best pleased with simple, rustic plainness. What do you, good Protector? What do you think of the King and his favorites?"

It was clear to me that we were being treated to a piece of high political theater. All the details and plans had been worked out before we had entered. These great lords were simply rehearsing their parts to demonstrate to their Captains that they had carefully considered an action on which they had already decided.

Plain Tom spoke up in his rustic Oxfordshire accent, "I salute your health, Brothers." He raised his goblet to everyone on the dais and Captains below. That got a cheer. Gloucester was always a favorite of the soldiers and, truth be told, he did have simple ways that were easy for a simple man to understand.

He continued, "I thank you from my heart. Your bravery and loyalty are a credit to the entire Kingdom. Now to answer your question Bishop, I swear before God that I don't rightly know what to think. These are dangerous times. I know you all are worried and discontented. But I urge you before God to hold back. King Richard loves us all. Believe me he's innocent of these black deeds and base conspiracies."

"You are too kind, My Lord," said Warwick. "We are all sick of these men around the King. We are afraid to lie down at night in case the King's dogs assault us."

Gloucester interrupted, "Enough my friend. Let me tell you that there is a sickness that pervades this Kingdom. King Richard is lulled and corrupted by these flattering sycophants. But he is not yet dead and may still be saved. If we bleed him a little, the sickness will be purged and he will heel."

"Then let's not waste any more time," said Mowbray. "De La Pole and Fordham are nothing but poisonous vipers to the King. You are the Protector, My Lord Gloucester, and only you have the authority to act to save the King from them. As we speak, the Commons murmur against the King. Treason is everywhere. Even the blind can see what is wrong. I must act."

Arundel took up the argument. He turned to Gloucester. "You are a prince of the royal blood. The people will follow you if you act."

Gloucester thought for a moment. "My friend, you are right. We must destroy these fuckers and tell King Richard that he abases himself by listening to them. But we must be careful. These bastards are powerful men and not easily taken. We need to make our approach gradually or we will scare them into action."

"If this is what you wish," said Arundel, "we will wait to hear what Parliament asks of the King. But while we wait, let us test the will of our Captains here tonight. What do you think lads? Do we, your lords and masters, reach too high, too quickly, or should we act now to protect the King from the nest of thieves, sodomites and flatters that have surrounded him?"

There were general shouts of "We are with you," and "Pull the bastards down." The men on the dais sat back comfortably, assured of their support. Then from the crowd My Lord Owain rose to speak.

"My Lords," he said, "I am Owain of Glyndyfrdwy, a captain in the service of the Earl of Arundel. I have risen to the top of his rolls through my actions in Scotland and Cadzand. I am a ready and willing servant to the Lord Protector. Yet I am concerned. I fear that when a man moves against a king he commits a terrible sin, for a king is a king no matter what we say and has been so favored by God. I am a Welshman, and my forefathers fought against the kings of England, but when we were beaten and our Princes were dead, we laid down our swords and took an oath to the crown of England. We dare not break that oath unless it is clear that the King has broken his."

"Master Glendowery is not only a solider but a lawyer, it seems," said De Grey scornfully. There was general laughter. The Bishop looked annoyed, but calmed himself and responded.

"Your loyalty and caution do you credit," said the Bishop. "For common men should not seek to follow the council of lords to act unless they know in their heart the way is true and the law is right. So let me speak and explain to you the law and precedent for our actions. Did not the King's own great-grandfather fall when he raised up his favorites over his right and proper lords? Did not Parliament and the Council come together as one and demand the King exile the hated Graveston or lose his throne? Did not all this lead to the tyranny of the great Mortimer and the execution of my own grandfather? I will not see this chaos come again. I will not see another King break his oaths and be led by his favorites into treason against his true people. I say the law and precedent are clear, and we must act before the King is further trapped by his favorites."

"But," Owain persisted, "in the case of Edward, second of the name, there was a clear heir, the King was in his majority, and he had repeatedly broke his oath. This King is barely of legal age, and his councilors are as yet unproven. We do not have proud Edward here, but a boy testing his strength and learning his ways. If your lordships oppose him now, it may create a sour feeling in him and when he comes to his majority, we may all come to suffer for our actions."

"Behold the disputatious Welshman," said the Bishop, "Ever was you race too in love with their words and too easily swayed by the sound of their own voices. Calm yourself, gentle Welshman. Your arguments have been heard. We do not aim to remove a King, but simply to use our power to save this King from his evil councilors. We only wish that he comes to manhood surrounded by the council of his good uncles and their friends."

Owain could see his argument was making no headway. "Then," he said, "I trust to my betters to know the way, for I am a simple solider and seek only the good of the King."

"Well said," said Arundel. "It is good that men should feel free to make such statements before their masters. It speaks well of your Christian charity and understanding, my dear brother," he nodded to the Bishop. Then, turning to the Captains he said, "You have all seen here tonight that we act only out of the gravest concerns to save the King. We have reviewed the case among ourselves, carefully considered the situation, and wish only the removal of the King's councilors, not the King. Make certain that your men hear this and all understand our intent, for lies and rumor may yet undo us."

He stared down at us to make sure his message was understood.

He continued, "Now we must leave you, but I urge you to continue at your table and enjoy your feast. I will call on you in the forthcoming days and indicate a place where all our forces shall assemble."

With that the worthies filed from the dais and left us to more ale and wine. As the Bishop drew next to Owain, he stopped and said in a voice that was barely audible to any of those around him:

"Master Glendowery, I urge you to proceed with the best care to your safety. Mischief is about, and who knows when steel may hit the unsuspecting? Avoid the day and be careful at night. We know not who our friends are yet and our foes have grown so mighty, so pray be careful."

Owain bowed slightly. "I have many friends in London, My Lord. I will stand against all dangers and watch for enemies, you may trust my word upon it."

The Bishop looked at him and nodded slowly. "We shall meet again I think, Master Glendowery" and with that he moved on.

We drank away the evening, but I noticed that Owain remained quiet. In the morning he kicked me awake.

"Come," he said, "let us go to Westminster and see if my father-in-law is there. I wish to hear his mind on the matters that were discussed last night."

We left the Bishop's Inn and made our way down the Strand to Westminster. Now at that time it was still common for the Parliament to meet in many places. However, increasingly it met at the Palace of Westminster in the great hall so better to accommodate the petitioners. Judge Hanmer had frequently been sent to Parliament from one shire or another along the border, and he was quickly found among the petitioners and knights assembled in the Great Hall.

He saw Owain and quickly fastened on to him. "My boy," he said, "I heard you were with Arundel and were come to London but feared I would not see you before I have to leave for Wales."

By this time, Judge Hanmer was a justice for all of the North of Wales and served upon the Great Commission for the Government of Wales. He was still endeavoring to push his mission of greater union between the peoples of England and Wales and the furtherance of good government within the March, but with as little success as ever.

Owain pulled him aside. "I would have a word with you in private," he said, "I heard matters discussed last night that are of great concern to me."

Judge Hanmer looked concerned and motioned us to follow him outside. There, Owain told him of what had transpired the night before at the Bishop's Inn.

"It is as the Lord Arundel says," said Judge Hanmer. "The Parliament is much displeased with the King. They have voted articles of impeachment against Fordham and De La Pole. If they thought they could get away with it, they would they would ask for De Vere's head as well."

"Has the King responded?" asked Owain.

"Very coldly," said Sir David. "He has denied the Parliament's impeachments and called for a deputation of forty knights to attend to him in his lodge at Eltham. His message was most tactless and rude. It did little to strengthen his friends' positions. He is still only nineteen, and the Protector can exercise his authority legally if he has the support of Council. The King acts as if he were the only power in the land and fully in his majority. I am trying to maneuver myself onto the deputation, for the King needs his friends. I feel that it would be better if at least some of those present were friendly towards the court."

Before we could continue, we heard a commotion and shouting in the Great Hall. Inside Mayor Exton was addressing the Parliament to great shouts and acclaims. He was guarded by a force of apprentices from the Drapers' Guild, all good strong men and well armed. It was a shock to see them in the precincts of the Palace, and it was a sign of how low the King's authority had fallen, for armed men were not normally allowed within its precincts.

"My Lords, Gentlemen of the Shires," he called out, "I have clear, undisputable evidence that the request for a deputation of forty knights to meet with his Majesty was not penned by the King, but by the traitor De La Pole. This very letter," he waved a piece of parchment, "bares the seal of De La Pole and orders his assassins to take the knights upon the road to Eltham after they have given up their arms to the King's Marshall. They shall then be murdered as a message to the Parliament that the King does not accede to your demands."

There was a great outcry. Judge Hanmer called out, "What manner of proof is this? How did you come by it and how can you vouch for it?"

"It was given to me by one of the men enlisted in the plot. His conscience got the better of him and, knowing that De La Pole is a false friend of the King, he sought me out. I have questioned this man in person and am sure of his honesty. Further, he has sworn a holy oath over the bones of Saint Sebbi at St. Paul's."

This impressed the crowd. However, Judge Hanmer was not to be put off. He continued, "I do not doubt the man's oath, but I do not understand what is to be gained by this. What would the killing of forty knights do other than to enrage the Parliament and pull the King's enemies even closer together? Is this man sure he is not the victim of some enemy of England that seeks to further weaken the King by spreading lies?"

That had them. It was a good point, for it was not clear what the King or de la Pole had to gain by this action. Then, just as Parliament's temper began to subside, the Protector himself entered the Great Hall.

"My Lords," he said, "I come straight from London where I have heard terrible news. The King has acted with willful rashness and reveals himself to be completely in the control of De La Pole and Fordham. This very day he has ignored all propriety and tradition and raised his friend, De Vere, to the Dukedom of Ireland. Further, he calls upon this Parliament to disband and for you all to return to your homes."

There was an explosion of anger. The Protector continued, "De Vere cannot hold such a title. Never has one so low been raised so high. The King grants him powers and revenues beyond even the greatest of the land. If he can do this, then he can take away any man's privilege and property. I see the hands of De La Pole and Fordham at work here. I call upon Parliament to charge me and my comrade, the Bishop of Ely, to attend the King. I will take my power, all my good Captains and those of the Lord Arundel and arrest the King's councilors, if you so direct."

There was general applause, and it was moved that Parliament should send Gloucester and Ely with their army rather than a mere forty knights.

Judge Hanmer pulled Owain aside, "Go back to your men. Make sure you are among the men Gloucester takes. Watch all that happens and report back to me. If they move directly against the King, you must act to protect him. Gloucester's and Ely's ambitions are bottomless. With Gaunt gone to Castile, nothing stands between him and the throne. Once the King is in his hands, it would be easy for some accident to befall him."

Owain nodded and we left quickly heading towards where Gloucester and Arundels' armies were camped to the north of London.

The next day the army moved off and crossed the river heading towards the Manor of Eltham. After a day, the army reached Eltham and readied themselves to make their powers known to the King. Arundel brought his captains in with him all armed and arrayed for war. Thus, my Master found the King's lodge in a most warlike state, and stood behind the Lords as they awaited the King. At the appointed hour, the King's Chamberlain walked to the front.

"Pay heed and show obedience to his Majesty King Richard, by Grace of God King of England and France and Lord of Ireland."

Then the King entered. He was very richly attired in fine French fashions and was surrounded by his body guard of Cheshiremen. The party bowed and he seated himself upon his throne.

"My Lords, why do you come to me in such force?" he asked.

Gloucester stepped forward. By God and the Virgin, he looked sure of himself. There sat the King, a thin, effeminate boy and opposite him the great man of battle Plain Tom, hero of all Englishman. He was a cocky bastard that day. He looked down from his great height upon the boy king.

"My Lord King, the magnates and lords and the whole Commons of your Parliament, with most humble submission, commend themselves to your royal dignity. We desire nothing but the triumph of your invincible honor against your enemies and the strongest bond of peace between you and your subjects."

Sweet Mary how the sarcasm dripped from his tongue. The King reddened knowing the bastard meant none of it. The Bishop of Ely could hardly control his grinning. They really thought they had the boy that day and they intended to enjoy every minute of it.

Gloucester continued. "We have come on behalf of Your Grace's subjects to remind you that under ancient law, which I am sure Your Grace cannot deny, that if the King should absent himself from Parliament for more than forty days, they are free to go home and may assume any request for a Royal subsidy to be annulled. Therefore, no man shall owe the King anything in subsidy or taxation. You have been absent from the Parliament for more than forty days and, as such, the Commons and the Lords wish to depart to return to their business."

He was a lying bastard of course. There was no such law or precedent. He was making it up as he went along. Furthermore, the last thing the Parliament wanted to do was leave before it had Fordham and De La Pole's blood, but Gloucester knew that Richard needed the money and he would get none of it if Parliament left.

I thought that Richard would back down. He seemed like such a small, weak thing. But Owain always said he was made of sterner stuff that revealed itself when he was pushed. Like a gambler who loses a run on dice and then goes all in, the King threw everything he had on the next roll.

In his nasal, midlands accent he said, "We have long been aware of our Parliament's treason and your concurrence with it, Uncle. We have absented ourselves because we feel that our heart is best with our French cousin."

There were shocked intakes of breadth around the room. He continued, "We have determined to seek his support and aid against our enemies. We judge that it is better to submit ourselves to him than to our own subjects."

Well fuck the Devil and all his friends, I remember thinking, there's something you don't hear every day. The King of England had just rolled back fifty years of war with France. In a few sentences he'd abandoned his title to the French throne, said he would invite the French into England and that he would take it up the arse from the King of France and submit to him if necessary. Considering that we had been fighting the French all summer and the Kingdom was in dread of French invasion, these were hardly politic or well considered words. I believe that this was the first time I began to doubt the King's sanity.

Gloucester rallied quickly. He was not going to let the boy get better of him. When he spoke, his voice was as cold as steel on a winter's day and all the flowery phrases had gone.

"That wouldn't be a sensible course. In fact, it would lead to your inevitable destruction."

I noticed there was no more "Your Grace" now it was just "you" and "your." He was letting the boy know who was in charge. Gloucester continued.

"The so-called King of France is your chief enemy and our greatest foe. If he ever sets foot in this Kingdom, he will work to undo you, usurp your kingdom, and kick you from the throne. I would ask you to remember how your grandfather, and my father, King Edward, sweated all his life to conquer France, which was his by right. I would also ask you to remember how the lords and nobles of the realm, the commons both of the kingdom of England and of France, and your allies have withstood the waste of war and fought with you for years. I would also add that the commons have poured out their wealth ungrudgingly to sustain this war. They have reduced themselves to poverty to keep our armies in the field and can neither pay their rents, nor maintain your household or provide for themselves the necessities of life."

More lies of course. Most people did very well out of the war.

"The wretched state of this kingdom has come about through your ministers' actions. They mismanaged your affairs and the affairs of the kingdom. They will continue to do so if they are left alone."

He let it sink in a minute and continued.

"So let me tell you one more thing on behalf of the Lords and the Commons. Let me remind you of old Queen Edward. Remember him? Your great-grandfather? Nice man they said, who had trunks full of pretty dresses and loved a nice tight arse." All the polite tone had gone now. It was Plain Tom who was speaking, not "My Lord Gloucester."

Plain Tom continued. "He was no good at listening to the Lords and Commons either. And guess what? Just when it was getting so that an Englishman could not hold his head up high, some clever lawyers found an ancient law. Do you know what it said? No? Well let me tell you. Apparently, it provides that if the king, having taken evil counsel as a willful, stubborn boy, should estrange himself from his people, and then it would be lawful to put down the king and raise another of the royal lineage in his place."

There, he had said it. If you don't do what we want, we will get rid of you and put one of your uncles on the throne. With Gaunt out of the country chasing the crown of Castile it was a good bet that Gloucester saw himself as the new King. He continued.

"So nephew, if you really want to stay on that comfortable throne, I recommend that you do as you are told, or there will be little I can do to save you from the anger of your own people."

He smirked at the King. He had him and the King knew it.

Richard looked around.

"Are you all of one will on this?" he said. "Elly? Arundel? You agree with this?" They said nothing. The King looked past them at the captains and knights who had come with them. He was desperately seeking one sympathetic face. He settled on my Master.

"You," said the King. Heads turned to look at Owain. "We know you. We remember you from our Coronation and our campaign in Scotland. You are a Welshman."

I'll say this for old Queen Dick; he had a bloody good memory. He just had to meet you once, and he remembered you forever. I'd normally say it's a good quality for a man to have, but it eventually was the downfall of Queen Dick. He never could forget a slight or insult.

"Owain of Glyndyfrdwy, Your Grace," said Owain.

"That's right," said the King, nodding, "You are Our tenant-in-chief. You hold your lands directly from Us. You have nothing to gain from associating with these men. Surely you do not agree with them?"

Arundel, Ely and Gloucester turned full on Owain. God's witness but I could feel the hate pouring out of Ely.

Owain spoke cautiously. "I am a loyal subject of Your Grace and would defend you to the death. But I am also a man of law and in this Kingdom; a King must be guided by his council and the Parliament. Thus, I must say that a King, especially one who has not reached his majority, is well advised to lean on the wisdom of older men, especially those from within his own family. I believe that Your Grace may risk civil war and internal strife if you persist in the course. This is not good for anyone. I agree with the Duke of Gloucester that an invitation to the so-called King of France would be disastrous. The French have been desperate for a foothold in this country for many years. Once they get it, they will never go home."

"So you take their part," said the King.

"Not so Your Grace," said Owain. "I simply beg Your Grace to consider the views of the lords and commons and act not out of threat but to preserve civil peace. Dismiss your friends, do nothing more. They will not be harmed. Let your uncles see to affairs until you reach your majority. Then with good heart they can relinquish their position. Let us have peace and all will be well."

"You may be right, Master Owain. Civil peace and patience may rule the day, and I believe I have much to learn from my uncles," he said.

He turned to Gloucester, "Very well, My Lord, you shall have Our friends, but they shall go unharmed and with pensions. We accept your guidance, but We ask that no more radical moves be made until my good uncle the Duke of Lancaster returns. He is the most senior of you and We would listen to him before We make further changes. We will write to him and ask his for council."

It was a good move. Letting Gaunt know that Gloucester had made a power grab would undoubtedly annoy Gaunt, and if he wasn't having any luck becoming King of Castile he would be back on the next boat.

The King extended his hand and Gloucester bent to kiss it.

Gloucester looked at the King. "I am pleased Your Grace has seen reason. The Bishop has the instruments of impeachment. I would ask that you sign them now and return with us to Westminster where we can explain this happy state of affairs to the Parliament and Council"

So back we went to Westminster, now all loyal servants of the reformed King. But it was clear that Gloucester's faction had no intention of keeping their end of the bargain. No sooner had they returned to London than they kicked out most of the King's friends. In place of his friends, Richard had to tolerate Ely as his Chancellor and all of Gloucester's men were put in high places. They put De La Pole and Fordham on trial, but the charges were so badly constructed that they got out of the worst of it and were packed off to imprisonment at Windsor rather than death. The King made a fool of the sentence by giving them the run of the castle and keeping Christmas with them there. He even went as far as to remit to them what they had lost in their sentences. After that we knew it was going to be long battle.

I remember Owain saying to me, "This will be the death of us all, Gwyn. Before the years out we'll be lucky if any of us keeps his life or his lands." He was always good at predictions was Owain. I never really understood why he needed Crach.

OUR TRAVELS WITH KING RICHARD

Owain was right. The King did not suffer his strictures well. In addition to the new ministers, he was saddled with a Commission of Government. Fourteen men, all of them part of Gloucester and Arundel's faction, were charged with exceptional powers to set the government of the realm to rights. Oh yes, they had royally fucked him up the arse. They didn't just have power to run the government, but they also controlled all the Royal jewels and goods. They were empowered to enter his palaces and bedchambers whenever they wanted, no doubt hoping to catch him and De Vere at it.

But there was a catch. The Parliament had only granted them these powers for twelve months. After that the King would come into his majority and they would disperse. For the Commission, it was twelve months in which they could try to tie Richard in so many knots that he would never escape them, or push him to some rash action that would force the Parliament to remove him from the throne. For Richard it was twelve months to cool his heels and wait. He knew that if he did nothing at the end of that year, the Commission would be gone and he could begin to take his revenge.

The Commission put its men in place to watch Richard. As one of Arundel's trusted commanders, Owain found himself one of Richard's minders. So for the better part of that year, we traveled up and down the breadth of the country with Richard while the King tried to find some peace from his persecutors and gather his forces for the inevitable battle we all knew must eventually come.

Richard left Westminster as soon as he could and moved off to tour his Kingdom. It was an awful gyration he took us on. We left just after Candlemass, around the Feast of Saint Agatha. The whole court moved with us. First we went up to Leicestershire then on to Nottingham. From there we were on our way to Lincoln and then back around the Midlands, then up into Cheshire and then down the English side of the March.

Owain was able to get away for a few days and visit Marged. It was enough time for her to get with child again. It was uncanny. They ended up with ten children in all, and most of them survived infancy. It was quite an achievement when you consider that Owain was basically never home for the first ten years of their marriage.

Richard was the opposite. Though he had two wives and seemed to love the first one very much, there were no children. Was he a sodomite? I have no firm knowledge of the fact, but I tend to think so. In general he was a most peculiar man and an odd end for the Plantagenet line. Many men have asked what he was like. I spent a fair amount of time in his company, and I formed quite clear knowledge of him. In fact so well versed was I in his habits and appearance that many years later, I was asked to determine the identity of the "false" Richard at the Scottish court.

The Richard that I remember was a tall, thin young man with long, rolling hair and a light beard and mustache. What really struck me about him was his face. He was one of the most beautiful men I have ever seen. I use these words well. I have rarely seen a man with any beauty at all, but Richard was indeed beautiful. His eyes were big and blue and seemed to swallow you up. His skin was as pure as a boy's and never showed the cares of aging. His mouth was full and thick, his nose was long and well formed, and the bones of his cheeks high and well pronounced. His face was long and angular.

The overall impression was very feminine. He strode that line between male and female that some men will walk when they are young. But for Richard, it never changed. In his whole lifetime he retained a strange, intermediate look that at one point made you see him as devotedly male or unmistakably female. At his whim he could move between those genders and present himself equally seductive to both men and women. This was his mystery. He was capable of being whatever you wanted him to be. To the ladies of court, whom he loved and kept with him always, he could be alternatively their sister playing with their paints and silks or an innocent, hurt boy requiring their love. To the Great Lords, he could be the young lion determined to avenge himself against the French, or the wise young King, cautious and ready to take council. To scholars, he was the perfect new monarch full of the newest ideas from Italy and France. To his men, he could be plain 'Dickin,' a simple man with simple tastes determined to share their struggles.

Whoever you were, he would go to great lengths to win you over and bring you into his world. Once there, he would fix on you as if you were the only person in the room. As long as you returned his affection he was fine with you. If you gave any hint you were moving away from him, he would fly into uncontrollable rages or crying fits, alternately begging you to stay or demanding that you leave. It produced quite an impression.

However, despite all of this drama, once Richard left your presence you could not but help being struck by the impression that you had dealt with something vague and insubstantial. His beauty and attraction stayed in your mind, but you had no sense that you had been in the presence of someone whose identity was solid. He only seemed to come into himself in times of crisis or great problem which demanded that he act. In time I came to suspect that he engineered these dramas to draw attention to himself. In these situations, he would display emotion beyond all reason. He would be either at the height of pleasure or the deepest well of pain. He was always very sensitive to criticism, but during one of his crisis he perceived threats from every direction and believed the whole world was his enemy. At the same time any friendship he had would be exaggerated. Make a friend of the King and he assumed an intimacy beyond any reason. A simple letter from the King of France could convince him that the two of them were born brothers, while the harsh words of the Arundels and Gloucester made them enemies for life.

All of these things made him poorly suited to be King of England. The English people expected their kings to be rough, tough-hewn warriors who cared little for the finer things of life. They expected the King to be firm and unchanging in his relationships and ill-disposed to any foreigner. Further, kings were generally distant from their people. They ruled through their great lords and allowed them to mediate the relations between the people and their ruler. To the average ploughman, the King was little different from God. He was a divine being who dwelled outside the normal world. If he was ever seen, he was surrounded by great men and rarely bothered to deal with his subjects directly, unless it was to lead them in war.

Richard was the opposite. He was soft spoken and loved the luxury and beauty of the court. He despised war and longed for a peace where the people of England would put down the tools of war and devote themselves to worshiping him. He was as changeable as a young girl or the summer breeze and loved drama. He wished to simultaneously draw close to his people and distance himself further from them. Thus he was at once their god and their friend. As all men will tell you, a man may be a leader and a god or a friend but he cannot be both. What is expected in a god will never be tolerated in King and what expected in a friend will serve only to undermine the godhood of a leader.

At the beginning of his reign, few knew him and assumed this would change. However, as his reign continued, more became aware of his strangeness and his inability to meet their needs as a king. Over time I formed the impression that Richard was at least two people.

First and foremost of these two identities was 'Queen Dick.' Queen Dick loved the ways of court, a womanish sod that spent his days adorned in finery and perfumes. He delighted in the ways of women and loved nothing better than to engage in arse play with his bum boys. The other Richard was "Dicken," the rough lad with a scheming mind and powerful constitution. He was the King beloved of his archers. They would follow him to hell and back. He spoke to them as he spoke to friends. He was a simple, ordinary man hell bent on retaining his rights and looking after his people. I think that 'Dicken' and 'Queen Dick' were forever at war in the King's mind. He could never on decide who he was or what he wanted to be. Therefore, he became exactly what you wanted him to be.

What I remember most clearly of the time after the Wondrous Parliament was the constant traveling. They do say that Kings must constantly go on these travels. "Progresses" they call them. Myself, I think they are bloody stupid. If the Kings of Wales were as rich as the King of England they wouldn't be constantly traveling. They would stay in their fine palaces and call all their high-men to come to them. Of course, Kings travel the country to show themselves off to their subjects and to saddle their high-men with the cost of keeping them. This weakens the rich and powerful. They are forced to spend small fortunes to entertain the King for a few days, which saves the King money that would be spent on keeping his own household. Clever buggers are English Kings.

Before long it became evident the young King had more on his mind than a normal progress. He did not accept his defeat by Gloucester and the Arundels, and he was testing his power. Everywhere he went he would hire more men who were ready to wear his livery and join his cause. It was an easy job as long as he stayed outside the lands of the magnates. I remember that Arundel caught a few of the King's agents in East Anglia and hanged them for doing their duty.

Once we got to Cheshire there were no restrictions on the King. Cheshire is a royal county; the King's earldom, his own principality. Inside Cheshire he could do whatever he wanted. He was lavish with money, handed out titles and jobs and did everything to make the people love him. Secretly, he had his agents collect men, mainly archers, because Cheshire is known for its bowmen. He also sent his agents into Wales and the March to pull out our warriors. Of course he had to talk to Owain if he was to raise any men from Powys.

The King came calling when we were riding as escort to the Queen's carriage. It was surprising to see a soft man ride like the Devil himself. That day he presented himself in his guise as a man of the people. No gold or silver, just his simple red and white livery and a solid English woolen cloak. He could be mistaken for some local lord on his way to a country fair or to hear court at some distant assize. He spotted Owain in the crowd of guards and signaled to him.

"Master Glendowery," called out the King, "I trust you enjoy our travels."
"Your Grace," said Owain bowing. "It is an honor to travel with you. I had thought never to see so much of this Kingdom."

"Indeed," said the King. "It is a great and varied place. I love the western part of Our domains. It is so unlike the rotting plentitude of the South. There is something obscene in the easy life of the Southern men. Give Us the hard rocky places and the thick forests of the west. Like your homeland, Master Glendowery, the West is a land that is older and more mysterious than ever was the rest of England."

"Your Grace speaks the truth," said Owain. "This is the place where the original Britons made their stand against the Saxons. This is where true Britain begins."

The King laughed, "The English and Saxons were an ill-bread lot. They were, and are, a crude inferior people. Not like ourselves. Are we not both inheritors of the Empire of the Romans? You Sir are the decedent of the Britons through whom the Romans ruled this land. We and Our House are decedents of Rome. It has been shown that the Plantagenets descend directly from Charles the Great, who is known to be the last true Emperor of the West. He in turn was assured that his lineage could be traced back to the great Caesar and before him to Alexander. The Pope blessed my ancestor the Great Conqueror to come to this land from Normandy and restore it to true civilization and the embrace of Rome.

"When we came, we easily rolled over the English but drew back when faced with the might of the Kings of Wales. We recognized our kinship with these fine fellows and determined that our battle would be long before we could judge them to be part of our Empire."

This was of course complete nonsense. The Plantagenets line could be traced back to the time of the Northmen. Back then the Plantagenets they were petty Franks who stole the Duchy of Anjou from the local Gaels and gained their loyalty by keeping the Norse out. When the Norse moved into Normandy, they intermarried with the French, and eventually banished the Dukes of Normandy and took their places. From there it was only a few well-placed marriages, the occasional war or two, and some broken treaties before they were Kings of England and pretenders to the throne of France.

How unlike my own Lord's genealogy, for it is well known that My Lord Owain could trace his ancestors back to Brutus of the Trojans who settled in this land after the great siege of Troy, and before him to Noah and the people of the flood. Still, Kings should be forgiven their illusions, shouldn't they? After all, they are poor fragile creatures not often given to proper thought.

"It was unfortunate that our people could not find some way of living together," said Owain, "and that war between our peoples became our way."

The King nodded. "It is unfortunate," he said. "We have often thought that Our great-great grandfather made a mistake when he spent so much time and effort on his Welsh wars. If it was Us, I would have been happy with homage. We have no taste for war for war's sake. We see too many good men dead. We would rather that Our subjects devote themselves to the industries of peace. If We had been my great-great grandfather, We would not have spent Our energies on the Welsh. Rather We would have joined with Prince Llewellyn and burnt out those bastard fiefs along the March." He said this with considerable venom. "Those lands are neither England nor Wales. They are a world unto themselves and a home to all manner of outlawry and evil. The lords who hold them act as if they are kings themselves and dare to challenge my own rights in Our Kingdom. We hate those proud lords and would see them brought low."

"It is a pity you were not King then, Your Grace," said Owain. "Were my people still Kings of Powys, they would have joined you."

The King smiled. "Perhaps those days will come again. There can be no retreat from my great-great grandfather's conquests, but if We had our full power We would end these silly limitations against Welshmen. We see no reason why a Welshman should not be able to rise as high as any in Our service or own land in his own country. We would build a core of loyal men around us in the West who are not restrained by the petty laws that the Parliament and the Lords of the March insist upon. Further, We would end the rule of the Marcher lords. When We have reached Our majority, We intend to do away with the Marcher holdings. We will take them into Our Kingdom proper and give them to those that have shown their loyalty to Us. Men such as yourself could rise high and regain your full title to the Dyffryn Clwyd and full title to Powys."

How clever was this King. He was bribing and seducing. He knew it was not enough to throw out the possibility of high office and new lands. To attract Owain, he knew he must show he knew the Welsh and our ways. He offered him the De Grey holding of Ruthin and cleverly referred to it by its Welsh name.

"Your Grace would have to deal with the Charltons and the Greys if you were to wrestle that land back Welsh rulers," said Owain.

"The Greys are in the pocket of Our uncle the Duke of Lancaster," said the King, "and the Charltons are nothing. They try to walk the line between the factions at court. They do not realize that the time for straddling loyalties is coming to an end. They must choose Us or the Appellants."

It was the first time I had heard the King use the name "Appellants" The King's opponents were becoming known as the "Lords Appellants" after their so-called "appeals" to the King to be reasonable in his selection of favorites and friends.

"It would be difficult for me to choose," said Owain, "since I am a loyal subject of both Your Grace and sworn man to the Lord Arundel."

The King looked at Owain oddly. "Master Glendowery, We do not know whether We are in the presence of the last truly honest man in my realm or a devilish conspirator."

"I would hope I am honest and true," said Owain.

"We shall see," said the King. "We would have you attend to Us when We come into our lands in Cheshire and hunt in the forest of Maccelsfield. Until then Master Glendowery."

The King turned around and faced his retinue:

"Come Lads, we will make Chester by nightfall," said the King to his escort, and with that he was gone.

Owain turned to me. "God's Bones, what am I to make of that?" he asked.

"I do not know," I replied. "I have no head for great politics and conspiracy." I was young and had yet to see that the ways of the world require all men who would serve their Lord to listen for conspiracy at every point.

"I will ask Crach to caste the bones to determine the proper way," said Owain. "Only the spirits can reveal the path forward."

There he was again, always with the spirits and the signs. The older Owain got, the more he came under the thrall of Crash and his prophecies. We dragged Crach around everywhere with us. Even as a young man, I remember Owain consulting Crach on business deals, the possible price of wool or cattle next season or the correct moves with his patron. He believed everything Crach said. I myself was never sure as to Crach's abilities. There was no denying he could have genuine prophetic flashes and was a true wizard, but he couldn't control as much as he pretended to. Many times when Owain consulted him, I could see that Crach had no idea what was about to happen and was making it up as he went along. Sometimes I would catch his eye over Owain's shoulder and he would wink at me. He was an awful old rogue and a man of genuine power and talent at the same time.

And so on we went to the town of Chester. We were no strangers to the place, for there is not a man of business or war in North Wales who does not visit Chester at one time or another. It is a fine old Roman town that still shows their mark. In our time it was a wild place where all manner of rogues and cutthroats could be hired. It became apparent that the King's purpose was to recruit such men into his retinue. During the Scottish Campaign the King had come to realize that while he remained dependent on the Great Magnates to provide him with men and arms, they would be able to use their revenues to recruit their own forces and provision them full time. Thus, Lancaster and Arundel turned up at Berwick with their own private armies, while the King turned up with a merged bodyguard provided from the Earl Marshall's men. Seeing this he determined to have his own men who would wear his livery and be completely loyal to him. Cheshire was a near principality within the Kingdom of England in much the same way as Lancaster and Durham were. However, unlike these other places, the King was master in Cheshire. So, like Johnny Gaunt in Lancaster and the Bishop in Durham, the King was unimpaired in his authority in Cheshire.

Now it is well known that all Cheshiremen are thugs and murderers, so it was to Cheshire that the King came to recruit his army for forthcoming battle with the Appellants.

It was at that time that we met our old friend Master Dodd. We were lounging in a tavern near the King's residence when who should walk in but our old friend.

"Davy" shouted Owain. "Davy Dodd. As I live and breathe, I thought you had followed Johnny Gaunt off to Castile."

Davy saw us and came over with a great infusion of emotion.

"By God's Bones," he said, "I never dreamed I would be pleased to see a Welshman. What brings you old thieves to Chester?"

"We have been in the service of the Lord Arundel," said Owain. "I married and inherited a broken down, old wooden castle. The remorseless demands of my wife to make it livable led me to enter service."

Davy laughed. "Women are ever the cause of work. If the world were left to men we would stay drunk and happy all of our days."

Owain continued, "Lord Arundel has detached a portion of his men to guard the King on his progress, although I fear we are more jailers than guards."
Davy nodded, "I know of the King's troubles. I was always loyal to his father, so when I heard he wished to establish his own retinue to stand up to the Arundel's faction, I retrieved my bow and came to join him."

Owain set down his tankard. "This is a bad business," he said solemnly. "I have taken oaths to both the King and the Lord Arundel. I have no wish to choose between them. No land ever benefits from civil war, and I fear we are moving down that path."

"It may be so;" agreed Dodd, "but a man must obey his Lord. I am a Cheshire man and thus sworn to the King. I have no option but to defend his rights. Double sworn men such as yourself are in a difficult position. If I were you, I would find an excuse to return to your estates and wait for these great men to resolve their quarrel."

Owain nodded. "I would if I were not an ambitious man. I have great hopes that I may rise in the service of either the King or the Lord Arundel. The King speaks of removing the barriers against Welshmen and allowing us full place in our own lands, and the Lord Arundel is the power in my corner of the world. If a man is to acquire any more for his family, he is forced into these combats."

"Then you may have to pay the price of ambition," said Davy. "You risk it all while humbler men, such as myself, are content for smaller things. We know the best things come from only doing well what we were born to do."

He was right. Men such as Davy and myself had no option but to do what we were told. I wished nothing for myself other than that I might serve my lord and finally manage a small living that would enable me to take a wife and raise a batch of children. Owain aimed high and risked everything. He was always ambitious and was a man of great abilities. It was his ill luck that as a Welshman he had a no outlet for those ambitions and was forced into the games of the English if he were to advance in any way.

We spent the night drinking with Dodd. We told old stories and rehashed old fights. Late into the night, after drinking much ale, he shared with us a dangerous story.

"Let me tell you about Katherine Swynford," said Dodd. "You remember when the King got delayed on his way up to Scotland? And there was a problem at Beverly? Well, here's the story as I know it"

So he started to tell us the story about Katherine Swynford and how she caused Princess Joan's death. Now let me give you a little background so you will better understand. Johnny Gaunt's first wife was Blanche of Lancaster. Nice girl by all accounts and, if truth be told, the origin of the Lancastrian title as her father was the original Duke of Lancaster, and Johnny Gaunt got the title through her. She had a bunch of children with Black Johnny. One of them was Elizabeth, a nice girl without much to commend her apart from a habit of outliving her husbands. Her second husband was John Holland. He was a son of Princess Joan by her first marriage; that is, she married her aunt's son.

Now, Katherine, who was one of Blanche's ladies, fucking hated John Holland. He stood for everything she disliked. He was close to the old court that existed before she came along, and she knew all those old fuckers with old names who hated her. She also knew that John was especially close to the Princess, his mum, and that if some misfortune happened to him, his mother would be devastated. So she came up with a plan to set the court at each other.

Davy went on, "Now then, I'm working in the Wardrobe when I hear that Katherine had decided that it would be in her interest if Queen Anne got into a little trouble. Anne would then be in need of friends, and Katherine could befriend her and get nearer Richard. Now truth be told, King Richard was as likely to fuck Queen Anne as a duck is to dance on the sun, so her plan involved making sure that Anne's womanly needs were met by a lover she could control. She had been raised a few times by young Thomas Stafford. He was the son of the Earl of Stafford who had been a good mate of Johnny Gaunt. So she gets the idea to put him in the way of Anne and getting the two merry."

He took a pull on his ale, wiped his mouth with his sleeves and continued.

"Then when Katherine knows they are in love and willing to do anything to stay together, she drops a word in John Holland's ear, "Do you know that Tom Stafford is fucking the Queen and cuckolding the King?" Gave him proof and everything. He goes off full tilt and gathers together some of his boys to rough up Tom Stafford on his way up North. Unfortunately, things turned bad. It turns out that Tom Stafford is handier with a sword that Holland thought, and one of Holland's top thugs gets killed. Things might have got hushed up, but the King arrived just at that moment on his way up to Scotland. So now he has to make a decision.

"Tom Stafford is clearly the guilty party, but the Queen frantically begged the King to let him off. 'Do not take my Tom away. He's such a great knight. I need him to protect me,' she pleaded with the King. Richard listened and agreed. He thinks, maybe its Johnny Holland's fault because he started it. When Joan hears this, she wailed, "Oh please don't take away my little Johnny. He's your half brother.'

"On and on they go for days. Eventually it gets so bad that Richard can't stand either of them. Now he knows that Tommy is fucking his old lady and is quite happy about it; after all, it means he can avoid having to perform and allows him to focus on buggering De Vere. So Richard decides to favor Tom Stafford, and he condemns Holland to death. Joan can't believe it and goes crazy with grief. She's screaming and carrying on like Judgment Day's arriving and Christ's knocking at the front gate. Anyway, she gets more and more worked up and begs Richard for four days straight. He can't stand it any longer. He's got an army in the Scott's Marches that costs a fortune every day it lies idle, and anyway, he's anxious to get back to a little cock play with De Vere. So he tells her to bugger off and he'll think about it. Off he goes to Berwick-on-Tweed, and she goes to Wallingford.

"Now while he's up in Scotland, Katherine Swynford comes to see Joan. She's sympathetic, saying, 'So sorry to hear about your troubles, it must be so hard.' Well, Joan sees right through her and calls her a whore and a strumpet and one or two words you wouldn't believe a great lady would know. Katherine tells her to go fuck herself and that she is the only person who can save her darling son is her, on account of her friendship with the Queen. She says all Joan has to do is to persuade Richard to make her children legitimate, and she will make sure Johnny Holland gets off with a couple of years in exile. Well Joan swore and cursed a blue streak; I thought her head would explode. Anyway, I suppose it did 'cause suddenly she goes all quiet. Then she starts to wobble and I sees her one eye go red and blood drip out. Then see falls of the floor. I rushed over and don't you know, she was dead as a door mouse."

Dodd looked around to make sure we were not being overheard.

"Katherine sees this isn't a good place to be, so she tells me that if I mention she was here she would have my balls. Now I know that a smart man doesn't fall afoul of a woman like Katherine, so I nod and make sure that all the servants agree they saw nothing. Off she goes and heads back to London. When Richard gets back to Westminster, he finds out his Mother's dead. 'Course he knows nothing about Katherine's visit and assumes it's his fault. He's broken hearted and commutes Holland's sentence to going on pilgrimage. Now Holland's out of the picture, so Katherine decides to turn her attention back to Anne. After all she's got something out of it. Anne loves her and thinks that she's saved her lover. So she spends her time smiling and making nice and waits for the next opportunity to arise."

There was silence between us.

"This is all true?" asked Owain.

"I swear it on my mother's grave," said Will.

"So is Katherine for or against Richard?" I asked.

"She's neither for nor against Richard. She's for herself and anyone who will help her advance her and her bloody kids. All I can say is to keep an eye on her. She will fuck you over the first chance she gets. So be careful. That's all I'm saying."

I cannot vouch for this story. I simply relate to you what was said to us that night. All I ask is for readers to consider how quickly Katherine rose and how strange it is that all her enemies died along the way.

I will continue with my story.

Once the King had signed sufficient indentures to start building his army, he set off for his forest at Maccelsfield to hunt. Maccelsfield was in that part of Cheshire where the land becomes hard and heavily wooded. It begins to rise up towards the great mountains that divide the North of England in half, where little can grow successfully. Princess Joan held lands there, and the King had spent many years there as a boy. As a result he had developed a special favor for the place and liked to return there whenever he felt pressured.

We followed him on many days and served him during the hunt. Crach was particularly interested in the greenwood. He always had a love of forests and would come out into the open whenever we stayed among them. I recall that one day we were at camp and Crach was casting bones when the King came upon us.

As before, the King was affecting the dress and manners of a rough northern lord and showed none of his fancy southern ways. He arrived with a group of his new Cheshire men, all archers, and arrayed in the red and white of his livery. One look and you could see that these were hard men used to the ways of war and willing to enter the fight at the word of the sovereign. He dismounted and made straight upon our fire.

"Master Glendowery, why are you and your men not with Us in the hunt?" he asked as he warmed his hands.

"Your Grace," said Owain, "I was awaiting your call. We stayed back not wanting to ruin your sport."

"You must never wait on Our call," said the King, "We are a straightforward man. If any man wishes to speak to Us, all he must do is walk up and state his business. We have no time for the Frenchified ways of court when We are with Our people. While We are at court, We must follow these customs. Once outside We are free to be Ourself and act as We wish."

He was very good at playing this role. You could almost believe he was the plain, common man he pretended to be.

"I will remember that, Your Grace," said Owain.

"We see that you still wear the livery of the Earl Arundel," said the King indicating our blue and yellow badges.

"I am sworn to him," said Owain. "I signed indenture to his Lordship for two years and am bound to serve and wear his livery."

"It is a shame," said the King slowly. "We had hoped that you would have taken to heart our conversation on the road and signed to wear the red and white while We rested at Chester," referring to his colors. "Our sworn followers take the badge of the white hart," he said. He turned and looked at the forest around us.

"We love this place," said the King. "We come here when We wish to return to the soul of our Kingdom." He looked around our camp and settled on Crach.

"Who is this man?" said the King.

"This is my prophet and cunning man, your Grace," replied Owain.

"A prophet?" said the King. "We have heard of these men. We know that Wales is full of seers and magicians." He turned to Crach, "You are a wizard, are you?"

Crach bowed, "Indeed, Your Grace, I have been called that. However, I am a simple man who knows little of the wisdom of my ancestors and provides advice to My Lord when he asks."

The King smiled, "What are you known as?" he asked.

"I am called Crach of the Fountain," he said, "although I have been known by other names in times past."

"Ah," said the King, "a man of mystery and multiple identities. All the best magicians and conjurors need to encourage doubts about their identity." He stopped and thought for a moment, "Are you skilled in the interpretation of dreams?"

"I have some talent in this area," said Crach, "although I leave it to the Holy Fathers to truly understand all knowledge that God reveals to us in our sleep." Crach was being cagey here. He had no faith in the Holy Fathers and was simply hoping to avoid any direct accusation of witchcraft.

The King waved aside his demurs, "Quite," he said agreeably, "We wish you to tell Us what a dream We have had means."

"I will do my best," said Crach, "but I am unfamiliar with the intricacies and wonderments of a King's dreams."

The King smiled, "You are quite the courtier, Master Crach. We appreciate your delicacy on this matter. However, tell Us your thoughts on this dream. The first night We came to this place We dreamed that We saw my mother walking with a white hart. All of England seemed to follow the hart, both the living and the dead, for We could see father in his great armor walking among the crowd. Then a group of huntsmen came forth and beat the stag back. The people cried out in horror but could not move to help. The huntsmen caged the stag, but one was killed in the fight. Then a wizard appeared and brought him back to life, and now the huntsman was unable to hurt any animal and grew horns. He ran into the woods and became as a hunted beast himself. When the other huntsmen saw this they set the stag free and bowed down to it. Then the people came forth to honor the stag as their King."

"A strange dream, Your Grace," said Crach.

"What does it mean?" asked the King. Crach bent down and waved his hands over the fire. Suddenly, he snapped his head backwards, let his eyes roll back into his head, and then snapped his head forward again to look at the King.

The Cheshire archers with the King laughed. "Quiet!" said the King and stared at them sternly. Crach began to speak.

"You are the hart. The great stag of the realm. The huntsmen are the great lords of this land. They seek to bind you and limit your powers. However, they lack the power of a true king. One will fall in the fight that is to come and when the others see this they will be frightened and end their fruitless opposition. The wizard is the spirit of reconciliation. He will rise from a fallen house, and your enemies will become your friends. Afterwards they will no longer be a threat to your Grace, and they will harm no one in your dominions. Then all the people of your lands will turn to you and recognize you as a great and powerful King."

The King broke into a broad grin. "That is exactly as We saw it. We know that all We must do is stand up to these proud Lords and they will collapse." He turned to Owain.

"Do you not see, Master Glendowery? We must pull down their powers and see them reborn as useless, merely decorative bodies. What think you, Master Glendowery, should a King rule or be the plaything of rich and arrogant men?"

"He should rule, Your Grace," Owain said. "There is no other way for a king to be. I know of no argument whereby a king should not be the active governor of his realm. To argue otherwise is madness."

"You are then of Our party, so why do you wear the badge of Arundel?" said Richard.

"I am of both yours and Lord Arundel's parties," said Owain. "I do not see the contradiction in serving you both. The Lord Arundel is a loyal retainer and seeks only to expand your Grace's glory."

"You are an innocent," said the King, "Arundel and Gloucester pray daily for my downfall. Gaunt would be with them too if he had not gone to France to steal the crown of Castile." He thought for a moment and turned to Crach.

"Perhaps Gaunt will be the fallen huntsman, and We will have all his lands?"

"It is possible, Your Grace," said Crach. "It is often difficult to understand the exact interpretation of dreams. I would always counsel caution."

The King waved Crach away, "The time for caution is gone. We have played the fool long enough. We have abased Ourself. We have lulled Our enemies to sleep. They think We are nothing but a base, womanish sodomite. But We have fooled them all. Now is the time to act."

I recall thinking he had done a bloody good job playing the sodomite. It must have been all that cocksucking he did.

He looked at Owain, "The time is coming to decide, Master Glendowery," he said. "We will call on you and your tribe when We have need and hope you will see the justice of Our cause."

He turned to one of his men. "Pay this man for is prophecy. He has settled Our mind upon a course of action We were previously undecided upon." He spoke to the greenwood as if informing his whole kingdom of his decision. "Tomorrow We will leave for Shrewsbury. We will call a great convocation of jurists upon a matter that has been on Our mind, and We will solve all problems that challenge our House."

He mounted and left our camp with immodest haste. His man flipped a silver penny to Crach, who caught it in the air and bit it quickly to determine its true value.

Owain turned to Crach, "Was his dream truly what you saw?" he asked.

"As truly as a man can see," said Crach, "The King will fight a battle, and a great lord will die."

Owain nodded, "If is to be so, then it will be so. These are dark times we live in." He walked away and began to arrange his belongings for the return to the King's lodge.

"Was it really so?" I said to Crach.

Crach winked at me. "The first rule of prophecy as applies to Kings and foreigners is to tell them exactly what they want to hear. Any fool could see the King has remembered and manipulated his dream in such a way that it pointed to fulfilling his will. I would have been mad to offer any other interpretation."

I shook my head. "There may be war as a result of your tricks," I said.

"There will be war whatever any of us do," said Crach, "but not for now. This King is weak and will come to a bad end. All that happens in the next few months matters nothing to the final outcome. I have said that the war will come. I prophesied such years ago when I met the Lord Owain. When it comes, it will plunge all these lands into more than a hundred years of war, and when it is over My Lord's decedents will sit upon Richard's throne."

"You grow madder every year," I said.

He nodded, "That is true. Do they not say 'the older the Welsh, the madder the Welsh?" he said. "But in my madness, there is truth," and he cackled as if he had made a great joke.

Looking back I see he was only partly right, for war was to come, but I do not see how My Lord's sons will ever sit upon the throne of England.

THE "MERCILESS PARLIAMENT"

The King was as good as his word and called a great convocation of all the judges in Shrewsbury. As was to be expected, Judge Hanmer was one of those men. At that time he had reached the height of his powers and was retained by half the great lords of England to aid them in their legal business, among them the King, the Charltons of Powys and the L'Estranges of Knockin. He was also paid a regular fee by Johnny Gaunt and the Earl of Stafford. Furthermore, even the Earl of the March and the Lord Arundel appointed him as a member of their council and called upon him to register legal opinion. Thus he was one of the few men in the realm who was trusted and whose expertise was counted on.

Owain met with Hanmer at an Inn in Shrewsbury. It was clear that he was not long for this world. He was an old man, and the years had been hard upon him. It seemed as if all his judgments and knowledge had weighed down on him and shortened his years.

At Shrewsbury the King called on all of his cronies and bum boys to attend on him. They were all there, the Archbishop of York, the King's lover Bobby De Vere, now Duke of Ireland, Mickey De La Pole, and the King's dog Bob Tresilian. I recall the great celebration when they all met there. The King had ensconced himself in the castle, feeling very much among friends. But like the fool he was, he made no effort to hide his will. I stood in the great hall with Owain and watched him come in.

Trumpets sounded and Richard and his bum boys entered the chamber. Richard was transformed into Queen Dick in gold and satin. He turned to his friends.

"My loves, De Vere, De Le Pole, and my dear Tresilian, embrace Us and Our friends." He indicated the youths who had entered the room with him. "These youths are a joy to my tender years and their beauty graces Our throne." He smiled as the gentlemen bowed. "Do not fear my uncles, lads," he said turning to his boys. "I will protect you."

De Vere walked forward, "Thank you, Dearest lord, let me have your love. I will stand with you like a rock and will defend you against all these proud peers and magnates."

De Pole, not to be out done, leapt in: "Your uncles want to overturn your state. They treat Your Grace like a child. If they had their way, Your Grace would be gone from your throne. Your Grace should let them know the power of your majesty."

De Vere nodded, "Your Grace is young, but able, much like a young lion, and may not the lion roar even though he is young? What are your uncles, aged elephants grown into oak and rotten in their bitterness? If you topple one, they will all fall."

Tresilian smirked. He was anxious to show his value as the legal mind behind the scheme. "The law is with you, Your Grace," he said. "The law can be used as a hammer against all those who threaten your sovereignty."

Queen Dick had just made Tresilian Chief Justice and was happy to hear he was doing his job as chief-finder-of-legal-excuses-to-rob-a-man. He smiled and went on.

"You are Lord Chief Justice now, and you know best," said the King. "What do you think of these dogs that would subvert Our authority?"

"Your enemies undermine your sacred state. Even the greatest prince or most powerful magnate is subject to your majesty. It is nothing less than capital treason," said Tresilian.

"Then attaint them, arrest then, condemn them, and kill them," said the King.

This was red meat to De Vere. He giggled, "We'll have them on the block and walk away with their heads and then, Your Grace may claim the whole government for yourself."

Queen Dick waved his hand, "See it be done, Tresilian, and speedily."

Tresilian bowed, a bit nervously. "That may be a bit too rash, Your Grace," he said. Queen Dick was not happy at that. He scowled at Tresilian.

Tresilian continued, "It must be done carefully or they will rise before we are ready to act. Furthermore, they have many friends in the land. They may muster them to their aid if we move against them."

The King brushed a speck from his sleeve. He continued,
"You have a point. The commons do like them. Lancaster has his claws into ever part of this land, and his idiotic expeditions provide the rougher sort with ample opportunities for profit. As for Gloucester, the rustics seem to think he is Christ come again. But mark my words, the time will come when we shall place a yoke on their necks and bend them to our will." He thought for a moment, "But how shall we do this, My Love?" he asked De Vere.

De Vere had all this worked out in his mind.

"Your Grace should think back to your ancestors," said De Vere. "There are many strange and wonderful precedents of how to end the treason of the overly mighty. Think back to your royal grandfather. He was young and took the Protector, the vile Mortimer, and dropped him from a gallows some fifty foot in height."

The King giggled at the image, no doubt thinking how much fun it would be to drop his uncles from a similar height.

"Well then, why should we not punish our proud Protector? His treason is viler than Mortimer's," said the King. "We would rule like an Emperor. All the Kings of these islands will attend me, and we shall be the Emperor of all. Our words will be law again."

Tresilian came forward. "You are done with their advice, Your Grace," said Tresilian. "Your Grace's majority is upon you, and it is time you shook off your uncle's protectorship."

De Pole had not said anything for awhile and was clearly anxious not be left out of the arse kissing. "Your Highness is able to rule without the advice of those who do not love you. Why should any of Your Grace's pleasures be curbed?"

The King smiled. At least there would be no trouble in the bedroom tonight. "My Sweet Love, we shall ride together and take our pleasures as we wish."

De Pole smiled, "Sweet King, we shall ride together and show ourselves in gold!"

Queen Dick responded with enthusiasm. "We will ride through London, so that our people can gaze upon us, and then on to Westminster, where ten thousand of the pretty boys of Our Kingdom will feast at royal tables, richly furnished. The world shall praise my bounty, state, and royalty. Let all the chroniclers know that We faced down these proud lords and restored the majesty of the King of England."

He turned to Tresilian. "Call for Woodstock to come to our court," said the King. Queen Dick's bum boys looked shocked. He held up his hand, "You know we hate him, but we must separate him from his friends before we act. We can restrain him at our pleasure," said the King.

That was that. Queen Dick had decided. Over the next few days, they sharpened their plan and, when they were ready, Richard called the judges together in his Chambers. The King asked them a simple question: was it legal for a King to oppose the laws of the Parliament if he had been coerced into agreeing to them?

Of course all the justices agreed that the King could revoke or change any law he wished, and that Parliament had gone beyond its authority.

The King had what he wanted, and swiftly moved forward. He and his inner council had drawn up a series of questions that they believed would show that both Parliament and the Appellants had acted entirely outside their authority. Like the fools they were, they believed that if they could show that Appellants were acting illegally, then the Appellants would roll up their tents, say "sorry to have bothered you", and head for home.

They completely misunderstood their enemies. Gloucester, the Arundel brothers, and the others were hard men. They were playing for keeps, and the law was not going to get in their way. They hated the King. They wanted a decorative, malleable king who would fight the French and do as they wished in their own lands.

They would have preferred to get rid of the King altogether and install one of their number on the throne. However, they could never agree who should be king in Richard's place. Of course the King realized that he needed a little more than the law on his side to win against his enemies. For that, he counted on his collection of retainers.

Despite his efforts, Queen Dick's men were far fewer than those pledged to the Appellants. Arundel alone kept more than four thousand men under contract, and Johnny Gaunt had been able to kit out an entire army for his trip to Spain in an attempt to steal that crown. The King had collected a bodyguard of not more than two hundred and fifty men around him. Even if De Verve, who had stayed behind in Chester to recruit more men, was able to call all the county levy out to support their King, he would have a hard time taking on the Appellants.

I recall watching the King pose a series of questions to the assembled legal wizards of England. Judge Hanmer was seated in the front row. It was plain that he was unhappy. Like all lawyers, he hated to be pinned down, and the King's mood foreshadowed a nasty session where the legal minds would be asked for straight answers to straight questions.

I won't go into all of the questions the King asked that day. There are other chroniclers who understand the questions and the import more that I, and I urge my readers to consult them if you have a mind for legal posturing. Needless to say the King asked the judges nine questions concerning whether the Parliament and the Appellants had acted within the law and whether the King had a right to do as he wanted. The questions were very cleverly put together and the justices had to agree that the King could do what he wanted and could tell the Parliament to go suck Satan's cock.

Once the King got the answers he wanted, they were dismissed and sent off with a warning that they would be called back later in the summer. Armed with this information, the King set off on another jaunt through the North to see if he could collect a few more supporters and then headed for Nottingham to continue his conversation with the judges.

It was high summer when we all came to Nottingham. It must have been sometime late in August, for the hay was collected and the wheat was near harvest. This time the King reconvened the judges and asked them to fix their seal to their answers. He was planning to move quickly, and he wanted to their decisions on parchment in case anyone questioned him.

Not surprisingly, there was an awful huffing and puffing over this. No lawyer is ever willing to commit himself to parchment when his own life is threatened, and these boys were just the same. One of the judges, a certain Sir Robert Bealknap, was particularly troubled, and it took a few blows from one of the King's Cheshire Archers before he saw the justice of the Royal argument. Then the King called in the Sheriffs from all of the northern and midland shires. He asked them what help they would provide their King if he called out the shire levies against the Appellants. He got a disappointing answer. Most of them said that the shire men would follow their own lord rather than the King.

That was the problem. Richard never could understand that to the average man, the King was a distant presence whereas his own Lord had a continuing presence in his life on a day-to-day basis. If you pissed off your Lord, you were likely to end up in the stocks or worse, but there was almost nothing a common man could do to even bring himself to the attention of the King. Faced with a fight between the King and his Lord, any rustic would side with his Lord over the King.

When he heard the shires would provide no support, Richard fired off a letter to the Pope in Rome to ask him to come to his aid and even considered asking again for aid from the King of France. Of course none of these entreaties were answered, so the King was stuck in Nottingham with his small force of Cheshiremen.

It was then that he had another foolish idea. Richard decided that London would be a good source of men in his battles with the Appellants. In particular, he determined that Fat Nick and his fishmongers would make an ideal army. Now I will be the first to admit that London Apprentice boys are good ones to have with you when you're in a fight, but street fighting is a long way from proper fighting. Londoners are all right for a barney in the lanes and alleys, but don't expect them to stand with you to face a man on horse.

I watched as they dragged in poor Nick. "Your Grace," he said.

Queen Dick looked at him. "We have a need for your support," said the King. "Our Uncles have grown too proud and We have decided to take them down by a head. We require that London provide Us with sufficient men to ensure the safety of the City and challenge Our Uncles in the field. How many men-at-arms can We expect from London?"

Nick took a sharp intake of breadth. "London may supply Your Grace, but I doubt the City will provide many men. London men are merchants and craftsmen. They will stand on the walls to defend their City, but I would not count on them to fight."

The King scowled. "We have supported you in all your battles," said the King. "When the drapers opposed you, We were with you. When the City turned against your man Northampton, I insisted upon him and secured the mayoralty for him."

Fat Nick looked down at his feet, "That will be the problem, Your Grace," he said. "The Appellants are aware of the faction within the City. While Your Grace has privileged the victuallers, the Appellants have favored the drapers and the craftsmen. The victuallers stand for the right to maintain our prices in food items and demand that the drapers and craftsman reduce the outrageous prices they charge for their goods. The Drapers and Craft Guilds, being thieves and liars, maintain our prices are too high and theirs are just and sanctioned by tradition. Unfortunately, while all men need food, few need the products of the drapers and the craftsmen. Thus, the small men who abound in London these days favor the drapers and crafts in demanding we lower our prices. The Appellants have seen this and favor them. While I might be able to raise some men from among the Fishmongers, I fear the bulk of the City will favor the drapers and the Appellants."

The King reddened. "The affairs of this Kingdom are to be decided by trade? By common men choosing fish over cloth? Meat over loyalty to their King?"

"It was ever so," said Fat Nick. "Men will follow their stomachs and their interests. As long as London rules itself in these matters, then we can expect such behavior."

"You are useless to Us, Brembre. Do not count upon Our support when We are victorious. I will end London's liberties. If the City will not stand with me, it shall cease to stand alone. It shall become Our plaything and adornment," said the King.

"Your Grace," said Brembre, "We can be of considerable help. I can raise loans; I can provide supplies. Surely there must be trained men at arms that Your Grace could employ."

"If this were a year ago, that would be true," said the King. "But my uncle Lancaster has taken them all away to Castile and my Uncles seem to have collared the remainder. I am left with what I can take from my Cheshire. I would have more from Wales, but the Marcher Lords prevent my messengers from moving freely to collect levies, and the Shire Reeves tell me that no one will rise with me."

De Vere intervened. "Take heart, Your Grace. All is not lost. Our plans are still secret. Perhaps we can trap the Appellants before they have full knowledge of Your Grace's activities."

Then the King, or maybe De Vere, had another bright idea. On the King's order, De Vere headed to London with a request for the Appellants to turn up at Waltham Cross in Herefordshire. He intended to trap and capture them there. At the same time, fat Nick Brembre was sent off to raise the fishmongers and seize London, while Tresilian went off to take the Tower of London for the King and all its stores.

It was a good plan and would have worked if the Appellants were idiots. Of course, the moment they heard the summons from De Vere, they realized what was going on. In response they mobilized their powers and marched up to Waltham ten thousand men strong and published a bill of treason against the King's friends. Queen Dick was stunned that his, or De Vere's, plan had been discovered and decided that discretion was called for. Still believing that the law was the best way forward, he appealed his case to Parliament and set off for Westminster. Meanwhile the Appellants caught the legal mania as well. Gloucester scurried across the country telling everyone that he wished to settle his argument with De Vere and the King's friends by recourse to chivalric combat. The whole realm was going mad. I expected that armies would begin to fight with quill and parchment and that affairs of state would be settled by jousts and witty remarks.

We would have been sucked right into it if, God Save us, old Judge Hanmer hadn't dropped dead from the strain. Owain had been named as his executor, so he had to go back to Shropshire and Hanmer to settle the estate. Now, as the entire world knows, a will is registered at a monastery or in a respected Church. When a man dies, his death must first be proved in Church court before his will can be read and executed. Sir David had registered his will with the Benedictines at Shrewsbury. Thus, it was to Shrewsbury that we went to settle Sir David's estate. As one would expect from the Judge, the arrangements were nicely done. He had paid the good friars to ensure that all went according to his wishes and there were no challengers. Owain expected to conclude work on the will within a few days and then return to his position with the King or Arundel. But of course, the way can never be clear in such times.

Owain was in the Chancery House when an agent of the Lord Arundel arrived with a message for him. We were all there; Crach, the Hanmer boys, Owain and myself. The old gang back together again. Owain broke the seal and began to read.

"What does it say?" I said.

Owain sighed, "My Lord Arundel sends his regret at my father-in-law's death. He says that he hopes the will is clear and that no troubles will follow. Further, he says, that while he is sure that a man as careful and ordered as Judge Hanmer would leave his affairs in a good state, he warns me to be careful as powerful men with evil designs may use their position to intervene in court to delay or steal an inheritance. He reminds me that in such uncertain times as these, the courts are particularly open to the pressures from such evil men. However, he assures me, as I am his sworn man, I need fear nothing. He will exercise his power and influence to ensure that all Sir David's inheritances are remitted as the will states. If I were not his sworn man, then he would not be able to exercise his influence. Thus, he wished to underline I may rely on him and need to fear nothing."

He looked around the room.

"Arundel's polite way of telling me to stay with his side or he will stick his nose in the will and make sure that none of us see a penny of the Judge's estates," said Owain. "I wish he would leave me alone. I am one man without title and with few retainers."

Crach stirred himself. "You are far more than that. While you have been charging up and down this Island, the bards have been at work back home. Your fame has spread. According to the bards, you are now the second coming of Arthur, a great warrior. If you were to listen to them, they would have that you single-handedly defeated huge Scots armies and cleared the sea of French pirates with a single blow of your axe. Everyone knows of you and admires you achievements. Combined with your family connections and the prophecies that have always followed you, you are the most important man in the Northern March."

"The barons and the Uchelwyr will follow you. They look to you for a sign of who to support in this conflict between the King and the Appellants. Most are like you, double sworn. They have allegiance to the King of England and their Lord; they know not which way to move. They await your sign. Arundel is no fool. He knows this. His agents will have been about and found the lay of the land. He is urging you to stay home and keep the March quiet. He doesn't need you to defeat the King; that will happen easily enough. He just wants to make certain that there is no rising for the King in Wales. If that occurs the entire West will be with the King's party. Most of the Appellants have their power base in Wales. If we go for the King, it not only grows his power, it diminishes theirs. They cannot allow this."

Crach paused and considered the situation. "My friend," he continued, "you have become the critical piece in the game. The death of Hanmer has provided some leverage over you. Arundel knows he can tie up the inheritance in court for years, if not steal it outright. Remember that the Lord of Ruthin is a friend of the Lord of Derby, Henry Bolingbroke. The Lords of Ruthin have long envied your lands. If you raise the March for the King and the Appellants win, then Arundel will support Ruthin in pursuing his claim to your lands. If you are declared a traitor, your lands would be forfeited and they could take them with the support of all the Lords of the March."

"Well that simplifies things," I said, "and removes any doubt over whether you should switch your allegiance to the King."

"Possibly," said Owain, deep in thought, "unless the King wins, in which case Arundel's patronage will mean nothing."

"But what are the odds the King will win?" I said, "He has no army and already the Appellants come close to capturing him."

"Aye," said Owain, "You are right. I suppose that when faced with this and my obligations to my wife's family, I must draw back from high politics and take the road of caution."

That's where it would have stayed if that giant prick De Vere hadn't messed everything up again. De Vere decided that now was a good time for a great gesture to show his lover his loyalty. He called up the Cheshire levy and marched on Westminster to free the King from his evil councilors. Rarely has a man shown himself stupider than De Vere at that moment. He knew as much about war as the average kitchen girl, and his main qualifications for heading an army was that he had sucked the King's cock. Nevertheless he believed his moment was at hand and headed off through the Midlands with his four thousand men.

They were a poor, mismatched force that had been brought together hastily with no real structure to command them. All the decent fighting men were either off in Spain with Johnny Gaunt or had been hired out by the Appellants. Those who were left were the dregs.

Owain heard of it when he was preparing the reading of the will at Hanmer. By that time the army was already in Shropshire and was heading down through the Cotswolds to the Thames.

"God's Balls," said Owain, "If this turns into a real fight, then I will be forced to choose between the King and Appellants."

"We should stay out of it," I said, "Let the English fight the English."

"I cannot," said Owain, "If I am not with Arundel, he will never forgive me, and if I am not with the King then he will have my head if he wins."

Crach shook himself awake from where he had been dozing in the corner. "The King is too weak. He will lose but will not be toppled from the throne. The Appellants hate each other. They'll keep him there because they won't be able to decide who should replace him. If he's smart, that will be his opportunity; all he will have to do is sit and wait. Eventually the Appellants will fall out with each other and he can play one faction against another."

"You have a point," said Owain, "Langley will do nothing so can be discounted. Gloucester hates the Arundel and has the best claim to the throne. But Arundel doesn't want a strong man like Gloucester on the throne. Once Gaunt hears what's going on, he will be back before you know it. He won't be able to stand the idea that there's trouble back here and that's where his opportunity will be.

"What shall you do?" I asked.

"I will do as I am sworn. I will attend Arundel and hope that De Vere shows some sense. But I will move slowly," said Owain. He turned to me. "You follow De Vere's army. Pass them and take a message to Arundel that I will perform my sworn duty but must first end the reading and proving of the will."

So I was off riding down the March after an army. As I went, Owain got Sycharth prepared for war and raised his tenants to rally after the King or Arundel, depending on how it was turned. I came upon De Vere's army just before Christmas. I should add that this further shows the idiocy of De Vere, for who campaigns in the dead of winter?

He had come to the Thames at Radcott Bridge in Berkshire when he met the Appellants. It was a vile day, cold and foggy. A man could ride out a few yards from the column and he would disappear. I used this to my advantage and skirted De Vere's army without being seen. As far as I could tell, De Vere's army was a poor thing, badly organized and stretched out along the road in a haphazard series of columns. I left them and moved east to catch the other bridges over the Thames. There I saw that things were not as the King's friends would have them. Each bridge I came to had been cut or was strongly garrisoned by men of the Appellants' households. I traveled on until I saw the banner of the Arundels at one of the bridges and came close, calling out I had a message for his Lordship and waving my badge of service. The guard spied me and let me through. I was directed up river toward Radcott where his lordship was holding court.

I found the Arundel and his retinue on the south bank and was ushered into his presence. I bowed. I saw he stood there with Henry Bolingbroke and De Grey. They were hunched over a map and consulting their plans.

"My Lords," I said, "I come from My Lord Owain of Glyndyfrdwy. He informs your Lordships that the Northern Marches are quiet. He has instructed his tenants and kinsmen to stay upon their lands and to ignore the commands of the Duke of Ireland. He says he will gather his men and proceed south as soon as he is sure of the peace in the area."

Arundel listened and turned to his retinue. "You see, not even the Welsh are mad enough to follow this foolish King," he said.

Bolingbroke spoke up, "Who is the Owen of Glendower?" he asked.
"He is a captain in one of my companies," replied Arundel.

"He has distinguished himself in our recent campaigns, and the King likes him. You make recall he spoke up against my brother at our dinner in London?" Bolingbroke shrugged.

It was clear that Owain had made little impression on him.
Grey interrupted, "He is a liar and a thief. He is known as one of the worst bandits in the March. Every year he sends his men to steal my cattle. He also claims a portion of my land. I would not trust a word he says. As we speak he is probably dealing with the King for some preferment."

Arundel waved him silent. "Master Glendower is of high regard to the Welsh. He holds some tribal title among them. If he keeps them quiet, we can be sure that De Vere will have no Welshmen with him."

He turned back to me. "What have you seen on the road?" he asked.

"I have seen the Duke's army moving south towards this bridge, My Lords," I replied.

"And what of their state?" asked Bolingbroke.

"Ragged," I replied, "They do not show good order and are poorly led. There are no men to order their march and they proceed through the fog with no pickets."

Arundel stroked his beard, "Well if they come we shall let them cross part way, but we shall be waiting as they come." He turned to the map and gestured to Bolingbroke.
"Post your men in the front part of the bridge. I shall destroy the way on the second bridge, for there are twin bridges at Radcott. I will place my archers upon the other bridge and

fire down on De Vere's men when your men stop them. I have messages from Gloucester that he has crossed the Thames and comes down from the east. If we hold De Vere here, Gloucester will come up on his rear and we shall have him."

Thus it was. From my position with the Lord Arundel's camp I could see it all. De Vere's men arrived at the Bridge in chaos and disorder. No pickets or scouts were present to tell them of what was to happen. Rain began to fall and the land was wet and muddy. De Vere's men poured down the road in the fog towards the bridge not seeing the spears and archers before them. As they closed in on Bolingbrook's pikes, they finally saw what was to happen and tried to turn back. However, the press of their fellows behind them was too great and they were pushed directly into the pikes without being able to move.

Then Arundel's archers let fly their arrows from the broken bridge and the other bank. Under the arrow swarm De Vere's men began to fall, panic and retreat. However, the men behind them came on unaware of what was happening. Thus as they came on they met the retreating men head on. As the press became greater, men began to fall over each other and panic and fight to escape. This further worsened their situation as more and more men ran in fear. In the crush some men were pushed into the Thames and drowned in their armor. Others were crushed as men fell upon them.

De Vere could be seen on his horse trying to rally his men. He might have done so, but the Duke of Gloucester's army arrived. We could see Plain Tom's banners waving and hear his horns blowing. When De Vere's men heard that, they realized they were surrounded and panic took over. De Vere tried to stop the retreat, but he could do nothing. One of his men, frustrated at De Vere blocking his way, stabbed up at De Vere's horse and toppled him into the crush.

Arundel saw him go down, "There!" he shouted, "see how the sodomite has fallen. The King is ours now."

After that the fight ended and the murder began. Most men threw down their weapons and begged quarter. Others ran to the west in the hope of escape. Most were trapped and left to the mercy of Appellant's armies. It was a bloody day, and not one I wish to remember.

Later that day De Vere's armor and sword were found near the Thames. At the time it was assumed that he had died in the press or drowned, but it turned out he had escaped. He was to finally reach France and died there some years later.
I returned to My Lord's home to give him the news of the battle.

"So the King's cause is lost?" he asked.

"If he was relying on De Vere, it is," I said. "His Cheshire men were poorly led and unprepared. It was less a battle and more a slaughter."

"And what of Arundel? Did he take my message as meant?" asked Owain.

"He saw you as a good defender of his interests," I replied.

"Well," said Owain, "I have thrown in with him, but I will not raise a hand against the King."

"What will you do?" I asked.

"I cannot go to London, for Arundel will require me to join him against the King. I shall stay here and play the role of the loyal Welshman keeping his land safe for the Arundels. If the King rallies his forces and builds an army that might challenge them, I will side with the King but until that day, I will wait here."

And wait he did. While we waited great things were done at Westminster. The King was now placed under Perpetual Councils. The Council would govern, and the King would be King in name only. They would have deposed him if they could have agreed on who would be King. Edmund of Langley was next in line, but refused to act. Plain Tom was ready but Arundel and Langley refused to support him and Bolingbroke had received a message from his father to prevent any disposition until he returned from Spain.

The Council was therefore unable to act and thus decided on the compromise of keeping the King a prisoner and a harmless decoration. But they were not finished yet. The Appellants brought the King's friends before Parliament. De Vere, de la Pole, Tresilian, and Brembre were tried, found guilty and condemned. They executed all but De Vere, and their lands were forfeited and given to the Appellants' supporters. Still they were not finished. They turned to the King's supporters.

One by one they went John Blake, the lawyer who had questioned the judges at Shrewsbury, guilty and executed. Thomas Usk the under shire reeve of Middlesex who had carried the King's messages to London, guilty and executed. Thomas Rushook, the Bishop of Chichester and the King's confessor (oh the tales he must have heard) guilty and sentenced to perpetual exile in Ireland, which is worse than death if you ask me.

The six judges who had sided with the King after his questions were sentenced to death, but reprieved then sent into perpetual exile in Ireland. Then the Appellants moved on the lower level of the Queen Dicks bum-boys, all his fancy knightlings that had decorated his bed chamber. Sir Simon Burley, Sir John Beauchamp, Sir John Salisbury, and Sir James Berners were all tried and found guilty. The King embarrassed himself by weeping and going down on his knees in front of all Parliament to beg for their lives. The Appellants argued over their fate, but the end was the same. They were marched off to Tower Hill and met the axe as all the others had.

That ended the formal killings, but there were plenty more informal ones. Arundel let his dogs loose in Cheshire, and many small men were run down and hung for their support of the King. Their lands and property were taken and given to friends of the Appellants. In London the drapers gained the upper hand and victuallers were to spend many years out of power. The Appellants secured the City in the clever move. The mob and the small people wanted cheap food and many worked hard for the craft guilds. By crushing the victuallers, they were able to push through price controls on food and win the support of the small people.

Finally, they brought the good will of the country as a whole by announcing a new war with France. Everyone loved a war and the chance of booty, so the country agreed to pretend that the King had been led astray and that justice had been done. So with that, the crisis was over. The so-called Merciless Parliament went home and the King retreated into court.

We all returned to our homes. Owain decided he could not safely serve the Appellants. He received a request from Arundel to go to France, but he pleaded to remain home and keep the March quiet. He had had enough of high politics and, having made a good income from his time with the sword, returned to cultivate his lands and repair his walls.

"I tell you," he said, "I have no taste for the English and their betrayals. I shall mind my own affairs for a while and raise my family. I have had enough adventure."

Crach laughed, "You may try, My Lord," he said, "but the bones have been read, the skulls have spoken, and the prophesies made. Your fate has been written already. You will be called when the time is necessary. Go home and enjoy your time but be aware that you will be called and you cannot resist what will come."

Crach was right, of course. Owain did go home but he

HOW TEN QUIET YEARS ENDED

For ten years My Lord Owain tended his lands. He became rich and successful. Sycharth became a fine place. The gate and walls were finally repaired, and the bailey became the envy of the entire cantref. At Marged's insistence, Owain had glass placed in every window and built more than nine chimneys. The land around the hall blossomed. He cleared the lakes and stream, stocked them with good trout, and built a fine mill. A dove cote rose above the walls, and he built a rabbit warren for winter meat. We parceled off a wood and park for the dear so there was always good hunting. Owain persisted with his dream of growing grapes and tried year after year to keep his vines alive before he finally giving up. Around the castle the land grew lush wheat fields, and his people grew fat.

He lived as his grandfather had before him, riding the circuit from Sycharth to Corwen to Glyndyfrdwy and back to Sycharth. He maintained his lands and dealt with the drovers and the bandits. He sold his wheat and cattle at Shrewsbury and Oswestry and, on occasion, even drove them to London. In time he even introduced sheep to the barren hilltops and trained his people in the ways of watching sheep and gathering wool. He became one of the richest men in Wales, and stocked his larders with fine foods, served good beer from Shrewsbury and even lay in a cellar of fine French wines.

Despite his wealth compared to the other Welsh barons, he was far from rich when measured against the great Magnates of the March. Compared to them, Owain was a beggar. He had to work his lands every day to maintain his position, while they sat back and lived on their rents. When he drank beer, they drank wine; when he ate rabbit, they ate beef; when he parceled out his salt, they used spices from the East. So while Owain was rich, it must be understood that he was only rich for a Welshman.

Marged was happy. She popped out one baby after another. Jane came first, but did not live. After her came the twins Gruffudd and Marged, after that Maredudd, Catrin, Alicia, Madog, Tomas, Sion and Dewi. They were a good brood and decent as children go.

All in all Owain maintained a fine court. Crach was always on hand to give prophecy, and Iolo Goch was a regular fixture to create a poem when needed. Every year he gathered his kinsman at Glyndyfrdwy to maintain their alliance and speak of the future. Every year the barons would come from all over Wales to pledge their allegiance to him. When Owain LlawGoch died at the hands of a Scots assassin in France, even men from Gwynedd began to come to swear their loyalty. However, Owain remained quiet, also keeping Wales and the March quiet as he was sworn to do and, in return, he received a subsidy from the Arundel and the King. He would say, "As long as the King and Arundel live, I am sworn, but when they die, I shall be free and can act according to my own mind."

But while Owain grew rich, Wales grew poorer. These were hard times in Wales. The Marcher Lords determined to wring as much profit as they could from their land.

Men would come to see Owain. "Uchelwyr" they would say, "The Foreigner Lord has imposed a labor fine on our tref and we need your help," or

"My Father has passed and the Foreign Lord requires service from me. I cannot pay," or

"I wish to move to the Englishry, for my skills are needed, but the Foreign Lord will not let me leave without payment and the English say no Welshmen may live among them in their towns."

Some would come at night running from the slave catchers. They would say,

"Uchelwyr I am bondsman but I am free. I wish to leave to work on the harvest in Oxfordshire, but my Lord says I am not free and must remain on his land and give him service."

And another said, "I was a blacksmith and worked for many years, but then an Englishman came and said this is English land and I am not free. I cannot own land because I am Welsh and must give my land and forge to him. Further, he may own me and hold my labor for himself."

We were no better than dogs to the English. They hated us and did all they could to bring us down the condition of slaves. Owain would do his best, but in all honesty, he could do little. More and more all he could do was help them escape to the boys in the hills. Where possible he let these masterless men sojourn on his lands. "Better they stay close and are my friends then that they run into the hands of the English," he would say.

In so doing he revived his grandfather's connections with the outlaws of the North and the highlands. Many were the nights when the guests to dinner would be men with prices upon their heads in the Englishries and the border towns of Shorpshire and Cheshire. Indeed, My Lord and I often rode out with those men and raided the cattle of the Carletons, the Greys, and the Mortimers.

All of this was the life of a Welsh Lord in the March. He must walk the line between the Welsh and the English, between the rich and the poor, between the powers of the Marcher Lords and the outlaws who stole and traded their cattle.

And what of me, you might ask? I took a wife. A good girl called Sara, simple and sweet. She gave me a son we called Daffydd. He was a funny little thing. When he was four, he got a cut in his arm. It was nothing to begin with but it grew worse and worse. Owain brought a doctor from Oswestry to look at it.

"He is a very sick boy," the doctor said. "I might be able to save him, but he will lose the arm."

I am ashamed to say I broke down and cried while my wife remained composed. "Nothing in my life has prepared me for this," I thought. "How do I deal with this?"

Sara told the doctor to do what he thought was best, so he took my boy's arm. He was in such pain. For a time he seemed to get better. Then the fever returned. He grew weaker and weaker. I remember walking him up and down our room. He kept whispering to me, "I'm better now, I'm better now. Can we play Da? Can we go out and play?"

He died just before the dawn. Sara never recovered. She fell into a melancholy and I, for my sins, spent much of that summer inside a bottle. Owain finally pulled me out and told me to tend to my wife. It was too late. That winter she took a chill and died. It seemed that one day she was well and the next day she was dead. That was it for me. I never found it in my heart to marry again. I have been far from celibate, but it was clear to me that I was not a man who could love more than one woman in his life.

May the Good Lord gather them to His heart, and may they be there waiting for me when I go to meet them. I will not write more of this.

The years ahead would have been much the same had it not been for the events of 1397. For ten years King Richard slept. He ruled with his Council, followed their direction, and curbed his appetites. But he was slowly rebuilding his power. Gradually he built up his supporters in those places he could call his own. When a minor office came open, he would place his man there, tell him to be quiet and follow the direction of the Council. When a higher office came, he would advance these men. The Council would see a man who had followed their dictates and would allow his advance. Slowly, without being noticed, the King built his power.

The Magnates grew bored of governing. They wanted power. They left court to pursue their ambitions in France or returned to their estates. Every time they left Court, the King would gain new power and new authority.

The only one of those great councilors who remained at court was the Lord Arundel's Brother. But he was no longer Bishop of Ely. After the events of the Merciless Parliament, he became Archbishop of York and, in time, he advanced to Canterbury. Now the whole Church of England was his. He was the King's Chancellor and sat at all Council meetings. He became the most powerful man in the Kingdom. But Richard was patient and remorseless and waited. Even Arundel could not resist the King's steady advance.

In the summer of 1397, Richard was ready. Gruffudd Hanmer had travelled to Arundel's Castle that spring to deal with some small matter and returned with a story.

"I tell you," he said, "there is some mischief about. All the Council was present; the Arundels, Gloucester, Mowbray, Warwick, and Bolingbroke. There were rumors that Gloucester is preparing for a final showdown with the King. He has woken up to the fact that Richard has revived his power. There was a great argument between him and the King over the loss of certain towns in France in January. Gloucester called the King a coward for not coming to his aid, and accused the King of loving the French more than his English subjects. The King lost his temper and screamed that Gloucester was a traitor and a liar. Gloucester and Arundel retired to the March to plot their response. I have it on good authority that the Appellants have sworn an oath to remove the King from power and imprison York and Lancaster. They will then execute the other members of the Council and place Gloucester on the throne."

"That makes no sense," said Owain, shaking his head. "Lancaster is Bolingbrook's father. If Richard was executed, Gaunt would be next in line. Bolingbroke would he Gaunt's heir; to raise Gloucester over Lancaster is contrary to his every interest."

Gruffudd nodded, "Bolingbroke is not the most intelligent man. He is a man who thinks more with his hands than his head. He cares more for the joust that he does for politics or governance. He may have been tricked into the plot by Gloucester or the Archbishop Arundel."

"Bolingbroke might be stupid, but even he has the sense to see this goes against his interests," said Owain.

"I cannot credit it," he continued. "Why would Archbishop Arundel agree to this plan? If Gloucester is king, he will no longer need Arundel. He will not want a strong Chancellor. Arundel knows well that while he might have the power to put Gloucester on the throne, he will not be needed to keep him there."

"I think perhaps this story must be put about by the King's agents," I said. "If it is believed, he could use it as a pretext to move against the Appellants. Perhaps he hopes to distract Lancaster and York's supporters and cause confusion."

I was right. Mowbray betrayed the alleged plot to the King. Armed with this information, the King acted. I recall it was around the feast of the Translation of St. Thomas the Martyr.[8] Richard, unlike his normal practice, was staying in Westminster. Since the events of 1387 he had avoided Westminster and London and continued his gyrations about the Kingdom. The Council allowed him to do so as long as he did not enter Cheshire where it was known that many of his supporters congregated. But at the beginning of that year, Richard had ceased his northern circuits and focused his travels around the South. Just after the Feast of the Martyr, the King gathered all his friends at Westminster. He sent a portion of his Cheshire bowmen off to hold the Tower, and others to close the main London gates.

Then he sent out his agents with specific instructions. A group of Cheshire archers arrested Warwick at banquet in London where he had been lured. Then the King mounted up and with a large force and road to Pleshey Castle in Essex. There he surprised Gloucester and took him into custody. Quickly he had Mowbray take Gloucester across the Channel to Calais where Mowbray was now master of the English garrison.

The King then rode onto Canterbury and took Archbishop Arundel. He persuaded him to arrange the surrender of his brother, promising him that he would maintain their estates and permit his brother to go into exile. Arundel, realizing the game was up, traveled with the King to nearby Reigate Castle where Arundel had retired to on his journey to visit his brother. The King's friends Rutland and Kent arrived with a large force and prepared to reduce the castle. When the Archbishop arrived at Riegate, he persuaded his brother to surrender and the party then progressed to the Tower where all the conspirators were being held. Thus, by the Feast of St. Metheldred the Virgin Richard's alleged conspiracy was over and all the Appellants had been arrested and his power was secure.

It was then that Owain received a summons to attend Richard at his Parliament in Westminster. Owain delayed until the harvest was finished and then travelled to Westminster, arriving just after the feast of the Nativity of Our Lady.

Westminster was much changed from the place of our youth. In the last ten years, Richard had turned it into a great palace on the continental model. We stayed in an Inn on the Strand the night before Parliament, arriving that evening with a gentle rain falling. What a beautiful place this world can be, I thought. The Parliament was held the feast of St Lambert[10].
We woke early and made our way down the Strand towards the Bar. It was a bright, beautiful, clear day of the kind one can get in September. Not a cloud in the sky. What could go wrong, I thought, this not a day for evil. Oh, how narrow and men's vision can be. But it was clear we were not meeting in the Palace.

Richard had erected a large temporary building in the Old Palace Yard where tournaments and other displays of martial splendor held. A great tented roof covered the structure with banners celebrating the King falling from the rafters. The walls were open. Inside a dais had been erected for the King with the Judges seated in front. As a minor Welsh Lord, Owain was situated towards the back. In front we could see the Lords and the Commons come together. In those days a man could only serve in the House of Commons once. As a result, the Commons was always a little chaotic. New men would arrive at the site of the Parliament with little idea of what to do. Of course the Lords were always there and knew exactly what to do. All the Lords were standing in the front with their retainers around them. If anyone seemed ill at ease, the fact the marquee was open and escape was easy calmed them.
Then the trumpets sounded and in came Richard in full Queen Dick mode, dressed in gold and silk. He was such a bæddel. With him was his child bride. Poor Queen Anne had finally died a couple of years before, and he had acquired a child bribe from the King of France as a present to cement their friendship. She didn't look more than seven years old. I suppose it was a way of putting off having martial relations with her for a few more years. They came in and sat down with great ceremony. Their thrones were placed on the dais where the court benches were normally set.

The King's bodyguard filed in with him. I noticed that the heir to the Earldom of Northumberland led them in. It was the first time that I had seen Hotspur close up since the Scottish War. His father had wheedled his way into the King's heart and had secured the position of Marshall for him. Those few Cheshiremen the King had collected around the time of Radcott Bridge had now swollen in number to more than four thousand. He had hidden them from the Appellants by stationing them in small groups around his castles and hunting lodges. When he was ready to act, he had pulled them all together and quite stunned their Lordships with the size of his force. They came in wearing red and white uniforms with white hart badges. Each man was armed with a long bow. They marched silently on either side of the pavilion until they had completely surrounded the tent. The crowd stirred, and for a moment it seemed that Richard was to order all our deaths.

Richard's new Chancellor, Bishop of Exeter, a certain Edmund de Stafford, then walked to the front of the dais, said a prayer and began to preach a sermon.

I can remember little of it apart from that it was from the Book of Ezekiel: "One King Shall be King of them All." He went on at great length, repeating the point again and again that the King's power belonged to him alone and those who threatened his power deserved punishment.

"Thus My Lords and My Good Gentlemen," said the Chancellor, "be it ordained that this Parliament should begin investigating all those who have undermined the King's power and regality. When you have reached the end of your deliberation, decide upon their punishment and then provide certain mechanisms to the King to prevent this from happening again."

He might have had more to say, but Queen Dick interrupted:

"Oh, do be quiet, Stafford. Enough with the Scriptures," said the King. He reached for a goblet of wine and sipped at it lazily. "We wish to see the proceeding ended quickly. We direct the Commons to provide Us with a Forespeaker as soon as possible."

He smiled and nodded at the Common.

"We wish to announce that with the exception of those men already taken and fifty others whom We have not yet named, We will pardon all those who have acted against Us in the last ten years. All We ask is that you acknowledge your crimes and ask pardon of Us by the next St Hilary's Day. So We bid you goodbye for now, and We will meet again tomorrow.

"Oh, and one more thing," he added. "We instruct all parties to surrender their arms when they arrive at the bar at Westminster tomorrow, and those great lords now present will remain with Us at Our Palace at Westminster. We would like offer them Our generosity. Discharge your armed men and retainers. From now on, no armed men shall be allowed within the precincts of the Palace." He stood, smiled and nodded. With that he left, and his archers followed him out.

There was silence for a moment, and then the assembly erupted in conversation and argument. My Lord looked to me. He indicated that we should move when one of Richard's guards came forth and grasped him by the arm.

"Master Glendowery," said the King's guard, "The King would meet with you," and he indicated that Owain should follow him. Owain looked at me and told me to wait for him outside the Great Hall.

"I will be back," he said, "The King is my friend."

"Good luck, My Lord," I said and watched him walk away, wondering if he was one of the unnamed fifty people who the King had promised he would not pardon. I waited anxiously for several hours before Owain returned. "We must leave," he said, "I have much to discuss with you."

At our Inn he told me of his meeting with the King. He had been taken to one of the many rooms that surround the Palace of Westminster. Richard had changed out of his gold cloth and had transformed himself from being Queen Dick to plain 'Dicken.' He wore a simple rustic surcoat and plain woolen stockings.

The archer led Owain forward and called to the King, "Dicken, your man is here."

"My Lord Powys," he said, nodding towards My Lord. Owain was stunned. No Englishman had ever acknowledged any Welsh title. Owain bowed, "Your Grace."

"Come sit with Us," said Richard and patted a chair next to his. He sat back and scratched his head. "God's Feet," said the King, "We know We play the part well, but the pageantry of royalty is very taxing. We would prefer to be back in Ireland with the Army or with Our hounds in Cheshire." He reached for his wine cup.

"It had been many years since We saw you, Owain. You have aged well. We recall when I was a boy you seemed a giant. We never saw a man so sure in his strength."

"I remember you too, Your Grace. When you faced Watt the Tyler at Smithfield, I swore that I would follow you to the end."

The King smiled. "That was a great day. I had been counseled to agree to anything until there were sufficient men-at-arms, but We saw my moment when Walworth struck down the beast. We have always meant to ask, was the man that shouted at Master Tyler with your camp?"

"It was I," said Owain, "and the truth of it was that I was not shouting at him but a member of his retinue, a notorious thief I had met in London."

The King laughed, "It was you? Why did you tell Us?"

"I have never believed that it was anything worth boasting about. After all, I placed Your Grace in considerable danger. Everything ended well, but it could have gone badly."

The King smiled, "We have never seen it that way. We were a young boy. We were terribly frightened. Unless you had spoken that day, Walworth would not have had the courage to act, and We would not have found the courage to stand against the rebels. If We had known We would have made you a knight right there. Why, We would even have given you manors and lands."

"I wish no reward for serving my sworn lord," said Owain. "I was sworn to you from the coronation onwards, and I will never act against you."

The King nodded, "You have been a good friend, Owain. All these years We have watched you. When that bastard Arundel urged you to rise, you kept the March quiet for Us. When he called you to his service, you remained still on you lands, and many of your kinsman came with Us on Our march into Ireland." He was referring to his Irish war that he had prosecuted several years before.

Owain tried to interrupt, but the King waved him away. "Do not deny it. We know you well. Your countrymen look to you as though you are the king of Wales. One word from you and not one Welshman would have rallied to Our standard in Ireland."

"You exaggerate, Your Grace," said Owain.

"No such thing. We understand the men of the West. We may be their King, but you are the one they look to. But do not fear. We have no jealousy. We are not Longshanks, and I have no desire to brutalize your people. "

"What do you desire, Your Grace?" Owain asked him.

The King looked at Owain, "We will count upon your loyalty. For years We have needed to hide. When We were young, Our Mother told Us to beware. She warned Us that Our Uncles would do all they could to destroy Us. She told Us to build Our power slowly. Act the fool, the sop and sodomite, she would say, do everything that you can to make them underestimate you.

"When We were young, We ignored her, rashly challenged them and almost lost Our throne. It has taken Us many years to rebuild Our power. All this time We have played the bæddel. Let them think that all We care for is fabrics and jewels. It bored and distracted them. While they grew bored, We plotted. At last We are ready and now We will act."

He supped on his cup, "But do not think that this means a return to ways of the past. We have a vision for what Our Kingdoms can become. As long as this Kingdom rests on the power of the South and the East, We shall always be weak. The Appellants draw their wealth from the wool trade and the continent. The east shall always be theirs. They count on March for men but the south for money. I intend to shift Our power to the West and the North. I will raise the Lords of Ireland, Wales, Cheshire, Cornwall, and Northumbria over the English. And let me tell you, there will be places for all men who support me.

"I will not repeat Longshanks' mistake. Longshanks tried to create one Kingdom with himself as King. In the process he nearly ruined this Kingdom. Why he could not even complete most of the castles he began building to keep your people down. He left his Kingdom so dependent on the great Magnates that his son was horribly slandered and deposed."

The King continued, "Our grandfather made a bigger mistake. He hoped to divert the Magnates with the troubles with France. All this accomplished was draining the treasury. We need lords who are firmly rooted in their land. They should have no need or desire to seek foreign wars. They should depend upon Us and Our good will. Thus, Our vision is simple. We will raise new Lords based in their historic land. They shall govern completely for Us. We will call on them to maintain order in Our lands in the south to forever control these grasping, proud magnates. The King of France shall be my friend, and We shall rule in perpetual peace."

He had that look in his eye that bespoke of the madness of Kings.

"You, Owain, can be my man in Powys. We will raise you up to your historic power. We will remove all prohibitions from Welshmen. Your people will be free as they were before Longshanks came. All you must do is swear allegiance to Us and agree to serve Our commands."

"I am already sworn to you, Your Grace," said Owain.
"But We need more. We need your total absolute loyalty.
All your heirs must swear to Us, in this life and the next. We need your oath sworn anew."

Owain thought, "Your Grace you have always had it. As for my heirs, that is for them. It is our custom."

The King toyed with his cup. "This is fair. Send them to Us. We will raise and educate them in Our Court as did Princes in past times. When they are with Us, We will confer and confirm your titles. We shall have a grand ceremony."

He smiled and slapped Owain on the back. "The wine and ale shall flow. We shall come to Wales, and all the Chiefs of your tribes shall come to Us. We intend to go to Ireland again when this unpleasantness is complete. We shall stop at Caerleon where Arthur held court and stage a pageant at his roundtable."

Owain said that Richard almost stepped out of character and let a little of Queen Dick out, but the King calmed himself.

"But wait, We are not ready. We must end these trials and We will have the Appellants done with. We must move against Gaunt and his idiot son. Once Gaunt and Bolingbroke are gone, We shall have their lands. Then We will be free to act."

He turned full to Owain and focused fully on him.

"Wait for Us and We will call. Stand clear of the enclosure tomorrow. There may be blood. We shall have one of Our men direct you to a safe place. Bring all the Welshmen loyal to you to that point and wait. You will still be able to watch but need not be in the killing ground."

"And then I left," said Owain as he finished his tale.

"There will be a killing tomorrow if the Lords and Commons do not vote with him," I said. Owain nodded.

"I would have you call upon the Welshman to rally to me in the event of trouble," he said. "Go find Dodd among the archers and arrange for him to let them through. Give my friends words that will show them to safety. They will say them to the archers so that they will know to let them through. Tell Dodd the word, "Plant Owain" – the children of Owain. That will be easy enough for Dodd to remember and easy enough for the English to say."

Thus it went the next day. Owain stood aside where he had been shown and one by one the Welsh barons came to him using the words they had been given to pass through the Cheshire archers. They were all insignificant men to the English, so they saw nothing. But to any man in the know, it was a clear sign. These dozen or so men represented all the Welsh knights and native born landholders who mattered. Together they could raise thousands of their kinsmen and tribesmen. A sharp eye might also have noted that not all of the Welsh came. A small band led by Dafydd Gam hovered around Bolingbroke. These were Bolingbrook's tame Welshmen. The Lancastrians always kept near them a small team of these monkeys who were sworn mercenaries.

Of them, Gam was the worst and was also thought to be their leader. I once paid a penny to see the great beasts in the King's zoo at the Tower of London. I saw an ape there. He was an intelligent beast but was profoundly ugly. Gam looked very like him, all hair and great dangling arms. His knuckles almost dragged on the ground. He got his name from his great droopy eye that was never completely open or completely close. What an ugly bugger he was. He was good with a sword though. His reputation with a sword was known throughout the March and Walli Pura.

I also saw that weasel Adam of Usk. He had spent his life sucking up to Gaunt and Bolingbroke in hopes of advancement. He was their pet chronicler and spent his life recording history according to their view. I hoped that an arrow would go astray and catch that little cunt before the end of the day's proceedings.

The Mummers Play continued as it had the day before. The Commons had retired the previous day and chose John Bushy as Speaker. Of course they had little say in it. Bushy was one of the King's boys. The King loved to have him nearby and kept him in good estate. I imagined that the King and his men had done quite a bit of arm twisting the previous day. It was also rumored that he had packed the Commons with his men. It might have been true. There were plenty of people there that day who were bought and paid for by the King. However, if they were all in the King's purse, why were the Cheshire archers there? I suspect that the King had bought all the men he could but still knew there were many shires dominated by the magnates.

Bushy stepped up to the throne. He had done his work and swung enough of the Commons behind him.

"Your Grace, you charged us to determine who has worked to undermine you majesty and regality." Bushy paused for dramatic effect. His words caused a stir. "Majesty and Regality" were continental terms. The King of France might use these words, but to our ears they sounded strange and suggested tyranny and an exaggerated view of a King's role.

Bushy went on.

We have studied the evidence and consulted witnesses. We declare that Thomas, Duke of Gloucester, and Richard, Earl of Arundel, in the tenth year of your reign, did treacherously force you, with the support of the present Archbishop of Canterbury, who was then chancellor, to grant them an unlawful commission to govern your realm."

That shut everyone up. You could a heard a mouse fart.

"In so doing they did you a great wrong that was prejudicial and hurtful to your majesty and regality."

Bushy had just attacked the most powerful men in the realm. They might be down but who knew if their supporters in the Parliament would still rally?

The King waved for him to continue.

Bushy continued. "I humbly beg Your Majesty to revoke all pardons and exceptions from these men for their actions at that time. Further I request that all acts and warrants issued in their names and in the names of the false councils they summoned, be withdrawn and annulled. I call upon this Parliament to recognize this action and similarly withdraw all legality from their acts."

Mighty Richard nodded. I saw then that this was a new character for him to play. The King had moved on past Dicken, Queen Dick, and even King Richard. He had become Mighty Richard the Tyrant and Lord-Upon-the-Earth. I saw in his face a new madness. I thought of what might come and trembled.

"I draw to Your Majesty's attention, and the attention of the Parliament, the role played in these crimes by the Archbishop of Canterbury. This man obtained a special pardon for his brother when he should have arraigned this man as a traitor."

Archbishop Arundel tried to stand to object. The Mighty Richard stared at him, "Later Arundel; maybe tomorrow." It was to be the last time that day that Arundel attempted to speak in Richard's presence.

Mighty Richard continued, "We will consider your request," said the King. "But We also want this Parliament to consider if this should set a precedent. In future, should any man who acts against Our regality and majesty be considered a traitor?"

There were some shouts of approval. "Excellent," said the King, "I do not think we require a full vote, do you Bushy? No? Good, let us continue."

Bushy turned to the Prelates and the Lords seated in the front rows. "Your Graces, in the past it has been required that all cases of treason be tried before your Lordships. I move that, in future, all cases should be tried by the King without your assent or involvement. How do you vote?"

At this, the Cheshiremen stood tall, drew their bowstrings tight, and notched their arrows. Richard looked at them,
"Calm down lads. No need for bloodshed yet."

Then he turned back to their Lordships. "Please let Us hear your votes."

Thus they voted, and the King gained another power. The session continued. The acts of the Lords were confirmed by the Commons. Then Bushy proposed that the Lords and Prelates should choose one of their number to act in their place. In future this one man would serve as the representative of the Lords and Prelates and could approve all of the King's actions as needed, rather than convening the full Parliament. There were rumblings, but the King knew how to silence them.

Mighty Richard held up his hand. "Several here have asked Us to name the fifty people excluded from the general pardon We granted concerning the sins and crimes of past Parliaments. We will not. This is Our business, and We intend to tell you only when We are ready. Further We add that anyone who asks Us to speak one of those names deserves to die. The only reason they seek confirmation is because they know they committed treasonous crimes and plan to flee or plan new crimes. The simple act of asking proves them to be traitors and marks them out for inclusion in the list." He paused for effect and looked around,

"Unless, of course, they are already listed."

He turned to the Lords, "Pray continue."

Their Lordships huddled and decided that it would make sense to nominate one of the King's friends. They chose Sir Thomas Percy, the king's steward, as their proctor and authorized him to agree to whatever should be done in Parliament.

Without a pause, Bushy jumped up, "Your Majesty, I would move a second article for this Parliament's consideration. That is, I ask that the Parliament consider the appropriate punishment for the traitors we have identified here this day. I also beg Your Majesty to allow me to proceed on a second case and to consider it as part of the previous indictment."

He turned towards Arundel. "I accuse Thomas Fitzalan, Archbishop of Canterbury, of treason in three parts. First, he worked with the traitors Gloucester and his brother the Lord Arundel to illegally govern this Kingdom. Second, he worked to undermine your power, honor, majesty and regality. Third, that during the period of his false rule, he treacherously put to death your knights and faithful liegemen, Sir Simon de Burley and Sir James Berners."

"Moreover, as this false Archbishop is a man of great wealth, family, and numerous connections, and is known to be an untrustworthy and vengeful creature, I beg also that, for the safety of your own person and your entire realm, and in order to facilitate the business of this present Parliament, he should be placed securely in custody until such time as judgment is passed on him."

Richard thought for a minute, stroking his chin. "We will think on this tonight. However, for now, We will take your advice." He waved to a Captain of Archers, "Take the Archbishop into custody. " They moved to take him. All of his allies moved apart and let him them by.

Richard turned to the Lords, "For those of you here who acted with Arundel in the commission of his crimes," he looked around the room, "We pronounce that you all acted faithfully and lawfully and are innocent of treason, especially Archbishop Neville, Archbishop Wykeman and my own loyal good uncle, Edmund."

The three of them fell on the ground weeping thanking him for his kindness. With that, the day was done and the Parliament ended for that day.

At night, the Welsh barons met again. More had come to Owain's banner. They realized the seriousness of the situation and saw that Owain had told the truth. It was agreed that they would follow Owain's lead, and all would support him in his directions.

Thus began the third day. The opposition to King Richard collapsed. The audience was now full of men dressed in the King's red and white livery. Everyone seemed to be sporting the white hart badge. The Earls of Rutland, Kent, Huntingdon, Nottingham, Somerset, and Salisbury, Lord Despenser, and Lord William Lescrope all decided it was now time to show they were the King's men. The King looked pleased. He signaled the guards. Arundel was dragged in. Like the others, he was dressed in red, only this time with a red hood to cover his face.

Then Bolingbroke stepped up. This is it, thought I, he finally got some grit in his arse. He'll show he's a man and stand up for his friends. But I was wrong.

"Remove his belt and hood. He is a traitor and should show his face," said Bolingbroke. Arundel looked at him in surprised horror, but Bolingbroke ignored him. Then Bushy read the charges.

Arundel interrupted. "I am no traitor. I have guarded this Kingdom all my life. When Your Majesty was seduced by false friends, I was strong enough to stand against them. I was fully pardoned by Your Grace and Parliament."

Before he could continue Bolingbroke piped up, "Traitor," he said, "Your pardon is revoked."

"Fuck you," shouted Arundel, losing all lordly grace, "You are a miserable lying fuck. I was never a traitor." In his fury, Arundel dropped the fancy speech of court and spoke in the rough language he habitually used.

Bolingbroke grinned, 'Then why did you ask for a pardon in the Parliament after you challenged the King at Radcott?"

"You know full well. You were there. You were part of this. The only reason I pursued a pardon was to silence my enemies." He looked at Bolingbroke, "And I see that you are now one of them. Let me tell you, Bolingbroke, when it comes to treason, you are the biggest fucking traitor in the world, and you need pardon far more than I do."

Richard grinned throughout this exchange. He was in heaven. His enemies had fallen among themselves. "Answer the charge," said Richard.

Arundel shook his head, "I can see that I am completely fucked. These people accusing me of treason are all liars. I never was a traitor. God's Feet, I insist on claiming the benefit of my pardon. You gave me that pardon of your own hand. You were fully grown and free to act."

Richard looked at him, "We granted it to you on condition that your pardoned actions had not harmed my interests. Since then We have considered your actions and concluded that you have consistently acted against Us."

Bolingbroke jumped in very pleased with himself, "Thus, the grant is invalid."

Arundel was now completely disgusted with the way the trial was going and began to see that all was lost.

"I tell you this," he said, "I did not ask for the pardon. It was given to me by Your Grace when I was out of the country fighting your wars in France. You gave it to me of your own free will."

Bushy was becoming impatient. "The pardon is revoked by the King, the Lords, and the Faithful Commons"

Arundel snorted, "Where are these 'faithful commons?' He looked at Bushy, "I know you and your fucking crew well enough and I know why you are here. You had no intention of giving me a fair trial. You do not represent the true commons. I know the common people. They love me and Gloucester. They will grieve if we are harmed, and they hate you Bushy. They know what you are."

Bushy shouted above the ensuing commotion, "You see, Majesty, how this traitorous turd is trying to stir up trouble between you and your true Commons."

Arundel screamed at them, "You're all fucking liars and bæddels."

Then Bolingbroke intervened again, "Didn't you say to me at Huntington that we should rebel against the King and that before we did anything it would be best if we seized His Majesty?"

Arundel shook his head in resignation, "Bolingbroke, you are lying through your fucking teeth. You are an evil shit and you know it. I never proposed anything like that. Everything I have done has supported the interests of the King." The crowd saw how things were going and started to boo.

Then the Richard spoke, "Did you not say while in the bathhouse behind the White Hall during that hateful Parliament that there were a number of reasons why Our friend Sir Simon Burley deserved to die?"

Arundel looked confused. Richard was on to something here. The King continued, "Did you not also say that you could see no reason why he should not die? Further, did you and your fellows then treacherously put him to death? Eh? No answer? Enough, I am convinced. He is guilty."

Gaunt had been quiet up to this point. Now he stood up. "His Majesty has spoken. That is good enough for me." The crowd erupted into cheers. He went on, "Richard Fitzalan, also known as the Earl of Arundel, sometime false steward of England, you are judged a traitor, and I condemn you, by final and definitive process, to be drawn, hanged, beheaded, and quartered, and your lands to be confiscated."

It was time for Richard to show his merciful side, "In recognition of your high birth, We will show you mercy. You are to be beheaded only."

"You do me wrong, Your Grace," said Arundel, "I have been the firmest friend of your Kingdom. These men who accuse me are liars and evil doers. I warn you that if you rely on them, they will have your throne. And you," he turned to his accusers, "if you are so willing to lie and follow this King," he nodded to Richard, "You will all be dead within the year." He was almost right.

Then the Earl of Kent and others of the King's bum-boys came forward and led him away to Tower Hill. I am told he behaved very well during his execution. He acted with bravery and humor on the block. He distributed all the money he had on him and forgave his executioners. "At least," he is rumored to have said, "You do your duty honestly rather than those lying shits at Westminster."

His body was taken away and buried at the home of the Augustine friars. It's strange how things go. Nowadays it is quite a popular gravesite, and many people go there to say a prayer for the old rogue.

There were more trials and denunciations. I will not bore you with all details. Let me just say that many men confessed crimes they had no business confessing to and accused men of crimes they could not have committed. At the high point, Richard stood up and announced that Gloucester was dead. Of ill-health he said while under Mowbray's custody in Calais. That got a stir. If Plain Tom was gone, then he did not need to fear the opinion of the common people. He was their hero, and if the King had killed him, they clearly feared no one.

Then the King announced that he had removed all titles and offices from Archbishop Arundel. He remembered the mistake that Henry Plantagenet had made with Saint Thomas Beckett and was not going to kill another Archbishop of Canterbury. He went on to proclaim that all Arundel's lands were confiscated. Then he took those lands and attached them to Cheshire, making it a full principality within his Kingdom.

Sufficiently full, he turned to his supporters. He rewarded them well from Gloucester's and the Arundels' lands. Gaunt and Bolingbroke did well. He raised Bolingbroke up to the Dukedom of Hereford and gave Gaunt a bit more here and there. He also made Katherine Swynford an honest woman. She had seen off Gaunt's second wife by poison or some other means and snared Gaunt in marriage. However, she still had a string of bastards from Gaunt and she was anxious to see them settled. Gaunt had made a deal. In return for his support at the Parliament, Katherine's bastards would legitimized and granted titles. Thus, began the rise of the House of Swynford, the origin of many of the Kings of England.

After that, Richard paid off Mowbray for doing in Gloucester. He gave him the Dukedom of Norfolk and a portion of Arundel's lands. Then the King took all Lords and Bishops to Westminster Abbey and made them swear on the tomb of his favorite saint, Edward the Confessor, to love him forever and follow his bidding. It was a touching scene. If only the Cheshire archers hadn't been there as well, it would have been almost believable.

Finally it was over. The condemned were exiled or dead, and the guilty had survived. The King looked out on the crowd, "We would warn you all," he said, "that any man who helps any child of a condemned man shall experience the same penalty as that man. These men have been condemned and are lost to me forever. All their descendants are forever disinherited. Let them become beggars in the street."

He smiled and looked around, "These proceeding are at an end."

I looked to Owain, "What now?" I asked.

"Go home and thank the Lord God we have survived this."

HOW THE HOUSE OF LANCASTER APPEARED LOST

We returned home to await the great changes that we all knew were coming. With the death of Arundel and the exile of the Archbishop, we saw the Arundel's inheritance and all the properties of the Appellants swallowed into Richard's new holdings. A whole new Principality emerged in Cheshire, and Richard crowned himself Prince of Chester. In Wales and along the March, loyalties that had seemed forever set shifted and changed. Men felt lost and adrift. After living all his life under the Arundels' thumb, Owain now found that he was within the King's domain. Like many Welshmen, Owain realized that now every inheritance and legal suit depended on the King, and every drop of service owed and patronage given would go to and come from the King.

"We are in the King's pocket now," he said. "What he says we must do."

Then, just when we were beginning to feel settled, Richard moved again. The next events in this drama occurred at Shrewsbury.

To show his commitment to the West, Richard held his next Parliament in Shrewsbury. He swore he would remove all government from London and Westminster, as he associated them with his years of powerlessness. He was as good as his word. He made it clear that from now on, the Parliament would meet wherever the King was, and that the Kingdom would shift to the west.

Owain received a summons from the King to attend him and bring his oldest son with him to enter into the court as a page. Gruffudd was about fourteen at that time and a fine lad. He took much after his father and was a credit to his line.

"I'll not have him go to that sodomite," said Owain.

"Richard may be a King, but he is not to be trusted with a good-looking young boy. I will find some excuse. I will send him on a pilgrimage to St. David's. Richard will hold back titles, but I will avoid sending my son into the lion's den until he is a little better schooled in the ways of the world."

So Owain went to Shrewsbury without Gruffudd. He did take his brother Tudur with him. Tudur had spent most of the last ten years fighting in various places. He had spent some time in France with Arundel and Gloucester and had gone over to Ireland with Richard. Like most second sons, he lacked the drive of his older brother. He was a worthy and competent fighter but lacked the qualities of leadership. All in all he was a solid and dependable man but lacking in imagination. He was always happy to find someone to follow.

His exploits did add a little to Owain's reputation. He was the image of Owain and people who did not know them well would frequently mistake them. Many men have told me that they saw Owain in France or Ireland, and that he was good fighter. I always did little to disabuse them.

The Shrewsbury Parliament was a quite an occasion. The people all turned out to see the King, and he did not disappoint them. He entered with four thousand Cheshire Archers and knights all clothed in red and white. The Lords and their retainers came in next followed by all of the Commons. Everyone hoped that the drama was over and we could return to more normal times.

The Parliament began out well enough. The Lords and Commons were still cowed from the events of the Westminster Parliament and were willing to vote the King anything. As a result, Richard was granted some impressive subsidies and duties on all the wool and leather for the duration of his life. These were almost unprecedented. No King in living memory had received a duty for life. If able to keep this money, he could use it to build a force large enough to overwhelm the Lords and Commons and shift the balance of power between them forever.

There was more evidence of the new regime. The King announced that there were fifty more unnamed exceptions to previous pardons and offered that previous potential offenders could confirm their pardons by paying a small fee. It was clear that the Westminster Parliament was the beginning of a new way of doing business and that all should fear the Tyrant.

The atmosphere was rife with fear. Every man considered betraying his fellows. It seemed as though the Parliament would burst when Bolingbroke stepped forward. He had seen Mowbray betray Gloucester, and knew that Mowbray wouldn't be able to resist turning on him. Therefore, Bolingbroke determined to reprise his role as a traitor that he had played so well at Westminster.

When the denunciations were at their highest point, Bolingbroke rose, and after some pretty words explaining how much he loved the King, he pulled the dagger out and went straight for Mowbray.

"My Lord Norfolk is a foul traitor."

Mowbray sensed the mood of the meeting and realized Bolingbroke had beaten him to the punch. He knew to survive he must up the bet.
"You Majesty, this vile shit is a liar," said Mowbray. "The accusation of treason must stick in his throat, for he is the real traitor to Your Regality. I piss on him. He is a coward and a turd. I challenge him to bring proof forward or stand in combat against me."

Richard must have thought he had died and gone to heaven. The two remaining Appellants were turning on each other and accusing each other of treason.

"You pale, trembling shit," stormed Bolingbroke. He turned to the King, "Mowbray is the coward and traitor. I will bring forward full proof and will defend it on the field of combat."

Poor Bolingbroke, such a Plantagenet. Challenge him and he's at your throat.

Mowbray would have backed down. He was never one for a fight if he could avoid it. He was more conspiratorial by nature, and preferred a good plot to a clean open fight. Now he was stuck. There was no way back for him. So, given the situation, he stood up and answered Bolingbrook's challenge.

"I'll take your challenge," he said, "and when I defeat you, the world will see you for the traitor and coward you are."

Richard could contain himself no longer.

"My Lords, the talk of challenges is quite wonderful, but do you not think it would make sense to first reveal your accusation? We mean, clearly the two of you have something to say but neither of you have quite managed to come out with it yet."

The two of them looked a puzzled. It seemed that both had forgotten that they had yet to properly express this challenge.

Bolingbroke was the first to realize his mistake and spoke up.

"Your Majesty," said Bolingbroke, "I will show that Mowbray has stolen coin; more than eight thousand nobles who were sent him for the defense of Calais. Further, I shall show that he worked with the traitor Arundel to undermine you over the last ten years, and that he conspired against and murdered the Duke of Gloucester before he could be tried."

The last accusation was a bit of a shock. It was a surprise that anyone still cared about Gloucester, and it was widely assumed that Mowbray had killed him on Richard's orders. But the Tyrant was a cunning man. He knew Gloucester was popular, and he must have encouraged Bolingbroke to accuse Mowbray of his murder. Then he could act innocent and blame some other bugger for something he had clearly ordered himself.

Bolingbroke went on. "He murdered him because a trial of the Duke would have shown him innocent of all charges and the guilty party was none other than Mowbray himself."

Now this clearly did not make any sense, but it seemed that we were beyond reasoned judgment and had fallen into a world of fantasy.

"Serious charges," said Richard, "and so passionately expressed. Has my Lord Norfolk anything to say?"

Now Mowbray was in a bit of a bind here. He could hardly say, "I only killed Gloucester because you told me to" and no one believed Gloucester had perished on his own. As for the money, well everyone stole from the Royal Treasury and the governorship of Calais was renowned as a way for a young man with the King's trust to make a little scratch. Still, Mowbray was good plotter, and he was not to be outsmarted by a plodder like Bolingbroke.

He turned to the King, "Your Majesty, if your clerks check the records of Calais they will see that all the funds in my control were apportioned as intended." This was probably true, as any thief worth his salt can arrange the account books to show that everything appears as it should. "As for Gloucester, I swear I did not murder him. When he arrived in Calais, his health had soured and he was dead before I could attend to him. In terms of my participation in the governance of the traitor Arundel, I was Your Majesty's agent throughout. I thought that the best way to protect Your Majesty's interests was to pretend to be these traitors' friends and so learn their secret councils. In this way I would know if they hatched any plan against your interest and warn you before they could act."

Richard waved his hand, "My dear friends, calm down. There is no need for all this anger." He turned to Gaunt, "Uncle, can't you calm you son? Say something to him and make him forget this silliness?"

Gaunt was more than happy to intervene. It was clear that something had been planned, but it had got out of control and Gaunt desperately wanted to reign in his son.

"Harry," said Gaunt turning to Bolingbroke, "Do not accept Norfolk's challenge."

Bolingbroke did not move. Richard shrugged and turned to Mowbray, "Norfolk, renounce your challenge. This is not the time for fighting."

Of course, both men would have liked to have backed down, but they were frightened that if either did it might appear they lacked faith in their cause and give Richard a chance to go at them.

Mowbray shook his head. He made the decision to go all in.

"Dread Sovereign, I throw myself at your feet." That was a new one I thought. "You know you command every aspect of my life, but do not ask me to swallow this shame. Having been so accused, it is my duty to clear my name. I am disgraced and baffled by this accusation. The Earl of Hereford has dishonored my name and I will be avenged. I demand we resolve this action."

Richard raised an eyebrow and looked back to Bolingbroke.

Bolingbroke answered, "I will meet this cowardly fucker on the field. I am not afraid of this coward. He is a liar and slanderer. I call upon Your Majesty to set the time and place for this quarrel to be resolved."

Gaunt saw that all was lost and sat down in frustration. Richard grinned like the cat that had got the cream.

"Well, if there is to be nothing for it, then We suppose the two of your must sort it out on the field." He turned to a clerk and consulting a list, "Shall we say at Coventry at St. Lambert's day? We do like Warwickshire that time of year and We shall be on progress at Coventry." He looked at both men and saw them nod.

Bolingbroke raised his hand, "Your Majesty, I ask that the traitor Norfolk be confined until the contest. I fear that if he is free, he will try to escape."

"The same could be said for Hereford," said Mowbray.
"No," said Richard, "We have my Uncle's word and We are sure that my Uncle stands security for Hereford's good conduct." Gaunt looked pained, but nodded.

"Excellent," said Richard. "Norfolk, My Lord Archbishop Scrope shall take you into custody until the contest. Hereford is released to my Uncle." He smiled, "We think we have done a good day's business here today."

How right he was. Whatever happened, he would be short of one more Appellant and, if he played it well, it was possible both might go down. Owain was a mere bystander to all this, but he knew what had happened. Everyone knew. The King had won another battle.

Just before he left, Richard caught Owain's eye, "Master Glendowery," he said, "Do you have your son with you?"

"No, Your Majesty," said Owain, "I came to say he is on pilgrimage to St. David's and will not be home until after the Parliament has ended."

Richard smiled. "It is good to hear the young are devout. However, We would have your son to secure our bargain. Attend to Us again at Coventry and bring the boy with you."

Thus Gruffudd was not to escape. Instead, he found himself trudging with Owain and his telu to Coventry to watch the King's games unfold. Marged made a great to do, wailing and stamping her feet, but nothing could be done. Richard was not a man to oppose, and if he wanted the boy, then he would have the boy.

Coventry was a fine city. It has a good, well-maintained wall and an excellent cathedral. I am sure that it will forever be a reminder to the people of Warwickshire of the ancient beauty and heritage of the county.

The lists were well set up. Banners drifted in the wind, and the normal crowd of spectators, craftsmen, trainers, supporters, hawkers and whores that always attend a tournament was there. At one end of the field we could see Bolingbroke all tarted up and ready for the fight. I hate the man, but I must say that he always looked good on a horse. At the other end was Mowbray, less impressive but still looking sharp in his jousting armor. Very modern it was, and very Italian. I think Bolingbrook's armor was German on account of all the crusading he had done with the Germans against the heathen Slavs ten years earlier.

They rode up to the King's stand and were about to ask his blessing when the King interrupted them.

"My Lords," said Richard, "We cannot in good conscience allow this to go forward. We have thought upon the matter and decided that there is truth in both accusations. Therefore, We have determined on a course of action that will resolve the problem without loss of life."

He turned to Mowbray, "Norfolk, We know that you were deep in Arundel's pocket. There is no hiding the fact. We have decided that you are guilty."

There was a sharp intake of breath from those closest enough to hear. See, while Mowbray had been locked up, Richard had had his clerks go over all of Mowbray's records and destroy anything that might have incriminated the King, while digging up evidence that might prove his guilt.

Further, Richard's agents had been out among Mowbray's retinue, making it known that Mowbray was going down and that smart lads would switch sides and make no trouble if they wanted to keep their heads.

As for their Lordships, Mowbray had always been unpopular, and there were plenty who were happy to see him go. When it came down to it, his endless conspiring meant he had fucked just about everyone over the years. And now that the King was out to get him, there was no one left to stand up for him.

The moment Richard realized that, he thought, what the hell, I might as well get rid of him. Of course, the Parliament had voted Richard the power to try and condemn traitors at the Westminster Parliament so he didn't have to consult them. He made the decision alone and signed the paper. However, he did not want him dead. There had been plenty of killing recently, and Richard saw that he had to slow the pace if the Lords were to remain compliant. Therefore, he decided on another strategy.

"Norfolk," continued Richard "We exile you from Our Kingdoms for life. All your lands and titles are forfeit. However, We will grant you £1,000 for life. We hate to see an old friend fall on hard times." That was hush money. Mowbray knew that if he complained that would be gone too. Before Mowbray could speak, a pack of Richard's Cheshiremen descended on him and dragged him off his horse. He was gone so quickly that if you had told me he had been on the boat to France that afternoon, I would have believed you.

Bolingbroke was grinning ear to ear. He thought that his father had swung it with Richard and got him off the hook. Richard has other ideas. He turned to Bolingbroke.

"Cousin," Richard said with an adder's smile, "We cannot in good heart believe that you are fully innocent. While you might have not been central to the Appellants' crimes, you were involved and did not act against them. Therefore, We sentence you to ten years in exile. If you return earlier, your life and lands are forfeit."

Bolingbroke moved to say something, but his father stepped forward and stayed him. "My son accepts your wise judgment, Your Majesty," said Gaunt. That was a good move. The field was surrounded by Cheshiremen and a challenge to the King would have proved nasty. Richard smiled. "Excellent," said the King. He turned to Bushy, who always now seemed to be with him, "See that it is announced to the people."

And so it was. There was some booing and grousing, but there's nothing more that the common people enjoy than watching two rich buggers beat the shit out of each other. They accepted the King's decision. Richard was clever enough to keep the entertainments going and made sure that plenty of wine and ale flowed. By the time the people began to consider what had happened, Richard had left Coventry and was on his way to Leicester.

We were as stunned as everyone else. I thought it might mean that Gruffudd was spared, but of course it didn't.

Dodd came up and found us. He was a Captain of Archers by then and was well regarded by Richard, "The King asks me to take make sure your son leaves with us."

There was a to-do but Owain realized he had no choice. He took the boy aside and had a word with him. Dodd realized Owain's doubts and walked over, "Don't worry" he said, "I'll keep an eye on the boy. Nothing will happen to him. He'll bunk down with the Cheshire lads. They're good sorts and they'll make sure he's safe. The King puts on an act for the common people, but he's plain Dicken with us. Gruffudd will be safe and a spell with good Cheshiremen might help him improve his English and learn to shoot a bow properly," he grinned. "You Welshmen are always boasting, but you know only a Cheshiremen can really pull the bow the way God intended."

Dodd smiled at Gruffudd. "Did your Da tell you I knew him in London? He was a lad then; not much older than you. He was a rum one. The stories I could tell you. In fact, the stories I will tell you." Gruffudd smiled and shook his father's hand.

"I will be safe," he said.

"Say close to Dodd," said Owain, "and make me proud."

Thus Gruffudd went off with the Cheshiremen, and we returned home to wait for word of any other happenings. We did not have to wait long. Within six months, black old Johnny Gaunt was dead. The old bugger had been with us for so long I assumed he would live forever, but even really mean old bastards like Gaunt go eventually.

Richard didn't wait long to act. Before Bolingbroke could petition to return, Richard declared him exiled for life, and that all his lands and titles were forfeit. As with Mowbray, he got an allowance, but the Lancastrian inherence was lost to him and fell into Richard's hands.

I remember Owain saying, "I say this for the King, he has balls. He's stolen half the land in England and Wales and not one person's stood up to him. Who'd thought a sodomite like Richard would have the stomach for this?"

Jenkin Hanmer was there when we heard the news. "I tell you Owain, he may be our friend now, but no one is safe."

"You may be right," said Owain, "But we are sworn. As long as we are sworn and he acts for Wales, what are we to do? We have no choice but to remain loyal. A king is a king. If our oaths are left to choice, then they are meaningless. A man must abide by his oath no matter the consequences. If not, we are no better than the beasts. As long as Richard is King, we are bound to him. I can see no way out."

Indeed at that time, we could see no way out, but within a few months, the ever unpredictable forces of war were to provide an unexpected solution to our dilemmas.

THE RETURN OF HENRY BOLINGBROKE

Now the world might have gone on peacefully had not the Lord of the March decided to challenge the Irish chiefdoms at a place called Kells. My knowledge of the battle is limited. Safe to say, the Lord of the March led armies of the English King in Ireland, and exaggerated his own strength and abilities. His army was defeated, and he was killed. As a result, the eight-year-old son of Roger Mortimer became Lord of the March and, as the great-grandson of Lionel Duke of Clarence, he now became Richard's heir.

The Mortimers were fabulously wealthy. They were the most powerful of the Marcher Lords and owned most of Wales. Richard was not going to let the Mortimer inheritance slip out of his hands or let someone else control his heir. He snatched up the boy and took the Mortimer lands into his safekeeping. Once again, Richard swallowed great chunks of England and Wales and no one complained.

However, this was not all that happened. Richard decided that the Irish must be taught a lesson. He assembled a great army and determined to take all his forces to teach Ireland a lesson once and for all. I should add that the Kings of England have been teaching the Irish a lesson once and for all for as long as any of us can remember and probably will be doing so until Judgment Day. The problem is the Irish never learn their lessons. They are an incorrigible people and will never lie down easily or for long.

The English need to learn from us. We and the Irish have been fighting among ourselves for as long as there have been people in these islands. We both know it means nothing. It's just a nice argument between friends. We steal a little, and they steal a little. At the end of the day, we shake hands, exchange women and go home. Nothing lost and nothing gained. We would no more try to conquer Ireland, or anywhere else for that matter, than go to the moon. The Irish might raid a little here and there and plant a town or two, but their hearts are not in conquest. For some God awful reason, they like their own rain sodden land and, we for own God awful reason, love ours.

Thus, we fight but accept that final solutions to problems are not the kind of thing to expect from the Celtic mind.

Richard did not grasp this. He assumed that a good fight would solve his problems. This gave him an opportunity to return to Wales and in doing so; he must have recalled his promise to Owain. He decided to meet with the native Welsh leaders during his progress across South Wales and called them all to meet him at the Arthur's table in Caerleon.

Richard was a clever man. None of the English were there, all the Welsh who mattered to the Welsh and none of the Marcher Lords or big land owners. All the Uchelwyr were there. I could see that old thief, Henry Dun from Cydweli, Rhys and Morgan Gethin from the Gower, old man Tudur and his boys, and Dafydd ap Ieuan Goch from Cardiganshire, back from the Holy Land and twenty years of fighting the heathen with every inch of his body burned from the sun and scarred from the fight. With them were Rhys Ddu the Sheriff of Cardiganshire as gloomy and despondent as ever, the terribly proper and courtly Dafydd ap Gruffudd Fantach from Dwygyfylchi, cautious and well healed Hywel Fychan ap Madog ap Hywel, Ieun ap Jenkin Kemys from Abergavenny, the richest Welshmen in the south, and that vicious bastard Hywel Coetmor of Nantconwy. Each man brought his telu, so there was quite a crowd.

Richard had also called the Churchmen. There were the heads of the Franciscans in Wales, known to be very sympathetic to Richard, the Cistercians and even a few Dominicans. The White and the Grey Friars had always been good friends of the Welsh. The Dominicans were a little dodgier but they could be counted on. This might have been the first time I saw Gruffudd Yonge. He was to be one of the most important men in Wales during Owain's kingship, but then he was young church man with a quick mind and was rumored to have great things in his future.

Bishop Trefor of St. Asaph was there. He was always a good friend of Owain's and would turn up to anything that would help Wales. Richard was even smart enough to pull in the great Anglo-Welsh families that had married into the Welsh. Thus, the Hanmers were there, as were the Plustons, Kynastons and maybe even some Scudamores.

Richard called us all together at Caerleon somewhere around the Feast of St. Gregory. We met in the early evening. He had the place decked out with banners and torches. We all stood around waiting for the King to come. Then a trumpet sounded and in walked Richard's Cheshiremen. They marched in good order and surrounded the table. Then in came Richard, dressed like a Welshmen with his hair long and braided and wearing the kilt and sandals. The crowd bowed deeply. Richard acknowledged us and said, "Croeso cyffeillion."

There was a thunderous shout of support and joy. He didn't get it quite right, but it was more Welsh than an English King had ever spoken. He quieted us and continued in French with a clerk translating.

"We do not speak your language as well as We would like. We look forward to spending more time in your lands and hope to learn more. You all know Our affection for the men of the West. You are the elder race of Briton, the true descendants of Arthur. When Macsen Wledig was Emperor, he ruled from these hills and passed the keys to Britannia into your hands for safe keeping when he went across the seas. Of course, he did not return and in his place came the Saxons. You stood bravely against them for five hundred years until Our ancestors came from France to return you, the men of the West, to the world of Rome. Since then Our forefathers have ruled over the Saxons to ensure that they remain as they should: slaves to all civilized men."

That drew a great cheer. This was red meat and fresh ale for us. We didn't like the French and the Normans, but we hated the English.

"Now in time the Saxons led Our ancestors away from the path of righteousness and persuaded them to make war upon the men of Britain. This was wrong. We are here today to tell you that that time is over. We have a new vision for the future. In Our vision We shall revive the Empire of Britain of Arthur and Macsen Wledig. In that Empire, all the peoples of Britain will share equally. The Princes of Powys and Deheubenth will sit as equals with the Lord of Northumbria and the Prince of Strathclyde. The Lords of Ireland will deal as equals with the

Dukes of Kent and Norfolk. All will be equal under a single imperial crown. We shall be your Emperor, and you shall be raised to your proper place in Our Empire."

Again there rose a loud cheer. Not many understood what it meant, but it sounded good. Richard went on.

"What will this mean to you? An end to bans and exclusions. A Welshman may hold any office. A Welshmen may buy, hold and sell any land that he wishes. You may hold land in the English, Roman or Welsh manner as you choose. There will be an end to the March; you will be ruled directly under Royal law. No more forced loans, fines or dues. You shall pay the same duties and taxes as any of Our subjects. Welshmen will be allowed to reside anywhere; the Englishries will no longer be for the English only. You may speak your language in official proceedings, and there will be no bias in favor of English, although of course French and Latin will remain the languages of state. We will create an Empire that is open to you all. Welshmen of talent and good breading will be welcome into my service and may rise as far as their talent takes them. This is what I offer you. Do you accept?"

There were shouts of joy and support. This was what Welshmen had begged for ever since the Conquest. It was not the return of our freedom, but it was the best we could hope for.

"All We ask of you is your loyalty, your sworn oath to support Ourselves and Our successors." There were shouts of assent. "We go to war in Ireland to bring the Irish chieftains into our Empire, and We will bring your men with Us. Further, We ask that while We are gone, you defend Our lands and titles against Our enemies." There were more shouts of assent.

Then Richard said, "When We return, you will join Us in Our further wars to bring the so-called King of Scotland to heel and establish Our Empire in the North beyond the Wall."

More shouts and agreements.

"Then, My Lords," Richard said, pausing for effect. Nice touch that; no Englishman ever called a Welshman 'my lord.'

"We ask that you come one by one and swear for your house, your kin, and your tribe to obey Us and Our successors and follow Us in all of Our endeavors."

One by one, they all came up. All swore and all agreed. If Richard was as good as his word, this was a new day. The world had changed that night. Owain and his telu approached. He kneeled in front of Richard,

"Lord Powys," said Richard, "Your son serves me well." He smiled and Owain returned his smile. "Our Captain of Archers tells Us he is a good man with a sword and will make a fine addition to Our armies."

"Thank you, Your Majesty," said Owain. "He is a good boy."

"Indeed," said Richard, "Will you be joining Us in Our campaigns in Ireland?" he asked.

"No, Your Majesty," said Owain, "I will stay and guard your interests along the March but I send my son and my brother, Tudur, with you." Tudur walked forward and bowed. "He has fought with you before in Ireland and is a good man. I commend him to you. He brings two score of mounted spearmen who will defend Your Majesty's interests. I have gathered and recruited these men at my own expense and will pay for them in the field."

Richard was pleased. "This is most excellent. When We return, We shall meet with you again. We will convey titles upon you and your kin."

Owain bent and kissed the King's ring, "My Emperor," he said, "I will be loyal."

Richard liked that. "We will count on you, My Lord."

Richard left the next day and headed to West Wales to take his ships to Ireland. Now many men have said that Richard was a fool to go to Ireland and leave so many dangerous enemies on the loose. Those who say this don't know what they are talking about. Richard was well aware of what he was doing. He knew that many of his enemies remained behind, so he took hostages with him. Henry of Monmouth was taken as hostage for his father Bolingbroke, the son of the Arundel for good behavior of his uncle the exiled Archbishop, Henry Beaufort for the good behavior of the Gaunt's widow and her faction, and the young son of the late Duke of Gloucester. The only faction that slipped the noose was the Percys. The King had requested that Hotspur accompany him to ensure the good behavior of the Earl of Northumberland, but as ever, the Earl delayed and managed to miss the King's sailing.

Richard took other precautions too. He put his cloth headed uncle, Edmund Langely, in charge of the Kingdom. You could count on Edmund to do as he was told. Richard knew he wouldn't have the gumption to challenge him, but would have brains to resist anyone who made a grab for the Kingdom. He also took with him all of the crown jewels. It was clever move. Put a crown on your head and the English will follow you everywhere. Also, it was difficult for anyone else to be King without the crown.

He left at the end of the month and landed in Ireland with all his army by the beginning of June. Owain returned to his lands and awaited the King. It was not to be, of course. In the first week of July we heard that Bolingbroke has returned to England. Rumor reached us that he and a band of his supporters, including the Lord of Ruthin and Archbishop Arundel, had landed at Ravenspur on the Humber sometime late in June. Bolingbroke had had extensive lands in Yorkshire, and this was no doubt the reason he landed there.

At first Bolingbroke sent messages about that he had returned only to take back his land and had no interest in challenging Richard. Gradually he moved across Yorkshire and gathered men as he went. Soon his thirty companions swelled to several hundred, and he began to pose a significant threat. Sometime towards the middle of the month he reached Doncaster. There, it was said that the Percys would challenge him. Of course, the Earl of Northumbria could never resist a good conspiracy or pass up the opportunity for betrayal. He and his son rode out and dealt with Bolingbroke to secure a higher place in the Kingdom if they supported him rather than Richard.

In years to come Henry Percy would always claim that he only changed sides because he thought Bolingbroke had been wronged and only sought the return of his lands. I find this difficult to believe. I think that Bolingbroke had enough men behind him by the time he reached Doncaster to demonstrate his intentions were more than a desire to reclaim his land.

Now Richard was in a bind. When the army arrived in Ireland, the fleet had been disbursed. It was impossible for him to quickly gather his army and return to Wales in force. He sent messages to his Uncle, the Duke of York, to gather all of Richard's forces in England and prepare to resist Bolingbroke. Poor dull Edmond had been made Keeper of the Kingdom of England before Richard left, and now Richard counted upon his to chase off Bolingbroke.

However, Edmund was forever slow and, as it turned out, easily swayed. He made for the west, timidly gathering his army as he went. Bolingbroke and Arundel realized they had a choice. They could either make for London and Westminster to secure the south and the wealth of the Kingdom, or they could continue west and try to capture Richard's inner citadel, the Principality of Chester. They were still debating the correct course of action when Edmund began to move.

Arundel proposed that they follow Edmund and catch him before he could link up with Richard. Bolingbroke, ever anxious for a keener mind to help him out, agreed and they caught up to him at Berkeley. There in the Church at Berkeley, Edmund, Bolingbroke, Arundel and the Percys met. They hatched a plot and made a deal. Edmund would support Bolingbroke in his claims against Richard. In return, Richard would remain King and would not lose his throne. Edmund really didn't have choice at that point. His army was beginning to desert to Bolingbroke, and only the diehards wished to stand up and fight. The two of them united their forces and marched on down to Bristol where the King's friends, Bushy, Bagot and Green were waiting. They could have put up a fight, but the constable of the castle surrounded them the moment Bolingbroke appeared and went over to the rebels. Before they knew it, they had fallen into Bolingbroke hands. He wasted no time in dealing with them. They were executed the next day, and a clear warning was sent out to all those who favored Richard: if you stay with the grand sodomite, the axe awaits you.

Owain rallied his kinsmen and his retainers, but the best of them had gone with Richard to Ireland. Messages began to arrive from Richard. The King had sent the Earl of Salisbury ahead of his return, and all loyal Welshmen were to rally to the Earl of Salisbury at Conwy. So we went and met with him there. Welshmen from all over the North came. All ready to follow the King. Day upon day we waited and no word came.

Finally Owain went to Salisbury.

"My lord of Salisbury," said Owain, "we have remained here for ten days. I can hardly keep my countrymen together. We have heard nothing from the King. People are starting to believe he will not return. They will disperse unless they have a sign."

Salisbury looked down, "Stay another day. I know the King puts all his trust in you."

"They are saying King is dead," said Owain. "There are signs." He had talked to Crach the previous night and was full of prophecy. "The bay-trees are withered, stars and meteors have been seen and the moon is red. I have consulted my seer, and he whispers that fearful change will come. All these signs foretell the death and fall of kings. If Richard is not dead, he will be dead soon. Bolingbroke is moving toward Chester and my estates. I will remain, but most of these men will return to their homes to protect my rights. They are simple men and need signs to convince them to remain."

And so Richard's army disbanded and returned to their lands. We continued to wait. Finally we heard that Richard had landed in the South.

"We will go south and meet him," said Owain. Thus Owain and telu rode south and met with Richard at Carmarthen. We had expected a strong defense, but we found Richard had left the castle and was in prayers at the Whiteland Abbey near the town. We were amazed to find that the stupid bastard had left his army in Ireland. He came back with half a dozen bowmen and a few retainers.

Owain walked up to him and bowed, "My King, what news do you have?"

Richard seemed confused and distant. "Lord Powys," he said, "We promised you a title and lands, and We shall give you them. We have heard from My Lord Salisbury that you have rallied out Welsh followers at Conwy. "

"Yes, Your Grace," said Owain, "but we must move quickly. Bolingbrook's agents are loose and are spreading rumors that you are dead or still in Ireland."

"We have heard these rumors. We sent Thomas Despenser to confront them. Do you know We have made him Duke of Gloucester? He has gone to Glamorgan to raise the county, but the tenantry has refused to rise. Can you believe that? We had planned to march through Glamorgan and challenge Bolingbroke in the south, perhaps at Radcott where he killed my beloved De Vere."

Richard trailed off, his words gradually losing focusing and energy.

"You Grace," said Owain, attempting to refocus the King,

"Who did he speak to? Did he speak with the men from Glamorgan who attended you at Caerleon? Henry Dun from Cydwehli or Rhys Gethin at Gower? These are the men who can raise the county for you. The English there are in Bolingbrook's pocket. That land has been in the hands of the Gaunt and his family for years."

Richard seemed lost. He focused on Owain, "I do not know. I rely on others."

Owain was becoming frustrated, "Where are your retainers? Where are the Archers that you ride with? Where is my son?"

"Your son?" said Richard, "Oh, he is in Ireland with my army."

"Why did you not wait and return in force with them?" asked Owain.

"We assumed that there would be adequate forces here" said Richard, "We did not imagine Bolingbroke would move so fast."

Owain looked directly at the King, "You Majesty, the English are too strong in the Southwest. If you stay here you are in danger. You must travel to the North. We are strong there and can defend you. The castles of the north can keep Bolingbroke out forever, and we will rally your forces to you and return the army from Ireland."

Richard seemed to shake himself. "Yes, you are right," he said. "We should travel to the north. Salisbury is there."

"We can take you north," said Owain, "Pick your most important advisors and we will go straight away. We will go by the paths that are known only to the Welsh. You must disguise yourself, Your Majesty. If word of your journey leaks out, then assassins and homicides will strike at you."

Richard began to wake up, "We shall dress as monks. We shall be a party of brothers returning from pilgrimage." That was Richard. Suggest dress up and you had his attention. I swear he was more interested in the exact composition of his disguise than in the location of his forces.

So together with the Dukes of Exeter and Surrey, the Earl of Gloucester and the Bishops of Carlisle, Lincoln and St. David's we made our way North. Richard made the mistake of leaving Thomas Percy, the steward of his household, behind. He was angered by what he saw as the King's desertion, broke his staff of office, sent messages to Bolingbroke at Bristol, and surrendered Carmarthen to the Lancastrians.

I have heard that he wept bitterly on hearing that Richard was gone and swore that Richard had betrayed his friends and that the end of his reign was near. Richard also made the mistake of leaving all the crown jewels and regalia. He had brought it back with him from Ireland. He assumed that Percy would keep it safe until he returned. Of course, Percy surrendered it to the Lancastrians although, as I shall tell you later, it was not to reach them intact.

We moved on far from where the English travel, up over the highlands that look down on Ystrad Tywi, through Ceredigion, to Strata Flordia and the Abbey of the White Brothers, and then up through Powys, to Harlech, Caernarfon, and into Gwynedd and Eryru before finally arriving in Conwy. At the same time, rumors came that we were being shadowed by Bolingbroke moving north through the March. We heard he was at Hereford, then Ludlow, and then Shrewsbury. Then we heard that Chester had surrendered. Bolingbroke sent messengers and the traitorous Sheriff Bob Liegh gave the city up without a fight.

At Conwy Salisbury came out to meet us. Richard rode up to him.

"My Lord, how far off lies your power?" said Richard.

"All gone My Lord. Yesterday there were twelve hundred men, but rumors abounded that you were dead. They all dispersed and fled. Even if Master Glendowery had been here he could not have held them," he said, nodding toward Owain.

The blood drained from Richard's face, "We are lost. Everyone who wishes to be safe should leave now."

A courtier spoke up, "Comfort, Your Grace, remember who you are."

Richard shook himself.

"You're right. We forgot Ourself. After all We are the King, and is not a King's name worth thousands of men? Don't worry my friends. We know Our uncle York. He will not desert me. He has power enough to save us. But where are Bushy, Bagot and Green?"

Salisbury looked down, "Bristol has fallen, Your Grace. Bushy, Bagot and Green have been taken. They are dead."

Richard wailed, "For the love of God, why?

There was quiet. Salisbury spoke up. "We must take refuge in Conwy. The castle is tied to the sea. We can bring the army from Ireland and then link up with your supporters in England."

Richard nodded. He was losing himself again. Salisbury and Richard's retainers looked at each other. They knew that they had to keep Richard moving or he would collapse.

In Conwy we began to ready the castle for a siege. Old Man Tudur was Sheriff of Anglesey by that time, and he arranged for corn and cattle to be brought across the Menai Straights to the castle.

Owain sent messages out across Wales, and we received notice that men were on the move to Conwy. Owain and Salisbury studied the routes that Bolingbroke could take and discussed how lightly armed Welsh raiding parties could harry and raid the English as they progressed along the coast road. At the same time, Richard sent messengers to Ireland ordering his commanders to prepare to return and send soldiers ahead to Conwy.

Conwy was a strong castle. Properly supplied it would take months to reduce it. If Bolingbroke attempted to bring his army into Gwynedd, we would destroy his supply lines and starve him out. By the time the castle was seriously threatened, the army would be back from Ireland and Richard would have been able to rally his forces in England. As long as we stayed there, we were safe.

Then one day, the Earl of Northumberland appeared at the town gates. He came alone with no retinue. We had intelligence that his retinue was somewhere over the estuary. However, his presence without armed men suggested that he had the King's best interests at heart.

Richard came to the gate and looked down on him. "What do you think, Salisbury?" asked the King.

"I believe he comes in good faith," said Salisbury. "Perhaps he seeks to mediate between Your Majesty and Bolingbroke? Whatever he wants, he is just one man. As long as we do not leave the castle, we are safe. I see no harm in hearing what he has to say."

Richard nodded and Northumberland was brought in. He was presented to Richard in the Great Hall.

"Your Majesty," said Northumberland and bowed deeply.

"Come to conspire further?" asked Richard, "Some new plot? Some new betrayal?"

"Your Majesty, I simply come to put to you the Duke of Lancaster's case," said Northumberland.

"We know no Duke of Lancaster," said Richard, "The last man We knew of that title was my uncle, and he died a few months ago."

"I beg your pardon, Your Majesty," said Northumberland, reddening, "I mean the Earl of Hereford."

"We know no one of that title either. We once knew a man of that title before We sent him away. We believe that he is now known as the exile Henry Bolingbroke."

Northumberland sighed, "This is the man I refer to."

"Have you come to offer Bolingbrook's surrender? Has my uncle York finally come to his senses and turned against the traitor? Or have you come to tell me he declares war on my Kingdoms and seeks to take for himself all my titles and processions?"

"Your Majesty," said Northumberland, "You misunderstand Bolingbrook's intent. All he seeks is the restoration of his lands and titles. If you will agree to this, then he will surrender his position and return to his estates."

Richard looked thoughtful, "This is all he wants?"

"Perhaps a few other minor concessions, but nothing significant."

Gloucester spoke up, "What other conditions?"

Northumberland looked at him, "Your Majesty cannot be seen to be at fault in these matters. The King cannot be wrong. Therefore, there must be someone made to take the blame for the actions taken against the Lancastrian inheritance."

"Whose heads do you want, Northumberland?" said Salisbury.

"You are too harsh," said Northumberland, "All My Lord Hereford seeks is for Your Majesty to renounce the powers granted to him in the Westminster and Shrewsbury Parliaments. He seeks a return to the status quo. You must convene the Parliament and allow Hereford to act as your Steward in Parliament. Exeter, Surry, Salisbury, and the Bishop of Carlisle must all stand trial, but I swear they shall not be punished beyond exile for ten years. The lands granted to them after the Westminster and Shrewsbury Parliaments will be surrendered, but they may keep all lands and titles that accrued to them before those Parliaments."

Salisbury exploded, "How can we trust you? Ten years? Living in poverty on the continent?"

"Please, you overreact," said Northumberland, "A pension can be provided for you as was provided to Mowbray. A comfortable life in sunny Italy might be preferable to civil war and spending a winter in these drafty castles."

"He is a liar," said Salisbury to the King. "Northumberland, you never said an honest word in your life. You are a lying fucker and always were."

Northumberland reddened. "And you are an immoral sodomite. You owe you power entirely to the unnatural love of patrons."

"Do you hear him?" said Salisbury, "He insults Your Majesty? He is not to be trusted."

Northumberland went down on his knees, "Your Majesty, I give you my word. I swear an oath by St. Cuthbert, the most

Holy saint of the Northlands that I will stand by you in all things. You will be under my protection. If Bolingbroke acts against you or stands for more than we have agreed to, then I will strike him down. Bring the Host to me now, I will swear on it. Bring the bones of any saint and I will swear on them. I will bring the Archbishop Arundel and Bolingbroke here and they will swear on the host too. "

"Arundel has returned too?" asked Richard. "We should have known it. Bolingbroke is not capable of dreaming this up himself. There needs to be a brain to move the muscle. We will think on this. Northumberland will wait with Us in this castle. We will tell you of Our decision soon. Wait outside until We have decided."

Northumberland left. Richard turned to his council of war: Surrey, Salisbury, Exeter, Gloucester, the Bishops of Carlisle, Lincoln and St. David's and Owain.

"We would take your counsel," said Richard.

Salisbury spoke up, "You cannot trust him. The moment you put yourself in his power, you are lost. Master Glendower's hillsmen tell us that Northumberland's men are out there. Within a few days Bolingbrook's army could be here. Once you leave these walls, you cannot be protected."

Gloucester interrupted, "Consider the advantages you possess now. We hold the castles of Beaumais, Conwy, Caernarfon, and Harlech. These castles are the strongest in Europe. Each can be supplied by sea. They can be supplied indefinitely from Ireland. If one falls, you may move to the next and continue the fight there. You possess a large, experienced army in Ireland. As we speak, it is being readied to return. The Welsh gentry and tribes are rallying to you. They know this country and can destroy any army that marches into these hills".

"You have hostages from most of the leading families and factions that oppose you, and they will not move against you as long as you hold their families. In England, you have thousands of supporters. Your party is strong and looks to you for leadership. Stand here and they will come to you. You have allies in the France and Castile. If all is lost you can escape to your lands in France and return with the support of your cousin the King of France. Everything favors you. We are safe now, and the longer we wait the more the situation will move in our favor. All we have to do is wait and Bolingbroke and his rebellion will collapse. I urge you to put no trust in Northumberland. It would be madness to leave this fortress simply on the word of a man who is a known plotter and conspirator."

"What do you think?" asked Richard, pointing at Owain.

"My Lords Gloucester and Salisbury are correct. Time favors you. As we sit thousands of Welshmen are converging on this area. You are their best hope in a hundred years. They will die for you if you ask them to. They know well who Bolingbrook's allies. Men like Ruthin and Arundel; these men are not friends of the Welsh. They know if Bolingbroke wins, it will not go well for the Welsh."

Richard spoke up. "Whatever happens We have no intention of agreeing to Northumberland's terms. It would mean a return to Our minority. Everything We have worked for over the last ten years would be gone. We may agree, but only to persuade him to stand down and to lure Bolingbroke to me. If We tell them that We agree as long as they come to Us in person and swear to fealty on the host, they might come. Particularly if they thought We were helpless and trusting in Northumberland. We could station men in hiding. When Bolingbroke and Arundel come, Our men could take them prisoner." He looked around questioningly.

"It is a dangerous course, Your Majesty," said Gloucester.

"We may take them, but it is risky to expose Your Majesty to danger. If would be much better simply to wait until our forces are all together. Remember, Your Majesty, that your cause was lost at Radcott Bridge when De Vere moved too soon."

Richard thought. Radcott was always a sore point for him. Then he brightened, "But remember during the Hurling Times when We faced the mob at Smithfield? We showed no fear and rode straight out at them. They were so overawed by Our regality that We were able to defeat a force of thousands of armed men with a single command."

"But Your Majesty," said Salisbury in exasperation, "There is no need to take this risk. You are safe here. Everything favors delay and caution."

So the argument went on until late into the night. Finally the King made his decision. He would adopt the risky strategy of pretending to trust Northumberland. Owain would station bowmen and warriors in the hills around the town. A meeting place would be arranged which seemed to favor Northumberland. Bolingbroke, York, and Arundel would be called to witness Richard's surrender. When they were in the trap, Richard would call and Owain's men would emerge and carry the rebel leaders back into Conwy. Once there they would be forced to order their forces to stand down and return home. They would then be executed, and the rebellion would collapse. The army would return from Ireland as planned, and Richard would make a great march of revenge against all those who had opposed him.

Richard called Northumberland and played the part of the defeated fool. He ate his breakfast mournfully and complained he had no appetite. He repeatedly asked for Northumberland's assurances that he would be safe and said how he looked forward to seeing his cousin Bolingbroke again. I thought he laid it on a bit thick, but he always was a little over the top.
While he acted out his part, Owain and some of the Welshmen slid out of the town. We moved to the arranged spot on the other side of the estuary and hid among the green wood. I would have wished for a few more archers with us. The bow is the weapon of the South. Northerners are good with the spear.

Northumberland left early on the pretext of arranging the meeting. He returned late in the day and said the meeting was arranged for tomorrow. The next day we saw them leave and cross the river as planned. Then Northumberland and the King made for east.

"I wish that he had agreed to meet with them at Conwy rather than over the estuary," said Owain. I nodded. The King showed too much confidence in crossing to the northern side of the river. We climbed the ridge and looked down into the valley below. We could see the road to the east and, clear as day, we could see Northumberland's retinue waiting.

"I see no sign of Bolingbroke or Arundel," said Owain
He looked closer, "I think it's a trap. We must save the King."

He ran to his horse. I shouted to the others to follow. Owain reached his horse and spurred it down the hill.

The King and Northumberland rode on. Owain began to shout that Richard was riding into a trap. The King saw Owain and halted. I could see him gesticulating at Owain. Northumberland's retinue saw what was happening and began to move toward the King and Northumberland. We raced on. Northumberland's retinue was not an overpowering force. If it came to a fight, we could take them.
Owain arrived and pulled up his horse, "Your Grace, this is a trap. Northumberland has his forces on hand and intends to take you. Bolingbroke and his friends are nowhere to be seen."

"Your Majesty," said Northumberland, "This man is mistaken. I have brought my retinue here to protect you and escort you to the meeting place. I assure you, you are under my protection."

Richard hesitated, "Do you swear?" he asked Northumberland.

"Yes, Your Grace," said Northumberland.

Owain interrupted, "Your Majesty."

The King waved him down, "We trust Northumberland. You may return to Conwy. We have spoken this morning and We have come to the conclusion that we are of the same mind."

Owain protested, "But why? I do not understand why you are doing this?"

The King looked at him, "You have been a good friend, Owain. We would have made great use of you, but We must go. We sense Our end is very near and there is no way to escape it."

"No," said Owain, "Nothing is inevitable. We make our own future."

"You know that is not true," said Richard sadly. "Our fate was made a thousand years before We were born. We shall rely on our Regality for protection. If it does not protect Us, We see no reason to possess it. If Henry would have Our crown simply because he is the better knight, more beloved or more competent, then what is to stop others challenging him? We will trust that he is intelligent enough to realize that once the golden thread is broken, once the magic and mystery are gone, then they will be lost forever.

"Henry may depose me and pretend to rule, but the crown will never sit easily on his head. A thousand challengers and pretenders will spring up. Perhaps even you, Master Owain? Kings are anointed by God, not made by the will of the people or the whim of powerful factions. If Henry does not yield on this point, he is a fool. Better to have a weak and unpopular but rightful king than a strong king who stole his throne. Such a king will never be safe. We will trust that Henry realizes this."

"You assume too much of men," said Owain, "Men act without understanding the consequences of their actions. The Devil is ever active. He has tempted Henry, and Henry is not strong enough to resist."

"Perhaps he tempted Us first?" said the King, "A more prudent prince might not have tempted the fates? Perhaps this is all some strange payment for the sins We have committed, or perhaps the Lord seeks to repay this sinful nation for the terrible crimes We have committed throughout the world. We do not know. Do not worry, Master Owain. When sins and merits are weighed, you shall be found to be a man who did the best he could. We shall recommend you to Henry."

And thus, his mind made up and sure of his course of action, Richard left. We watched as he rode away. "I never saw a man so happy to go to his death," said Owain. I agreed.

"What do you suppose he is thinking?"
"I believe he is losing his mind or perhaps is possessed. Perhaps some malign magic? I am at a loss. When the history of this day is written, no man will ever be able to explain what happened here."

I looked at Owain, "I tell you something, My Lord, I never heard him speak more sense or with deeper understanding,"

I said.

"Perhaps wisdom only comes when we truly face our end," he said. He shook his head, "I just wish I understood why he became determined on this course."

To this day I cannot account for Richard's actions. He had every opportunity to escape, and yet he went. Perhaps it was magic. When I met Northumberland years later in Scotland, I asked him what he thought happened. He had no explanation either.

"I was as surprised as you," he said, "I expected he would turn and run back at any moment. I just kept talking, and he kept going. I couldn't believe my luck. I have never been able to explain it."

Such are the strange histories of Kings. The entire history of Britain hung on that moment, and there is no good explanation why it went one way rather than another.

What happened next is well known. Richard went to Rhuddlan and then on to Flint. At the same time, Bolingbroke moved his army to Flint and Richard fell right into his hands without a fight. With no leader, Richard's forces broke up and returned home. The army sat in Ireland waiting for orders and gradually fell apart through Bolingbrook's subversion. We returned to Sycharth and waited for Gruffudd to return. It was clear that a new age had come, and we needed to prepare for it.

HOW HENRY BOLINGBROKE STOLE THE CROWN OF ENGLAND

The next few months were confused. Rumors were everywhere. The King was dead, and then the King was alive. He had run to France or Scotland or was imprisoned in Flint or the Tower. Nothing seemed certain. Then, one day in September, I saw a group of riders coming toward Sycharth. I called the watchmen, and we stood upon the gate awaiting them. As they came close, I saw that Gruffudd and Tudur led the group, and I ran down to meet them.

"Gruffudd" I called to him, "It is good to see you returned, and you Tudur. Owain will be anxious to see you and hear your report."

"Do you have no words for us?" said one of the other riders.

I looked and saw that Dodd was among the riders and leading the pack were the Tudor brothers.

"What a gang of thieves and liars," I said, "I would lock you out forever if I did not think that you had news for My Lord."

They dismounted and we embraced. I took them to Owain. Marged made a great to do at Gruffudd's return. She always spoilt the boy.

That night Owain had a few good pigs killed and brought out his best Shrewsbury beer. We sat up late into the night and heard the story of their adventures in Ireland.

"We landed in Waterford on the first of June," said Dodd, "It was a great army. Beyond anything assembled by a King of England in Ireland, and perhaps the greatest force ever seen in Ireland. We were stuck at Waterford for six days waiting for the Duke of Albemarle to arrive. I think he may have been in league with Bolingbroke and sought to confuse and delay the King while the fleet broke up and sailed up to Dublin."

He took a gulp of his ale.

"We began to march inland toward the Black Mountains where the Earl of Kilkenny was hiding. Again Albemarle trailed behind, and we waited two weeks for him to catch up. The MacMurrough[1] held back and began to strike at our supplies, retreating into the mountains whenever we pursued. The King sent out messengers offering pardons if he would surrender and proposing a generous peace. The MacMurrough laughed at him and said Richard would starve and rot before he was able to catch him.

"It was decided that Richard and the bulk of the army would push on to Dublin where they could be resupplied, while the Earl of Gloucester would track down the MacMurrough and negotiate an end to the war. At Dublin the army waited and starved. Albemarle had been charged with bringing supplies from England, but again he had delayed. He finally arrived with a hundred-ship load of supplies, but only after many in the army had begun to question the wisdom of the King's strategy. By then the King had lost patience. He decided that there would be no more negotiations and offered a huge bounty on the MacMurrough's head.

"Richard sent parties out beyond the Pale[2] to bring the MacMurrough to justice, but none came. At that time a great storm appeared on the sea between Wales and Ireland, and no ships could travel for more than six weeks. Of course in this time, Bolingbroke travelled from France and established himself in Yorkshire. However, because of the storm, we did not hear of Bolingbrook's return until mid-July when he was already at Bristol. The King was hot for returning with the whole army to Chester or Wales. However, Albemarle had treacherously dispersed the fleet, and it had returned to Waterford. Thus the King decided to send Salisbury to rally support and await his arrival.

"Even if he had wanted to return, the army was stretched out all over the Wiklow Mountains hunting MacMurrough. It would have taken weeks to concentrate at Dublin and even more time to bring the back. Messengers were sent to tell the army to return to Waterford and then prepare for the return to Wales."

He paused and poked the fire.

"Albemarle promised the King that he would return with the army the moment it was ready to move and persuaded the King to return to Haverford. He said that our forces in England and Wales were melting away for lack of Richard's royal presence, and that he must go to reassure his supporters. Richard took his advice and left with all the loyal captains, leaving Albemarle in charge. The moment the King's ship was beyond the horizon, Albemarle deserted to Bolingbroke. He dispatched the fleet again to Dublin and waited for news to arrive."

"What did you do?" asked Owain.

Gwilym ap Tudur answered, "What could we do? We knew nothing of what was happening. Albemarle did not come straight out and proclaim his disloyalty. He acted sneaky like. We were told to wait and rest and recover our supplies as the campaign we were about to proceed upon was likely to be long. The movement of the fleet was explained by the need to go fetch the supplies from Dublin that had been delivered there in July. It all made sense."

"He sent loyal men out into the mountains to collect the stragglers and protect our rear," said Rhys ap Tudur, "We were chasing around the Wiklow Mountains making sure everyone was safely returned while Albemarle was bribing less honest men."

Tudur nodded, "It's true," he said, "We rode out of a loyal camp on a Monday and returned to find a camp of traitors on a Friday."

"What of the Cheshiremen and the Welshmen?" I asked.
"They were boarded on ships as if they were to return. The Albemarle sailed them out into the bay and kept them there. They were trapped below decks with no food or water. He simply withdrew the crews and kept the ships at anchor far from the land with the loyal men caged below decks."

"The bastard," Owain swore. "Christ's balls, but Albemarle will pay for this."

"So how did you return?" I asked.

"When we returned to camp we saw what had occurred," said Dodd. "Rhys and Gwilym had the idea that we must return quickly. We found a fishing boat and persuaded an Irishman to take us across to Haverford. He landed us at some miserable place on the coast. There we heard of Richard's capture and made out way back here."

"A good story," said Owain.

"But it is not over," said Rhys with a gleam in his eye. "We came upon an interesting find on our way home. We were riding on the path North when we came upon that slimy bastard Thomas Percy. Had all the royal regalia with him he did, taking it to Bristol to give to the usurper. So we played the outlaw and deprived him of it."

"The Crown and all?" asked Owain.

"Well, not the big one they keep in Westminster," said Gwilym, "but the one that Richard traveled with and the all the other stuff."

"Where is it?" I asked.

"Hidden in every robber cave between here and the Twyi," said Rhys.

"And hidden it will stay until Richard wants it back," said Gwilym.

"That's right," said Rhys, "We'll keep it all until the usurper is defeated. Then we'll show the King what good stewards we are and he'll reward us."

Owain rubbed his head, "I'm not sure if you can trust our people with such wealth. They're good with small things but that much gold would tempt a saint."

"Too late now," said Rhys, "It's already out there. Anyway, let's forget all that and discuss how we intend to free Richard."

Dodd spoke up, "I've been thinking on this. From what I hear, Richard is in Flint and will be transported to London to stand trial in front of the Parliament. Now, I say we get some of your lads and some of my boys together and we take him when he crosses Cheshire. His home territory and our local knowledge favor us."

It was a good plan and all agreed that it made sense. As we gathered our forces, more information began to come in regarding the King's whereabouts. They took the King from Flint to Chester. At Chester they said that the people booed the King when they paraded him through the city. In truth they booed his jailers, for he came into town surrounded by men at arms, his chains hidden under his robes. From Chester they moved southeast. The normal route would have been down through the March to Shrewsbury, cutting across at Watling Street. That would have kept them in our territory for too long. So they decided on a route that would take them out of our land as quickly as possible. They cut right through Cheshire toward Nantwich and then down through Staffordshire and on to Warwickshire. From there they could pick up Watling Street and head down to London.

North of the Trent they were in our territory. We would be sure to find plenty of people who favored Richard or who would at least provide us with shelter. It was decided that we would hit the royal party at a Cholmondeston. Dodd sent out messages for returned guardsmen and archers to rally to Nantwich. Owain called out Welshmen from all over the March, the Tudurs brought some men from the Northwest, and the Hanmers and Plustons brought some of their tenants who were ready to fight for the King.

The plan was that we would take Richard and spirit him to Sycharth. From there we would carry him across the outlaw paths to Anglesey. Richard could then take a ship to Ireland. There were still loyal forces at Dublin. They could be marshaled and returned to Wales when they were ready. Owain proposed that Richard could send messages to the Popes, there being two at the time, Lords of Ireland, the King of Scotland and the King of France. Hopefully they would provide some men to challenge Henry's hold on the Kingdom. When we were strong enough, we would hit Bolingbroke hard and scatter his forces. Richard would know he had been reinstated on the throne by men from the West, and we would be in charge. Richard would be our King, and he would do our bidding.

So up we went from Sycharth to Hanmer and then on to Cheshire. There was a good track that led up from Hanmer through Maelor to Cheshire. Cheshire is generally flat but is cut in two by a sandstone ridge that rises about five hundred feet. Near Cholmondeston the ridge is cut in two and a road way cuts through the gap. We determined to wait in ambush at either side of the gap.

Dodd had sent messages before him to his kinsmen calling on them to come and share their news. Two boys came down from the North. One was a skinny, dark-haired lad that I imagine had a bit of Welsh in him. The other was pure Saxon; blond and blue-eyed. I will say he had the slyest eyes I have ever seen. That's the thing with the Saxons: bunch of bloody liars. Absolutely no way you can trust them. They rested by our fire and dug into our food.

"Not eating much boys?" asked Dodd of the two lads.

"Nor much to eat," said the blond one. "King Bolingbroke has seen to that."

"Aye," said the dark one, "They fucked everything up. King Bolingbroke comes to Chester and the lads there tell him to fuck off. Well, King Bolingbroke loses his temper because he's been told that Chester was ready to surrender. So he tells his lads "havoc," and off they go. Let me tell you Sir," he said, nodding at Owain, "they picked the county clean. They broke down the door to our Church and stripped it clean. Nothing left except the doors and windows. They would have taken the lead if they could have moved it. The fucking church, can you believe that? That's not right."

"He's right," said the blond one, "They burnt the fields and houses, smashed up all the Squire's things. Didn't matter who it belonged to or whether they were for King Richard or King Bolingbroke. They just destroyed everything. Whole fucking county was on fire. I tell you, night was like day. They killed every fucking cow they could find, slashed my mum's pig, and strangled all our fucking chickens. Fucking Southern cunts, I hate them."

We grunted in agreement.

"The Sheriff of Chester gave in, didn't he," said the blond one, "Fucking coward. But Pete Liegh didn't. He fucking stood up to Bolingbroke. Told him to fuck off, called him a treacherous cunt."

Owain looked at Dodd questioningly. Dodd explained, "Peter Liegh was a Captain of Archers in Ireland. Good man. Richard sent him ahead to Chester to take the mood of the city."

The blond one looked at Dodd, "Well, he won't be doing nothing no more. King Bolingbroke cut his fucking head off and stuck it on the gate."

Dodd shook his head, "This County doesn't deserve this treatment. This is bad boys," said Dodd. "How's your mother Peter?" He said to the blond boy.

He turned to us, "He's my sister's boy" he said by way of explanation.

"She's all right," said the boy we now knew as Peter, "She took us off to the Edge and we hid the caves."

Edge was a strange place. It was like a sea cliff that was marooned in the middle of the Cheshire plain. It was full of caves and old mine workings. There were some who said Merlin slept there. From the top of the Edge you could see all of Cheshire. It was a good place to hide.

The boy went on, "Steven's brother," he nodded at his comrade, "went off with Big Eddie the German to look after the squire's land. They chased off some of King Bolingbrook's riders for awhile, but then they came back with some knights so they went to ground until the knights left. They came back to the Edge and told everyone to wait and stay hidden until we heard news that King Bolingbroke had gone. Even Big Eddie said it would be better not to fight."

"It gets worse," said the dark one. "Everyone knows that King Richard kept all his money and supplies out at Holt. There were a hundred men looking after it. King Bolingbroke sent his army up there and the fuckers guarding the King Richard's treasure scarpered. Bastards, it's a bloody shame."

Who could deny that? Cheshire could have held off Bolingbroke for a year, but it folded and fell without the King.

The boys stayed with us and in the morning left to go back to the Edge. We hunkered down and waited for Bolingbroke to come.

The plan was simple. The Cheshiremen would lay down fire from their bows. We would swing behind and cut the retreat. Then some men at arms would ride down and seize Richard in the confusion.

That was the plan at least. We waited until we got the signal they were coming. Dam if the fuckers didn't come on strong. There were more knights and men-at-arms than I had seen since Scotland. I could see it would be a hard fight. They drew abreast and the Cheshiremen let fly with everything they had. Arrows flew down from the sky. Wasn't the arrowstorm that you'd see in a big fight, but it was something to see. I'll say something; those Cheshire boys are good with a bow. No match for the lads from Gwent and the South, but good all the same.

The column stared to shout and mill about. Men tried to form a defensive line. A few of the men on horseback tried to ride up the side of the gap, but it was almost a dead drop and they had no chance. Then Owain gave us the nod. We rode down on our ponies like heathens. We cut down through the undergrowth waving our axes and clubs. Owain led the charge. We hit them hard and cut our way through the baggage. But Bolingbrook's boys were tough buggers. They were well armed and rested. We were lightly armed and had been traveling in the rough. We cut and pushed our way through. Owain got close to where they held Richard; I think he even saw him. Then we had more knights arriving.

"God's teeth," said Owain, "we're going to be stuck here."

We pulled back and retreated up the hills. The Cheshiremen covered our retreat, and Bolingbrook's knights on their big chargers could not get up the ridge. We went straight up and backed off into the greenwood along the ridge. We heard them shouting and screaming, but we lost them and waited for the column to calm down so we could continue to stalk them.

On they went. At Newcastle-on-Lyme they were joined by Warwick and his retainers. We were going at them every chance we got, at least as far South as Coventry. We harassed them mightily, but there was no real chance of getting Richard. After Coventry we were in hostile country and had to back off. Owain sent most of the Welshman home.

"Go look after you homes, boys," he said. "There's going to be trouble, and you will need to look after you families. Wait there till I call. I fear it won't be long."

Thus they left and on we went, just Owain and telu and Dodd and his boys.

The last opportunity we had to spring the King was at Lichfield. The company stopped there for the night. It was a strange place to stop. Richard had liked the hall there and had celebrated Christmas there for the last two years. He knew the house well, and we thought there might be a chance to get him out. Dodd and some of his boys got into the grounds and located Richard's room. They signaled to him, and he opened the window and tried to do a runner. He almost got to them when his guards saw him. By then he was guarded by a dozen bruisers, big tough fuckers. They caught him running across the courtyard in his nightshirt and dragged him back. Dodd's boys were stuck on the other side of the ditch watching it happen.

I heard that a delegation from the City of London arrived the next day and begged Bolingbroke to behead Richard there and then and bring him no further south. Bolingbroke decided to keep him alive. He was still styling himself as "Duke of Lancaster, Earl of Derby, and Steward of the Kingdom of

England" and wasn't quite ready to become King. Archbishop Arundel was working on him, though it was clear that he'd make up his mind on the subject by the time they got to London.

After Litchfield we shadowed the column but gave up any attempt to free Richard. Dodd and his boys decided to go home and see if any of Richard's friends were collecting to challenge Bolingbroke. There were rumors the Franciscans were backing Richard and opening their houses to anyone that swore to support the King. Dodd figured it would be good to move back to Cheshire going from Franciscan house to Franciscan house. That way he could spread the news of our efforts to free Richard and see if the opposition to Bolingbroke was growing.

We continued on and entered London a few hours before Bolingbroke and his party. We passed ourselves off as Welshman from the South loyal to Henry Bolingbroke. Some Southerners were big supporters of the House of Lancaster. They had sworn to them eighty years ago when the then Duke of Lancaster rose against the English in opposition to Edward the Sodomite.

Anyway, we were among the crowd when the Mayor and the Council of London were escorted through the City Gates. The Mayor was Tommy Knowles. I can't remember much about him. He was something of a nonentity. The real power at the time was the City's greatest man, Master Dick, the King of Cats himself, the great Wittington, our once and future Mayor-for-life. There he was in all his glory at the height of his powers, the richest merchant in London, the only man elected four times to the Mayoralty, and the man most beloved man by the City. He met Bolingbroke all swathed in red velvet and gold. As with all things, they were perfect. No expense was ever spared on the King of Cats garments. He was London. He dressed to show all what London was and what they could be.

I will say that on that day there was no sign of his famous cats. Wittington had a strange love of these evil beasts and, unlike other Christian men who avoid them as much as they can, he courted their affections. It was impossible to go to his counting house without seeing these beasts strolling about and rarely could a meeting with the great man proceed without a cat snuggled up upon his lap considering the finer points of the conversation. Thus, the origin of his name, for while he might be the Master of London, it was said that he was truly King of Cats.

Londoners let you know when they don't like you. They screamed themselves hoarse for Henry and booed and hissed at Richard. Bolingbroke took Richard straight down Cheapside to St. Paul's. There Henry went down and prayed at the tomb of his father. He then walked out to the crowd and produced Richard.

The crowd booed. "Good people, I have here Richard of Bordeaux sometimes called the King of the English," said Bolingbroke.

"He has granted me the stewardship and protectorship of this Kingdom." There were cheers and applause. People shouted "Take the Crown", "Fuck Richard", "No Sodomites on the Throne."

"I make no judgment as to his future. That will be decided by a court of the Church, the Lords and the Commons at Parliament."

More cheers. Parliament was back in the mob's favor.

"But before I ask the courts to consider the plight of this poor soul, I ask you, citizens of London, what should I do? What do you believe this man deserves? Should he keep his throne? His Life?

"Look at him," said Owain, "He's like Pilate, "My hands are clean, I am innocent of these actions."

The crowd erupted and shouted, "No". Bolingbroke smiled and waved them down, "I have heard you, my people. Off to the Tower with him."

They applauded and cheered. Richard was dragged off and led to the Tower. I heard someone shout, "Now we are revenged of this wicked bastard," and spat on him. The

English love their kings until they hate them; they a disloyal bunch of bastards.

Bolingbroke backed off and headed out of the City to St. John's Priory at Clerkenwell. Over the next few days the usurpers met at the Bishop of London's house. Arundel sat as Chancellor and was made Archbishop of Canterbury again. It was a bold move. There was still a sitting Archbishop at Canterbury and as far as Arundel knew the Pope in Rome, who the English temporarily supported, still backed him. The usurpers formed a temporary council with Bolingbroke, placing Arundel at its head, and kept Richard imprisoned in the Tower while they decided on his fate.

Owain dispatched most of his telu back to Sycharth and moved down to Mistress Wrigley's Inn. As ever, I followed him. London was a dangerous place to be, but there was still hope of freeing the King and anyway, he didn't want to miss what was going to happen next. After all, it isn't every day you see a king thrown off his throne.

All of the old gang was back at Mistress Wrigley's. Owain walked through the door and was greeted with a huge roar.
"Master Owain!" A great mass of fat and fur moved itself from a place near the fire and barreled over to us. My God, I thought, can that be Fat Johnny himself? The years had not been kind to him. The elegant knight was now a mass of fat. Drink and loose living had destroyed him. He was a man when we were boys, so I suppose he must have been in his fifties then. The rest of them looked equally disreputable. Nam, Bardolph and Whistler looked as if they had been soaked in alcohol for the last twenty years. Peto, Gadshill and Ned Poins eyed us. They remembered us from the trouble we had caused in the Hurling Times and were not happy to see us again.

Mistress Wriggly looked as old as ever. How can there be some people who seem ancient all their life? I asked about Eleanor. Mistress Wriggly told me she had married a man who lived in Calais and ran an Inn there. Strange marriage, I thought, but decided not to comment. After all the world is full of many strange things.

"So where have you been?" asked Owain, "The last we heard you were with Johnny Gaunt in Castile."

"Ah," said Sir John, "A good time for us. We made a fair bit of scratch. Have you been to Castile Sir? An excellent place; I believe that if the English could spend a few weeks there basking under the Mediterranean sun, this would be a better country. They do a decent red wine, a little harsh, but interesting. We earned a bit and moved on to Aquitaine; again an excellent place with enormous profit for a man with gumption. We made stayed there while the late King experienced his unpleasantness with the Archbishop's brother. I thought that it might be politic to remain in England's other realms until things had smoothed themselves out. Of course, Queen Dick was interested in fixing Aquitaine as Johnny Gaunt's principality and severing it from France, so things looked good for men who served Lancaster. We had hopes, Sir, hopes of great wealth. Of course, Queen Dick decided on peace and Johnny Gaunt returned home and dragged us with him."

"And since your return?" I asked.

"Drinking and experiencing the joys of London. Queen Dick had little use for soldiers, so we have been pursuing opportunities for profit around City." He smiled and winked, "There's always opportunities around London. Peto, Gadshill and Poins have turned out to be excellent acquirers of opportunities. Further, the late Duke of Lancaster and our dear Mayor Wittington had many missions for us. Believe me, Sir; the war against Queen Dick has been active for a long time."

"And did you follow your Master to France during his exile?" asked Owain, referring to Bolingbrook's time in France.

"No Sir. We stayed to protect our patron. After all, once Johnny Gaunt was deprived of his son, the old boy needed the protection of loyal knights and men-at-arms such as us. Further, I was entrusted with keeping an eye on young soon-to-be Prince Hal. Johnny Gaunt was a little too worried that Queen Dick might take the boy into his tended graces."

"I assume you were fast to Ravenspur though?" Owain asked.

"Oh, most certainly. Once the Duke had landed, a man would have been a fool not to swim to his standard. Let me tell you Sir, there were many who were of two minds as to Henry's challenge, but the moment they saw that London and the Northerners were moving towards him, they swallowed their doubts and moved off. Of course, we were delayed by numerous events and did not arrive until the Duke had arrived in Cheshire. Again, enormous opportunities for profit after Harry cried "havoc." Excellent plunder to be had with the King. Once we heard that Queen Dick was captured, we saw the action was over and decided it was best to leave for London and carry the news of our victories to the south."

I should pause for a moment to translate. Fat Johnny and his gang plundered, pillaged, and lazed under the Castilian sun. When the chaos of war was over, he decided on more plunder in Aquitaine. After that he and his gang returned for a few years playing the footpad and the highwayman around London. During this time he remained an agent of the House of Lancaster and the King of Cats doing in their enemies around London. When Bolingbroke returned, they waited until they were sure he would win and then joined in the pillaging of Cheshire. After that they ran back to London to bask in the credit as heroes.

"I am surprised to see you though," said Fat Johnny. "I had heard that you, and all Welshmen, were good friends of Queen Dick?"

"Yes," said Poins, "a risky place to be."

Nasty little gnome. I have always wished for a bad end for him.

"Silence Poins," said Fat Johnny, "These are our friends. I am sure they are loyal."

"I am here to protect my interests," said Owain. "I don't need to tell you that these are uncertain times. A man needs to keep a careful eye on his interests."

Fat Johnny supped on his ale, "Indeed Sir. A man needs to watch his interests. Have you heard that certain potential enemies have already been dealt with? I hear that there have been killings. Arundel is not a man to hesitate when it comes to revenge. I would hope that you have not crossed him in the past? You were his brother's man for a long time, so it might be worth reminding him of your previous service?"

"I may visit," said Owain, "but I feel he might be too busy what with the settlement of the kingdom under his consideration."

"You have a point, Sir," said Fat Johnny, "Whatever you decide, know that you are under my protection. I recommend you stay here. We have various missions to undertake for the Duchy of Lancaster and need to be in and around the City."

And indeed there was much work for Johnny and his gang.

The House of Lancaster had many enemies and small scores that needed to be settled over the next few weeks. As Fat Johnny said, this was not a good time for enemies of the Arundel and Lancaster.

We waited and watched the deposition. First, they considered allowing Richard to continue to rule, but placing him under a new continual council. However, they remembered the lesson of 1398 and decided that Richard could not be left with any opportunity to renew his power. Second, they considered trying Richard before Parliament. They liked the idea, but it was recalled that Richard was an excellent performer and the end of such a trial might be unpredictable. Further, they were not anxious to suggest to Parliament that they had the power to make and unmake kings. As such, they decided they must depose him through more traditional means.

They considered canonical precedents. Apparently, a Pope had got rid of an Emperor once, and they thought that it could be a good precedent. It turned out to be a bust, but the City was full of talk about canonical law for a time. Next they explored whether the deposition of Edward the Sodomite was a good precedent. Superficially, his case was like Richard's; he had pissed everyone off, he was a sodomite, he made peace with foreign enemies, and he spent too much money. The problem was that Edward the Sodomite abdicated in favor of his son, not his cousin, and unfortunately for Bolingbroke there were the Mortimer heirs between him and the throne.

Faced with these problems, they decided to move to more radical alternatives. Arundel and Lancaster floated the idea that Richard was not Prince Edmund's son. They claimed that Princess Joan was a whore and that she had conceived a child with a random minstrel. They further suggested that Edward Longshanks was also a bastard and that Bolingbrook's mother, who was descended from Henry III's second son Edmund Crouchback, was really the legitimate heir. According to this theory, everyone since Henry III were usurpers until Bolingbroke came along to restore the Plantagenet line. This argument was too complicated and also too stupid for words. A few idiots might believe it, but it strained credulity.

Next they suggested that perhaps they deserved the Kingdom by right of conquest. This was the best argument so far, but they didn't want to look like the footpads they were. They proposed many other things, such as Richard took the crown jewels out of the country, Richard levied too many taxes, Richard had broken his oath. On and on it went. These were all good reasons if England had been a republic, but it was not. Kings gained their authority from God and the oaths sworn to them. If an oath was conditional, or if God's favor changed, then the question became who was to decide when the King had broken his oath or when God had deserted him. Whatever the answer, it implied there were power and right beyond the King. No man was prepared to say what that power was, but all seemed to agree that it was there.

In the end they settled on a twin strategy. Richard would be isolated and browbeaten into abdication and would renounce his crown. Once the throne was vacated, Bolingbroke would claim the crown and ask Parliament to confirm, not approve, his action. It was a dangerous course, but it was the only chance left.

In late September we heard that the King had renounced the throne. Whether he did or not I do not know, but it was widely put about. The heralds announced that a great announcement would be made at the Great Hall in Westminster. It seemed as though all of London made the trek there. We got a good place toward the back of the crowd. It was high drama. I think that some of Richard's palace queens must have remained in residence, because I doubt that any of the thugs surrounding the House of Lancaster had that kind of taste.

The empty throne draped in gold cloth proclaimed that the king was gone. The Parliament was there and called in Richard's name. Legal minds might have noted that a Parliament could not be called without a king, so that this could not be a Parliament. The Archbishop of York got up and mumbled something to the effect that Richard had resigned his throne, as if such a thing was possible. Arundel was clearly becoming impatient. He jumped up and shouted, "Do the Lords and Commons accept this end of Richard of Bordeaux's authority?"

There were a few murmurs. Arundel looked around. The Bishop of Carlisle arose. He was a doddering old fool, but I give him his bravery that day.

"My Lord Archbishop," he said, "are we sure of these claims? Could not the King," a bad choice of words, "be brought here to confirm his resignation? I feel we must explore the background of these events. I am concerned that the Duke of Lancaster may be as guilty of the crimes he levels at the King as the King himself. Further, how can a King renounce his thrown? God makes Kings, not men."

"He'll be dead within the month," whispered Owain, gesturing toward the Bishop, and I had to agree.

Arundel stared at him. He waved a scroll and pointed it at the Bishop. "I have the King's resignation here in my hand. I believe that it is enough evidence for this assembly. As to your accusation concerning the Steward of the Kingdom, I wonder that you have the gall to make such claims."

The Assembly then voted and, as one would expect, they accepted the King's resignation.

Arundel moved to the front again. "I call upon the Bishop of St. Asaph to read the articles of deposition."

This was a shock to us. John Trefor was a good friend of Owain's and was thought to favor Richard. "God knows what they have threatened him with for this to happen," said Owain.

Bishop Trefor got up and read the thirty-three articles of deposition. Throughout it his hands shook and his voice cracked. He repeatedly glanced towards Arundel. Each time

Arundel smiled and prompted him to continue.

When he was finished, Arundel stood. "I ask members of this assembly, singularly and in common, to give their public assent to this act."

First they voted in common in a voice vote. Then every man was then polled as to whether he approved. Arundel wanted every man's hand on the document. None of them would be able to claim they had not voted against Richard.

"Excellent," said Arundel. "As head of the Council, I call upon the Bishop of St. Asaph to form a commission to decide the future of Richard, formerly King and now styled as 'Sir Richard of Bordeaux,' a common knight."

He looked around at the assembly. "Now My Lords and Gentlemen let us turn to the matter of the throne."

At that moment, Bolingbroke walked from the side of the hall to take his place behind the throne. He was no longer the dashing knight of his youth. He was short, stout and barrel-chested and slightly bow-legged. His eyes were heavy and swollen, and he wore a thick red moustache that ran down to a neatly clipped beard. He wore a hat, but I recall he was quite bald by that time. He was not an impressive looking man. More like a distant uncle who might have done well overseas in the wine trade and returned home only to find that he had nothing much to do and his youth had deserted him.

I realize now that he must have already been quite ill. Not three years before he had been one of the finest jousters in all of Europe and was still thought to be a well-made, handsome man. In fact, I remember him at Richard's last Westminster

Parliament as a fine-looking specimen. He seemed to have lost a few inches in height since then and had the rosy cheeks and red nose of a man who had spent many years at the bottle. However, the English like these plain, bluff types, and he played well with the crowd that day.

He hobbled to the throne and spoke in plain direct English, no Latin or French, to the Assembly:

"In the name of the Father, the Son, and Holy Ghost, I, Henry of Lancaster, challenge this realm of England and the Parliament with all its members and appurtenances to accept my claim as King. I state that I am descended by line of the blood from the good lord King Henry III. Further that my right comes from God's good grace, and that He has sent me, with the help of my kindred and my friends, to recover this realm that is rightfully mine. Be it known that I have returned to claim this right because this realm is on the point of being undone for default of governance and undoing of God's laws."

There was a silence and then Old Man Percy stood up. "I charge the Lord and Commons, will you accept Henry as King?" he said.

There was a general assent, and Henry sat his arse down upon the thrown. Scrope and Arundel went down on their knees and kissed his ring. Northumberland followed suit. The assembly then stood up and cheered.

"Let's get out of here," said Owain "I think we know what comes next."

We turned and began to leave. Just at that moment we saw Reginald de Grey, "Going so soon, Master Glendower," he said.

"We were just stepping outside for some air," said Owain.

"I understand," said De Grey. "Such emotion. I take it you will return? The coronation will be within the week."

"I imagine we shall be here," said Owain.

"Good," sneered De Grey. "I believe our Lord the King has concerns as to the loyalty of the Welsh and wishes to see a strong turn out."

"I am sure all of Wales loves the King," said Owain.

"Ah," said De Grey, "but which king? These are such strange times."

Owain nodded. We bowed and left.

"Where shall we go now?" I asked.

"Home," said Owain. "The Uchelwyr must decide how to respond. After all," he said, "Richard still lives and we are promised to him as King."

HOW MY LORD DECIDED TO DECLARE HIS KINGSHIP

I won't bother you with the stories of the coronation. Needless to say, it was quick and messy. The highlight was the crowning. It turned out that the crown was full of lice, and Bolingbroke was so shocked he ripped it off his head and threw it into the crowd. Not a great start for a new king. Ruthin got a good part. He had the important job of holding the King's slippers. Nice to find challenging work. Richard was taken up to Pontefract Castle right in the middle Lancastrian territory. We went home, and Owain decided to keep our heads down.

Now around Christmastime travelers began coming through our lands. All of them were saying that trouble was brewing. It seemed that many people were waking up to what they had done when they had undone King Richard. People were also considering what it meant to have Archbishop Arundel back in a position of power. They knew he was a revengeful bastard and they began to think back to the events of '97.

Many men who were now supporters of King Bolingbroke realized that they had been strong supporters of Richard at the Westminster Parliament when Arundel's brother had been beheaded. Now while it was true that Bolingbroke had also been on Richard's side and had been the main accuser of Arundel, he was now king. But other men who had been good friends of Richard were not similarly blessed. They thought that the Archbishop might decide that to reenact that Parliament and deal with those who might not be as loyal as they could be. So these men decided on a plot.

As we learnt later, the conspiracy involved the Earls of Rutland, Huntington, Kent, and Salisbury, the Lord Despenser, Sir Thomas Blunt and Roger Walden, and old Thomas Merks. Their idea was to capture Bolingbroke and Arundel while they were at Windsor celebrating Christmastime. While the Royal Family were drunk and exhausted from the Christmas revels, Richard's supporters would sweep down on them during Epiphany. They would arrive in disguise pretending to be part of the Twelfth Night reveals. Then they would infiltrate the Castle, seize Bolingbrook's family, whisk them away to Cheshire and hold then until Richard was free. The plot was to be supported by risings across the country. Huntington would take London and issue orders for risings all around England and Wales.

It wasn't a bad plan, apart from a few essential details. Most importantly, they told no one of the planned risings. There was a network of Richard's supporters that would have been ready to act, but these fools didn't bother to reach out to any of them. Further, they made no plan to free Richard. Thus, it was quite possible that even a successful plot could have ended up with the two factions holding each other's king and no way to break the stalemate. The final fuck-up was the fact that while they told no one who might have helped them, they told plenty of people who could betray them. In particular, Rutland told Arundel, and Huntington's wife got scared and told Bolingbroke.

Now say what you want about Bolingbroke, but when he realized he was threatened, he always moved quickly. He sent messages to London and the Midlands, ordered the raising of bands of armed men to support his cause, and sent word to close the ports in case Richard escaped and tried to run to France. Then he and his family took off for London and settled in the Tower. The plotters found themselves in possession of an empty Castle at Windsor. With the plot failing, they decided to send out messages for the rising. We got one in February after everyone had been executed.

When they realized what a balls up they had made, they retreated up the Thames Valley and established themselves at Cirencester. There were a few sparks of support. Men from as far away as Derbyshire began to march on Cirencester to support the rising, and a few towns in the West Country came to life. However, it was really a cock-up. Salisbury and Kent didn't even have enough men to fight off the townspeople in Cirencester. They turned against them in the morning and took their Lordships while they were trying to escape. They hacked off their heads and hung them in the town square. Huntington escaped down the Essex coast in a fishing boat but was forced ashore by high winds, captured and taken to Pleshy and beheaded. Dispenser was captured in Cardiff making for Ireland. He was taken to Bristol and beheaded by the freedmen of the City in a gesture of loyalty to their new king.

Unfortunately, news of the plot reached Cheshire. The county had taken a beating and was ready to strike back. It rose on mass. People dragged out their white hart badges and marched on Chester expecting to see the King. They took down Peter Leigh's head from Eastgate walls and ran as a mob through the City calling on all loyal men to join them. Within a few days they were possession of much of the county. Then they got word that the rising had collapsed in the south and Richard was still at Pontefract. Bolingbroke pulled together a small army and began to ride north. Without good leaders, the people decided it would be a good idea to go home. Slowly the rising melted away. By the time Bolingbrook's forces arrived, there were no rebels to be found. But Bolingbroke decided that the county needed another bollocking and cried "havoc" once more. I tell you they did some harm to Cheshire. I went through the County thirty years later and saw plenty of ruined building from those years.

Of course all of this made it clear to Bolingbroke and Arundel that they could not let Richard live. I have heard that they met in council and sent a servant, a certain Thomas Swynford, to Pontefract with orders for the King's keeper, Sir Piers Exon, to do him in. Most people believe that Exon chopped his head off with a poleaxe. I know this to be false. This Thomas Swynford was none other than the oldest son of the famous Catherine Swynford, or the Dowager Duchess of Kent as she was then styling herself.

Years later I met a woman in Oswestry who was a poisoner in the pay of Archbishop Arundel. She told me that Swynford had stopped on his way up north to see her on the instructions of his Mother.

"I knew the Lady Catherine for many years," said the poisoner. "I had been attached to the Duke of Lancaster's household for many years as a midwife, and I knew the Lady Catherine back when she was governess to the Duke's children. She was a nice girl. I became right friendly with her. She was very interested in the ways of poison and charms. She said a woman needs to know such things if she is to prosper in this life. Especially if she wishes to catch the eye of powerful men and play the game at court." She supped on her ale and considered. "And she was good at it. Had a real talent, she did. It's served her well. Look where she is nowadays."

I looked surprised. "You say she used her skills to advance in Johnny Gaunt's household?" I asked.

"Well, I wouldn't know," she said, "but I tell you this. There were two women between her and the Duke, and they have been dead in a box for many years. Both of them were healthy women when Catherine came to the Duke's household, and both were dead within a few years. And who looked after them and nursed them when they were sick? Why Catherine, of course. She knew that the best way to see someone off is to nurse them. I taught her that myself, I did. After they were gone, she was able to get Johnny Gaunt for herself. She's a good looking woman, but she had plenty of charms to make sure Gaunt stayed with her. I mean, Gaunt could have had anyone, couldn't he? And why would he have married a lowborn woman like Catherine? Gaunt was a greedy bugger who would have taken some rich lady for her lands, wouldn't he? So why did he do it? Well she used her magic, didn't she? She came to me and asked me direct,

"How can I tie that man to me?" she says.

"I tells her heart of dove, liver of sparrow, womb of swallow, and kidney of hare will do it every time. She goes off and it works, but not good enough. He's still got an eye for other women. So she goes back,

"What have you got that's stronger? I need something that will make him follow me and put him completely in my power."

"Now I hesitated, because it can be dangerous to give out such powerful remedies, but she had always been good to me so I tell her: black dust of tomb, venom of toad, flesh of outlaw, lung of ass, blood of blind infant, corpses from graves, and bile of ox. Off she goes and she gets the stuff, mixes it up, and feeds it to him. See what happens? He can't leave her. He follows her everywhere. He's in love with her. So much so that when King Richard sent Archbishop Arundel to France, Gaunt makes a deal with Richard to make her kids noble. She's a smart girl, is Catherine. She knew that she had to make her kids titled or they'd be shit-arsed after she died. I mean, look at poor Alice Peters children? Terrible what they did to her when she died."

So there was the truth. Catherine was a witch and whore.

"Anyway," she went on, "when Archbishop Arundel comes back, he sent me up here to keep me out of the way. I thought that they'd forgotten me. But not Catherine. She remembered me. When they needed to off the old King, she sent her boy to me for a good potion. She sent a message with him saying the poison must be slow acting and must make it appear that he was very ill. Well I knew immediately, death cap's the thing. Give it to someone and they will be dead in ten days. They'll be off their food and sick as a dog. So I fixes him up a batch and off he goes to Pontefract. A month later I hear that the King is dead and I think, 'Well that's that, the lad did his job right.'"

"There are not many people who get the chance to see a king off, and I count myself lucky to be one of them. Of course, there were a lot of people in those days who did things they would not normally have done, what with King Henry coming in."

So there it was. Catherine had Richard killed using Arundel's poisoner. It'll bet that Arundel and Catherine decided to do Richard in. Henry was not too smart, and always had to be pushed to do what needed to done.

News of Richard's death reached Sycharth just after St. Valentine's Day. We sat in the tower on the mount at Sycharth going over the account and discussing whether it made sense to bring the herds from Cowen down early as the winter had been mild and the spring might come early. A tinker arrived from Oswestry with the news. The watchman had realized its importance and sent the man directly to Owain. He told the tale. Richard was dead and taken from Pontefract to London for all to see. There was no doubt about it.

Bolingbroke had sent out a proclamation to every sheriff, and Arundel sent a message to be read in churches that Richard was dead and all were welcome to come to London to see the body. He had been denied burial in his tomb at Westminster and was buried at his uncle's tomb in Langley. It was a poor end for a man who had cared so much for his appearance and the beauty of the things around him.

Owain looked grim. He stared down and then walked over to the window of his tower. The land was cold and hard. There was still snow on the mountains. The cattle were down on the valley floor picking at the winter fodder, and the plowmen prepared the ground for the land. It was a February like any other February I could remember.

He turned back to me.

"Well," he said, "I am free. If Richard is dead, my oaths to the King of England are over. I am free to act and may follow my destiny."

Thus it was that that Owain decided that the time had come to prepare for his kingship.

THE EVIL OF THE HENRY BOLINGBROKE

On the day that My Lord heard of Richard's death, he sent out messages to all the Lords of Wales. He called all the Bards to his seat and told the time had come. The Franciscans and Cistercians were warned that tumultuous times were coming and they should prepare the way. He called down the boys in the hills and told them that soon it would be time to prepare to leave their hiding places and strike down on the English. He even made contact with some of Richard's supporters in England and Chester and made new alliances against Bolingbroke.

Gradually messages trickled back to us.

"Yes," said Old Man Tudur, "the time has come. I'll send my boys."

"I'm with you," said Henry Dun. "Give me a year, and I'll be ready."

"Call on us when you need us," said Rhys and Morgan Gethin. "The Gower is ready."

"I will read the signs," said Crach.

"Always with you," said the Plustons, Kynastons and the Hanmers in Flint.

"I'll wet my axe," said Cadwyn of the Southern Valleys. "The valleys will rise."

"My boys will stop their murderous ways for awhile and come down from the hills for you," said the outlaw Gruffudd ap Dafydd ap Gruffudd of Geiriog.

"We are ready to burn the English out," said the Red Bandits of Powys.

"We will pray for you," said the Cistercians of Strata Florida.

"My sword is yours; I will fight the English with the same passion I once brought against the Saracen," said Dafydd ap Ieuan Goch.

"I suppose this is not the worst time," Rhys Ddu; that was the happiest we ever saw him.

"It is proper and legal," said Dafydd ap Gruffudd Fantach.

"I will write poems and songs that will praise the achievements of our armies," said Iolo Goch.

"My purse at your service," said that old moneybag Ieun ap Jenkin Kemys.

"Let's kill some Saxons. I thirst for the blood of foreigners," said Hywel Coetmor.

Finally it was decided that there was sufficient support to act. Now all that remained was to cast the signs and determine the future course of events. Owain directed Crach to call the spirits and the People of the Beautiful Tribe together to tell them of our decision and ask them what would follow.

Thus, Crach looked and listened and took the signs. Finally he declared the hour was right to read the signs. He pulled us all together at Owain's Mount near Sycharth. When we were all assembled, and the fires burned high, he began to chant in some unknown language.

Nothing came. He turned to us.

"These are some of the oldest words in the world," he said. These spells were brought to these Islands by the first men. They were used to chase the great ice away and they hold all the mystery of the world in them. I traveled once to the land of the Great River beyond the country of the King of Persia and heard the Priests there speak them. I was even able to converse with the Lords of the High Mountains in those lands using these words. These spirits have been asleep for a long time. They are the oldest beings in the world. I have heard it said they were made by God before the angels. They have not been called on since the time of Arthur, and we may need more powerful magic to call them to reveal the future to us. They may be too far gone in their sleep. I perhaps need stronger words."

He looked around and began to try again. Still nothing came.

Now he grew frustrated. He looked up to the sky and shouted something in an ancient language.

The sky began to change. In the darkness a ripple of color came down from the north. Crach looked to us, pointed and nodded with a satisfied smile on his face. More words.

Another pause; the lights became brighter and he continued in Welsh,

"Gwalt, Crwyn, Gwaed, Braster, Cnwad, Gewyn, Asgwrn, Cymal, Mer.
Gwalt, Crwyn, Gwaed, Braster, Cnwad, Gewyn, Asgwrn, Cymal, Mer.
Gwalt, Crwyn, Gwaed, Braster, Cnwad, Gewyn, Asgwrn, Cymal, Mer."

The light grew and he continued, raising his arms to the sky,

"Hair, Skin, Blood, Fat, Flesh, Sinews, Bone, Joint, Marrow.
Hair, Skin, Blood, Fat, Flesh, Sinews, Bone, Joint, Marrow.
Hair, Skin, Blood, Fat, Flesh, Sinews, Bone, Joint, Marrow."

Slowly raising his voice, and beginning to scream,

"Where is he that killed the horse-devouring, man-devouring, dragon?"

His voice was all consuming, reaching everywhere, as the light grew stronger, blinding us,

"Come now slayer of the great dragon
He who smashes first his weapon down on beast and man"

The wind blew and howled. Clouds gathered in the sky running in from the North. The wind grew and the lightening crackled. The rain poured down upon us. Throughout Wales the dragon began to move and uncoil himself. Everywhere mountains rippled as the dragon moved and the horse slayer awoke. Crach raise his staff and pointed at the dark clouds.

The rain fell harder. The mud boiled and the grass turned gold. From the earth the spirits began to rise. The fire grew and burned red and gold, denying the rain. It formed a glowing, burning bubble and rose into the sky. In that sphere, we saw all that would come.

We saw great battles and fights. Kings charged and Kings fallen. The Lords of North and the Lords of the March kneeling before the King of Wales. My Lord in gold and red riding down the Brecons toward the Seven Seas and smashing the castles of the Saxon as he went.

Heads were taken and lined up along the wall.

A forest grew up along the land and swallowed an army.
Storms came, the valleys turned to lakes.

Dragons came from the sea, belched fire and broke down the walls of castles.

Bowmen fired arrow upon arrow at the mounted knights who fell in their thousands.

The House of Lancaster brought low and a Welshman on the throne in London.

The images hovered for a minute. A voice said,

> "Owain was and will be once again.
> The time has come
> The time has come."

Then the bubble of light rose higher from the mud and fizzled in the rain. Slowly the rain stopped and the clouds parted.

Crach collapsed. Everything was quiet for a minute. Then Crach picked himself up and wiped himself off.

"That was quite good, I think," he said "Did anything manifest?"

Owain explained what we had seen. Crach rubbed his temples.

"It is a good sign. You shall fight and win. The forests and storms of Wales will swallow any army Bolingbroke sends against you. The Dragon is Wales. All the strong places of the Saxon will fall. You will become King of all of Briton or perhaps your son. That is too complicated to say for sure."

Owain nodded, "Good enough. We will act."

Poor Crach, he really did see the future, but he never could understand what he saw.

So the plans were set. The rising would occur in the spring of the Year of the Lord 1401 on St. David's Day. At once all the men of Wales would rise and seize the castles and strong places of the Saxons. Our lads would find excuses to infiltrate the Englishries, and on that day burst out and burn their towns. At the same time, we would sent messages to the Kings of France and Scotland and the Lords of Ireland to support us. The Cistercians would intervene with the Popes and gain their blessing; there being two Popes at that time.

Gradually, we worked. We stored our weapons, prepared caves and hiding places and made ready the rising. We hoped to take the Saxons by surprise and break open their castles and strong points before they could turn against us. All the Saxons would be killed. If any remained they would be pushed out of our holy land before they could react.

Of course, some of the English got word of our plans. We intercepted messages from the Englishries saying something was afoot. English churchmen complained we conspired at night and called the Devil to kill the English. But though they complained, no one believed them. We had been quiet too long, and the hard men in London were too busy tracking down Lollards, Arundel's new obsession, or Richard's supporters, Bolingbrook's obsession. The Welsh seemed distant and exotic. As long as Richard's name was not mentioned and we appeared orthodox in religious matters, we were left alone.

Everything was going well when Ruthin decided to raise his ugly mug and ruin everything.

As I said at the beginning of this chronicle, there had been many arguments over the years between the Earls of Ruthin and Owain's family concerning the placement of boundary markers and the ownership of certain pastures. It was well known that Grey was Bolingbrook's chief fart-snifter, and we expected that King Bolingbroke would raise this bastard to new titles. As we expected, he was placed on the King's council and given the title of Lord High Admiral of the Seas, no doubt because he had never actually seen a ship. The Saxons are a stupid people.

Grey was never a man to ignore an opportunity for profit, and he used his new influence to lay claim to the disputed lands. He sent his bailiffs in our trefs to throw off Owain's people. He seized our cattle and drove them to his barns and grazed his sheep on our pasture. Owain rode out and moved the boundary stone back. He drove off their sheep and sent men to guard our trefs. Grey's men came back. They moved the boundary stones again, they fought our men, and they burned what they could.

One night Bishop Trefor arrived from St. Asaph. The Bishop was a clever man and had changed sides many times in recent years. He was now highly placed with the Lancastrians and had just returned from a mission. Archplotter Arundel had sent him to Spain to ensure that the King of Castile knew that Richard was dead. Thus, we treated him carefully and avoided direct talk of the politics of the day. He drank our ale and supped on our wine, but it was clear he had some other mission. After the women had gone to their beds, he addressed his points.

"I hear you have a dispute with the Lord of Ruthin," he said.

"I have no dispute with Ruthin. He has a dispute with me. He tries to take my land and cattle," said Owain.

"It is said that men have died over these disputes," said the Bishop.

"Men always die in these hills," said Owain. "Not a year has gone by since the Flood when men have not died because of some argument."

"You are playing a dangerous game," said the Bishop. "Grey is well placed. This is not Richard's time or even Edwards.

The Greys have been second rate lords for as long as anyone can remember. But they have risen greatly now and you have no protection. Your family always had the protection of the Arundels or the King to scare off the Greys. Now De Grey sits on the King's council. He is one of the King's closest friends, and you are known to have been a friend of Richard's. If you push him, he will have no trouble painting you as a rebel and taking everything."

There was silence at the table. Owain considered his ale for a moment. The he looked up.

"But Bishop," he said, "I have friends at court. You are my friend and are you not well placed?"

The Bishop nodded, "I am your friend, Owain, but my power is limited. Let me tell you, when I saw that Richard was doomed I decided upon a course of action that tore my soul in two. I would support Henry on condition that he left Wales unharmed. He was as good as his word. Look what happened to Cheshire. I was there, I saw what they did. That could have been Wales. I would not see that happen to my flock. But let me tell you, there are people close to Henry who cannot wait to end our agreement. If they are given any excuse, they will turn on us and this country will go up in flames. Your argument with De Grey could be the excuse they need to show Henry that the Welsh cannot be trusted. I urge you in the name of Christ; avoid any direct confrontation with De Grey."

Owain thought for a minute. "What would you have me do? Give in? Roll over and let De Grey take everything?"

"Follow you Father's path," said the Bishop. "He was always a man for the law. Judge Hanmer was his best friend, and he is still well remembered in Westminster. If you put your case before the Courts in Westminster, you will receive a fair hearing. If Henry and Arundel see that Welshmen are still committed to the law, it will strengthen our position."

Owain was silent. The Bishop continued, "Owain, I know what you are planning. I have heard the rumors. I know what the bards say. I beg you to consider this course carefully. You cannot win. You have no idea of the power the Saxons can bring against you. Whatever happens, Wales will be the loser. They will burn this country from one end to the other. Nothing will be left. Every time we have risen against the Saxons, we have lost. They are simply too strong. Our future lies in making an arrangement with them. If we show we are loyal and they have nothing to fear from us, they will begin to ease their prohibitions, just as Richard promised. If we oppose them, they will crush us and laugh as they do it."

"They are not as strong as you think," said Tudur. "I have fought for the Saxons' King. Their armies depend on us. Without Welshmen to fight their wars, they would be nothing. The Saxons have become soft. All they want to do is sell wool and steal from the French."

"Weak are they?" said the Bishop. "You have seen them in France. Remember Crecy and Poitiers? There were plenty of Welshmen, but the English were there too. I give you that the Southerners are not as used to war as we, but look at the Percys. Would you face them? They have been fighting the Scotts for five hundred years. Only a fool would willing go to war against Northern men."

"But they are disunited," said Tudur. "There is no better time than now. The Percys will fall out with Henry. Old Man Percy can't resist scheming. There are still plenty of people who supported Richard and believe that Bolingbroke is a usurper. The Mortimers have their own claim on the crown and will eventually rise against Bolingbroke. There are Lollards everywhere. Arundel can't move without finding some new nest of heretics planning some mischief. All we have to do is give then a good push and the whole rotten house will come falling down. I tell you, we will never have a better opportunity than now."

The Bishop shook his head. He turned to Owain, "Is this what is passing for good counsel among your telu?"

"My brother has much to commend him," said Owain.

The Bishop turned to me. "Gwyn you have always been a sensible man. Surely you do not advise this course of action?"

"I follow My Lord," I said, "He is free from his oaths. His destiny calls him. The prophets confirm that this is the right time."

"Prophets," spat the Bishop. "This country has been more grievously harmed by prophets and windbags than by the Saxons. It is the greatest weakness of the Welsh to listen to any man who can turn a phrase. We love words too much, and they always seduce us.

"I know your man Crach. I have a thousand complaints about him. I could have had him burned as a witch any number of times. Yet I have restrained myself because I know he amuses you. I beg you not to listen to this fraud. You are a good man. You have a good life. Ignore these stupid prophets. Accept what God has ordained for you."

Owain looked at him. "You want me to accept this. Why should I? Why should I always be the one who missed out? Why should I always be the one who falls short of what has been promised? For forty-five years I have done as I was told. I have followed the path that was expected. Each time I have been close to seeking glory or following ambition, I have watched as something has intervened to snatch it away from me.

"I have been a lawyer, full of logic and high sentence, but I was doomed to practice that craft in a time of petty tyrants who use the law as a common whore. I have been a soldier, but I have fought in a time of peace. I have played the courtier, but the lords I followed were butchered, exiled, or overthrown. I have been a prosperous landholder, the patriarch of my family, admired by my friends and kin, and now I see that all I have achieved can be snatched away from me. I was promised so much and have been delivered so little. Fate has denied me all that I am owed. So now I will act. No longer will I wait for others. No longer will I follow the path laid out for me. I will follow my instinct."

The room was quiet.

"Please, Owain, one more time. Please try the courts," said the Bishop.

Owain looked at him. "For my Father's sake I will try once more. But Bishop, you must promise me this. If I go to the courts, you must agree to stay quiet about our plans. And if they turn against us, will you give us you blessing?"

"I cannot give you my blessing, but I cannot turn against you. I have been a good friend of your family for too long. However, I will say a mass for you when the Saxons bring your body back and will intervene to beg for your body to be buried intact."

So it was that Owain went to Westminster one last time. I shall not bore you with the details. We went, he presented his case, they pretended to listen and then they threw out his case, called us Welsh dogs and tossed us to the street.

So in Sycharth we continued our plans. We sent out messages. Prepare for the rising. The time has come. Get ready lads, we said, the rising will be on St. David's Day 1401. Then that prick De Grey came again.

Henry decided that it would be a good thing to start a foreign war. He knew that a good war always pulled the country together. George Dunbar, the Earl on the Scottish side of the March, had a daughter who was betrothed to the heir to the Scots' throne. He decided to ditch her when Archibald the Grimm offered a daughter with a bigger dowry. That was enough for Dunbar to sign a treaty with Henry to start a war, invade Scotland and force the heir to wed this daughter. Such is the way of kings. At best they resemble a drunken quarrel between turf cutters on a Saturday night, and at worst like two dogs fighting over a bone they stole from their master's table.

Anyway, Dunbar gave Henry the war he needed and so sent out the call for the Feudal levy to assemble to invade Scotland. De Grey received the call for North Wales. Rather than passing it on to Owain, he kept it to himself. When the time had passed for Owain to assemble with the King, he sent a message saying that Owain had deliberately refused to order assembly. He received a message back, "Arrest the traitor."

De Grey knew that a frontal attack on Owain at Sycharth was out of the question. Owain was surrounded by his telu and his tenantry, and to defeat him would require larger forces than De Grey had at his disposal. Thus he sent out a message to Owain, "Let us meet at Glyndyfrdwy to resolve our differences. Man-to-man."

Owain received the message. "I will go," he said. "We are not ready to move yet. I need to buy a few more months. Then the preparation for the rising will be complete."

So he sent a message back, "Come and speak, but bring no more than thirty men, I will bring no more than thirty and will dismiss my tenantry from the house."

We waited in Glyndyfrdwy for De Grey to arrive. It was a clear day in early September.

"Why do things like this always happen in September?" Owain asked. "Richard's last Parliament in Westminster, the condemnation of Bolingbroke, and the fall of Richard. It always happens on my birthday. I am at a loss to understand why."

We saw the riders in the distance. They were not wearing armor and seemed peaceful enough.

"What do you think?" said Owain.

"I think we should have brought at least sixty men," I said.

"Nonsense," said Owain, "we must give the impression we are weak and seek a peaceful solution to our problems. All we need is a few more months, and we will flay that bastard alive for his insults."

They arrived and De Grey dismounted and walked up to Owain.

"Master Glendowery," he said, "I am glad to see that you have decided upon a peaceful way to resolve our differences. One hears such terrible rumors these days."

"That is true, Lord Ruthin," said Owain. "These are terrible times. Please bring your men into the courtyard and join me in the Hall for a cup of wine. I will have my bard, Master Iolo Goch, come and provide music for our entertainment."

De Grey was pained by the idea of Welsh music, but he swallowed his dislike and followed Owain into the Hall. We went into the Courtyard and watched De Grey's men. I thought back to that day years ago when I had waited in the courtyard at Glyndyfrdwy for the party to return with Owain after we had escaped from De Grey's castle. How strange is life?

Now as luck would have it, Iolo Goch was late to that meeting. He had stayed late at a house nearby. He was riding along the bandit track in the forest when he looked down. He saw a large party of armed men riding down the road from Corwen to Glyndyfrdwy, and at first he assumed they were De Grey's men. Then he looked closer. He did not see De Grey's standard. There were more than fifty men, and they were very heavily armed. He realized that De Grey must have betrayed his agreement with Owain. So he rode faster and arrived at the manor.

I saw him come in. He dismounted and came to me and embraced me. He whispered in my ear, "We are betrayed and outnumbered. De Grey's men are on the road."

I leaned back and said in Welsh, knowing that De Grey's Saxons would not understand. "We must warn Owain. De Grey's men are in the courtyard and he is with De Grey. We cannot hold them all off."

"Have your men leave slowly. I will warm Owain. Let us all meet at the place you played as a child."

"You must find a way to warn Owain that will not alert the English."

He smiled and walked toward the hall. "I have a good song for Owain today," he said for all to hear in English, "Listen well to the words."

I turned to the men, "Come on boys, and let us attend to the horses." I led them to the stables. Inside I told them the situation. One by one I had them go out through the windows and off to Owain's Mount.

I was about to leave when I heard Iolo's voice strike up a most beautiful song. It was an englyn concerning the death of the Lord of Denbigh. The englyn is a complex form, and even those who are native speakers may have difficulty understanding it. De Grey might speak a little Welsh, but he would never be able to understand the music's full complexity. The story of the Lord of Denbigh was famous. After he had been executed, his heart was thrown into the flames. It has resisted the fire and jumped from the flames, blinding the executioner. However, Iolo changed the story slightly. As he sang Owain began to notice the difference and began to listen more closely.

> "Think on the death of Chief Llewellyn that night
> The murder that they planned was in full sight
> The plan betrayed in 'Mwythig's Keep
> The burning heart escaping as it leaps."

Owain nodded, "It is a good song, Iolo." He turned to De Grey, "Let us break from our discussions for a moment while I relieve myself. Too much ale and need a piss." He patted his stomach. "I grow old." He turned to Iolo.
"Take a break also, old man" he said to Iolo. Iolo bowed and moved out of the room. De Grey bowed to Owain. Owain walked to the kitchen. He pulled the window open and eased himself into the moat. I could see him from my position on the Mount. He swam across the moat and reached the bank. I saw him easing himself out and disappear into the trees. Just as he reached the tree line, I saw the second party of De Grey's men arrive. They burst in expecting to find us

unprepared and lost. All they captured was an empty manor. Owain joined me.

"What now?" I asked.

"We will wait for them to leave. They will gain nothing by staying. He has declared a war on me. It shall not stand. I shall have his head. The Prophet told me that an enemy would come to try to take me at my home one day. He said that a curse would fall upon my house if I did not avenge the insult. I will take his head and give it to the Prophet. He will make it speak and beg forgiveness from me," he said.

"But then what?" I asked.

"We must bring forth the day of the rising. Send messengers out to rise on the 16th of this month. I shall make myself a birthday present."

THE BEGINNING OF THE MY LORD'S KINGSHIP

Owain was right. De Grey left. He knew that we were warned and he would need a stronger force to take us, so he sent to Henry to request more troops. We went ahead with the rising. I remember the day. All Owain's closest friends and telu were there. His brother Tudur, young Gruffudd, Phillip and Gruffudd Hanmer, and Lowri's husband Robert Plustons. The Bishop wouldn't come, but he sent his Dean, Howel Gyffin and two of his nephews, Evan Fychan and Gruffudd ap Evan. Madog ap Evan ab Madog came from Powys and a Franciscan John of Astwick. Crach was also present. I was there with Owain's telu and his men-at-arms. We waited until the sun began its descent.

Owain remained in his chapel praying. I went to find him and discuss his plan. I needed to make certain that he was committed to this course and that the day for killing the English had arrived. He confirmed that the time had come. Crach entered and said all was ready. Owain nodded, crossed himself and walked out towards his coronation. We walked out to the mount slowly, each of us lost in our thoughts. Ahead we could see that all of Owain's tenants and kinsmen were there. The telu was assembled and a great fire was burning.

He walked with solemnity. Each man held a torch. He came to the Dean and kneeled in front of him.

"I ask for you blessing," said Owain.

"I give it willingly," said the Dean. "We have waited too long for you."

Other words were said and the oaths were made. Owain then turned to his people. For the first time he avoided a speech. He nodded at his men.

Then he turned to me.

"It has begun," said Owain. "Wales will be free and whole."

I nodded and prepared myself to head to the North and to fulfill My Lord's destiny.

2494503R10201

Printed in Great Britain
by Amazon.co.uk, Ltd.,
Marston Gate.